I0762021

SHATTERED HEART

SHATTERED HEART

Guardians Trilogy — Book 2

Stefanie Dawn

This book is a work of fiction. Any references to real events, real people, and real places are used fictitiously. Other names, characters, places, and incidents are products of the author's imagination, and any resemblance to persons, living or dead, actual events, organizations, or places is entirely coincidental.

Disclaimer: The material in this book contains sexual content and is intended for mature audiences ages 18 and older.

ISBN eBook: 978-1-7636644-5-6

ISBN Paperback: 978-1-7636644-6-3

ISBN Hardcover: 978-1-7638705-4-3

Book Design by Angels and Fire Books

Paperback Cover Design by Artscandare

Hardcover Cover Design by RJ Creatives

Published by Angels and Fire Books

Also by Stefanie Dawn

The Unearthly Sins Novels

The Demon in Me

The Angel in Her

Lure of a Demon

Dark Angel

Touch of a Demon

The Demon in Him

The Elements of Abduction Novels

Savior

Rescuer

Redeemer

Liberator

Releaser

Freer

The Guardians Trilogy

Rogue Heart

Shattered Heart

Reborn Heart

Novellas

Demonic

Daemonia

For Chris and Kate.
For when I say I don't know where I'd be without you, I mean every word

Guardians are incapable of love.

Until I met Anahera–a half-human, half-Guardian–I believed it too. Despite being an outcast, she's lived with me in Lucidis for years, and having her by my side is a bliss I won't ever give up.

But something is happening to Ana's powers. She grows stronger each day.
And more unpredictable.

Our son, Samael, is coming of age. I want him to embrace his Guardian heritage, but being part human, it's difficult for him to simply observe and protect humanity when he feels their pain—and their love.

How can I tell him falling in love with a human is wrong when my son is a reflection of me?

When the Tenebrian Guardians launch an attack to create chaos on Earth, I'm convinced there's more to the assault than it seems.

And when Samael goes to Earth against my wishes and Ana wants to follow, I must fight to protect them from outside threats...
and from themselves.

Contents

Fullpage image 1

1. Prologue 3
2. Chapter One 9
3. Chapter Two 17
4. Chapter Three 25
5. Chapter Four 35
6. Chapter Five 45
7. Chapter Six 51
8. Chapter Seven 57
9. Chapter Eight 77
10. Chapter Nine 97
11. Chapter Ten 105
12. Chapter Eleven 115
13. Chapter Twelve 127

14. Chapter Thirteen 147
15. Chapter Fourteen 155
16. Chapter Fifteen 169
17. Chapter Sixteen 179
18. Chapter Seventeen 189
19. Chapter Eighteen 197
20. Chapter Nineteen 211
21. Chapter Twenty 219
22. Chapter Twenty-One 227
23. Chapter Twenty-Two 233
24. Chapter Twenty-Three 247
25. Chapter Twenty-Four 263
26. Chapter Twenty-Five 265
27. Chapter Twenty-Six 267
28. Chapter Twenty-Seven 269
29. Chapter Twenty-Eight 271
30. Chapter Twenty-Nine 273
31. Chapter Thirty 275
32. Chapter Thirty-One 277
33. Chapter Thirty-Two 279
34. Chapter Thirty-Three 281

35. Chapter Thirty-Four 283
36. Chapter Thirty-Five 285
37. Chapter Thirty-Six 287
38. Chapter Thirty-Seven 288
39. Chapter Thirty-Eight 289
40. Chapter Thirty-Nine 290
41. Chapter Forty 291
42. Chapter Forty-One 293
43. Chapter Forty-Two 295
44. Epilogue 297
45. Acknowledgements 297
46. Bonus Chapter — John 298
47. Connect with Me Online 298
48. About the Author 298

Prologue

Cael

Now...

Ana sighed as she leaned her head against my chest, melting into me as I pulled her closer and relished the feel of her wrapped in my arms. We swayed in slow circles to the music my community played a short distance away on an assortment of instruments—some obtained from Earth and others fashioned using the materials from Lucidis.

Guardians didn't always approve of or understand dancing, but it had been many years since Ana first called Lucidis home, and I smirked, knowing she was far beyond caring about some members of the community's disapproval of humans and their love of dancing. The fact that music was now an integral part of the Lucidian lifestyle was a far cry from where we were generations ago, as elements of human nature had begun to infiltrate our existence. But while music was here, dancing was still mostly looked down upon. It was okay to enjoy the music, but not to get lost in the feeling of it.

To feel was human, a weakness.

Luckily, Ana no longer gave a damn.

At least most of the time.

I stroked her back with slow, sweeping motions of my fingers and hummed my contentment as her large, ice-blue quills flattened under my touch. It had taken her a long while to get used to her new appearance after her skin changed. When her life on Earth ended, her Guardian half had become dominant.

She looked up at me, her face lit by the moonlight as she gazed past me to watch the purples and reds of the galaxies beyond the stars shine against the black backdrop. Over the hours, they would shift across the sky so slowly that it was imperceptible at any moment but made for an incredible night, lying in the fields and watching their progress, which we had done with our son Samael on many occasions. We wouldn't talk much. We would simply lie there and hold hands, allowing the energies passing between us to say all they needed to, and recharge each other in a way that only love could. The moon was bright and large, and its healing light pooled onto us as we danced through the grass, the dampness from the condensation cooling our naked legs, the strands occasionally snagging briefly in our scales.

"Your dancing has improved," Ana said, smiling against my chest.

I chuckled. "I had a good teacher."

"I've seen you teaching Samael and some of the younger Guardians to dance." When I didn't respond, and my back stiffened involuntarily, she grinned. "So, it looks like the student has become the teacher."

"They still sometimes ask why humans dance."

"We dance for the same reason we sing, paint, or play music. It's an expression of joy or sorrow. A creative outlet for emotions when they get too much to keep contained within us anymore."

"The Elders don't always approve. Dancing involves *feeling* the music, not just listening," I said, although I knew we'd had this discussion several times before, and many similar to it.

Ana shook her head, rubbed her cheek against me, and stopped to inhale against my skin. "You said yourself that emotions are a strength, not a weakness. Maybe the Elders aren't right about everything."

"You can't change thousands of years of opinions and culture overnight, Ana."

She huffed quietly but didn't say anything, and I rested my chin on her head as we continued to move together. It must have been hard for her to adapt when she found herself alone in a strange place. A different realm that she had only recently learned the existence of.

But she had proved herself stronger with every passing day.

Her resilience was inspiring and only made me love her more, if that was even possible. I hoped that all these aspects of her nature would be passed on to our son as he reached adulthood.

Ana was right in her views.

Many Guardians' attitudes had started to shift as they recognized that humans were stronger and more complex than we had originally given them credit for. They were more than simply tools or obstacles for maintaining the Balance. Humans were aware of things the Guardians had not been aware of until recently.

I believe that my reappearance in Lucidis after being away on Earth for so long and my subsequent relationship with Ana played a pivotal role in this change. Over time, this could revolutionize how Guardians interacted, influenced, and maintained the Balance. However, all these high hopes and changes depended on Tenebrians doing their part to help, along with the Elders from both realms accepting that the old ways needed to change.

While the Lucidian attitudes seemed to change, the Tenebrians were going in the opposite direction, behaving increasingly erratically.

A change was coming, and it was in the air across all three realms.

Ana opened her eyes and stared into the distance. A grin lit her face, one that I couldn't help mimicking, knowing that somewhere just beyond the circle of light around the community was our son and a small group of other youths.

Dancing.

Chapter One

Vikt

Then…

My feet pounded across the red dirt of Tenebris as I ran, pushing beyond the pain of the stitch in my side. There had been a change in the air, a shift created as someone came back through a Gateway into the realm. I recognized the energy pattern immediately, and I turned and bolted. I wanted to be close when he came home, but I had no way of knowing exactly where he'd reappear or if he would have any control over the location if he were forced to leave Earth abruptly.

Ignis.

I was fast, but I wasn't fast enough.

As I cleared the broken branches of a patch of black bushes, I ignored the rough scrape against my naked legs as the Elders surrounded Ignis. He was on his knees, looking at them defiantly.

"No!" I cried out, bursting into a sprint.

The Elders ignored my cries for them to stop. There were no words spoken, no trial or argument. They were judge, jury, and executioner all in one, and according to them and their outdated views, Ignis had crossed a line while on Earth. The line itself was vague and unclear, and I thought it ironic that in the beginning, they had made little effort to stop Ignis in his quest but were keen to kill him the moment he returned home.

They claimed their actions were to maintain the Balance, but they weren't as pure as they pretended to be. Ignis threatened their power, and their motivation for his removal was less about his actions on Earth and more about his influence at home. Ignis had a small following of Guardians in Tenebris, which grew with every passing day, of which I was the first to be a part. Once there were enough of us, even the Elders' experience and matured powers wouldn't be enough to control us. By sheer numbers, we would take over the realm.

Then Earth would follow.

I was mere feet away when the moonstone blade was thrust in and out of Ignis's chest in one smooth motion. I could almost hear the sound as the blade punctured his skin and the resulting ooze as blood followed the blade's departure from his body.

Despite their age, their speed had not failed the Elders, and together they stabbed Ignis twelve times before I reached them. During the assault, his human form melted away as his strength to maintain it left his body with his life's blood. At my cry of rage, the Elders scattered with no particular rush but no intention of dealing with my futile objections.

Falling to my knees, I skidded along the dirt for the final stretch, welcoming the pain as my knees were cut. The wounds would heal quickly, but right now, I felt I needed to repent for not being able to save him. I caught Ignis as he collapsed backward. His head fell into my lap, his legs bent at uncomfortable angles he could no longer feel. He had not uttered a single sound during the assault on him, but now a low, gurgled moan escaped his lips, followed by a cough of blood that sprayed against my chest.

"You got yourself caught, you fucking idiot," I whispered.

Ignis smiled and grabbed at my neck, pulling me close to his face with his last remnants of strength, enough to cut off my air supply briefly.

For a moment, I thought he was going to kiss me. It would seem uncharacteristic, even in his moment of death, to do anything to display any emotion, any sign of the connection we shared beyond what we would ever dare say or admit.

Ignis spluttered. "What we seek, I found a way, but she was taken from my grasp."

"What was it?"

"Not what. Who. A half-breed."

My body tensed, and it felt like my chest caved in on itself.

A half-breed?

"She lives?"

"No." Ignis shook his head as he drew a death rattle of a breath. "Find another way, and bring them all to hell with us."

His full weight collapsed into my arms, and I shoved his body from my lap to the ground, heavy in his death. Standing, I looked away even before the dust had settled around his motionless form. There would be no funeral, and his body would be left to rot where it lay. I glanced at him as the glowing edge of his orange quills faded with his life force, and he became dull in color. A dead Guardian was a wholly unimpressive thing. Ignis had been proud and wouldn't want to be seen this way.

I resolved to come back at night and burn his body.

Turning, I walked back across the plain with no particular

rush. I'd come from one of the many forests full of trees and plants, uncomfortable to touch and tough to eat, but they sustained us. My current residence was in one of the old communities, where I lived alongside some of Ignis's other followers. Tenebris had not maintained communities for many centuries. We were not equipped to live together in groups, and it often resulted in fights and deaths. We came together for sex, sometimes willing, sometimes not, for the weak didn't fare well in Tenebris. If we needed or wanted to change the Balance, we might work together, but then we would drift apart again.

As I left the shade of the forest canopy and emerged into an opening, Culo appeared before me, his eyes already holding the accusation before his words presented it. "Did you get him?"

I glared at him. "Do you *see* him?"

"So, you were too slow."

"None of you are faster. The Elders were too quick. He's dead."

"Pity."

I shrugged. I wouldn't mourn for the loss of my lover—he was one of many—but he had played a pivotal role in the changes occurring in the realm. Over the generations, Tenebrians' concern for the Balance had become lax. Humans caused themselves enough issues without needing much intervention from us, and, at this point, Tenebrians mostly came to Earth for our pleasure at the expense of humans.

Any mess we made would be cleaned up by Lucidians, anyway.

Dropping heavily to the ground in a huff, I rested my chin on my palm. Now that Ignis was dead, leading the rebellion was up to me. Luckily, I had a plan.

"What now?" Culo asked.

I took a deep breath. The air was stagnant and saturated with negative energy. It was a vicious cycle living here—the environment directly reflected the beings within it, and, in turn, it had a further negative effect on the Guardians.

There was no reprise, no escape, and maybe this was part of what we were rebelling against.

Did we need a reason, though?

I didn't think so. The humans were tools for the Balance, but why couldn't they be tools so we could feed off their pain? Why was human suffering more important than our pleasure?

"Now…" I started drumming my fingers against my chin as I considered how much to tell him. A change such as what Ignis and I had hoped for would take many years, even decades, and the others would grow restless quickly. Better to drip-feed them information enough to keep them compliant and pliable. "Now Earth becomes our playground. Do what you want, but keep the activities scattered, as we don't want too much attention from Lucidis."

"That's it? What about the one who killed Ignis?"

"If we find them, they will pay. Their imprint was all over him when he came through the Gateway, and I'll know it when I feel it again. But it's not worth putting our resources into finding his murderer."

The Elders may have been the ones wielding the blades, but the actual murderer of Ignis was whichever Lucidian had forced him through a Gateway from Earth. Doing so had doomed Ignis to death, and I do not doubt that whoever took that action knew the consequences. They were responsible, and if I found them, they'd pay for it.

Culo shrugged and moved away. As he looked around, he rubbed himself, searching for a suitable mate for the next few hours. He knew better than to try for my physical company. He'd tried to force me once, and it had not ended well for him. But the attack had served its purpose and had established my dominance, if nothing else.

I watched the Reflections of humans move about in the distance, afraid and injured from previous tortures.

The Reflections were no longer enough to satiate us. While they responded to emotional and physical torture like humans did, they weren't real. Their imprints didn't bleed their pain into the air to be absorbed, as humans did. There wasn't the satisfaction of sensing the slight shifts in the Balance when they cried out in terror. The Reflections served their purpose, leaking their terror into the souls of humans.

But they wouldn't do for us anymore.

We wanted the real thing.

Chapter Two

Ana

Clutching at my chest, I groaned as I woke, feeling like a thousand hangovers were pushing against the inside of my skull all at once. A chill spread across my skin and into my being, creeping into my body through a wound that was no longer there. Then, the cold sensation stopped, and even as my fingers continued to wander across my skin, searching for the arrow wound that had pierced through me, I found nothing.

It had happened. I knew it was real. I'd felt the arrow push its way through my chest and then felt nothing more. There was no pain now, no blood or bruises, and when I looked down at my hands, expecting to find them caked in my blood, I cried out in surprise. My palms were a pale blue, and the backs of my hands were covered in sharp scales of varying shades of blue and white that seemed to glimmer in the sunlight like crystal. I started to tremble as my fear spiked, trying to make sense of what I was seeing. The scales straightened and sharpened as my breath quickened, and I stared at them, unsure if I should try to swat them flat or ignore them. Standing, I hastily attempted to cover my body when I realized the sharp quills had mostly shredded my clothes. The same scales on my hands curved across my arms and down over my breasts and stomach. The remaining skin that still resembled mine was blue and had a slight glow in the rising sunlight.

Looking around, my heart thumped in my chest. I didn't recognize this place. For a horrid moment, my heart skipped a beat when I thought that somehow Nathaniel had transported me to Tenebris again. But this place felt different—the air and sense of it were lighter, it was quieter, and my skin didn't tingle unpleasantly. However, the fear of the unknown was still deep within me, and I fidgeted with discomfort as my eyes scanned the unfamiliar terrain.

I needed something, *anything* familiar I could grab onto to keep my sanity.

Again, I pushed my palms to my chest, flexing my fingers against my skin. Maybe I'd missed the wound in my panic? But no, there was still nothing there. Curling my toes in the grass, I squeezed my eyes shut momentarily. Every sensation was amplified—this body was mine, and I was alive. But how or why, I couldn't explain, and a seed of doubt that grew like wildfire in my veins told me I couldn't really be sure of anything. My eyes started to sting as tears formed. The sights and smells of this unfamiliar place, coupled with the touch of the air on a body that didn't look like my own, were overwhelming.

"Kyle?" I called out, but not too loud, afraid of what lay beyond my range of vision.

When there was no response, I allowed the hopelessness to overcome me as my legs shook.

I considered sinking back to the ground and waiting for whatever fate fell upon me.

A shuffling of grass confirmed my suspicions that someone was approaching. I sensed it, but then ignored the sense because I couldn't understand how I could *sense* someone was coming. The feeling was almost of an invisible wave, gentle and soothing, that pushed through the air toward me, and I'm sure if I could see it, I could reach out and touch it. I looked up, and three creatures were standing a few feet away. I made eye contact with the closest one and retreated backward with several tentative steps.

They had the same skin as this new body of mine, but their eyes were all a bright, vivid blue, and there were no parts of their skin that resembled human. Instead, their entire bodies were covered in quills or scales. The one closest to me tilted her head, and I guessed it was *her* once I allowed my gaze to travel over her body, noting the two small swells on her chest that indicated breasts beneath her scales. Her legs were strong and athletic, and her feet and hands were large. Once I studied her face, it appeared distinctly feminine, at least more so than the two creatures standing to either side and slightly behind her.

But despite the different colorings, the similarity to the creature I encountered in Tenebris couldn't be ignored.

My fear spiked, and my heart rate rose in tandem. At the exact moment, the female flinched and then resumed her study of me. Did she feel my fear? Was she a Guardian? I sensed no ill intent from them, but they were tall and intimidating, and I didn't know if I should run or attack. To try to attack seemed futile and foolish, but my scales stood up on end involuntarily, and I glanced down in surprise at my body's reaction.

I intended to ask one of the thousand questions running through my mind, or at the very least introduce myself, but instead, I said, "Don't hurt me." My voice sounded small and weak. I had failed miserably if I were trying to show I could hold my own or that I was willing to fight for my life.

The female approached me with a palm held out and slow steps that were unnatural for her height, as though she were intentionally trying to appear as less of a threat. While I'm certain I was practically a trembling mess at that point, I couldn't find the strength to stop it. The female with the long face and striking features gazed at me with those bright blue eyes that seemed to see straight through me.

My shoulders slumped, and almost subconsciously, I decided that if this being attacked me, I wouldn't resist.

I was dead, anyway.

"We are not going to hurt you." The voice was deep and soothing and distinctly female. I nodded slowly as her eyes glanced up and down my body.

"Where am I?"

"Lucidis." She frowned at me, and her facial features became familiar with every expression. The knot between her brows made her less intimidating, more relatable, more... human.

Almost.

I needed anything to cling to, and the flicker of fight within me flared. I wanted to live.

"Who are you?" she asked.

I returned her gaze, feeling insignificant next to her almost seven-foot frame. "Ana. Anahera."

A look of understanding passed across her features, and it was my turn to frown. Did she know me? Did she know why and how I was here? I needed answers.

I pressed a hand to my chest. "Do you know me?" Taking a bold step forward, the female didn't retreat and watched me curiously. "You do, don't you?"

"You are the one who was with Cael," she said, but she was holding something back.

"Cael? Is he here?" I looked around as if he was going to materialize next to me. She shook her head and continued to watch me as though I were a curiosity to behold.

"You're the half-human, half-Guardian."

"Yes." But she didn't tell me how she knew or what was on her mind, and frustration began its slow claw at my skin. "Is Cael coming here? I need to see him."

"Cael has work to do on Earth. There was a considerable disruption to the Balance, and he needs to right it."

"Send me back. I can help." I didn't know how, but I would rather be there helping Cael than here with these strange beings who kept staring at me.

"That is not possible. You will be a distraction to him. He has work to do."

"Who *are* you?" I demanded, trying to keep my frustration down but failing. I didn't want to be given information in dribs and drabs. I wanted to know what was going on, and I wanted to know *now.*

And I wanted Cael.

"I am Monia..." When I continued to stare at her, my frustration ebbing away and being replaced with fear and confusion, Monia added, "I am Cael's mother."

I gasped, my face crumpled, and the tears came through no matter how hard I tried to keep them at bay. I wanted to say something meaningful and ask so many questions, but they all choked up in my throat. Instead, it took all my willpower not to break down and sob, a thread I was barely holding on to.

I was alive and in Lucidis. I was in Cael's home, which meant he would return at some point.

I was alive.

But while I was safe, I was far from calm. I opened and closed my fists a few times, my palms sweaty despite the cool breeze that brushed my sensitive skin. I needed someone to hold me, to calm my nerves, and to tell me everything would be okay. There was only one person I needed at that moment.

"When will Cael be home?"

"He has work to do on Earth to restore the Balance," she repeated without enlightening me further. Monia held out her hand. "Come." Monia froze and stared hard at me as I took her hand, her gaze moving swiftly up and down my body before settling on my widened eyes. Something passed between us, and a warmth that felt like pure power swept my being on a level that couldn't be seen or touched. "You are with child."

The tears came through, thick and fast, tears I was still trying so hard to hold back.

Nathaniel's words echoed in my mind as my memory crawled with the sensation of his hands on my stomach, his fingers twitching in glee as he asked, "*Do you know?*"

Is that what he meant? A baby?

"What?" There was too much to take in at once. I trembled, and Monia gripped my hand lightly, steadying me when I felt my legs would give way underneath me.

Monia touched her fingertips gently to my stomach, her touch fading away the memory of Nathaniel's assault. "You are with child," Monia repeated, looking at me with her large blue eyes that seemed almost sad. "You are so young yourself. Not even in your third decade."

"That's not possible."

Monia frowned as if she didn't understand my denial, so she repeated her statement a third time.

I cupped my hand over my stomach and focused all my attention there. When I felt a slight pulse in response, I jumped and snapped my eyes up to Monia's.

"What do I do? I need Kyle." I shook my head and corrected, "I need Cael."

"He is the father." It wasn't a question, but I nodded anyway. Monia ran her thumb over the back of my hand, and I watched as my scales flattened, and I felt calmer. The quills on my shoulders and back relaxed against my skin as they responded to the calming touch and comforting presence of a mother figure I had missed so much. "We will look after you. You are safe, be calm. Please, come."

After the first step, which seemed to take forever, I walked with Monia back toward the others. The two male Guardians stepped back as I approached, as though I were somehow contaminated. Was it me they hated because I was a half-breed? Or my child? Ducking my head down, I cupped my hand over my stomach again, protecting the light that would turn into my child soon. Monia shot her companions a warning look, and they fell into step behind us.

Chapter Three

Ana

The first few months in Lucidis passed in a blur, and I didn't understand why Cael didn't come for me. Monia tried to explain, but her reasons were rooted in a logic I couldn't grasp. She hadn't told him that I was alive and here. Surely, he'd prefer to know I was okay? As I could neither create nor pass through a Gateway myself to see him, I asked Monia why someone couldn't simply tell him of my presence here. But no, the work to restore the Balance was more important than Cael and I, as individuals, and our *personal plight,* as it was put to me. I desperately wanted to try to contact him, and at night, when I was lying in bed, I would think of his name, think of his face, and picture him touching me as hard as I could, hoping he would pick up on it with those Guardian senses of his. I got no response or flicker of a feeling that told me he was also thinking of me.

I did my best to understand. Since this place was to be my new home, I at least tried to fit in, which is more than I tried to do on Earth. But it wasn't easy. I was used to forging my path and forcing the world to fit around me, and if it didn't, I'd move forward anyway. But here, I was alone, and everything was strange and new. I might as well have been on another planet. I knew that Earth existed through a thin veil that separated the realms, and with the right powers and teachings, I could reach through and touch Cael. But I did not have the skills to do it, and Cael still thought I was dead. It broke my heart to think about it, so I tried to focus on literally anything else.

Unfortunately, the Guardians weren't much for talking, which usually would've suited me, but I had so many questions that went unanswered. I didn't want to continuously bother the few Guardians who spoke to me freely lest I wear out my welcome.

I got the impression there were complications due to my mixed heritage. I overheard a conversation between Cael's mother, Monia, and some old dude who I assumed was an Elder, some of the Elders apparently made it clear I could be of no use at all. I couldn't help maintain the Balance, so I was an accessory, an being out of place—a mere human in a world where my species was considered inferior than Guardians.

They also said I'd never be able to produce a Gateway, and that was like waving a red flag at a bull. Thoughts of how I could achieve it consumed me whenever I wasn't thinking about Cael, which wasn't very often.

If they would allow me the time and maybe help me, rather than brushing me off, I could be taught. Surely the only reason I couldn't master the skills of influencing and creating Portholes and Gateways was because I'd spent my life as a human on Earth. The Guardians weren't *born* with the knowledge of creating Gateways and influences, but with the power that could be molded through education. It made sense, and I tried to reason with the Elders. Still, the rare times they allowed me to speak to them directly—usually when I caught them in passing through the community, they certainly wouldn't grant me counsel—they again told me to await Cael's return. The two of us could figure out my place in the community together.

I wasn't worth the Elder's time.

If every community were like this one, they would all consist of a few hundred Guardians spread out over a large area, coming together only in the evenings to feast and share news of the state of the Balance. They came together to court, and I'd sit by the fires and watch them pair up, usually right before they slept. That part seemed the most human of the behaviors I'd witnessed. One Guardian would approach another, regardless of gender, and attempt to court them. Granted, the courting consisted of openly asking *Do you want to have sex with me.* But to a certain point, I could relate to it, and I was searching for anything familiar to keep me sane. I wanted Cael to be here, to remind me that I wasn't crazy, that all of this was really happening, and that the man who had become my rock was real and with me. But even when I asked Monia about him, she would brush off my concerns. She may have done it more gently and with something closer to a mother's care, but it still dismissed my concerns.

So, I waited.

And I watched. Despite my confusion and constantly feeling out of place, the Guardians were fascinating. It did somewhat churn my stomach to realize that we humans lived our entire lives with another species, unearthly beings watching us from another realm and influencing us. But there wasn't anything lurid about it. It was their duty.

Monia explained that each community responded to changes in the Balance felt within its immediate local area. However, from what I understood, they could reach out across great distances with the Gateways, focusing on a feeling or energy rather than a geographical location. The only reason they kept it localized was so they didn't get overwhelmed by the energies from the humans.

There must be hundreds of thousands of communities across Lucidis and Tenebris, each doing their part. A month after I arrived, several Guardians departed the community with unceremonious goodbyes to their companions. Monia said they occasionally moved between communities to avoid inbreeding.

"Wait," I said, waving my hand at the retreating backs of the Guardians. "How was it decided who was to leave? Is it just a random draw? Do they make the choice themselves? Didn't they miss their families?" On the occasions when I got to ask questions, it was difficult not to let them all spill out in a verbal vomit. There were too many things I wanted to know, so any question would come out in a rushed jumble as I tried to ask several things at once.

Monia looked confused when I asked about missing their families, and I dropped my hands to my sides. "Don't you miss Cael?"

"He is my son," she answered.

I shook my head. It didn't answer my question, but I don't think she understood.

I left my questioning there, but I still wanted to know if there was communication between the communities or if they kept to themselves. Do the new Guardians rock up and say *Hey, I'm a part of your community now?*

More questions I'd add to the list of things to ask Cael

when he returns. A pen and some paper would be a blessing at this point. I had a literal list of things to ask. It wasn't so much that the other Guardians were cruel, but I constantly felt like an imposition. Absentmindedly, I'd rub my stomach and stare out over the community, watching everyone go about their business. I never thought I'd be pining for a place in a community.

I hoped my child didn't feel as much of an outcast as I did.

Occasionally, when I couldn't take being alone anymore, an issue I never thought I'd have, I'd sit with some of the Guardians while they monitored the Balance and disturbances. Although I couldn't—*yet*, I was determined one day I would be able to—see what they could, I could feel the energy transfer as it passed through the air, across the realms, from Earth to Lucidis. Sometimes, I swore I felt the essence of the Earth around me, as if I could almost hear the traffic and the birdlife and feel the thickness of the city air.

Perhaps I was hoping to have a place in the community so much that I imagined I was home.

Eventually, I forced my way into a group of younger Guardians, with whom I spent most of my time while waiting for Cael's return. They were aged between thirty and fifty years old, young by their standards, and this group included Sasha. They were not quite as strict on the old beliefs about humans being only scum on the bottom of their bare feet and were more open to include me. It became easier to ask questions, and they took me at face value. It was oddly reassuring not to have to behave a certain way. Much of what I said and did was considered odd by them, so my jokes, which no one got, weren't anything out of the ordinary. Strangely, sometimes I felt more understood and accepted by this group of young Guardians than many people on Earth.

There was much talk among them about Cael and his time on Earth. No Guardian prior had spent that much uninterrupted time away from their realm, I was told, and they were keen to observe its effects on him. At first, I thought they pitied him, and I was ready to grow angry and defend him, but it was nothing more than a static curiosity.

And a hint of awe.

What took the longest to get used to was my appearance. I knew Guardians could shift between their human and Guardian forms, and although I squeezed my eyes shut and gripped my hands into fists, I couldn't seem to change my skin from blue back to its natural hue. Guardians were always naked and showed no concern. The scales at least gave me some sense of being covered, but I had fewer than the full Guardians. It was like constantly wearing only a see-through, skimpy, scaly bikini.

When I finally worked up the courage to look at my complete appearance by leaning over the edge of a lake to see my reflection, I wasn't prepared for the size of my pregnancy bump in relation to my small frame. Delicately, I traced my fingers along the curve of my stomach, stopping where my belly button now pushed outward. The baby kicked, and I flinched, before I smiled and patted my belly.

"Don't worry, baby," I whispered to myself. "I'll find my place here before you're born. I promise."

Monia and I sat by the still-warm embers of a previously roaring fire, surrounded by a circle of rocks and sand. I poked the remains of what was our dinner with a stick, now burned beyond recognition, and watched while Monia peeled fruit.

"Sorry," I apologized for the fourth time for ruining our dinner. It was challenging to adapt to cooking in Lucidis. I'd never been camping as a child, and had no vegetable garden. Hell, even my cooking skills were limited with all the utensils and appliances in my apartment kitchen. Another reminder that I had no skills to apply here. I wasn't accustomed to sourcing food from gardens and trees and cooking it over an open flame or buried in the ground with hot stones. Besides, even if I had, the plants here were unfamiliar—large trees that fruited only at certain times of the day, or root plants Guardians dug up with their bare hands and ate raw after rubbing away the rich soil.

"You do not need to apologize, Anahera."

"It must be frustrating for you, teaching me like a child."

Monia looked at me from under her brow, her head tilted slightly to the left. My lips curved. She looked like a curious puppy if it weren't for the patience of a mother in her eyes. "I do not know why you would think that."

Of course, she wouldn't know why I'd think that. "I don't like being an inconvenience," I explained.

"You are a misplaced being, finding yourself in a new home. A period of transition is to be expected."

I huffed out a breath. "Well, it makes sense when you put it like that."

My emotional responses to situations were out of place here, and I would never have pegged myself as a particularly emotional person. But here, every emotion beyond mild irritation, and I might as well have thrown a full-blown tantrum. Things in Lucidis either were or weren't, and that was all there was to it. While I'd noticed the younger Guardians tended to react and engage with each other more passionately than the older ones, it wasn't a *human* level of emotion.

And no matter how long I'd been here, it didn't dull my surprise every time I witnessed actual anger or true happiness, so rare and out of place that it stood out like a beacon and a reminder of Earth.

A hint that maybe deep down, we weren't so different.

From my point of view, it seemed the Guardians were almost taking on some human qualities—actually *feeling* the emotions they were trying so hard to suppress. Perhaps it wasn't a matter of them *not* having emotions, but rather a *choice* not to display or acknowledge them.

But so many of them still treated humans as inferior and looked down on me. As though they could pick and choose desirable qualities and display only those. But anger wasn't a desirable quality, and I'd seen that flare in the eyes of some of the Guardians at my sheer presence in their community.

"I'm not used to this style of cooking. It's so strange to me that you don't have electricity or technology," I said.

"We do not need it."

"Don't you have magic or something to make things easier?"

"Magic?" Monia stopped peeling and raised a brow at me.

"You know... magic." I wiggled my fingers toward the embers, resisting the urge to mutter some magical words to emphasize my point. "Like a wizard." Monia's expression was so reminiscent of Cael's when I'd first quoted a movie line to him that I laughed. "Never mind."

Monia finished peeling and handed over a bowl of fruit pieces. "You are so strange."

"Funny, I was strange on Earth too."

"Well, then..." Monia said, placing the knife down and picking up her bowl, "... maybe you are the bridge between realms."

Chapter Four

Ana

My pregnancy frightened me, and I feared for my child. I had no idea what to expect.

Were Guardian pregnancies the same length as humans'? Were the babies the same size? It's not like I could check myself into a hospital and have a C-section if something went wrong. There'd be no drugs, no nurses. Only the Guardians. Who, while they'd done this before, never with a mixed breed.

God, I missed Cael.

I kept telling myself that my mom had gone through this same situation with an unknown outcome, giving birth to me. But I'd learned that the environment impacted the beings within. The fact that I was a half-Guardian was only part of the factor. I was conceived, born, and raised on Earth. My mother was on Earth throughout her pregnancy with Earth's energies and influences surrounding her. A Guardian on Earth, too long, could lose their powers apparently, so it stood to reason that a part-Guardian would grow up differently in Lucidis than they would on Earth. So, *my* birth, childhood, and life could be no point of comparison for that of my child.

My child would be three-quarters Guardian, born and raised here. So maybe they would be more Guardian than human. Perhaps the human part would barely be a part at all.

The thought both comforted and saddened me.

When I expressed my concerns to Monia, I was told we couldn't know what would happen. I knew that, but I didn't want cold facts. I wanted comfort. I wanted someone to tell me that everything would be okay. Monia tried to reassure me and lay her large hand on my shoulder, reminding me I had support. But Monia couldn't do as humans would and assure me everything would be okay because Guardians didn't lie.

Still, I waited for Cael.

Sitting across from Sasha and Esco—another female Guardian who had taken the time to welcome me into the community—I rubbed my stomach, now so large I couldn't see my feet when I stood. I was five days over nine months and constantly on edge. I sought comfort from my unborn child, leaning forward and whispering to them, asking them to tell me they were okay. They'd kick, and I'd sigh, taking that as the comfort I needed.

The baby was a boy. I didn't know how I knew. I just knew. I *felt* it. Something about the energy he exuded and how he moved. Something that would have sounded crazy if I tried to explain it back home on Earth, but here, energies were like a language unto themselves. Given how long I'd been in Lucidis, I thought that perhaps my body was leaning further into my Guardian side, and maybe I was picking up on some of these energies, too.

Sasha reached over and rubbed my stomach. "He will be an interesting child."

I nodded in agreement and didn't question her choice of pronoun. She felt it, too, then, that he was a boy. That helped me feel a little less crazy.

"Will he be okay, do you think?" I asked.

Esco tilted her head. "He is alive. He is okay."

"That's not what I meant."

Esco made a noise of acknowledgment, and I didn't push the matter. I appreciated that Esco tried to connect with me. She was quiet and gentle, and while she frowned a lot when I talked and tried to understand why I would say or think some things, she never criticized me. And like Sasha, she never looked down on me as though I were weak or a lesser being.

On those rare occasions when I caught a glimpse of the Guardians' more human reactions, such as a smile or even anger, it was enough to keep me going and continue trying to fit in with the community. It was enough for me to have hope that even if my son displayed human qualities, he would be at home here.

"Do you know what his name will be?" Sasha asked.

I made a non-committal gesture with my shoulder. "I have some ideas."

"Call him Novus," Esco said.

"Why?" I asked. She offered the name as if it were the most normal thing in the world or something I should have already considered.

"That is my father's name." Esco's bright eyes studied me.

"Why would I name him after your father?"

"It's a good name."

I smiled at the simplistic answer. Of course, that's the reason. *Why else, right?* "Yes, it is."

While there were enough Guardians who accepted me for who and what I was, and a greater circle who were fascinated by my existence and impending child and treated me well enough, I still couldn't wait for the day when Cael returned. I missed him as if I were missing a part of myself. I couldn't observe Earth as the others could. I'd tried to mimic the creation of a Gateway a few times, sure that I'd seen a flash at one point, but no one believed me. They told me to wait, always to wait for Cael's return. He'd teach me if I could be taught and help determine my place in the community.

At least I could work in the gardens now, Monia had shown me what to do, and it was nice to have *something* to do.

Cael had been gone so long, and as much as the thought filled me with dread until I felt as though I couldn't breathe, sometimes I thought maybe he had been killed. What if Nathaniel had returned somehow and executed Cael as revenge? Monia assured me he was okay, and I guessed she must be checking up on him somehow, but I wouldn't feel whole again until he was here with me, until I saw him with my own eyes and held him again.

I'd hoped he'd be present for the birth of our child, but the reality that it might not happen haunted me with every hour that dragged on. It was an ever-present thought I didn't even try to express to the Guardians since they wouldn't understand my need to have him close for the birth anyway.

Surely, I was close to the end of this pregnancy soon, which was frightening enough, but more so was the prospect of doing it without Cael.

Several community members were gathered around a Porthole—a partially formed Gateway not used for transport and created only for viewing and, when required, influencing. They milled around, muttering about increased disturbances to the Balance across the country.

I hovered around the edge of the group, wanting to ask questions, but instead watched and listened, hoping to learn.

The disturbances were spread out over vast distances, each on its own would certainly draw the Guardians' attention, but not necessarily the level of reaction that passed through the community now.

Something was happening, something bigger than they were telling me.

Although many things happened that they didn't tell me.

So, I listened.

"These disturbances, while physically far apart, all follow a similar pattern. A single act creating a ripple of grief and pain."

"So many in such a short time?"

"Unusual."

"Should we involve the Elders?"

"It is too soon to conclude anything. We will deal with this."

"How many are dead?" A Guardian, I didn't know the name of, asked no one in particular as he entered the area where everyone was gathered.

"Fifty-seven and counting," Sasha answered without moving

her eyes from the Porthole. I couldn't see what they could—the air shimmered, and the Porthole's energy made my fingers tingle, but that was all. The Guardians were working, and I didn't want to interrupt.

"The number of dead is irrelevant..." Ferox chimed in, "... only the subsequent effect."

"I'm not a fool, Ferox." Sasha's lips pressed together as though she were barely containing her anger. "But the number of dead *is* relevant as it affects the number of grieving."

"You only say that because you have a weakness for the humans."

"I say that because we need to know how to deal with this."

"There are other Lucidian communities closer to the area," Ferox said. His voice carried a dismissive tone as he grew tired of the conversation. "Let them deal with it."

"But haven't you noticed a pattern? Doesn't it seem that Tenebrians are more active?"

He waved a hand at her, brushing away her words. "They are *always* active. As with much else, it has always been the way. They will never stop, and neither will we."

"I know, but—"

"Stop arguing with me."

"You're overlooking the issue here!"

Ferox scoffed at her outburst and turned away. Sasha straightened her shoulders and lifted her chin slightly, wiping her face of expression as Ferox continued, "If there were a bigger problem, the Elders would tell us." He left it at that while Sasha's hands curled into fists. I couldn't stop my eyebrows from raising. She was trying to calm herself internally, having been denied the opportunity to speak her mind. I *knew* it. I could *feel* how she felt as clearly as if the feeling had been my own. The revelation excited me, but I said nothing. There were a few moments of silence as everyone continued to watch the event unfold through the Porthole, and I desperately wanted to know what had happened.

Coming up behind Sasha, I stood next to her. Her pupils darted about as she took in the scene before her.

"Am I failing?" she whispered. I didn't know if Sasha was talking to me, so I said nothing. Sasha shook her head. "If a Tenebrian caused such large-scale pain and death, then have we failed in our duty to protect the humans? Should we have seen this coming?" Her voice dropped again until I could barely hear her. "I can't believe the Elders would not be in control. Maybe Ferox is right. Maybe I care too much. I should only care about the Balance."

She trailed off and said nothing further, lifting her hands to help push positive energies through the Porthole with the other Guardians, trying to even out against the fear and grief of whatever had happened.

I had to know. "What's going on?"

"Ana." Sasha turned to me as if seeing me for the first time. "You shouldn't be here."

I'd seen the Guardians agitated before, but not like this. Looking around at the group gathered, their nervous energy pulsated around them. "Tell me what's happening. Is Cael okay?"

"Cael is fine. There's been an accident on Earth, far away from him."

"Accident?"

"A thirty-two-car pile-up on a major highway."

I looked over Sasha's shoulder to where the Guardians still watched. "I can't see anything."

"I don't want you to see it."

I couldn't help it. I started to tear up, cursing at my hormones and emotions as I swiped the tears away angrily. I wanted to help, and this was a duty to them. The Guardians weren't getting upset. They were doing their jobs—the death and destruction in front of them didn't change their expressions. With every tear I shed, I highlighted myself as an outsider.

"Did the Tenebrians do this?"

Sasha placed a hand on my belly, her voice soothing. She showed none of the emotion that welled within me, although her eyes betrayed her. "Please, stay calm for the child."

I rubbed my stomach subconsciously. "I'm scared."

I didn't even know what I was referring to. Was I scared of the Tenebrians, the chaos on Earth, for my son, or all of it? Sasha's expression tightened when she sensed my uncertainty, and her first instinct as Guardian was to calm me. Her hand grew warm against me as she forced energies into my being to soothe me.

I grabbed Sasha's hand and shoved it away from my stomach, ignoring the stab of a cramp that gripped my abdomen.

"Stop. No influences." I glanced over Sasha's shoulder again. "Your energy is needed elsewhere."

Chapter Five

Ana

Images of car accidents and death infiltrated my dreams and flooded my soul with fear, forcing me to wake. Instinctively, I held my belly with one hand as I sat up, slowly arching slightly to stretch out my aching back. I was drenched in a cold sweat, and my light blanket was strewn across the floor of my sleeping quarters.

I spent my nights in a large hut shared by several others and wondered briefly what had woken me from my nightmares when the noises of two Guardians having sex three beds over made their way to me. My brows furrowed. I'd mostly learned to sleep through the sounds of others having sex, so I wondered why—

A piercing stab of pain shot through my gut, causing me to curl over, groaning loudly. When the pain reoccurred, I clutched my swollen abdomen and cried out, "Mom!" and a sob wracked my body as I realized the mattress and my legs were wet, how did I not feel that before?

My water had broken.

I wanted my mother.

Monia appeared moments after I cried out a second time and rested a hand against my forehead before touching my stomach tentatively and closing her eyes. I breathed shakily through the next contraction as Monia channeled energy through her palm. For a moment, I thought she was trying to calm me and was about to protest at being manipulated when I cried out again.

"It is time, Anahera."

As Monia helped me stand, I started to cry, and I hated the tears that came. It wasn't only the pain that forced the tears to come. I was frightened. I'd only had fleeting thoughts of having children when I was on Earth, and now I was faced with the reality of having a child to care for in a strange world.

Without Cael.

We walked slowly into another community building, and Monia was forced to pause every time a powerful contraction struck me, and I had to stop. I cried out with each sharp pain and gripped Monia's hand, biting my lip after each shout as though that would somehow make me feel stronger. The pain was intense, and my fear increased. Was something wrong with my baby? Was it meant to hurt this much? When I started to sob again, Monia squeezed my hand.

"Calm yourself, Anahera, everything is okay."

Guardians don't lie.

A few more steps, and I had to stop again. The contractions were getting closer together. Monia's brows drew together when I clutched her fingers.

"Very strong..." Monia muttered, and I lifted my face to hers, aware of the sweat on my forehead despite the cool chill of the night.

"W-what?"

Monia patted her free hand on top of mine and urged me toward the community hut. "Your grip is very strong."

"I'm sorry," I whispered, wheezing slightly through another shock of pain.

"It is okay. I am strong too."

When we reached the community building, Monia helped me to the ground where simple bedding was set up—*had Monia been expecting the birth tonight?* She laid a blanket over my stomach and another by my feet. When she gently guided me to bend my legs, I cried out, "Cael, *please.*" before another particularly strong contraction had me again calling, "Mom!"

She wasn't here. No one was here. Not Penny. Not Cael. Not anyone I had loved.

Tears streamed down my face, and I gave up trying to stop them, looking at Monia as she gripped my ankles. Her face seemed almost sympathetic, and I felt a pang of guilt, crying out for my mother when Monia was here, trying her best to support me.

I wanted to thank her, but instead, I asked, "Have you done this before?"

"Many times."

But she was still frowning and took a deep, steadying breath before she looked between my legs.

"What's wrong?" I gasped, gripping the blanket and my teeth through the pain.

Monia offered me a small glance. "You are different." Yes, yes. I was different. I'd heard little else from the Guardians for almost ten months. Again, I opened my mouth to say something, but couldn't get the words out.

Monia patted my leg. "I forget sometimes you cannot control

your wordless communications. You are calling to me."

Was I? I had called for my mother. That didn't mean her.

Monia looked sympathetic again and touched her chest. "Here. You are calling for me here."

With another pang of guilt, I let my head drop back against the pillow. This wasn't only my child, this was Cael's as well, and Monia's grandchild.

We were family.

As I lay on the ground, Monia at my feet and contractions ripping through my core, I still felt separate from Monia, from this community, from this realm. I looked down into Monia's eyes, and for a moment I could've sworn her passive exterior dropped, and I felt a wave of affection radiating from her. Was that in my mind? Did I just *read* Monia? She was, at her core, a mother herself, and I shouldn't forget that.

Through our eye contact and Monia's hand on mine, there was a connection between us.

And that was the comfort I needed to get through the birth without breaking down.

After several hours of agony and as the sun dawned on a new day, with one final exhausting push, my son was born into the realm of Lucidis.

The hours of childbirth were nothing compared to the enhanced agony of those few seconds when I waited to hear him cry. Nothing else mattered at that moment—not the place I was living or who I was with, nor the community members I didn't even know who had come to witness the birth. None of that mattered. The moment that baby boy was placed in my arms, his face scrunched up as he wailed, my heart felt whole again. I smiled, seeing his blue skin and the shine of his still-wet scales.

He cried, but not for too long, and a connection formed as I looked into his eyes. Was this something all mothers on Earth felt? I couldn't know. But something passed between us—a bond that filled the air and enveloped us both. He was Cael's son. He was far beyond human or Guardian or anything I had imagined possible, and he was mine.

I held him close to my chest as he fumbled for my breasts with his chubby fingers, and as he looked up at me, I watched him feed and felt the wisdom that was born into him through his genes.

I was overcome with nothing but hope for the future.

For our son, Samael.

Chapter Six

Vikt

We met in a small group in a clearing in Tenebris. We kept our gatherings brief and infrequent, as several Guardians had already been killed over minor disagreements. I had used Ignis as much as he had me, for sex, for gathering followers. But he'd been too far gone to gain much momentum with other Guardians, too extreme, too dark, labeled wild before anyone had even listened to what he'd had to say. Ignis hadn't understood that even here, we had to tread carefully. There were Tenebrians—although in dwindling numbers—who still cared for their duty above all else. I managed to gain support from more Guardians than he ever had, although Ignis held the charm and the power to loom over everyone. While we were still seen as his supporters, half of them wouldn't have known Ignis existed without me.

Besides, he had been a good fuck, so I was happy to hang around. At first, I ignored his ramblings about the injustices of our existence, but the more time I spent with him, the more I realized he had been right. Our home was a nightmare fueled by the negative energies of the humans we were bound to protect—and for what? So they could live in blissful ignorance of our existence and the teetering point our realms existed on.

It was time to shake things up, but as Ignis was prone to do, he launched into it headfirst. He had no plan and headed straight for Earth, causing as much damage as he could. Of course, he was bound to gain the attention of the Lucidians. But I was smarter than Ignis. If we wanted to make waves, we needed to spread our attacks. Cover distance and time. Create ripples until those ripples of negative energy collide with each other.

Until the Balance was interrupted.

Then we could push it further and further.

Until ultimately, it would Shift.

"There were several Lucidians at the site of the accident. I think they are becoming suspicious," one of the followers said. I hadn't bothered to learn most of their names as it seemed pointless. I knew their faces, and that was enough.

I shrugged. "They respond to all disturbances."

"No, this was different. There were energy patterns from several communities. They were viewing the accident through Portholes. They are connecting the incidents." His eyes darted around as though the Lucidians may be listening right now, and I scowled at him. A connection wasn't possible from one of our realms to another, only through Earth. He knew this. "Perhaps they suspect a rebellion."

Unfortunately, in this case, he may be correct. But I lifted my chin. I'd rather cut off my fingers than admit someone else was right. This was my mission, *my* time to take the metaphorical reins and make a change following Ignis' death. To finish what he started and do what he didn't have the foresight to plan for.

"There is something else."

"What?" I snapped, turning toward Culo, my second in charge, as he spoke up.

"Did you feel the disturbance? A few hours ago."

"Of course I did."

"It felt like pain and fear. Intense enough to flow directly between the realms and a strong life force, almost splitting in two."

My lip twitched as I listened to Culo's explanation. Why was he breaking it down as though I were a child? But I understood as my eyes scanned the remainder of the small group. They didn't understand what he was referring to. They were too young and inexperienced to differentiate that sense from the regular unease that settled over Tenebris daily. "What do *you* think it means?"

"I don't know..." He hesitated. "You don't think it was *her,* do you? The half-breed?"

I *did* think so, but she wasn't our priority. Ignis had said she was dead, but if she wasn't, she was as responsible for his death as the Lucidian was. "If it were, we'll kill her."

"How?"

I scoffed loudly. "Keep your mouth shut until you have something useful to offer." He looked as though he was about to question me again, but a lift of my lip to show a snippet of my bare teeth was enough to make him back down. The half-breed wasn't important. If we had come across her, I would have sought my revenge then, but while Ignis had seemed hung up on her and the part she played, I didn't see the significance. We were working on my plan, and it *was* working.

But the others were right about one thing—the Lucidians were beginning to suspect something. We had no deadline, and

I could be infinitely patient. "We'll back off for a while," I said, rolling my shoulders and stepping back. The meeting was over, but I raised my finger to hold their attention for a moment longer. "But we are not done yet. Don't get complacent, and don't think for a moment a break means we're backing away from our goal."

There were a few nods, but mostly dark eyes as they watched me, waiting for me to say something further. With a wave of my hand, I dismissed them, and the Guardians scattered to go about their pleasures, done for now with any mission or responsibility.

Chapter Seven

Ana

As I had been doing for months, I continued to watch the Lucidians as they observed humanity. The spikes of negative energies felt across the realm's walls were investigated and corrected if required. It was still strange to me that humans could be observed at any time—it seemed such an invasion—and I tried to hide my disgust in the early days when I thought of a Guardian catching a human in a compromising position. However, as the months passed, I realized it was done passively, and it began to feel less like an invasion and more like beings simply doing their jobs. More like... Guardian angels, I guessed. Chuckling to myself, I shook my head—the irony of the comparison wasn't lost on me.

Lucidians and Tenebrians, the proverbial angels and demons on humanity's shoulders.

Sometimes, they almost looked like angels in the right light, with the sun behind them streaming across their ice-blue and white spikes. The ridges in their skin sat nearly flat like scales when they were calm, only rising when they sensed the disturbances in the Balance.

Scaly and spikey angels, but somewhat like angels nonetheless.

On the days when I was alone with my thoughts, which was often, it was difficult to stop my thoughts from wandering to the topic of religion on Earth. Did someone sense the Guardians watching us? Were Tenebrians the real-life Devil? Whispering in our ears and encouraging us to be the worst versions of ourselves?

Or did God exist beyond all three realms?

Questions too big for me. So, I continued to watch. I couldn't help them, although sometimes my fingertips would tingle as they corrected the energies.

I reminded myself to ask Cael when he returned home if he had seen me before we met. It was unlikely, and I was being foolish even considering it. But the thought had crossed my mind more than once, and I had to know. I'd noticed some of the younger Guardians occasionally watched humans' interactions around the negative energy pulses—watching the humans' reactions and actions as if they were a reality television show. My stomach churned when I first saw it, but it seemed so few of the Guardians, and they were so young, looking like teenagers and, I guessed, behaving as such. I tried my best to understand—they were still learning, after all, about what it meant to be human.

Maybe that's what they were doing—learning about humans, and I'd hate to discourage it.

The Guardians were raised being told that humans were lesser life forms, weaker, and of lower worth. They played their role in maintaining the Balance and not much else. It was like humans watching mice. However, I knew from conversations that the attitude within the younger generation was shifting, and they were witnessing human interaction with less of a formal approach and more interest in their emotions and how they cared for one another.

This is where my one use in the community came into play.

I'd become the go-to for questions on humanity. Guardians had questions about *so* many things, and I did my best to explain them in a way they could understand. Things I never thought I would have to explain, and sometimes, it was like talking to aliens. There were parts of being human that just... *were,* and how to find words to explain those things when I'd never had to before?

Relationships and breakups were big ones, along with weddings and parties.

"*Why stay with one partner?*"

"*Why the term 'wife'?*"

"*Why raise your children at home, then send them to a school to learn together?*"

Sometimes I struggled to answer seriously when my default on Earth was to be sarcastic. But I tried, I *really* tried. For the first time in my life, I tried to fit in and wanted to be part of something. Without Cael, I was a fish out of water. It wasn't easy to learn when so few were willing to teach. Sasha, Esco, and Monia were kind to me, but it felt like I would bother them by bombarding them with questions when they had work to do. There were a lot of humans on Earth, after all, with a multitude of emotions and energies, and the importance of maintaining the Balance was stressed to me several times.

So, usually, I tried to learn the same way the young Guardians did, by watching.

But today, I'd made sure I was alone. Today was the day I was going to try to open a Gateway.

I'd seen the Guardians doing it often enough now, and Samael was with the community's other infants today. I wanted to be with him constantly, to keep him to myself, and find a quiet place to play and rest. But, as part of my initiative to be part of this community, although they continually insisted I wait for Cael to return, I relented, allowing Samael to be raised with the other children.

Most of the time.

Some days it was just the two of us, and those were my favorite days.

Although I longed for the days when the three of us would be together.

Standing alone in my sleeping quarters, I spread my hands in front of me, picturing the Gateway in my mind as I remembered it from the night I saw one with Nathaniel. I hadn't yet been able to see one here, but I'm sure that was due to a lack of training. If the others would take the time to *show me...*

No. Being angry wouldn't help.

I wasn't exactly sure what I was supposed to do, but I followed my instincts and imagined Earth. In my mind, I could see my old apartment and the city streets, and smell the coffee in the air from the shop on the corner. I could hear the tram passing by, and how the sound was muted when I closed the windows. I could feel Seamus rubbing against my ankle and his whiskers against my skin as I reached down to pet him, and he'd push his face into my palm. Then Penny's subsequent laugh when I'd come home covered in fur.

My face scrunched up as the tears welled in my eyes—fuck, I

was getting too detailed, too specific to my life.

My *old* life.

I needed to picture the city and, more importantly, *feel* it. Blinking away the memories, I shook my hands and tried again. Using my fingers to feel the air, I tried to sense what it would feel like in the city, the way the Guardians did. Was someone in trouble or hurt? Was a family grieving? A slight static shock hit my fingers, and I jumped in surprise.

"That was it," I muttered, feeling a bit silly at how excited I got from the tiny spark. But that could have been the beginning of a Gateway. That feeling, I needed to focus on *that*.

Repositioning my feet, I tried again, forcing my hands to stop trembling and relax. Moving my hands through the air, slowly, in cautious circles, I paused whenever I felt a brush against my fingers that had nothing to do with the breeze. It was as though I could feel the edge of the realm itself, an invisible force that held the realms apart, and all I needed to do was find a loose thread and pull.

After several minutes, when nothing had happened, frustration bloomed in my chest, and I took a few deep breaths and repositioned my hands—this time, as if I were trying to poke a hole through the air. The quills on my back stood up, and I tried again, attempting to force a reaction between myself and the air around me. I imagined the air was *hiding* the Gateway, and all I needed to do was push it aside and find it, like clearing fog from around a signpost. Flattening my palms, I clapped my hands against the air before me as though it were a glass window.

Then it happened.

I was thrown off my feet.

Blinking a few times, I shook my head. One moment, I'd been standing in the middle of the room, and the next, I'd been thrown against the wall. Turning my head, the wall had been damaged with the impact when I'd hit it, and the supporting post splintered where it had cracked.

Holy shit, just like in the movies.

Stretching, I groaned but didn't feel like I was too injured beyond a bit of bruising, although I rubbed my hands over my arms and legs to be sure.

My neck tingled, and I straightened and stared in front of me. The air rippled and shimmered, shifting between blue and a deep orange, and it made my skin crawl whenever the color changed. An abrupt wave of fear washed over me, and scrambling to my feet, I pushed myself back against the wall, away from the apparition.

This wasn't a normal Gateway. I didn't know what it was, but it wasn't normal.

Should I call for help? Would they be angry at me? What if I had endangered the community in some way?

A small group of young Guardians ran into the room, one shouting, "What is going on?"

Of course, they would feel the disturbance, and I cursed under my breath for not realizing they would.

They all turned simultaneously toward the failed Gateway and, without hesitation or another word, worked together to close it, spreading their hands, palms flat, and closing the space between their hands in a measured movement that finished in a quiet clap. The Gateway disappeared after a thin line of white and orange shimmered as if holding on to the connection.

"What did you do?" Ferox turned aggressively toward me as I

remained pressed against the opposite wall, staring at where the Gateway had been.

"Back off," Sasha snapped, moving forward to help me to my feet as I slid down the wall. My skin was still crawling. What had I done?

"What was *she* doing?" Ferox demanded, pointing at me but looking at Sasha.

"*She* was attempting to make a Gateway." I straightened and faced him.

He approached and towered over me. Ferox was a darker shade of blue than Sasha but with vivid streaks of white. I was told he was immensely popular with the females. I didn't see it, but I had no interest in anyone except Cael. "You have no business doing such things. You were told to wait."

"Told to wait, always wait. *Wait for Cael to return*, he'll know how to handle the half-breed."

Sasha placed a hand gently on my arm, ending my rant. "Ana..."

"No," Ferox smirked. "She is right."

I stared him down, trying desperately to fight the rage burning inside me. But there wasn't only rage. There was fear that *he* was *right*. No one knew how to handle or what to do with me, nor where I fit into the community.

If I could fit in at all.

Where did that leave me for the rest of my life? And a more horrifying thought, one I had been trying to stamp down since the day it first formed in my mind, stronger and stronger every day I waited...

What if Cael never came back?

Sasha turned to me, and I pressed my lips together. No doubt she could sense the shift in the air at my emotions—emotions I couldn't hide. Because at the end of the day, I was still half human, and constantly trying to be something I wasn't, only forced me to push everything down inside. Then, at times like this, it would boil over. There was no hiding from the Guardians. They knew what I was feeling all the time. It was humiliating.

The quills on Ferox's back quivered. "You are scared."

"No," I mumbled with little conviction.

"You are afraid of me."

I scoffed. He could sense my fear, but one thing they couldn't do was figure out *why* I was feeling something. "I'm not afraid of *you.*"

"Typical *human.*" Ferox practically spat the word out.

"Enough!" Sasha stood between me and Ferox, lowering her voice. "That's enough."

She placed a palm on each of our chests, forcing her calm through us.

Ferox slapped Sasha's hand away. "Do not touch me," he growled out and left, followed shortly by the rest of the group, who had no interest in the situation beyond repairing the failed Gateway. Although one or two threw a curious glance back at me, and I hated to think what was on their mind.

Freak. Dangerous. Stupid human.

I closed my eyes and allowed Sasha to calm me. I needed it, and she was my friend, at least I hoped she was. Did Guardians have friends? Another thing I couldn't find the words to ask. The warmth spread from Sasha's palm through my chest, and while it soothed me, it also morphed my anger into despair. When I opened my eyes, they shone with tears.

"Why are you so nice to me?" I whispered.

"Because Cael is my friend, and he loves you, so you are my friend."

Oh. "It can't be that simple."

"Really? I think it is that simple."

"Guardians don't believe in love," I said.

"Cael does. Maybe he knows something I don't."

I shook my head and dropped myself heavily on the edge of a nearby bed. "You're all so confusing. Just when I think I understand something about you..."

After a brief silence, Sasha asked, "Why were you trying to open a Gateway?"

I huffed and looked away as though that could stop her from reading my emotions in the air between us. "I don't know. I'm trying to figure out where I fit in here, in this place." I looked at my hands, at the skin I barely recognized as my own. Shifting my gaze to my feet, I swung my legs out from the side of the bed. It was too high for me to touch the floor while sitting.

Because Guardians were tall, and I wasn't.

Blue feet with scales. Not my feet. "I'm not human. Not anymore."

Sasha sat next to me. "But you are not quite a Guardian, either," she said it without malice. It was just a simple fact, but it still stung.

"So I've been told," I mumbled as I looked at the floor. Again and again, I'd been told, through words and glances, through the way I sat alone, and the way they watched me when I disappeared to spend some time alone with Samael.

"That Gateway was unusual," Sasha muttered, her brow furrowing. "The orange..."

"I didn't mean to do it like that." Sasha stared at the space where the Gateway had been, held her hands in front of her face, and glanced between her fingers and the emptiness before her as if expecting the Gateway to reappear. When she didn't speak again, I sighed and dropped my chin to my chest. "Everyone keeps telling me to wait for Cael, like he will have all the answers. But I think it's because no one knows what to do with me." I turned toward Sasha. "What if he never returns, and I'm alone forever?"

"He'll come back." Sasha glanced at me before she stood abruptly. "I need to go."

"Where are you going?" I stood with her. She was one of the few Guardians I felt I had something that resembled a friendship with, something I'd tried to nurture more than I ever did with anyone outside of Penny on Earth. But whenever I spoke with Sasha about Cael, she would leave, sometimes for days, and it was difficult not to stomp my foot like an angry teenager vying for attention. "You disappear all the time."

"I'm just helping where I can." Sasha touched me gently on the shoulder and hesitated, all the things she wasn't saying poised behind her lips and conveyed in her eyes. A rare glimpse of compassion shimmered through the blue of her irises. She squeezed my shoulder before dropping her hand, and I glanced at the spot where the brief contact had disappeared, thankful for this small gesture to show she cared. "You're not alone, Ana."

One of the most difficult parts of getting used to life in Lucidis wasn't the other Guardians, the lack of electricity, or their strange social etiquette. No, the hardest part was the human Reflections in the realm. I understood their purpose and knew they weren't real. Or they *were* real, just not *really* humans. If I thought about it too much, it made them seem strange and intimidating, like they were monsters. It was easier to think of them as humans, even though I knew I probably shouldn't. I liked to watch them go about their time, and when I was at my lowest, and Earth seemed like it didn't exist beyond my memories, they made me feel less alone. I could pretend I was in a crowd of people, and although they didn't see me, it didn't matter. If I zoned out, I'd feel like I was on a break from my job at the bar, people-watching like I used to.

The Reflections wandered around the realm. They would play in the river, climb trees, or pick flowers. Their play was almost childlike, pure and innocent. They were all ages and genders. Sometimes, they walked close to each other but never seemed to interact much. They were here to absorb the positive energy the realm of Lucidis offered. They were a connection to the souls of humans, yet they did not truly exist themselves. They had no names, no history, nothing. They simply... were.

At one point, I'd followed some of them as they wandered along the river's edge and had been led to a magnificent waterfall. I stopped dead in the grass and stood in awe. The rainbows created from the sunlight as it filtered through the mist from the falling water were nothing short of breathtaking, like a painting you'd find tucked away in a second-hand store, just sitting there waiting to share its magic with someone. The trees surrounding it were dense, and the rocks were in perfect formation, allowing one to sit and watch the water.

Later, I asked Sasha why she'd never shown me the waterfall, and Sasha tried to explain that it didn't exist as it was seen. I sort of got it. It was like the torture devices I'd witnessed in Tenebris—purely for the Reflections, created by the energies of the realm and fed back through them in a never-ending cycle. The environment was molded by the Reflections as much as the Guardians within the realm. The waterfall existed, but its positive energies magnified its beauty.

The Reflections had no outside distractions, no fighting or hate, and their souls could absorb all the warmth and energy from the realm. In turn, this would soothe the souls of those on Earth through the invisible connection that wasn't quite understood but never questioned. The Guardians paid them no mind, and there was no need for them to because their presence in Lucidis was enough.

But I paid attention to them because, without being able to use a Gateway or a Porthole, they were the closest connection to home I had.

Sitting in the damp grass, I shivered at the memory of Tenebris and how they'd treated the Reflections in their realm. The Tenebrians worked hard to break the human spirit, as they had to because humans were stronger than they would ever admit. While the Reflections in Lucidis could simply exist, in Tenebris, they were tortured to counteract the positive energy.

To keep the Balance—I'm sure that's the excuse the Tenebrians would use. But how much torture was necessary, if any at all? Was the energy from Tenebris itself not enough?

I think they just enjoyed it.

I felt lonely when I wasn't with Samael and disconnected from the community. I understood they wanted to raise him alongside the other children, to train him to hone his powers as a Guardian and perform his part in the duty to protect the Balance.

But without him, I was lost.

So, I had the crazy idea that I'd try to approach one of the human Reflections. I'd resisted communicating with them as I'd wanted to respect the way of the Guardians. But the Guardians were not human, and they didn't seem to understand how much I missed human company.

Which is something I never thought would be a problem.

To me, they were more than just *my kind*. They were friends, family, and all my memories, even if they were nameless. I wanted to reach out to them to talk to someone who understood what it was to be human and wanting to enjoy the small things like singing while driving with the windows down.

This was the next best thing.

Standing, I made my way toward one of the Reflections.

"Hello," I said, hoping my smile was inviting. I waved as I approached a young woman who looked to be about my age.

As I got closer, the woman's image visibly solidified, and the edges shimmered before her image was so sharp I wanted to reach out and touch her to prove the woman was actually in front of me. Why were the emotions always creeping up my throat? I tried to blame it on hormones, but I didn't think that was the answer. Even though I considered myself relatively unemotional on Earth, here I might as well have been flapping my arms about dramatically every time I spoke.

I frowned as the Reflection's image cleared. The Reflections in Tenebris had been so strong that it was hard to believe they weren't physical presences, weren't real people in pain needing help. But the Reflections in Lucidis were lighter and softer, and I'd never seen one change before.

So, I could only conclude that she was changing because I got closer, and I wasn't sure if I should worry about that.

The woman stepped back from me as I came to a stop, her voice ethereal as she said, "Who are you?"

"My name is Ana. I just wanted to talk to you, say hello, and ask how you are."

"No..." The woman shook her head and took another step back, her eyes darting up and down my body. "No. Leave me alone." She held her hands up in surrender for an attack that wasn't coming before hissing the words through her teeth, "*What are you?*"

When I opened my mouth to answer, the wind was knocked from me as I was tackled to the ground. I went to shout, but a hand clamped over my mouth.

"Stay down," Sasha whispered urgently as she scooted back, dragging me with her until we were both hidden from the Reflection behind some trees.

The woman followed our progress with her eyes. But after a moment, she looked back at the river, and her gaze scanned the horizon. The air changed, shimmering slightly, and it took me a moment to realize Sasha was silently directing her energies toward the Reflection. Slowly, the woman's face lit up with a small smile, and she resumed her walk along the riverbank, her image fading into slight transparency as the sunlight cascaded gently through her body.

"Wha—"

"Ana," Sasha cut me off. "Do you not think you might be alarming to a human?"

Looking down, I turned my hands slowly, watching my scales flatten as I calmed. Squeezing my eyes shut, I willed the tears to stay at bay. I'd already spent too much time crying, and it bothered me how often I was upset. "I'm not human anymore," I said, voicing my thoughts. It hadn't occurred to me that the Reflection would see me as a monster.

Sasha embraced me as my voice cracked, and I stiffened in her hold. "You are one of us."

While I appreciated the rare physical comfort and took the chance to hold Sasha for a moment, I gently pulled away. "I don't want to forget who I am."

"I do not want you to, but you must understand you look different. The humans here are not real. They are here to soothe and balance the souls on Earth. If you interact directly with them, they see you as you are, not as a human or just a background figure, but as a creature they cannot comprehend. They are still human. They do not understand and can be frightened, and we cannot have that here. This is a positive place, and they must not be afraid or feel unsafe."

"I'm sorry. I didn't think... I'm sorry," I whispered, unsure what else to say.

Sasha shushed gently and reached out to touch my arm before pulling her hand back, still unsure what was and wasn't acceptable in comforting practices. She'd already pushed her boundaries with the hug and was figuring out where to go.

"It's okay. I'm sorry you are not being told everything. To us, this is all second nature."

"Do I have to ask you before I do anything?" My voice betrayed my stress, teetering on the edge of breaking again. Everything I did here was wrong. Samael would grow up and fit in, and then maybe he wouldn't want to be around me any longer. If Cael never returned, and Samael grew up thinking I was a freak, I'd be alone forever.

I never realized how much I relied on other people—on simply having them around—until they were no longer there.

Sasha leaned back slightly, an automatic response to the waves of negative emotion that coursed through the air as my loneliness and hopelessness overtook me.

"Of course not," Sasha said, finally deciding and reaching out to place her hand on my arm. "But, if you want to ask anyone, you can always ask me. Or Monia."

"I miss Cael."

"I know you do, but he will be back soon."

I nodded, but I'd been told this many times for months.

I tried to believe it every time, but it was hard to keep faith that I'd ever see him again.

When Monia told me she'd felt Cael pass through a Gateway and return home to Lucidis, I grabbed Samael from the community group and ran in the direction she indicated. The closer I got, the more my body responded to his presence, and my quills rose as a streak of familiar electricity passed across my skin. I didn't need to see him to know I was getting close. It was the feeling I'd had when I was on Earth, but amplified a thousand times. Almost as if I could reach out across the air with my mind and heart and link to his. He was reaching back, even though he didn't know I was here. We were connected, but he'd been gone so long that I'd forgotten how he made me feel, how my heart skipped a beat, and how his chest felt against my ear as he held me.

As his presence was being healed in Lucidis, so was the strength of his emotional imprint, and I almost cried with the feeling of it. He grew stronger every minute, recovering from his extended stay on Earth.

When I saw Cael in the distance as he basked in the sun's warmth, I stopped, unable to take another step. My legs became leaden, and Samael looked up at me as I squeezed his hand. I smiled down at him, and he returned the look, unsure what to make of the confusing wave of energies flowing from me—*elation, uncertainty, bliss.* But so much at once, I felt like crying, like my heart couldn't take it.

"Everything's okay, Samael," I whispered, and I felt him calm even at the sound of my voice. "We will wait here for your father."

My voice, his mother's voice.

Soon, he would meet his father for the first time.

I could feel Cael's strength building, knowing he needed this. He needed a little bit of time, and thankfully, he wouldn't need long because I didn't think I could give him much longer before I went after him. Cael needed a clear mind to absorb the realm's energies.

So, I waited for him to come to me and used all my determination to allow him this time so he could feel like himself again.

I couldn't imagine what he had been through. He thought I was dead. Did he blame himself?

Cael finally approached, and my hand shot to my throat as I

tried to contain my emotions. A small part of me wanted to keep my emotional imprint hidden as if this were a surprise party and not the reunion of two beings in love.

His deep voice warmed every part of me, and I teared up as he said, "You waited for me."

My resolve gave out shortly after, and I threw myself into his arms, holding him tight. Too tight as it turned out, and Cael gently loosened my grip, laughed through his tears, and coughed slightly. "Careful, I can't breathe when you hold me that tight."

"I'm never letting you go." My words were muffled as I nuzzled into his chest, breathing in his scent, his essence, and letting him heal my broken heart.

"I don't want you to." He wrapped his arms around me and pulled me close again, our bodies fitting together as if we were meant to be. I sighed.

We *were* meant to be.

"You waited for me," he said again, as his emotional imprint became a confusing jumble of love, loss, and hope.

"*We* waited for you."

"We?"

Reaching out, I pulled Samael into our embrace, somehow keeping my voice almost steady as I said, "Meet Samael, your son."

Cael kneeled and touched Samael's shoulder as they looked at each other, the energies passing silently between them as they recognized each other as kindred spirits, as family. Samael reached up and wrapped his small arms around Cael's neck, and Cael's tears returned.

"My son," he whispered.

I kneeled next to them, wrapping my arms around them. "My

family."

Chapter Eight

Cael

"This is so *frustrating*."

I touched Ana's shoulder and smoothed out her quills as they spiked in response to her emotions. Her anger filtered through the air between us, and I hid the desire to smirk at her subconscious need to announce what she was feeling, as though I couldn't read her without any words needed at all. I'd wanted to wait to teach her to focus enough to generate Portholes and Gateways, but Ana had insisted on getting started almost immediately after my return to the realm. I understood her needs as they filtered from her as clearly as her anger did now. She wanted to feel useful and needed, and currently, the only time she felt like that was when Samael reached out to her. She would light up then, falling into the role of mother so perfectly I couldn't imagine anyone being better.

When I returned to Lucidis after being gone for so long, I wasn't prepared to find Ana waiting for me, much less a son. As I'd gathered them in my arms, I never wanted to let them go, and I hadn't for a long while as we sat together and bonded through an unspoken connection. I took Samael in my arms and felt his essence, innocence, and confusion, but I reassured him without words, and he knew who I was. Ana had placed one hand on my shoulder and the other on Samael's back, strengthening the connection between us.

She'd been practicing focusing her powers. Practicing alone without much guidance, but still practicing. Desperate to find herself within this new body now that she was no longer a human on Earth. My jaw clenched as I thought of how long she struggled without me, my grief forgotten in the wake of her suffering. While I understood my mother's and Sasha's motivations for not telling me Ana was alive, it didn't take the sting away, and I had no idea how long it would take for that to be repaired.

Ana still had much to learn, so we might as well start by learning to open a Gateway.

I watched her as she shook her arms out. A changed woman, physically halfway between human and Guardian, and emotionally still learning to live in Lucidis as one of us, when deep down she felt she would never truly be.

She ignored almost as many emotions as she acknowledged.

Humans were complicated.

"It's okay," I said, squeezing her shoulder. "It's going to take time. We practice for years from when we are children. So breathe, and try again."

Ana ran her hands vigorously up and down her face before taking a deep breath to maintain her calm. But the forced façade of her calm was surrounded by the jagged edges of her frustration. It seemed her practices hadn't involved controlling her emotions.

"It's not working, Cael. I can't feel anything."

I paused before answering. "I've been thinking about this... and I think your human half might be holding you back."

Ana stared at me for a beat, the tension thick in the air between us. "You sound just like the others."

"You know I didn't mean it like that."

Ana sighed, leaning into my hand as I brushed her cheek, the slight physical touch enough to smooth the edges of the tension around us. "I'm sorry, it's just... I know what they say about me as if I'm some experiment. I have friends in the community..." She glanced behind her to where we could see the edges of the community from where we stood at the riverbank. "But it doesn't make the whispers hurt any less."

"Hold out your hand."

Ana glanced at me, and a smile formed on her perfect lips as her cheekiness peeked through her frustrations. "Oh boy, a present."

I smiled back at her. There she was, the Ana I fell in love with from the moment I saw her. The woman who exchanged sarcastic banter with me during our first conversation, while hiding beneath layers of attraction, was a connection she couldn't begin to understand. It was comforting to be reminded she was still the same woman inside. She'd receded into herself—an act of self-preservation, I imagine.

Ana was holding her hand out, palm up, practically bouncing on the balls of her feet. I smirked before I placed her mother's necklace in her hand.

My smile dropped when hers did, and Ana stuttered through several words before she stopped trying. As Ana worked her bottom lip between her teeth, a wave of emotions spilled into the space between us, and I leaned into them, determined to feel what she was feeling.

Surprise. Hurt. Frustration. Fear. Guilt. Love. Gratefulness.

"Oh, Cael," she whispered, curling her fingers over the necklace. "I thought this was lost on Earth."

"I took it after you..." I swallowed heavily, closing my eyes for a moment and trying to shake the image of Ana dead in my arms from my mind. "... I took it." While she turned the stone over in her fingers, I felt the need to explain myself as though keeping such an important possession was somehow a betrayal. "In the end, I needed to use it to come home. I ah... cleaned it," I added as I rubbed the back of my neck, remembering the feel of the stone slipping into my wound.

Ana's eyes started to water as she put the necklace on, letting me help when her scales and claws got in the way of the fiddly clasp. She tried not to let her irritation show, but she'd already told me it felt like learning to walk again—a new body, home, and a son who relied on her and always came first.

She turned to watch Samael, who was playing in the grass near our feet as the pendant fell into its familiar place on her skin. Automatically, her fingers found the stone, and she twirled it. There was peace within the familiarity, and her quills flickered before smoothing and settling against her skin.

She was so beautiful.

"I'm sorry I didn't give it to you straight away." I watched her fingers as she twirled the stone, just as she had the first time we'd met. "We don't usually have possessions or gifts, and I didn't expect to find you here." When Ana smiled genuinely at me, some of my guilt abated, and I tried to shift my focus from my final days on Earth back to the training Ana wanted to do. "If we integrated moonstone into the equation, maybe it would override your human half... or at least help." I shrugged. "Or something like that. I don't know, Ana. I'm just making this up as I go along."

"That's comforting." She chuckled, nudging me playfully on the shoulder. I stumbled back on one foot with the force of her push, and a shadow of a frown passed over my face before I smiled at her, teeth bared and head bowed. I shoved her back, testing her and holding back on most of my strength.

She barely registered my touch.

I was still processing this when Ana grinned wickedly and launched herself across the grass at me, and the impact of her body colliding with mine knocked me off my feet.

She was *strong*.

Samael giggled as he watched us wrestle in the grass, while Ana's and my laughter was fueled by our son's joy, which permeated and lifted the air around us. It was innocent joy, so pure that I couldn't keep my thoughts straight as I tried to consider the implications of Ana's increased strength.

The ground shuddered underneath me as Ana pinned me down. When I couldn't get my hands out of her grasp, my mood unintentionally shifted.

So much stronger.

"What's wrong?" Ana's brow furrowed. "You're upset."

"Nothing."

"Is it because you're a sore loser?" she teased.

I smiled and allowed the residual effect of her joy to wash over me, soothing my concerns. There was time to consider those later. All the time in the world because now it was just Ana, me, and our son.

Perhaps my mother had noticed something while I was gone.

"It's okay." I lied. I was bothered she'd been able to overpower me, but I certainly wasn't going to let her know. I took advantage as her hands gripped my wrists and spread both arms out in one rapid movement, causing Ana to fall on top of me. I nipped playfully at her shoulder. "I let you win, anyway."

"Liar." She leaned down to kiss me, the heat from her skin fueling my desire as her soft lips pressed to mine, teasing me. Her passion as a human was *nothing* compared to her passion as a Guardian, and a shiver ran through my body as I responded to her. Ana giggled against my lips, sensing the change.

It would take me a while to get used to knowing she could read me as well as I could her.

"We can't," she whispered, even as her fingers flexed where they still held my wrists. I couldn't help my body's response to her, pressed against me while she had me pinned down.

So maybe I didn't mind so much that she could overpower me.

"Not here. We have Samael."

"Yes, but tonight he will be with the other children..." I nipped at her shoulder again, loving the way her scales flared with the flush of arousal, "and you'll be all mine."

Ana ran her tongue across my bottom lip, grinning when I shuddered again. She released my wrists and sat up, straddling me as I relaxed into the grass and linked my fingers behind my head.

"Does monogamy bother you?" Ana asked after a beat.

"No. Why do you ask?"

"I know it's not your way here." She stared into the distance, where the heart of the community was centered. "I thought maybe it would annoy you, me insisting that we be together, just us. Like I'm holding you back from your natural self or something."

Sitting up, I pulled Ana against me, my chest pressed against hers as her thighs gripped me. "It's not you insisting on anything. You are the only woman I need or want."

Ana smiled, then the smile dropped from her face just as quickly as it had appeared. "I don't think the others approve of how much Earth changed you."

I shrugged. "I'm not so sure it did change me all that much. I think I just learned a lot."

"Well, that's one way to look at it, but look at what it did to your powers."

I didn't want to think about how it felt to have my powers drained, how Earth had taken everything from me until I had nothing left to give. And I'd let it take, thinking I deserved nothing less for Ana's death. I shook the thoughts away. "Yes, but my powers are restored now. It didn't take long after coming home to return to my old physical state. Yet, I still feel the same about you as I did on Earth. That hasn't changed at all."

Ana looked around, taking a long visual sweep of the landscape as she nodded. Lucidis was a beautiful place. The sun was different here than on Earth. The brightness almost dulled so you could look directly at it without discomfort. But its light was warm and comforting and never burning. The plant life was spectacular, as if it were designed to sustain life and enrich the soul through its aesthetic beauty.

But Ana still missed Earth. I could almost feel the ache that resided deep within her being, and I wondered how much she struggled with the concept that this ache might never be fulfilled.

"Do you worry you'll outlive me?"

My brows furrowed with concern as I rested back on my elbows. "Why do you think of such things?"

"I'm always thinking of these things. It's hard not to. You could live decades longer than I. What's the average for Guardians? One hundred and twenty? One hundred and fifty? We don't know what my lifespan will be. I might only live as long as my human half allows."

"On Earth, yes, but we don't know that here. You don't know that I'll outlive you."

Ana frowned. "Of course you will." She gave me a sad smile, and my chest ached for her. She was constantly plagued with such negative thoughts. Too much time alone in her head. Guilt stabbed at me. "But at least I know that Samael will have you."

My lip lifted into a smirk. "I don't know, Ana, I'm pretty stupid. I could get myself killed after some reckless act."

Ana laughed. "That's the worst comforting you've ever done."

"But it made you smile." My tone dropped, and I rubbed her arm. "Ana, how about we just enjoy the time we do have? If you worry this much, you'll make me worry. I already lost you once, and I don't want to spend the rest of my life wondering about it happening again." Before she could answer, I bucked my hips. "Now get off me, and let's try again."

Ana climbed off my lap and held out a hand, yanking me to my feet with uncontrolled strength. She apologized as I stumbled, and I mumbled about missing my footing, internally cursing myself again.

Eventually, I would have to talk to her about how she was changing. But first, I needed to speak to Mother. Every day I put off this conversation, it ultimately made it harder. Ana wasn't stupid, and she knew her body had changed, but I didn't know if she realized the limits of her new strength, and I had no way of knowing how much stronger she'd potentially get.

What effect would further years in Lucidis have on her? Decades?

Would she become a danger to herself?

She needed to learn control, and I'd help her.

"Ready?" I asked.

Ana nodded and squared her shoulders, rubbing the pendant between her fingers briefly before she splayed her hands out in front of her.

"Picture Earth and picture a tear in the air itself... just concentrate on the feeling of it. While you picture Earth, feel the air on your fingers, work it around your hands, and... pull it open."

Ana frowned. She touched her fingers together and slowly spread her hands apart. She jumped and closed her hands into fists when a small white spark flickered between her fingers. "I felt it. I felt something!"

I smiled at her eagerness, the negative energy receding from her as she became excited. "Good. What did it feel like?"

"Like a static shock on my palms."

I nodded. "Okay, that's good. Now focus on that feeling."

Ana faced the riverbank and went to move her hands again, but stopped. "Wait."

"What's wrong?"

"Won't people on the other side be able to see the Gateway appear? I don't want to scare anyone."

"Humans can't see Gateways the way we do."

"But I saw one..." She stopped speaking when she saw the look on my face, a reaction I couldn't control. "Right, right, I'm not human." She huffed. "What do they look like to *normal* people, then?"

"Mirages sometimes, like hot air lifting off a scorching road. Or tricks of the light. I couldn't be sure exactly what you saw that night, but the scale of the Gateway showed it had been deliberately opened to spread negative energy and not to be used. I assumed you were attracted to the feel of it."

She sighed and went back into position, then hesitated again.

"What's wrong now?" A half-smile played on my face. She was my life partner, but she had so many questions like a Guardian child. I considered teasing her, but stopped myself. I didn't want to upset her intentionally, even though seeing her pout and cross her arms was fun.

But I knew what it was like trying to understand a strange realm.

"What if I open a Gateway to Tenebris by mistake?" Ana asked.

"You can't. Tenebris can only be accessed from Earth. We can't travel directly from our realm to theirs and vice versa." Ana nodded but didn't look convinced as I continued, "When opening a Gateway on Earth, we almost always have to open both simultaneously and then close the one we don't want."

Ana dropped her hands. "Wait, what? A Gateway to Tenebris?"

I inclined my head. "At the same time, yes. It's not as easy to control on Earth, so it usually opens both when you create a rip to make a Gateway."

"So, you could just... go to Tenebris? Just like that? Or they could come here?"

I frowned at her, considering. I'd never tried to go to Tenebris. Why would I? "There would be resistance, but I suppose it's technically possible. I suspect this realm holds no interest to the Tenebrians, plus they know they would be forced out. As for going there, I wouldn't want to. Would you?"

"You don't even need to ask that," Ana mumbled. I nodded again and lifted my hand, moving my wrist in small circles to indicate she should keep trying. Distraction, before the strength of the negative memories of her time in Tenebris could take hold of her again.

Ana straightened her back and spread her fingers again. This time, when she moved her hands away from each other, a small white and golden tear appeared before her, stretching like a piece of thread from her fingers. Ana gasped when the thread didn't break immediately.

Instinctively, she stepped back from the apparition, tripped over her feet, and fell to the ground. The movement caused the tear to follow her hands, creating a large rip in the air that snapped open to reveal a Gateway as it swept along with the motion of her arms as she fell.

The Gateway shimmered momentarily, and then the city street appeared in front of us, so close we could almost touch it and smell the car fumes. The Gateway waivered, then disappeared in a cloud of blue dust with a loud bang, throwing me off my feet.

"Whoa." Ana pushed herself up on her elbows and looked over at me. My anger surged, I couldn't help it, and I gathered Samael in my arms, checking to see if he was okay as Ana jumped to her feet.

"I did it. Did you see? I did it!"

"Yes." I stood, holding Samael while he played with the agitated raised scales on my shoulders, unbothered by the commotion. "But I think that's enough for today. We need to step back and work on your control more."

"Oh, come on, that was *brilliant.*"

"Ana!" She stopped her excited pacing and looked at me. Her face fell at the shock that radiated from me, but there was something underneath the surface I couldn't control, and she picked up on it before I could mask the emotion.

Fear.

I struggled to keep my voice level. "That could have been very dangerous. You need to be able to control your powers." She opened her mouth, and I cut her off. "Promise me you won't practice unless I'm with you, so I can help steady your energies."

The Gateway had collapsed in a powerful surge of energy, and I ground my teeth together. I should've been using my power to stabilize hers.

Was the Gateway's instability a direct reflection of Ana's inner volatility?

"But—"

"*Promise* me."

"All right, I promise." She threw her hands up in frustration. "I'm not a child, you know." She took Samael from my arms and planted kisses all over his face, making him giggle and squirm.

I rubbed Samael's back before kissing Ana's cheek lightly, letting my lips linger, and my frustrations ebb away. "I know. I'm sorry. But we're playing with unknown forces here. We need to be careful." I frowned at the spot where the Gateway had been.

Ana watched my face. "I'm sorry too. I just got excited."

"And you should be excited. That was a huge step forward."

She kissed me quickly on the lips and smiled. But behind the smile, a whirlwind of thoughts and emotions was swirling. I followed her back toward the community, both lost in the possibilities.

"Ana is an unknown, an anomaly, and there is much more to her than we realize." I watched my mother, Monia, as she spoke. I didn't call her *Mom* or *Mother* as Ana did when she spoke of her mother. I called her Monia. Because family was different here, we were a community, and knowledge of each other's parentage was only used to prevent inbreeding.

But Monia was my mother, and I felt a tie to her I had never considered verbalizing before my time on Earth. I knew she could feel it too. When I approached her a moment ago to discuss my concerns about Ana's strength, she touched my arm in a nurturing gesture she'd never displayed before, and for a moment, my words were lost.

"You make her sound like a science experiment." I failed to keep the emotion from my voice, the need to protect and watch over Ana practically running through my veins.

Monia's lip twitched into almost a smile before the moment was lost. "I simply meant being born on Earth and then residing here in Lucidis may affect her in ways we can't predict."

I briefly told her about my experience teaching Ana to open a Gateway, and she nodded. "Perhaps we should ask the Elders."

"Agreed." Cordus was wise, and while betrayal stabbed at my chest at going behind Ana's back, we needed their thoughts on her growing strength.

Stepping into the Elder's hut without an invitation felt like an intrusion, although our home was open to all. The power radiating from the beings here was unmistakable—a shield of power and experience that enveloped the structure and spread outward. When I walked through the doorway, my step faltered as I crossed the threshold, but I pushed through, unwilling to show weakness.

Monia took the lead in the conversation, and as she was older than I, I was in no position to interrupt. "Ana is showing strength beyond her mere humanity. I think she is changing, and we need to discuss the implications of this."

"Interesting..." Cordus cut Monia off as she opened her mouth to continue, "... maybe in time, she will be like us."

A flicker of irritation radiated from Monia, and I snuck a sideways glance at her as she tried to maintain her grace. She didn't always agree with the Elders, neither did I, but they had several decades on us and the wisdom of previous generations, so we needed to trust their judgment. I glanced around the small room as four of the six Elders stood before us, and every one seemed to remain impassive to our concerns about Ana's powers.

I didn't want Ana to be *like us.* I wanted Ana to be Ana.

"I am not sure it is that simple. I believe her human half might make her stronger than us," Monia continued.

Cordus's eyebrows flickered up, a movement so fast I started to doubt if I'd seen it before he spoke, "Impossible. Humans are weaker than Guardians, not stronger."

"But the combination of her parentage—"

"Is nothing to be concerned with." Cascus fixed her with a dark stare, one of his eyes milky with age, and his quills losing their glowing edge. Yet his strength radiated from him in waves, compressed by time into a fine point rather than dulled. When Cordus spoke, he looked between us, but Cascus would give me nothing more than a passing glance. "We have prevailed as a superior species for thousands of years, and I find it hard to believe a single human will derail us."

Cordus nodded. "I understand your concerns, Monia and Cael, but I must agree with Cascus. This is not the first time such a being—"

Cascus shot Cordus a warning look, and the air in the room changed. The Elders fell silent. They stared at us as though there had been no interruption, and the disagreement and tension between the Elders weren't practically visible in the air. I stared back, waiting for them to continue. I knew better than to push the matter. The fact that we had managed to talk with most of the Elders was more than I thought we would gain.

But they weren't listening, and I hadn't even begun to tell them of Ana's attempts at making a Gateway.

At that moment, I decided I didn't *want* to tell them.

I could protect Ana myself, and I didn't need their help, especially if they didn't want to give it.

It was Monia's turn to glance sideways at me when she felt the shift in my emotions and body. The tensing of my shoulders was the only physical sign of the mental barrier I had erected around my family.

When no one spoke, Monia continued, "But Anahera is not only a human. She is half of us and, therefore, half of everything that makes us. Cael believes that humans possess a strength we do not. If there is truth to that—"

"Cael is young and inexperienced."

"He has experienced much." Monia clenched her fists as she redirected her stare to Cascus, but only for a moment, unwilling to hold his gaze lest he view it as a threat to his position. They spoke about me as though I weren't there, and I willed my quills to stay flat and not add to the waves of anger I was already barely able to contain.

Monia had always believed the Elders to be wiser than the rest of the community, but sometimes wisdom meant taking new information on board and growing with it. The Elders were stubborn in their ways, and although Monia wouldn't say it, I'm sure she, as I did, suspected they knew much more than they were letting on.

And now, the same pattern presented itself with their views on Ana.

One day, that information might come to light, and it may not be in a way the Elders would approve. Wouldn't it be better to share what they knew with us?

I huffed out a breath through my nostrils. Of *course*, they knew more than they expressed. They were the Elders for a reason, and information passed down through the generations occupied their minds and souls. Each group of Elders merged their essence with those intended to take over from them and planted their knowledge deep within the other being.

They were under no obligation to share everything with the community. A Guardian's duties could be performed without complete knowledge of every detail about their existence.

But this was about Ana. *My* Ana.

If I pushed, I risked inducing their wrath and wouldn't stand a chance against their strength.

A shadow of a crease crossed Monia's forehead when they spoke down about me, and I was almost overcome with the desire to take her hand and squeeze it briefly, the way Ana did for me when she felt I was troubled. A small gesture to say *I'm here.*

"Do you believe Cael's feelings for a human are a revelation, rather than what it truly is—a weakness he succumbed to?" Scae asked, a female elder, shorter than her comrades, standing at six feet three, but as powerful.

I'd had enough.

"We must learn from the humans," I said.

"We know all we need to know about humans, as we have watched them for thousands of years. I am surprised we are having to cover this ground. Especially with you, Monia." Scae bowed her head briefly, and Monia returned the gesture.

Cascus inclined his head, barely a nod. "The humans are still today as they were the day they came to be... tools, a minor inconvenience, and a duty. Did you come here to question us, or to ask us a question?"

Monia retreated conversationally. We were pushing too hard. "Perhaps..." she paused, searching for the words, "we could use her power..."

"Use her?" Cordus's voice rose. A rarity that made me shudder.

"I simply meant—"

"That is enough, Monia."

Monia's eyes narrowed as they spoke to her as though she, too, were a child.

I took charge, undeterred by the fact that they barely acknowledged me. This was unlike Cordus. He usually spoke to me as an equal, and I'm sure that if this were a conversation between him and me without the influence of the other Elders, it would have been entirely different. I thought that out of respect, we should at least try to talk to a few of the Elders, but now it felt like a mistake, and even heavier than the regret of not going directly to Cordus was not including Ana.

I straightened my stance. "If I talk to Ana about it—"

Cascus cut me off. "You will do no such thing. You and the half-breed can sort out how you want to live out your lives in the community. You can try to teach her to control her powers if you can. But neither you nor Monia is to interfere or plant ideas in her head that she is stronger than she is. She is still half-human and, therefore, weak-minded and can be influenced as such. She will stay in Lucidis and be grateful for it."

The dismissal in his words was powerful enough without how he turned his back as he finished speaking. There would be no point in continuing to try to converse with them. I glanced at Cordus, and he offered me a slight nod. It wasn't much, but it was enough.

I would try to talk to him another time, alone.

Monia and I left the Elders' hut and returned to the community center.

"I wonder, Cael," Monia started, her voice strained and her neck muscles working around every word. I raised my brows. My time on Earth had affected her more than she let on, and I knew she had seen the change in me. But she never once suggested I try to change back to who I was, instead embracing all the new parts of me I had learned about. "I wonder how

Anahera was born without the Elders' awareness. And what of her father?"

I pressed my lips together. "Ana says he left when she was young, and she hasn't seen him since."

"Why did he not bring her here?"

"I don't know. We may never know."

Monia hummed in response, and I understood. I hated not knowing as much as she did, but there were more pressing matters. I needed to continue working with Ana on controlling her growing strength, which I could do while teaching her to use Gateways and Portholes. But I was still a Guardian, and my duty came first. Nothing was more important than maintaining the Balance.

I would talk to Ana about her growing power, one day when she had it under better control and when it wasn't so responsive to her emotions.

Before we parted ways, I reached out to touch Monia's arm. "Thank you for helping... Mother."

Monia held my eye contact momentarily, and the corner of her lip twitched before she nodded and walked away.

Chapter Nine

Culo

The city lights glimmered and flickered when viewed from a distance, as if the entire town was moving faster than the rest of the world. A living, breathing being in itself, every light was a synapse connected to another. The city was a living organism, held together by the interconnected emotional network of the humans inhabiting it.

I stood with a small group of Tenebrians atop the low hills at the city's edge, overlooking the lights. I could sense the energy pockets where we had been earlier that night, and the footprints of our negative influence interrupted an otherwise peaceful space. Like water flowing over stones on a riverbed, the chaos we had caused created upsets in the otherwise neutral energy. Naturally, humans' energies would mostly balance each other out, with the negative and the positive forces evened out to keep them together.

Mostly.

But we were on a mission—one that started with Ignis and was refined only after his death. Vikt liked to think she was the driving power behind it simply because she and Ignis fucked more than he fucked anyone else. Pathetic.

We'd created bouts of pain and fear in the city, keeping them close enough together to weave a net of negative energy over the space but not so close that they'd alert the Lucidians to our actions.

Not yet.

When the time came, the fogs created would be joined, and the Shift would begin.

We stood in the suburbs, an area of peaks and valleys with winding roads that gave residents a sense of privacy and the illusion that they were further from the city's hustle and bustle than they were. They could maintain the creature comforts of city living while having a *country feel,* and often endowed their homes with decorations implying they were country folk, which fooled no one.

The hills cut out a lot of the sound of traffic from the city streets, and I smiled as they also cut out a lot of the sound from one suburban house to another. The hills did funny things to the sound around here—a car pulling into a driveway three houses down could sound like it was outside your front door.

Similarly, a scream from next door could sound like it was over the valley.

Several screams from multiple houses at once created a chaotic mix of sounds that residents struggled to identify accurately during their calls to the local police force.

"Are we ready?" I asked the group with me. They nodded their affirmation, and I turned to the humans behind us, bound and thrown into the bushes that hid us all from the roads. I hadn't stopped smiling, and my teeth poked out between my menacing lips. Taking the humans from their homes had been easy. Humans were weak, anyway, especially in their sleep with their false sense of security.

Now came the fun part.

Turning to the nearest human, I crouched down, grasped the young man's chin between my thumb and forefinger, and forced him to look into my eyes. With a finger from my free hand, I traced a line from the man's forehead down over his cheek to his chin. The man didn't take his eyes off my face, the soft intimacy of the touch somehow more terrifying than the abduction itself.

A touch that promised pain.

His feelings were so strong, rolling off him in waves, and I could practically read his thoughts. I bet he had always considered himself a protector, a *man's man* who wanted to protect his wife and children from danger. Of all the horrible scenarios that he, like many other humans, ran through his mind night after night as he lay awake, none of them involved something happening to him, but always to his family.

But as he looked into his kidnapper's eyes through the strands of hair covering his face, his vulnerability showed through. He was powerless as his vision blurred with the slight sheen of tears. I knew he couldn't understand *why* he feared me over other men.

I'd already decided. This one was mine.

The human screamed into the gag as a knife slashed across his back between his shoulder blades. The cut wouldn't kill him, but the stinging pain was enough to unleash the tears he had managed to hold back until now. Looking up at my impatient comrade, I chuckled before breathing in sharply through my teeth as the spike of fear radiated from the humans around me.

We'd taken seven from their homes in this area, one for every Tenebrian in the group.

Keep it concentrated in one area, Vikt had said. *It does more damage that way, and it feels better for us.*

She was right. The terror from the kidnapped humans mingled in the air, along with the fear and confusion from those left in the households that had been hit, wondering where their loved ones were and if they were okay. It had begun to fog the area and my senses, and I breathed it in again, letting it fuel me further.

I wanted more.

We were taught as young that we shouldn't take pleasure in feeding on the negative energies of humans. We had a duty to do—to maintain the Balance. The fact that it felt good to inflict pain and bring grief when it was needed to right the Balance was simply a bonus.

But for a lot of us, that wasn't enough anymore.

I grinned again. By the night's end, these humans would be at least alive. I couldn't vouch for whether they would be *okay* as such, but I didn't particularly care.

"For Ignis," I said, raising my fist. "For showing us how to make the most of our talents and all the delectable fear we had been missing out on." General chatter and laughter sounded among the group, and I stood, glancing at the humans. "Take one, do with them what you will, then dump them. But not this one." I brushed my fingers through the human's hair before me, a shudder running down my spine as he trembled at my touch. "This one is mine."

The humans all began screaming as, one by one, they were selected and taken away from the group by each of the

Guardians. They all thought they were to die, and we would use that fear.

Don't let them think for a moment that they will live through this.

There'd be many moments where, during the pain, they would wish for death.

My selected human strained his neck, looking around him as the others were taken. There was movement, but it was too fast for him to see clearly, and each motion spiked his fear further. There'd be someone beside him, and the next moment they'd be gone, with only the echoes of their muffled cries left behind as they were pulled into the woods.

He trembled when he realized he was left alone with me. I kneeled before him, taking his face in a vice grip, and leaned in until his lips were a breath away from mine.

Smiling, I whispered, "I guess that leaves you and me."

The humans were tortured, each to the specific desires of the Guardian who had them in their clutches. When their fear had run out, and they had resigned to the fact that they were to die that night, they were let go, forever to live with the memories and scars of their ordeal, both physical and internal. Those scars would cause a ripple effect of negative energy through them, their families, and everyone who heard of the attacks.

Humans are emotional beings, driven and fueled by their emotions. They were *empathetic* and felt each other's pain.

Another bonus for us.

They did our job for us simply by feeling bad for each other and fearing what would happen next.

I dragged my human victim by his hair back into the driveway of the home we'd taken him from, my fingernails caked with drying blood, and the only sound from the human was his body dragging over the gravel.

This was fun, and waiting some time before the next step would be painful.

But our plan required patience and precision.

We could wait.

Chapter Ten

Cael

Ana ran her hands down my chest and over my stomach, and my scales flattened beneath her touch. When she grasped my cock between her hands and rubbed me, it elicited a sound between and growl and a purr I couldn't control. Ana smiled, a look somewhere between pleased and wicked. Sometimes, when she caught me off guard, she could make me produce sounds or speak words in the ancient Guardian language.

She'd chuckled. "It's not exactly a romantic language, is it?" She produced a series of grating but quiet screeches and laughed again. "But I love it because it means I'm still able to make you lose control."

"You'll always be able to make me lose control," I whispered, eyelids heavy as she continued to stroke me between her hands.

We were together in the sleeping quarters we shared with eight other Guardians, who often swapped sexual partners. It used to bother Ana to share sleeping space with others, but nudity and sex didn't faze us the way they did humans, and Ana eventually got used to it.

She grinned as she watched my face, and I battled to keep my eyes open while I got lost in her touch. I wanted to watch her face, to see her beautiful blue lips smile, or her tongue dart out and run across them in her desire. Ana used to make us sneak off to a quiet grassy area or the woods to make love, but now she just took me in our room. No one paid us any mind anyway.

Although sometimes hiding in the woods and taking her against a tree was a welcome change, it felt like we were doing something wrong by sneaking off, as though we were adding to the already taboo nature of our relationship by hiding. I growled again, gripping her arms on the areas of smooth blue skin between her scales. Instead of being entirely covered in scales and quills, she had stretches of soft, blue, human-like skin. My cock twitched as she rubbed me in long, slow strokes, mimicking my touch on her arms.

Ana lifted one hand to my neck and pulled me toward her for a kiss. It had also taken her a while to get used to sex with my natural and her new appearance. But she learned quickly that our scales and quills flattened against our skin when relaxed or aroused and looked much less intimidating.

I grabbed her hands, stilling them, and she looked at me quizzically. She started rubbing again when my grip loosened, and my concentration became lax. "What's the matter, Cael?" she purred at me, her grin giving her intentions away as she increased her grip.

I drew in a sharp breath and gritted my teeth. "Not yet," I managed to whisper.

"Well, that all comes down to your self-control, doesn't it?" she teased.

I growled again, low and menacing, reminding myself that sometimes Guardians were more animal than not, more animal than human, definitely. Pushing Ana back onto the bed, I pressed my body on top of hers. Kissing my way down her body, I nipped at her skin, causing her to squeak quietly with delight. She loved it when I took control, and I could feel her relaxing as I took over. Ana tried so hard to control herself at all other times, so when it was just us together, she wanted to relinquish that part of herself.

And I was the only one she trusted enough to come undone with.

I was the only one allowed to touch her like this.

She was *mine.*

Playfully, I pinned her down, gripping her waist and teasing her breasts with my mouth. It was getting increasingly difficult for me to hold her still, and the muscles in my arms flexed as she bucked against my grip. I marveled at how the fusion between human and Guardian had created such a divine creature as I ran my tongue back down her body. Ana's stomach had maintained her smooth skin and waist—she didn't have the hardened armor-like covering Guardians do. Spreading her legs, I groaned in appreciation at her scent as the waves of arousal flowed from her into the air around us.

Burying my face between her legs, I worked her most sensitive area with my tongue, using my hands to hold her legs apart roughly. Initially, I had been overly gentle with her, but now that her strength had grown, I no longer held back on my own, knowing she could handle it. Every push of her legs, trying to close them, only made me push back harder, and with an angry swipe of my tongue over her clit she sighed and relinquished that control to me.

As Ana got closer to her peak, her breathing became heavy,

and she grabbed the back of my head, pulling me closer and crying out as she came. I wasted no time, moving up over her body until I was lying on top of her, and pushed my tongue into her mouth as I guided my cock into her heat. Ana moaned against my lips as I thrust, burying myself deep within her.

"Cael." She gasped as I increased my pace.

"Say it again," I grunted out, punctuating the words with another thrust.

"Cael!"

The air was thick with her arousal, and the other Guardians present picked up on it, the mood in the room changing as several of them paired up. One of the males pounced on the almost asleep female on the bed next to ours, and she responded with vigor, pulling him down on top of her.

Ana ran her hands down my back, flattening the large quills against my skin with her touch.

When she gripped my hips and pulled me into her harder, we groaned together. I matched her pace and dropped my body over hers, crushing her beneath me, and drove her down against the soft mattress with my thrusts. Her passion released something inside of me, and I leaned down and bit her neck slightly harder than just a playful nip. Ana cried out and returned the gesture, biting into my shoulder as another orgasm built inside of her. I pulled out after she came with a cry and spilled my seed onto the sheets before collapsing on top of her.

Ana stroked my back until my quills softened post-climax, having raised at the moment of release, and my breathing slowed, my arousal spent.

For now.

It started to rain outside, and gentle droplets of pure water hit the roof.

Ana smiled against my shoulder. "I remember the first time I experienced rain in Lucidis," she whispered, and I hummed to show I was listening, but didn't move from on top of her. "How it had been such a surprise, as if this utopian land couldn't possibly be sullied by something as plebeian as rain." She chuckled, and I huffed out an amused note through my nostrils. We lay together, and her fingers danced up and down my back, touching and smoothing my quills.

"Do you miss Earth?" Ana whispered into the darkness.

I rolled over onto my back, pulled her toward me with one arm, and tucked her against me. "Sometimes. But my favorite thing about Earth is right here."

"Sometimes I wonder..."

"You do that a lot."

She gave me a withering look before smiling. "Sometimes I wonder what would have happened if we had never met. Would I have eventually known I was different?"

"There's something I've been wondering too."

"What's that?" Ana raised herself onto one elbow.

"Why haven't you asked about your father?"

Ana remained silent for a long time, and I watched her as the moon's light streamed through the open windows.

"Because I'm not sure I want to meet him..." Pausing, she added, "... if he's alive."

"I'm sure we could find out everything about him if you wanted. It might be a good thing. He obviously cared for your mother and you."

"I'm not so sure it's *obvious.*" Her tone changed, and she dropped back down next to me. "Maybe he just stuck around through some feeling of obligation."

"That would be very out of character for a Guardian. He must have felt something for your mother, like my feelings developed for you, or he would have left before you were born."

"Maybe he was interested in me as an experiment."

"*Ana.*"

"What? It's entirely possible. I'm sure many in the community see me that way."

"That's not true." I huffed.

Ana looked at me hard. "Tell me that again, but look me in the eye this time."

I hesitated. "Okay, fine, but not many of them."

Ana sighed. "Anyway, I haven't asked because I don't know how I feel about it. When I find out why he left, I'll either like the reason or I won't, and either way, I have to live with it. Besides, I think there's something you're not considering."

"What's that?"

"I don't think it'll be that easy to find him. Did anyone here even know I existed?"

I remained silent for a beat. "I don't know."

"Anyway, I'll think about it."

I tilted my head, resting it against hers. "Well, if ever you decide, just tell me, and we'll do whatever you want."

Ana kissed me quickly. "Ah, just as a relationship should be."

I laughed, but my smile dropped as I rubbed her arm absentmindedly. The air thickened between us as memories I could never erase rushed back.

"Do you have any idea how much it hurt when I thought I had killed you?" My voice was ghostly quiet, fading into the space between us as it filled with the pain I had lived with those many months on Earth.

I could feel Ana looking at me as I stared determinedly at the ceiling. She hadn't seen me cry since the day I returned, but sometimes, like now, I struggled to contain my emotions.

"I'm sorry, Cael, I'm so, so sorry you went through that. I wanted to tell you I was here, but couldn't." She rubbed her thumb around the inside of my wrist in small circles. She whispered, "Do you think of that day often?"

"Do you?"

It was Ana's turn to be silent, as perhaps she relived the physical torture Nathaniel had inflicted on her. I could feel her feet flexing next to me. The Gateway can heal many things, but can't regrow a toe. Eventually, she said, "Killing me was the only way to get rid of Nathaniel. I think I was dying, anyway..." She shuddered at the reminder of the feeling of weakness after losing so much blood. She'd tried to explain it to me once, but there were no words to describe the sensation of the life draining from your body. "I'm sorry," she repeated.

"I don't blame you," I murmured.

"I think it was my fault, though. I think, at least partly, I made you do it."

I had thought of that and remembered the feeling that surged from her when she had screamed *Take the shot*. Had she controlled me as I had her earlier? Was that the first sign of the strength of her influence? "I'm not convinced you had that level of control over your powers."

"Maybe. Maybe I didn't do it consciously, but I made a decision, and I'm sorry for the pain it caused you. I thought it was the right thing to do... the *only* thing to do."

A tear traced down my cheek. "It hurt so much, Ana..." I

paused after her name. I was still relishing being able to say it to her when, for so long, I thought I never would again. "I've never felt pain like that before. It's like I was being torn apart inside, as if my soul was being shredded. I was in pieces and didn't think I would ever be whole again."

Ana moved until she was cradled against me, her form folded perfectly next to mine. She wrapped her arm across my chest, pulling my cheek against her face. Ana shushed gently as I tightened my grip with my arm, pulling her into an embrace that would've crushed her in human form. She was comfortable and safe here with me. I could feel it through her and the tiny air space between us as she got as close as possible. Feeling safer with me didn't mean she couldn't care for herself. It simply meant that we were two parts of a whole, stronger together than apart. Ana was everything I was not, and vice versa.

"It's okay. We're together now, we have Samael, and that's all that matters."

In the darkness, I reached out with my senses to the community area where the children slept. I could feel Samael's emotional imprint from a distance as clearly as I could when he was near. My son was calm, sleeping, and dreaming. I sighed, letting the contentment of our family flow through my body. I felt Ana next to me, helping me along, using her calmness to calm me.

Using her powers in a way I hadn't trained her to, she had figured it out herself.

I nodded but didn't speak. If I spoke, I wouldn't be able to stop the tears from escaping further. Despite the progress made in the community, it was still a sign of weakness to be seen crying openly. Slowly, Ana's stroking of my shoulder and arm stopped, and the change in her breathing, in turn, had a soothing effect on me.

We fell asleep together, still holding on to each other.

Because I never wanted to let her go again.

Chapter Eleven

Ana

Despite my years in Lucidis, there were moments when I still felt like a circus freak.

Desperately, I clutched onto what remained of my humanity. I knew myself well enough to know that I didn't have to change for peer pressure, even if I had to alter my actions for general social acceptance.

But coming into a different realm was a next-level adjustment.

On occasion, I'd noticed Ferox watching me. He was always frowning, and while I had no idea what I'd done to offend him so much, I suspected my sheer existence did it. I always felt exposed around him, due more to the look in his eyes than my being naked. He looked at me as though I were a display piece, a plaything—not enough human to be useful, nor enough Guardian to be respected.

Walking along the river's edge toward the gardens, even as I tried to keep myself occupied while Cael was on Earth teaching the younger Guardians, I still hated these moments without him. We didn't have to be together every second of every day.

Still, there was a difference between him being elsewhere in Lucidis and him being in an entirely different realm that I was yet unable to reach by myself.

Ferox approached and stopped in front of me, making me come to an abrupt standstill and immediately putting me on edge.

"Can I help you?" I asked.

"There is no need for the attitude."

I didn't apologize. Ferox had been nothing but rude to me. My having to make leeway for a Guardian's nature was one thing, but treating me like I was a waste of space was something else entirely. I crossed my arms and waited for him to say something further, expecting a slur toward my uselessness here.

After a beat, he asked, "Cael gone?"

The question caught me off guard, and the scales on my shoulders shuddered as I tensed. "Yes. He's on Earth with our son."

"You know, you haven't been with anyone but him since you came here." His words were casual, but his eyes never stopped that wandering gaze of my body.

"I have no interest in being with anyone but him."

He continued to eye me, allowing his gaze to linger over my chest, following the line of my deep blue scales as they traced around the curve of my breasts. Smoother blue skin covered most of my torso and stomach with a scattering of scales tracing down my pubic bone. I wasn't entirely covered as the Guardians were, and I always assumed this disgusted him and others.

Turned out I was wrong.

Ferox ran his fingers down my arm, quickly pulling his hand away when my scales rose in defense, and I yanked my arm away from his touch.

"I like your eyes," Ferox said, a deep growl rumbling through his voice.

"Thank you?" I tried not to sound too annoyed, although surely he could pick up on the changes in my demeanor and emotions as Cael could. Ferox had given me no reason to trust him.

"Brown eyes. They are almost non-existent amongst Guardians, and it is striking. You are a fine specimen."

My eyebrows flickered up and down in one quick motion, and I glanced around to see where the nearest populated area was, but I didn't respond.

"You are different, and I want to have sex with you," Ferox continued.

"No, thank you."

"Don't you want to experience real power?" He stepped closer to me. I took half a step back, torn between wanting to stand my ground against Ferox and escape him. Glancing down, I couldn't help but notice he was aroused, and I felt sick.

"Leave me alone. I said *no.*" I took another step backward. "Stop looking at me as though I'm a piece of meat."

Ferox brought himself to his full height. "You are not one of us, and you are not human either. I owe you no protection."

My jaw dropped. "Are you threatening me?"

Ferox looked confused. "Not in the slightest."

"I thought Lucidis Guardians were supposed to be good?"

"We are the ultimate good."

My stomach dropped as I stepped away from him again, realization slamming into my stomach like cement that this wasn't something I could talk my way out of. Deep down, I tried to believe he wouldn't do anything to hurt me, but his proximity and aggression were unsettling. "Don't touch me."

"But I want to. I could make you feel so good."

It wasn't spoken with malice, but it still made the lead weight in my stomach harden. "I'd like to see you try," I said, speaking more confidently than I felt. When he stepped forward and reached out to grab me, I instinctively pushed hard against his chest, knocking him off his feet.

Ferox fell hard and looked up at me from the ground before he stood, disgust etched across his features. "You are a freak."

As I watched Ferox slowly stand, I shifted my gaze to my hands.

I had done that—I had knocked him to the ground without even trying.

Rage bubbled up inside me, melting the leaden weight in my stomach and churning the acid. I remembered how Ed had attacked me, how helpless I felt when I couldn't shift his weight from me. How weak I felt around him, and the sensation of his body pressed against mine, knowing I wasn't strong enough to stop him, made me sick.

And Nathaniel... the things he had done to me when I was too weak to fight back.

There was an aura of power surrounding Ferox. Physically, he was huge, and coupled with years of honing his powers as a Guardian, it felt like there was resistance before I had even touched him.

But I *had* touched him. More than that, I had pushed him from his feet.

I could sense his energy shifting, and it created a hostile presence.

What would happen if I *tried?*

Crouching slightly to lower my center of gravity, I took a half-step forward, thrusting my weight as I pivoted on one foot and shoved Ferox hard in his shoulder. He spun as he fell and grunted as he hit the ground a few feet away, a cloud of dust dissipating after being disturbed by his heavy fall. Ferox didn't speak, but the confusion on his face turned to rage as he jumped to his feet and charged at me in one smooth motion.

I crossed my forearms before my face and leaned forward, meeting his charge with my force. I managed to stand my ground as he collided with me, and we wrestled for dominance in that position. My feet slid in the grass as I tried to hold my own against his frontal assault.

I may be unable to hold him back forever, but even he was startled by how much I resisted. His shock came off him in a wave, and I gained an inch of ground.

"You think you can beat me?" he sneered.

I only grunted in reply as again I was pushed backward when his rage took hold, and I slid further along the grass. I dared not move my feet in case I lost my footing and ended up in a vulnerable position on my back. When I felt I was about to fall, I kicked out at Ferox's shin, and he went down again, but not before he grabbed my arm and took advantage of my lost footing, bringing me crashing to the ground with him.

We were both back on our feet and poised to strike when a shout distracted us.

"What is going on here?" Monia came running toward us, her large feet slapping on the soil as she ran purposefully. She was a force unto herself, and I hadn't seen her move so quickly before.

I looked between Monia and Ferox before turning on my heel and running back to the community center.

Monia sat next to me without saying a word. She was going to ask about the encounter with Ferox. I knew it, yet I didn't feel like discussing it. I was experiencing a different type of weakness now, one of having power and exploiting it, not truly knowing my limits. On one hand, I was protecting myself, but on the other, even though it was self-defense, I struck first. This was all levels of confusing, and if I was confused, I couldn't imagine trying to explain the emotions behind this to a Guardian.

But Guardians also didn't ignore these things. Conflict was handled head-on, and everything was discussed, regardless of the discomfort. Although emotional distress wasn't much of a consideration for them.

"What are you doing?" Monia asked.

"I'm sorry, I didn't mean to fight with Ferox. He's had a problem with me since I got here, and when he touched me, I just lost control a bit and—"

"No," Monia pointed to my hands. "What are you doing with that?"

I stopped and looked at the Rubik's Cube I'd been playing with.

"Oh, just trying to solve it. I was never very good at these things." I looked at Monia, who was watching me curiously. My brow furrowed momentarily, but then I relaxed in her presence. There was no tension radiating from Monia, not that I had ever been able to read much from her, I certainly didn't feel as though she were ever hostile toward me. I was a curiosity to Monia, but not an experiment. "Sorry..." I said, turning the cube over in my fingers. "Was I not supposed to take it? It was with all the other human stuff."

Monia was still watching my hands. "You can help yourself to those items."

I glanced at the pile of things. I'd been here often since I discovered it shortly after Lucidis became my home, but I'd never asked about it. "Where did it all come from?"

"Occasionally, Guardians bring things back from Earth, mostly to learn... books, musical instruments... things like that." Well, that explained where they got the instruments from that they occasionally played around the fires in the evenings. I'd wanted to know, but my list of questions about this place never seemed to end, and it was a constant matter of picking and choosing what was most important to ask and leaving the rest until it came up.

Monia perused the pile of Earth items before she returned her gaze to the Rubik's cube as I held it out to her. "Sometimes things are in shops, and we might buy them, not knowing why."

"Did you buy this one?" I asked.

"Not me, but one of my generation, yes. Not too long ago... maybe two decades or so."

I smirked at the idea that a few decades was *not too long ago*, and I could have sworn that for a moment, I saw the shadow of a grin on Monia's face. But then it was gone.

Monia accepted the cube from my outstretched hand and turned it over in her long fingers. It suddenly seemed so small in her large hands.

"Humans are so strange." Monia turned to me earnestly. "You must believe I do *try* to understand. Tell me, why do you collect such things?"

"You ask some hard questions, you know? I never thought I'd have to explain humanity." I sighed. There were many things I *did* as part of my everyday life, and when faced with the question of *why*, it was sometimes nearly impossible to explain. "I guess these items can be attached to a memory, or maybe they were a gift from a loved one, or sometimes they are just fun or quirky and make us smile." Monia stared at me blankly, and I wasn't sure if she understood, but the fact that she was trying was enough.

"So, how do you work it?" Monia asked.

I pointed as I explained the goal of solving a Rubik's Cube and watched as Monia tried it. She seemed to be doing exactly what I had—randomly turning the sides, hoping they would match up.

After a few minutes, she said, "I do not understand."

I laughed, the soft sound a shadow of my usual loud laughter, but still, it was a laugh. "Neither do I."

"Well, then, I guess that is something else we have in common." Monia handed me the cube back. "Maybe it is magic," she added.

"What?"

Monia wiggled her fingers at the cube in my hands. "Magic."

This time, when I laughed, it was genuine and loud—the single *hah* that Cael said he loved so much. And this time, the corner of Monia's lip *definitely* twitched. I watched her as she stood. "Monia?"

Monia turned and faced me. "Yes, Anahera?"

"Am I okay here? I mean, am I a disturbance for you?"

"Of course you are not. This is your home."

"Monia?"

I was sure I saw a smile pass across her face as she turned again to answer me. "Yes?"

"Thank you for everything, and uh..." I looked at the ground. "... I love you," I mumbled.

There was a silence that I hoped would only last a few seconds, and perhaps it did, but those few seconds seemed to drag out into eternity. When I couldn't stand it any longer, I raised my eyes to Monia's. She was the closest thing I'd known to a mother in years, the one who had taken me in and nurtured me without question when I appeared in her world. She had delivered my child, her grandson. How else could I explain to Monia how I felt without using those words? I said it more for myself than Monia, knowing she wouldn't understand. But to have it hanging between us was hard to bear. Tentatively, I tried to control my senses enough to reach out to Monia to see if I could *feel* her response without her having to say it. I wanted to know if I could connect with her like Guardians. When Monia started slightly, I retreated as though she felt my intrusion into her emotional imprint.

Our eye contact was intense, and then I felt it like a brush of air under my skin. Monia reached out to me with her senses, encouraging me to pick up the connection I had intentionally dropped. I did, slowly and clumsily, but eager to feel what Monia was feeling, even if her emotions were more neutral than the wild chaos in my mind.

Her imprint was calm on the outside, nurturing, but when I probed a little further, there was a fire, a desire, an intention.

Monia severed the connection, and we stared at each other for a long while. Monia's face changed, betraying her inner battle.

Until finally, she said, "I love you, too."

I was glad I was sitting down, and Monia smiled softly as my jaw dropped.

A Guardian, admitting *actual* emotions.

We looked at each other for a beat longer before Monia nodded slightly and left.

Chapter Twelve

Cael

Six years later

Running after Samael, I realized I needed more speed to keep up with him as he grew. Samael was small but fast, faster than the other children.

He was almost eight years old now. Ana liked to celebrate his birthday, a ceremony that thoroughly confused the community, although each year, more Guardians took part out of curiosity. I had the sneaking suspicion they actually enjoyed themselves—watching Ana sing the happy birthday song with more enthusiasm than was required, with a huge grin on her face at the look of bewilderment from the community.

She'd accepted that there were some who would never truly accept her, and she made it her mission to bring as much human culture into the community as she could and confuse as many Guardians as possible.

She was good at it, too.

I was proud of Ana for allowing Samael to be raised and taught with the other children by the community as a whole, as was our custom. She seemed to have found a comfortable balance between integrating with the other Guardians and keeping her stubborn strip of humanity. I was glad of this, as it was when she was at her most human that I'd fallen in love with her.

Even though at the time, I didn't know what true love was.

Still, Ana and I often snuck off with Samael to enjoy a picnic, a hike, or a swim, just the three of us, and I couldn't deny those were my favorite moments.

With a wave of my hand, I generated a Gateway in front of us as I shouted, "Now, Samael." I followed him through it, both of us changing our appearances to our Earth forms. We had dressed in our human clothes before we started playing this morning—every community kept a ready clothing stash.

For a while, Guardians had gone through the Gateways naked, and while they may have gotten away with it in some places in the sixties, we certainly couldn't have gotten away with it before or after the era of free love.

I chased Samael as we wound our way through the streets of the small country town. I'd chosen a rural area far enough from the city that we were unlikely to encounter anyone who would recognize me from my extended visit to Earth.

Some humans had excellent memories for faces, and it could be troublesome.

Catching up with Samael, I swept him off his feet and held him close to my chest, having put on a burst of speed when I felt Samael's breathing becoming ragged. Hushing and patting him gently on his back, I cradled him against my shoulder as his breathing slowed.

A middle-aged woman approached us. "Is he okay?" she asked, worry written across her features to match the concern washing from her in waves at Samael's flushed cheeks and unsteady breathing.

I flashed her a brilliant smile. "Yes, he's fine. Just got a little overexcited in his play, is all."

She smiled and nodded knowingly, giving Samael a reassuring pat on the back before moving on. Walking to the corner of the street, I sat on the curbside and pulled Samael onto my lap.

"The air is different here, Samael. You must take deeper and longer breaths."

"I know. You told me." He pouted. "I just forgot."

"It's okay. That's why we have these practices, and you will practice with the other children, too."

Samael took a long, loud, steadying breath, pushing the air out of his lungs just as hard. His little nose wrinkled. "It tastes different."

"Describe it to me."

"It tastes like... heavy." He looked at me for approval of his assessment of the air.

I nodded. "Yes, it does taste heavy. It feels heavy, too, don't you think?" I looked at Samael's blue eyes and held out my hands as though I could weigh the air with them. "You need to focus on that feeling and notice how it shifts around people as they move. It changes with the things they say and do. That is the Balance."

"How will I know if the Balance changes?"

"You'll feel it. With practice, you'll feel it."

"Does it feel like your fat head?"

I recoiled, studying his face as his impish grin grew. Guardian children didn't talk like that, and he'd caught me off guard. I stared, open-mouthed, at Samael for a beat, relaxing and smiling only when Samael giggled at the look on my face.

I had to remind myself sometimes that Samael was Ana's son, too, and boy, did she rub off on him.

"Why don't you tell me?" I squeezed Samael lightly against me and kissed his cheeks.

Samael squirmed out of my grip. "You're gross!" He laughed before running away.

I took chase. The sound of my son's laughter lifted me. In this realm, it also lifted the mood of every human we encountered. Locals smiled as Samael and I played our way through the streets, working out of the small town into the surrounding farmland. We didn't need to stay close to where we had arrived, as I could open a Gateway to home based on the distinct emotional imprint of the community where I had grown up. It was a part of me.

I didn't want to keep Samael on Earth for too long while he was young and learning, but I had an idea. Gathering Samael in my arms, I spun him to end another bout of chasey before I lowered him to the ground and took his small hand in mine. "I want to show you something."

Samael was still catching his breath, but nodded and followed me along a deteriorated picket fence, scuffing his shoes in the loose dirt. Stopping under a tree, I lifted Samael again and rested him on my hip.

"What is that?" Samael squealed.

I shushed him as the animal approached us. "This is a horse. There are animals on Earth as well as humans, and they have their own emotions."

"Do animals interfere with the Balance?"

"No, they are in harmony with it. Here."

I took Samael's hand and placed it on the horse's cheek. Samael giggled at the feeling of the short-bristled hair under his fingers. "It feels funny."

"Yes, it does. But feel her *imprint.*"

Samael pressed his palm to the patch of white hair on the horse's forehead, and the horse let out a quiet whinny, causing Samael to lose concentration and giggle again. Seeing the look on my face, he turned back to the horse and focused his energies as best he could. I helped him along, using my energy to balance his out, and felt what he did as he took a reading of the horse's imprint.

Samael's eyes widened when he experienced what the horse was feeling.

She initially felt confused and fearful, but that was quickly replaced with calm as she felt no threat from Samael, only the love and curiosity of a child. Her mind may not have been as complicated as a human's, but she felt love and grief like they do. She had watched her foal grow and mourned when she was sold.

Deep inside, she still mourned.

A tear trickled down Samael's cheek, and he hastily wiped it away. Guardians feel what others feel, but they don't feel themselves. He had learned that much from being with the other youth. But being part human, he couldn't help taking the feelings on board.

I knew sometimes he wished he wasn't different from the others.

I also knew this broke Ana's heart.

The shifts in Samael's mind were as precise to me as if Samael had spoken his feelings out loud.

"Don't be afraid to feel, Samael," I whispered.

"The others don't."

"I'm not so sure. Maybe they hide it."

Samael shook his head but didn't answer. He patted the horse's cheek again, his small fingers curled in the wiry hair of her mane. He perked up. "Can we keep her?"

I laughed. "No, son." Lowering Samael to the ground, I retook his hand. That was enough for today. Each time we would stay a bit longer, as he got older, we would train him more intensely to focus his energies. They were a part of him, basically another limb, and he could learn to control them as such. "Let's go home."

On the bus, I stood holding onto the support strap and smiled as the group of young Guardians looked out the windows eagerly. Seeing Earth through a Porthole was one thing, but it took a while for the novelty of being here to wear off, if it ever did. As they grew, they would see things differently each time. This group, consisting of two females and three males, was in their late teens and had come here on a short trip to brush up on their social cues, and, I grinned, to be thrown into the thick of it and think on their feet. To learn to react and hold their reactions in equal measure when surrounded by a large group of humans' emotional imprints, each conflicting and rolling over each other. A place where the fog of their energies could be overwhelming for an inexperienced Guardian.

But they had to learn somehow.

This was the part Ana was most interested in—when the Guardians grew and truly began to learn about humans and Earth. She helped in Lucidis with information, but I could see the pain on her face whenever she waved me off as I left to mentor another group.

She wanted to be here, and my chest ached to keep telling her she couldn't.

Not yet, maybe not ever.

Upon my return from Earth all those years ago, I'd been keen to volunteer to assist with the training of the younger Guardians. Since then, many have requested me as their guide, knowing of my past and now infamously extended stay on Earth without respite in Lucidis.

"Where are we going?" Dita asked as she ran her fingers up and down along the railing before her. She had been doing so since we boarded the bus. Things felt different through human skin, and she moved her fingers in measured inches, twisting her hands around the cold metal.

"There's an art festival in the parklands, many people to talk to, and a joyous atmosphere," I answered. If we were going to be surrounded by many humans, I wanted the general vibe to be positive, especially for their first time in such a large crowd. I didn't want them to fight to maintain their internal balance.

Dita nodded, and I could feel the nervousness radiating from her. In her human form, she was slight, and although she stood over six feet, her face had soft features. She had opted to wear glasses, liking how they made her face look, and altogether gave her the look of someone who was shyer than she ultimately was.

She looked back at me, and her expression lit up. "Are we going dancing?"

The other youth looked at me hopefully, and I smiled. "Not today."

The mood visibly dropped, and I chuckled and glanced out the window to watch the scenery fly past as we moved down the main street. My smile fell after a moment. The Elders had reprimanded me for teaching the younger Guardians to dance, and although this hadn't stopped me, much to Ana's delight, it certainly took some of the fun out of it. Dancing could be helpful while on Earth to fit in, but the issue the Elders had was that I was teaching them to *feel* the music, notice the change it had on human moods, and get swept up in that magic.

As I had been constantly reminded, the Elders didn't take kindly to that.

If Guardians start to experience emotions as strongly as humans, who will maintain the Balance?

As the bus pulled up to our stop, I held up my hand and leaned forward to the group. "Remember, we are here to learn, not influence. Interact only."

We disembarked and walked the short distance to the festival, accepting several brochures along the way, which the younger Guardians read with interest.

Dita and Nicus, a young male Guardian whose hair in human form toed the line between blond and red, stayed close together. I watched them with interest, certain there was something between them more than the usual interactions of two youths. Exclusive and monogamous couplings were still rare within Guardians and bordered on non-existent. But again, I wondered, as I often did while observing the younger generation, maybe things were changing.

Motioning with my hands, I gathered the group together.

"I want you to split into two groups, get a drink, find a table with some empty seats, and start a conversation with the people there."

They nodded with looks of determination that reflected much more serious missions than what they had been handed, and I repressed a chuckle as they made their way into the crowd.

I waited, leaned against a tree, and shoved my hands in my pockets, trying to blend into the background to observe my students. After a tug at my elbow, I looked down. An elderly lady looked brightly at me, her lips stained with red lipstick for the outing.

"Excuse me. Your eyes are no doubt better than mine. Can you save me wandering around the area and tell me which of these food trucks is the pizza one?"

"Of course."

I scanned the food trucks dotted around the area, occasionally looking back at the lady who would smile pleasantly at me. Her presence flooded me with memories of a similar interaction when I was on Earth, trying to stop Nathaniel, and helping a woman cross the street near the hospital. At the time, I had viewed humans as weaker beings who simply required my protection and strength. But I knew so much more now, and looking back on those memories was like observing another person rather than a past version of myself. I knew the complications that lay beneath the surface of every human, their hidden strengths, and how they utilized those strengths to conceal their weaknesses when someone else was in need.

I viewed this woman differently than I would have back then. She wasn't as weak as years ago I'd have assumed she was. She held inside her a strength that I was only scratching the surface of.

Locating the food truck, I bent to point it out to the woman. "Are you okay to walk there alone? The ground is quite uneven."

She chuckled and patted my arm, and with the brief contact, I felt flashes of who she was, and her life before age had begun to deteriorate her body. She had a strong heart and much love left to give. "I'll be okay, love, but you're sweet for asking. My husband is waiting for me there."

"He's a lucky man."

Her laugh was loud and genuine, reminding me of Ana's. "Don't give me cheek," she said, pinching my arm gently in a playful manner. She continued to chuckle as she walked toward the food truck I'd indicated. The smile on my face warmed my body, and I wished I had allowed myself to experience emotions and humanity sooner.

But I was thankful for the opportunity to help the younger generations do just that.

Locating the other Guardians, Dita, and Mica—the other female in the group—had made quick friends with a group of young women who were getting into the spirit of the festival with the locally produced mulled wine, and by the looks of them, had been enjoying the beverage for hours. After only a few moments of conversation, there was laughter, and one of the tipsy human women stood and threw her arms around Mica's neck, hugging her tightly. Mica stiffened and awkwardly patted the woman's arm. But I felt the moment she relaxed and opened herself to the woman's energies before she smiled and laughed, hugging the woman back and tilting her chair as the woman almost tipped forward onto her. This was met with more laughter before my students excused themselves and crossed the grass to me.

"She hugged me," Mica said.

I laughed. "I saw."

"She was so warm, like a real nurturing warmth."

"There's a lot of good in people."

Mica nodded with a frown plastered on her face, deep in thought, a result of the complicated senses she had gathered from the intimacy of the hug. I knew that look. Thanks to her developing powers and increasing understanding, she was viewing humans in a new light.

Dita pressed her lips together. "Now I would also like a hug."

"It felt like this." Mica turned and hugged Dita, using her essence to replicate the warmth she got from the human as best she could. Dita stiffened in the same way Mica had at the physical contact, but there was a smile on Dita's face when she let go.

I found the group of male Guardians easily. They'd also selected a table of women to join.

But something was off.

Frowning, I noticed all the Guardians were sitting on one side of the table, giving a wide berth to one of the women. Bringing my fingers to my lips, I whistled to gain their attention and pointed to Victio, beckoning him.

Victio trotted over.

"What is wrong with that woman? Why are you sitting away from her?" I asked, and Victio visibly shivered.

"There is something off about her. Whenever she looks at me, I get the unnerving sensation of a negative presence."

"She may be hurt."

"She looks fine."

I shook my head. "I mean, she may be hurt inside, like with heartache or grief." I placed my hand over my chest, pausing for the briefest moment when I realized I had picked up Ana's gesture. "Talk to her."

Victio's brows furrowed, and he returned to the group, sitting next to the woman. To be sure, I did a mental sweep of the area as I had done many times since we arrived.

I detected no Tenebris interference in this area.

The conversation picked up again, and as the woman started talking to Victio, he placed his hand on hers. I watched Victio's expression as he felt who the woman was. He wasn't influencing her, as I had instructed, and he felt who she was.

As he touched the woman's hand, she looked around nervously, and I frowned as I picked up on the energy transfer.

He *was* influencing her.

So much for having the respect to follow my wishes.

Before I moved to intervene, Victio stood, still holding hands with the woman, and approached me and the girls.

I folded my arms over my chest. There better be a good reason for this. We weren't on this trip to chase the pleasures of the flesh from humans.

The small conversation between them tapered off as they approached me. "This is Nadia," Victio said. "She feels unsafe here and needs to get home. Can we escort her?"

A rush of pride filled my chest, and I caught the lift of Victio's lip as he recognized the emotion from me, one I should have had the self-control to hide from him. "Of course." I held out my hand to Nadia. "Kyle. Are you all right? Do you need anything?" When she took my hand, I understood Victio's reason for using his influence to calm this human. Her fear shot through her veins like needles, each one a stab of pain at the contact between us as she constantly scanned the area as though looking for an attacker. I allowed my influence to trickle through my hand to her, ignoring the looks the female Guardians gave me as I did the exact thing I had told them not to.

I introduced the girls, beckoned the boys over from the table, and waited as Nadia trotted back to tell her friends she was going home.

As we approached the edge of the park, a young man blocked my path, and in my peripheral vision, I didn't miss as Nadia shrank behind Victio.

"I'll take her home," the man said.

Glancing between Nadia and the man, I didn't need to be a Guardian to see the fear in her eyes.

"Go away, Nick," she cried, her sharp words contrasting with her physical stance, still hiding behind Victio. "Just leave me alone."

As Nick moved toward her, I stopped him with a hand on his chest. "No."

"Excuse me?" Nick's stance was immediately filled with aggression. Through the contact between us, my stomach lurched. The vibes from the man were wrong—he was one to make himself feel powerful through the ill-treatment of others.

I scoffed at the human, *how Tenebrian of him*.

"Leave now, leave us alone, and you will never bother Nadia again."

The group of students watched in awe. To Nadia, it would

appear only as if I had spoken normally. But my students felt the change in my voice and the vibrations in the air as my power passed through my voice to Nick. The strongest influence through the slightest touch. The ability to make him *act* on my orders. Nick stared at me momentarily before turning on his heel and leaving. Nadia's mouth was agape when I held a hand out to her and beckoned her to come around from behind Victio.

"He won't bother you again."

We escorted Nadia to her home and ensured she was safely inside. She thanked me but gave Victio a hug and a small kiss on the cheek, and offered him a small smile before closing the door. Victio rested his fingers on the place her lips had been on his skin, warm from her touch. Her imprint had changed, warming between the time Victio brought her over to me and when we left her at her home.

Smiling, Victio turned toward me. He didn't need to say anything. I could feel what he was feeling. I *knew* what that felt like. *Paying it forward*—showing kindness and expecting nothing in return, knowing that humans would pass the kindness on to someone else.

The ripple from the act helped keep the Balance and created an ever-growing circle of care that deflected the negative energies that could stain the air. It was *exactly* what I wanted my students to see. But more than that—much more than simply the effect on the Balance—I wanted them to *feel* the difference they could make to humans. I wanted them to understand why these energies were so powerful, to absorb the positive emotions, not just for the power and how it recharged us, but because they wanted to help.

Turning, they all stared at me as if I held the greatest secret known to Guardian-kind. This lesson would be unlike the ones they would get from other teachers. Others would focus on controlling their powers, which, while also important, wasn't what I wanted to teach them.

I smiled at their expressions. "You understand why I care about each of them."

The younger Guardians went on their way immediately after we stepped through the Gateway back into Lucidis, chattering excitedly amongst themselves as they stripped off their human clothing before returning to their natural forms. I stayed still for a moment, the remnants of the Gateway lingering behind me after I closed it, having generated it at the edge of the park where the festival was held.

They did well, really well. They learned more than I could've hoped.

I knew it wasn't my place to question the Elders and the teaching methods that had existed for generations. Still, every fiber of my being told me I was part of something bigger—raising a new generation of Guardians who could be more powerful, effective, and empathetic than ever before.

Turning to head toward the Elders' quarters, I stopped when a pain of discomfort shot through my shoulder. Pausing, I turned toward where the Gateway had been, and the pain came again, stronger and more insistent this time.

Something was wrong.

Hastily opening a Porthole, I shifted to view the festival where we had been an hour before. Flashing lights from the local police cars and ambulances filled the sky around the festival as people scrambled from the area, arms around each other, some limping, and many crying.

My hands clenched into fists by my side, and I waved over a group of passing Guardians, instructing them to do what was needed to control the effect of this attack.

I had seen enough to know that the group that entered the festival went there with more than the intent to harm and cause chaos.

The Tenebrians had grander plans, and the Elders needed to be informed.

Walking through the light rain as it started, I approached the Elders' quarters. Today's experience on Earth with the young Guardians only reinforced my belief that we should revise our teaching methods.

Raised voices greeted me as I approached the edge of the community, and I paused mid-step, torn between wanting to assist, given how unusual the shouting was, and not wanting to intrude. I shook my head to myself. No, I *must* interfere. There shouldn't be fighting in Lucidis if it can be avoided. Moving to the edge of the hut, a part of me teetered between wanting to help and wanting to leave until I crossed the threshold.

"I do not agree with your methods. I never have." I recognized Cordus' voice and froze. "I think there is a pattern here, and we need to include the others."

"I am more experienced than you. How I run the community works. I get the right result, and that is all that matters."

"It is not *all* that matters. There are other things in play here."

"It is not for you to decide if one needs protection over the others. She is not worth the effort."

My brow furrowed. *She* spoken with that tone meant they could only be talking about Ana. Any guilt I had about eavesdropping was quickly set aside. I should be included in all discussions about Ana. Ideally, Ana should be, too, but it was a matter of taking small steps with these things.

"Beyond her being *in* danger, she could *be* a danger. Do you not understand?" Cordus insisted.

"Enough, I will not have you question me."

I turned the corner to see a frown deepen on Cordus's face. "You—" he started, but he was promptly cut off as Cascus raised a hand to him once he spotted me, and walked away without a word.

I approached Cordus, my head bowed. "I apologize. I heard raised voices and wanted to see if everything was okay." I pressed my lips together to avoid saying more. I was certain Cordus would know my interest was piqued, and my intentions skewed the moment I realized Ana might be the topic of discussion.

Cordus sighed. "You are good, Cael."

"Is everything okay? Was that about Ana?"

"How did the youth go on Earth today?" Cordus ignored my questions, and internally, I flinched as I regretted having asked. It wasn't my place to probe the Elders for information. They would tell us if there was something the community needed to know.

If there was something I needed to know, they would tell me.

Surely.

While Cordus and I shared a bond, it didn't extend beyond his duties as an elder. My skin tingled as I sensed the barriers

Cordus was putting up against my attempt to read him, but they were weaker than he should have managed with his power.

As if he were unsure that he wanted to hide from me.

"Good..." I answered, watching Cordus wearily for signs that he was open to more questions, "...they learned a lot."

We stared at each other. I didn't tell Cordus about the growing respect for humanity among the youth and my role in it, and Cordus didn't ask any further questions. He was already distracted, and his mind was elsewhere while he looked directly at me. We_looked at each other for a long while, and Cordus opened his mouth several times, then he closed it and shook his head.

Tentatively, I reached out with my senses. The barriers were still there.

"I will always try to help where I can," I spoke into the silence. There was obviously something Cordus was debating on telling me.

Something about Ana?

"You are good, Cael," Cordus repeated. My lip twisted. I didn't like these small reminders of Cordus' age. "But I must respect my fellow Elder."

"May I speak to you about Ana?"

"No."

"May I speak about Tenebris? I feel something is happening."

"That is for us to discuss, not you."

I gritted my teeth. "May I speak to you about the teaching of the youth?"

Cordus's lip twitched, as close to a smile as I'd ever seen. "Soon, Cael. I am tired and must rest."

I nodded and watched him shuffle out of the room, but I

wouldn't soon forget the words that echoed in my mind.

Beyond her being in *danger, she could* be *a danger.*

OUTLET

Chapter Thirteen

Vikt

Standing off to the side of the chaos, I tilted my head toward the sky. People didn't pay me much attention. I didn't look like a threat in my human form and blended in with all the other onlookers who came to see the commotion. A small group of Tenebrians had gone into the festival and emerged nine minutes later with an artful masterpiece of blood splattered on their clothes. I hadn't taken part this time. I only observed and stood on the sidelines, drawing the humans' fear and confusion into my system, letting it pulse through my veins and strengthen me.

Letting it poison the area.

Three beings running through a crowd of people, brandishing small but sharp knives, could inflict much damage in a short space of time. My comrades sliced some people with the blade along their backs, legs, or palms if they put their hands up to defend themselves. Others they stabbed as they skipped past, sliding the blades in and out in one smooth motion before moving on. Mainly, they aimed for the torso, an easy target that effectively brought people down. The neck was as effective and a little more theatrical. Some of the group chose to get more creative and sliced at the humans' Achilles tendons, ears, or stabbed through the soft skin at the back of the kneecap. It was pathetic that such vital body parts were so poorly protected by the humans' soft skin.

As I moved away from the commotion, something else caught my attention. It was faint but detectable—the emotional imprint of a Lucidian.

But not just *any*, I recognized that scent, and it was difficult not to fly into a frenzy of rage as the taste of the imprint hit my senses. This was the being who had been near Ignis when he was sent back to Tenebris before he was killed. The Lucidian's imprint was all over Ignis at his death. No matter the years that passed, I'd always recognize those imprints—the Guardian who brought Ignis down and the human half-breed they had been saving. I could feel the Guardian's sense, though he was long gone from the area, but it was still like acid in my nostrils.

This was the one who had forced Ignis back into Tenebris using moonstone, interrupted his fun, and put him at the mercy of the Elders.

And was therefore responsible for his death.

My lip turned into a scowl at the idea that I had been so close and missed them. There wouldn't be much left of them if I'd been here earlier—a chance to kill the one responsible for Ignis' death—delicious. But if they had been here before, they'd come back again. I took a moment to try to solidify the feel of their emotional imprint, to burn it into my skin so she could track them. But it was nearly impossible. It was only a shadow of a sense, to begin with.

All I could get was one piece of information—*male.*

I flexed my hands before I turned and swept away into the surrounding darkness. I had someone to meet and couldn't spend more time on a fruitless endeavor. He'd be back on Earth at some point, and I'd be ready.

But he had better hope I never got hold of him.

The Guardian I was meeting kept their cloak on while on Earth, and even in human form, they kept their face hidden from me. I could tell little to nothing about them. The voice I didn't recognize, nor could I tell gender or age.

But the power radiating from them was unmistakable—no human could feel like that. To have waves of power surging from them, made my skin crawl if I stood too close for too long.

"Why did you call me here?" I was immediately aggressive. While I had enough respect for this Guardian not to challenge them too far, I didn't particularly like being told what to do. They had been summoning me for months, whispering in my ear through Portholes while I was on Earth. Initially, I ignored them and tried to put up blocks so I couldn't be contacted, but I could no longer ignore their calls and eventually agreed to meet.

"I have been watching you, observing what you are doing here."

I scoffed, already feeling as though this was a pointless conversation. "If you are here to tell me to stop, you are wasting your time."

They chuckled under the hood, a soft sound filled with hidden menace. "No, not stop, only refine."

"Get to the point or fuck off. I don't have time for this."

They laughed again, louder. "You have had all the time in the world and have done nothing with it. How long have you been messing around trying to shift the Balance? Years? And how much have you achieved?"

Their hum of acknowledgment told me I hadn't managed to mask my surprise fast enough. This Guardian knew what I was attempting to do, and there were very few I'd told the ultimate goal—to bring on the Shift.

I made a sound of impatience with my tongue that turned into a growl. "Speak."

"Your plan of organized chaos has no end game. You run around on Earth seeking and increasing negativity, creating pain, and feeding off it."

"We do what we do because we want to. We have a plan. It will take time, but it will work. So far, you have told me nothing I do not already know."

"We are slaves, did you know that? *All* of the Guardians are slaves, and we've had enough."

Growing tired of riddles and half-truths, I snapped, "Speak what you mean."

"Patience."

I recoiled, taking a step back. The word had been spoken with an undercurrent of untold power, and I fell silent, rubbing my arms as if trying to brush away the remnants of the power that had washed over me—a threat, not too subtly hidden—*I am stronger than you and could end your life.*

"I am sure some misguided loyalty to Ignis and whatever his motivation was drives your actions now, but I am telling you there is a way for you to have more power, for us *all* to have *more power*. If you listen to me and follow my plan, it may take a while, but we will be unstoppable once it all comes together."

"You're speaking of the rewards we would gain after the Shift. I already know this."

"The Shift is a slow process. After the initial crack, it seeps out over time. We could make it explosive, and the effects would be felt across the globe all at once."

My eyes narrowed, and again, I was careless and didn't cover my disdain fast enough.

Before I could open my mouth to speak again, the Guardian sensed my insubordination and intent to disobey. Faster than I could react, they had a hand around my throat and squeezed as I was pushed up against the bricks behind me. The wall shuddered under the impact of my body, and the dust settled around my attacker's feet. The stranger allowed their hand to change back into Guardian form and let their claws dig into my neck, my human skin vulnerable, and forced me to release a humiliating sound of protest as I fought for air. I couldn't see the hand around my neck with my head tilted toward the sky, but I felt the scales and claws, their strength against my skin, and swallowed heavily around the pressure.

"Listen to me, you pathetic being." They snarled. I wasn't often afraid, but this was a power I had not been faced with before, not with Ignis when he was angry, not with the Elders when I disobeyed them in my youth. "I am offering you a better world, power, and all the human suffering you can stand to absorb. You can do this my way, or I can work around you, and I can assure you that would be worse for you."

As I struggled to breathe, I kicked out at my attacker. Grabbing their hood, I pulled it back and tried to yank them away from me, using the clothes as leverage. While the human form of the Guardian's face meant nothing to me, I was surprised at their appearance. It wasn't the face nor the build I associated with the power I felt coming from the being.

The sort of human you wouldn't look twice at. They held no threat.

It was the best disguise.

Guardians had no control over our human forms, which meant this unassuming figure was simply who they were.

On the outside, at least.

They dropped me to the ground while they stepped back and adjusted their cloak over their head. I coughed and rubbed my throat. Rage burned through my pupils as the black spread across my eyes, and I stared them down as I stood. While there was no immediate physical recognition, I knew why they hid when I looked into their eyes.

I acknowledged their emotional imprint and what it spoke about them, and I wondered how I hadn't noticed it before.

Lucidian.

I was in more danger now. They knew that I knew their secret.

To spare my life, I was left with little choice.

"So, what is this plan?" I forced control back into my voice and through my veins and ignored the discomfort that lingered on my skin from the Lucidian's touch. "The negative fogs we've created have grown. The effects are visible within the human race."

"There needs to be better organization, timing, and well-chosen locations. There are places where you can choose to make the most impact. Information that only comes with age.

And..." They paused, and I arched a brow and waited. "There are further elements to the plan that will be revealed to you when the time is right."

"And what do you get out of this?" I asked.

"That is not of your concern. Partially the same as you—a new world—but more."

I stood still, wary of the stranger, but it could mean my demise if I were to back down now.

But I was also intrigued by the offer of power, however aggressively it had been delivered.

Tilting my chin upward, I ignored the throb of the bruises as they formed on my neck. "Tell me what to do."

Chapter Fourteen

Ana

"What's she doing now?"

"She's just sitting there. Give me a second."

Bouncing on my toes, I moved around Cael, using his shoulders for leverage and trying to see past him. He turned to me after a particularly enthusiastic bounce left him stumbling forward. His lip twitched as I smirked. Had I intentionally pushed too hard to break his concentration because he can be funny when mad? Maybe.

"What do *you* see?" he asked.

I stopped bouncing and came around in front of him. Cael lay his arms casually around my neck and kissed my cheek before looking forward again at the Porthole. What could he see, I wondered. A crystal-clear vision like looking through a window? A distorted dream? I frowned. Whatever it was, it wasn't working for me. Not yet.

"Not much," I answered, trying not to let the disappointment wash away my excitement at checking in on an old friend. "It's like bad reception. There's so much interference."

He chuckled. "It's not a TV, Ana."

Ignoring his cheek, I leaned forward to stare hard at the flowing white substance before me. The image flickered. It was a split second, but I gasped and reeled back against Cael. "I saw her." I pointed. "For a second, I swear I saw her."

I couldn't yet summon Portholes or view through them properly, so I relied on Cael to regularly check Penny and Henry. My fear that a Tenebrian would come for them dissipated as time passed.

But it was never completely gone.

Leaning back against Cael, his arms tightened around me to steady us both.

"Tell me about her," I said, sighing.

"She's in a different apartment, but there's someone else there. A woman with red hair."

"Lynn," I offered as emotion twisted in my chest.

"They're on the couch together, and they look happy."

Closing my eyes and tilting my head back against Cael's chest, I smiled. Penny and Lynn must have moved in together. This was the best news I could have received. I could only speculate on most things. This was the first time we had caught Penny at home in a long time, as her shifts were difficult to predict, and we could tell nothing about her life while watching her work. Lynn was good for Penny, and I'd always hoped Penny would better balance her career and personal life and let Lynn into her life in a more permanent capacity. Thankfully, Lynn had been patient enough to wait for Penny to be ready for that stage in her life.

"The ginger cat is there."

"Seamus? Really?"

"He looks old," he added softly.

My nails dug into Cael's arm as sadness overcame me. The pull of Earth had me leaning toward the Porthole, wishing I could see.

"But he's happy, right?" I whispered through the emotion I struggled to keep at bay.

"Yes, he is very happy. He's content and comfortable, curled on the couch beside them."

I needed to change the subject. "What else do you see?"

"They're reading something. It's a brochure. It's..." When he stopped, I turned desperately toward his face, expecting something terrible, and was met with a brilliant smile. "It's an adoption brochure, Ana. They're looking at having a child."

A small *oh* escaped my lips as I clasped a hand to my mouth.

This was a tough one to deal with.

I wanted Penny to have a family, whatever family she wanted.

But I would never meet Penny's child, just like Penny could never meet Samael.

My hand migrated to my chest as an ache grew beneath my ribcage before it evolved into a sob that escaped my throat.

Cael spun me to him and pressed me against his chest when he felt the shift in the air between us, picking up on my emotions before I had even made a sound. I never needed to tell him what I was feeling, and while being so open and transparent would have sounded like a curse when I was on Earth, it was a blessing here with Cael.

"That's enough for today, I think," Cael whispered and waved his hand, closing the Porthole. I felt the change in the air as it closed, even if I couldn't see it.

"But, Henry?" I pressed my face against his chest, wanting

to check in on my other friend but not wanting to let Cael go. Images of Samael playing with a small child with dark hair played across my mind before they shattered into static. That is never to happen.

"We'll check on him another time."

I sighed. "I wish I could go and see them, even if they didn't see me."

"You know you can't."

"I'm getting better." The words came out as more of a plea than I intended. My home was here with Cael and Samael. But Lucidis was not Earth, and I didn't know if I'd ever be able to shake the feeling that this realm wasn't my true home.

Cael shook his head, his chin moving against the top of my head. "You cannot hold your human form. Last time, you flickered back and forth, but that's as close as we've got."

I nodded sadly while Cael stroked my back as I wrapped my arms around him and squeezed, causing his spine to straighten against my grip.

"Ana..."

"I know," I said before he could finish as I loosened my hold. "I'm an unknown entity, and it's a risk we can't take bringing me to Earth. I know." I huffed out a breath against his skin. "I already know all that."

I felt Cael's jaw stiffen, then he sighed again. He didn't need to tell me what I already knew—I couldn't fully control my powers, my human form was out of reach, and not to mention, I was dead on Earth.

But all these facts didn't relieve the ache in my chest.

We did check on Henry regularly.

He lived in the same apartment for a long time, and when Penny was working, Lynn helped him with his shopping. They continued to support him even after they moved out of the building. I wondered if he thought of me as I thought of him and if perhaps he could feel me watching.

Unfortunately, although he was still happy, Henry's body betrayed him with age, and he resigned at Penny's insistence that he move into assisted housing. His children visited regularly, and his two eldest were staying with him for a month when the reaper's soft touch came for him at night. The nurses talked, and I listened through tears as Cael told me one evening Henry had simply said to his children that he loved them and their company, but he was tired and wanted an early night.

He then passed peacefully in his sleep.

I cried for days, clinging to Samael, his thin arms wrapped around my neck and his worried face peeking over my shoulder at Cael. He was unsure what to do to make things better. I could feel the uncertainty in him. While he was perfectly capable of feeling the pain that seeped from my being and flowed around us both, he didn't know what to do about it.

He didn't understand that this pain couldn't be fixed.

My little boy Samael didn't understand why his mother was crying, and every time I opened my mouth to explain it to him, I cried some more.

"I love you, Mommy," he whispered, and in my peripheral

vision, Cael nodded stiffly at his son, an unspoken communication passing between them. The reasons for my crying were a conversation for later, but now, I only needed a hug.

When Samael squeezed harder around my neck and nuzzled my cheek, I let out a watery chuckle. "I love you too, Samael, and Henry would have loved you so much, my little boy."

Cael whispered, "Yes, he would have."

I sniffled loudly, straightened my back, and allowed Samael to climb onto my lap as I leaned against the wall.

"Oh, Cael." I sighed, stroking Samael's back.

Cael slid down the wall and sat next to me. "I know." I didn't need to say anything more. Cael could feel my pain as it poured out with my tears, blanketing the air around us. It must pain him to be next to me like this, feeling my grief so acutely. I wished I could turn our connection off because I didn't want him to suffer too. There wasn't anything Cael could say to make it better, and while he could ease my pain using his powers, he wouldn't.

I didn't want him to ease it. I didn't want him to fill me with his calming influences. Because Henry deserved better, he deserved my tears and my love, and I wanted to grieve for him.

I *needed* to grieve for him.

Cael sighed, reached down between us, intertwined his fingers with mine, and simply felt my pain with me.

Lying on the floor of one of the community huts, I sensed

Cael as he entered, flicked a small toy car away from me, and watched its progress across the uneven ground. With one arm outstretched, I rolled onto my back to watch him enter, but I didn't get up. The air in the room was thick with my sadness. It was all-consuming, and Cael's step slowed and hesitated as he entered the space where my emotions spilled out. His gaze traveled around, taking in the things strewn across the floor, and I clenched my teeth. I wasn't proud of the temper tantrum I'd thrown, but sometimes the emotions were too much to handle, and I didn't know how to deal with them. It was different here than it was on Earth—my negative emotions created a bubble around me, which could start with only *one* bad day, then I absorbed and released more and more negativity until I couldn't break free from the cycle.

I could feel what Cael was feeling, and we held eye contact for a strained moment. I didn't break often, my moments of despair further apart the longer I lived here. But the dull ache that was me missing Earth never truly left. A sting of sour guilt crossed the barrier of my emotional cage as Cael watched me. He'd been visiting Earth with Sasha, Samael, and a small group of young Guardians.

"Ana?" He approached with tentative steps. "Are you okay?"

When I sat upright, I rubbed my hands over my face. My cheeks felt warm where they were flushed, and my eyes were probably red-rimmed from rubbing them as I tried to push away the emotions and the tears themselves. "I bet I look amazing," I muttered, dropping my hands into my lap.

He crouched in front of me. "Always."

I reached out to him like a lost child, and he kneeled by my side and held me when I leaned against him. "I miss it, Cael."

He nodded against my head. "I know."

I didn't want to tell him I was having these feelings, and I'd hoped he never found out I still had a hole in my heart from Earth. I was living in another *realm,* and with the time that had passed, I thought I would've gotten used to it by now. The presence of Cael and Samael made my life worth living. They were my family. But I had lost everything I'd ever known, been thrown into a different world, and told to make do.

Cael started stroking my back as I sighed. "I can't ever go back, can I? I mean, I'm dead there."

"There are many reasons you can't go back."

I sniffed. "What if I learn to control my powers? What if I hide from sight?"

Cael hesitated, and I wiped my eyes again before looking at him. His eyes betrayed his indecision, even if his essence hadn't done it. "I'm always honest with you, Ana, but you can be stubborn."

Immediately, my spine stiffened under his touch, and I was about to correct him and then tell him to blurt out whatever he was trying to say. But the swirl of hesitation, love, and concern that surrounded Cael—my life partner—calmed me instantly, and I let out a hollow laugh.

"I don't know what you mean," I said, and he chuckled as he squeezed my upper arm with his fingers.

"You have not yet mastered your human form. You are..." He searched for the words, apparently trying to find a delicate way to say what he needed to. "... You are an unknown entity. We don't know how you will react if you are to go to Earth."

"Plus, I'm, you know..." I waved my hand around. "Dead."

Cael smiled when I gave a small watery laugh. "You are

incredibly resilient," he said, kissing the top of my head. "Your mother would be proud of you."

I lifted my eyes to his. "What makes you say that?"

"You said you always hoped you had her inner strength, and maybe you're starting to realize you always did."

This elicited another sob from me. How dare he say something so sweet that it catches me in the heart? Oh hell, life was easier before I *felt* so many things.

Cael cradled me again and allowed me to grieve for my lost home.

"Can we practice my human form more?" I asked after a short while.

"Of course, we can, but..."

"I know, I know. You still don't know if I can ever go back."

He nodded sadly. "I love you, Anahera."

I snuggled into him. "I love you, too, but I could go for a whiskey right now."

Cael laughed. "Me too. I'll bring you some back from Earth next time."

The following morning, I was jerked awake.

Well, I was gently shaken away with a soft hand on my shoulder, but it was still enough for me to shriek and jump from the bed I shared with Cael.

Sasha stood above me. "Are you okay?"

I glanced over at Cael's sleeping form. "Apart from my heart attack just now? Yes," I whispered, rubbing my eyes. "What's wrong? Is Samael okay? Are you okay?"

"I heard you were upset yesterday."

My lip twisted. "News travels fast, eh?" My emotional reactions to situations were still the fodder of Guardian gossip. Despite thinking themselves so high above humans, they weren't above chattering among themselves.

Sasha looked confused. "Everyone felt the waves from your emotions."

"And yet no one did anything to help."

"They didn't know what to do."

"Or they didn't care." It was difficult to keep the bitterness from my voice, which I instantly regretted when Sasha's brow furrowed further. Penny had tried to make me more aware of this behavior in myself, pushing people away when they were doing nothing to deserve it.

I sighed as Cael rolled over and groaned, and I pressed a finger to my lips before I stood and led Sasha outside. We sat together in the dew-touched grass, a few paces from the entrance to the hut. The sun was barely visible over the horizon, and a chill was in the breeze from the night air. I took a deep breath and let the sense of the realm fill me.

No matter my qualms about missing home, this place certainly had a magic of its own. The sun, the moon, and the air themselves could calm.

Sasha reached forward and touched my necklace. It glowed slightly where her finger met the moonstone, and she moved her hand away. "Why do you have this?"

"It was my mother's, and Cael ensured I got it back."

"It is a nice stone... useful," she said, nodding curtly. It was as close to a compliment I could expect from a Guardian, and I smiled. She was trying.

"It's pretty too," I added.

"Yes, it is." Sasha studied the pendant. "Why do you give gifts?"

"For a race that spends all its time watching humans, you sure have a lot of questions." I regretted the words the moment they left my lips. Sasha had been accommodating to me, answering all my questions about her realm, questions she probably thought silly and petty when she had better things to do than cater to me like a curious child. She didn't deserve such a rude response, but Sasha showed no sign of being offended.

"Just because we witness the acts does not mean we understand the reasons behind them."

"You're right, I'm sorry." I tilted my head as I thought about it. I'd gotten better at explaining things I never thought I'd have to explain before, since being in Lucidis. "It's to show someone you care about and love them."

"But don't they know you love them, anyway? You tell each other all the time."

"Of course, but it's that bit extra to show them you're thinking of them even when they're not there."

"I think I understand. It's a nice thought."

"*It's the thought that counts,*" I chimed in a sing-song voice, and smiled at Sasha's confusion before I explained the meaning behind the saying.

We sat silently for a moment, and I twirled the grass around my fingers. "So, you were worried about me?" I teased.

Sasha smiled. "You are always so sure that we all feel nothing. I have told you before that you are my friend. I am sorry I wasn't there to help."

My brows furrowed even as a smile played on my lips. "You are all so strange, yet sometimes you surprise me."

"Ana, I know things are different here than on Earth, and we are different beings, but perhaps you need to give us more of a chance."

"The Elders literally won't look directly at me... like I'm a disease."

"Yes." The disappointment was evident in Sasha's voice as her tone dropped. "The Elders are... very set in their ways, but also wise and good. Do you think perhaps you are judging all of us on the few? Are you allowing your negative experiences with some of the Guardians to give you an excuse to shut off from the rest of us? Or..." she paused as though she was forming the thoughts as she spoke, "... perhaps you are almost doing it on purpose, and using it as an excuse not to open up."

My eyebrows shot up, and I placed a hand over my heart. *Ouch, called out.* "That's an incredible insight," I said tightly.

Sasha laughed then. It was a soft chuckle, barely more than a smile, and a single note of amusement. "We are empaths. Insight is what we do."

I placed a hand on Sasha's. "Thank you for caring."

Sasha smiled again. I liked it when the Guardians smiled. The snarl I'd witnessed all those years ago from the Tenebrian I realized now wasn't a smile, but was intended as aggressively as it looked. When Guardians smiled—*really* smiled—the change was visible in their faces, as though there was an inner part of them that was human, and allowed to shine through at that moment.

Chapter Fifteen

Ana

Five years later

The concern that Samael would become an outcast never left me, although I didn't fully express this to Cael. It felt wrong not to tell him exactly what I was thinking or feeling, but I clung to the hope that Samael, being three-quarters Guardian and having been born and raised in Lucidis, wouldn't be ostracized. With every passing day, Samael grew, progressing at the same rate as the other children. Thankfully, I could still see his humanity, of which I was immensely proud.

I wanted him to fit in and be happy, without losing sight of his identity. It was a fine line to tread, yet he seemed to find the balance better than I had.

Samael was quiet, which wasn't unusual. Guardians often became more stoic as they aged, losing any childlike playfulness they had early in their lives. But he was also sensitive to others and genuinely cared about how they felt.

I encouraged this.

Samael was also a curious, yet somewhat naïve child. There were things the other children seemed to know from generations of ingrained knowledge that Samael didn't understand—mostly their attitude toward humans and how they looked down upon emotions as a weakness. For the most part, humans were still considered a lesser species, and emotions were nothing more than tools. Samael didn't understand this, but he did understand that beyond being useful for a Guardian's duty to the Balance, emotions could be felt and experienced on a deeper level.

Why not feel joy for yourself rather than simply use it?

Why deny yourself the sensations of having these emotions inside you?

I encouraged this too, and I grinned to myself. It felt like a small bit of rebellion, but Samael was *our* son, and the community could shove their opinions up their ass. I did my absolute best to let him have the most *normal* childhood he could for a Guardian, but I wasn't going to let him go as if our relationship was completely void.

We were family.

Guardians are considered mature at twenty, and while they were old enough to procreate at this age, it was discouraged until they were around thirty or forty years old. However, they were physically capable of having children well into their sixties. Many Guardians had only one and rarely more than two children, and some waited much longer than others. But as the population of Earth grew, so did the need for more Guardians to maintain the Balance, so breeding was encouraged.

But no one encouraged me to have more children, which was fine with me. I'd stick with my little rebellious family, thank you.

Samael was thirteen years old today, much like his other

birthdays, and to the complete bewilderment of the Elders and much of the community, I insisted on celebrating it. I'd sit there with my family, a few curious Guardians, and children who wanted to join the celebration, singing 'Happy Birthday' as loudly and out of tune as possible. Samael would laugh, and I'd sing louder, and even Cael couldn't keep the smirk from his face as the community watched with polite but confused expressions.

"It never ceases to amaze me your perseverance with human customs," Cael said once the song was finished and cake was being shared. "You seem to ignore completely... or at least pretend to ignore... the community's disinterest."

"And yet..." I waved a finger at him. "They still eat cake and play some of the games. So, they can put up with the stuff they don't understand." I added under my breath, "Lord knows I put up with their shit."

Cael chuckled and kissed me on the head.

As we watched Samael play kickball with the other children using a large red ball I'd found in the stash of human items in the community, I squeezed Cael's hand. "He's so cute, I just want to *squish* him," I squealed, my eyes following his progress through the grass. Though I'd never say it to his face. Samael was a teenager, and I needed to start seeing him less as a boy and more as a young man. While Samael had yet to roll his eyes at me and exclaim *Moooom* as I embarrassed him, I was trying hard not to push him to that point.

So, instead, I told Cael all about Samael's squishy cheeks and how I wished to smoosh them.

Cael gripped my hand. "But you won't, though, right?"

I laughed, a single loud *hah*, and Cael relaxed and allowed the smile back onto his face. "Why? Afraid I'll embarrass our son?"

"I'm afraid you'll squish him too hard."

I laughed, then frowned at Cael. *Was he being serious?*

"Sasha brought you back a calendar," Cael said.

I smiled up at him. "Oh, brilliant, I needed a new one." I gasped loudly, and Cael jerked toward me as I added, "We should start celebrating *your* birthday!"

Cael shrugged. "For what purpose?"

"It'll be fun."

"I'm not playing ball games or pinning a paper tail on some unfortunate animal image."

I laughed again. The joy I felt during these moments, when I managed to let my guard down and my human half could come to the forefront, was invigorating. "Those games are just for children's birthdays. For adult birthdays, we used to go out drinking or for dinner." I looked around. "Although I'm not sure what the equivalent is here."

"Con the community into cooking for you?" Cael smirked, then his eyes widened as I ran with the idea.

"*A feast.*" I clapped my hands together. "We could do a big community feast. *Everyone* is invited."

"Ana..."

I smirked. "I know, I know, you're all party-poopers."

"We are an ancient species—"

"An ancient species of party-poopers." I cut Cael off with a finger to his lips, then sighed. "I know all that, Cael, I'm just playing with you." I kissed his cheek. "Sort of." Before he could protest, I continued, "But, while I think of it, I don't know *exactly* how old you are. I know the Elders are over one hundred and thirty, maybe more. Your mother is around eighty, although she looks half that." I'd never really thought about how old Cael was because to me, he was just Cael, *my Kyle.* "It's still hard to take in, how long you live, how young you look until you're well past one hundred."

I assessed Cael now. He had hardly aged a day since we met. Guardians maintained their looks and physical grace most of their lives, only declining in their last decades. I wondered how much of that was the absolute control they had over their beings to keep fit and lean, like their ability to have unprotected sex without risk of an unwanted pregnancy. They could simply... *switch it off.* Their bodies were in as much control as their minds.

"I hope I live long so I can spend as much time with my boys." I sighed as Samael bounced the ball to one of the other children.

Cael's head snapped toward me. "You want another son?"

I smiled. "You and Samael are my boys, you idiot."

Cael laughed, and when we fell into silence again, I prodded him with my elbow. "So, how old *are* you?"

Cael looked thoughtful. "As of this year, that would make me... sixty-seven."

I tried not to stumble as my mind hurdled over the thought.

"That's uh, a lot of birthdays," I said, regaining myself.

Oh my God, I've been sleeping with an old man.

When I looked at Cael again, certain this time I would see wrinkles on his perfect face, I noticed a smirk instead.

I sneered. "You're messing with me."

Cael chuckled as I crossed my arms. "You're much better at playing jokes than taking them." He placed an arm around my shoulders and shook me slightly. I stayed resolutely still, holding my pose and trying not to smirk at the cheeky bastard. "I'm surprised you didn't immediately do the math based on my mother's approximate age." When I continued to stare at him with stony eyes, he added, "I'm in my late-forties... I guess."

"You guess?"

"We do not keep track." He shrugged. "So, I can't be sure. It's not important."

"Sixty-seven," I muttered, "I can't believe I believed you." I nudged Cael gently with my elbow again and continued to watch Samael as he stopped playing to wave to us. Samael's skin glistened in the sunlight as the children ran through the dappled shade from the trees. I liked watching the young Guardians play. It was more human than I had witnessed as they got older, and I could only hope that as Samael got older, he wouldn't lose the ability to feel emotions himself, as the others did as they refined their powers.

But looking at Cael, surely that wouldn't be the case.

I smiled as Samael tagged a child and ran away laughing.

I hoped he lived to be well over a hundred, but, more importantly, he enjoyed every moment.

The party was winding down as the air cooled with the gentle breeze that accompanied the approaching evening. As the stars started to make themselves seen through the haze of the setting sun, I was approached by an older male Guardian. I watched him cautiously and glanced at Cael as he observed from a short distance away. Cael didn't appear to be bothered or threatened, so I relaxed. Cael would have done something if I were in danger and unable to get an accurate read on a Guardian myself.

Some of them were just so *good* at hiding their emotions and their essences. They could make themselves almost invisible to my senses. I knew I was still developing my abilities as a Guardian—I'd started from scratch as an adult, so it was slow going—but I hadn't managed to master the part where I could control my emotional imprint with such accuracy as to hide.

As he came level with me, I looked up into his face. His quills and scales were a sky blue that was only slightly starting to betray his age. He held a bag, and I eyed it suspiciously as he handed it to me without a word. Opening it, I took out a small hand-woven pillow.

Oh my God.

It was a *gift.*

I smiled at the stranger. He had used different colors of natural thread to create an intricate pattern.

"It is for Samael," he said, his voice not quite a whisper but soft like silk. He was a gentle being. I could feel that much about him. "For his birthday."

A gift.

A gift.

I couldn't keep the smile off my face. Every moment like this was a treasure, where a Guardian took a leap and tried a human custom. They stepped away from the community and *tried,* and this... *this* was something I would never have expected.

Handmade, it must have taken hours.

"Thank you," I whispered, clutching it to my chest. "He will love it. It's beautiful."

Although maybe I love it more.

It's the thought that counts.

"I did not want to interrupt their playing."

I held out my hand. "I don't think we've officially met. I'm Ana."

He looked at my hand for a beat while I waited patiently before he slowly took it in his. We didn't shake, but held hands for a moment and assessed each other so I could get a reading on him. Something about him felt familiar, like I'd met him before, but had forgotten. "Novus," he said.

"Oh! You're Esco's father."

He lifted a shoulder. "I am also Cael's father, but the children are raised as a community."

The pillow almost slipped from my grip as I momentarily forgot about it. Regaining myself, a prominent thought passed through my mind—*damn, guess it would've made sense to name our son after him then, but how was I supposed to know?*

I stuttered. "Yo-you're Samael's grandfather?"

"I suppose I am."

I dropped the bag and the pillow then, and without a further thought, threw myself forward and wrapped my arms around Novus's body. He stiffened with his arms pinned to his sides and glanced at Cael as he laughed. Novus looked down at me, but I didn't let him go. The hug had drawn the attention of a few nearby Guardians, and my spine stiffened as I felt Novus's nervousness filter through. I kept hugging him. The familiarity I felt must've been because he was Cael's father, and perhaps that's what I picked up on.

But there was something else inside him, something distinctly human...

Novus pulled away as he moved one hand and patted my arm. Chuckling, I glanced at the uncomfortable expressions of the onlookers, and I let Novus go and stood back.

"I'm sorry," I said, picking up the pillow. "I miss my family."

"I understand."

I laughed. "No, you don't."

A breathy chuckle escaped Novus's lips as they curved into a small smile. "No," he admitted. "I guess I do not."

I shook my head, still smiling. "I can't tell you how much I appreciate the gift. It means the world to me that you thought of Samael on his birthday."

Novus tilted his head as he maintained intense eye contact with me. "We are not all so judgmental. Some of us are trying, you know this?"

My smile was sad. "I know."

Chapter Sixteen

Cael

Ana sat with a circle of the younger children around her. She had found some children's books and, over the years, convinced Sasha to bring her back more. When she ran out of stories, she'd make them up, and the children loved how animated she was in her storytelling, putting on voices and occasionally acting out the scenes for them.

Sometimes, Esco sat in on story time, her eyes wide with fascination. Ana had admitted to me that this pulled at her heart, and promptly shoved me with her shoulder when I'd teased her. As I watched Ana's story time tonight, the grin I had at the memory of the conversation dropped. It had made me realize that Guardian children were perhaps not so different from human children in some ways. But as we commenced our training, we lost the curious and spirited part of being a child, and became the apathetic beings who so steadily guarded and monitored the Balance. Ana said she understood the importance of this task, but still didn't understand why it had to be undertaken at the cost of our potential humanity.

If we let our emotions run wild, then who would monitor the

Balance?

The children laughed while Ana pretended to have a sword fight, but the laughing ceased when the elders Cascus and Pernax, a female elder with gentle eyes in contrast to her tough stance on the community, emerged from the shadows. My back stiffened as they stood silently on the precipice of the light cast from the fire. Ana looked up when she realized the children had stopped laughing, and they scattered as she straightened before the Elders.

"Anahera."

"Hello." She nodded at them. Her shoulders shifted back slightly, and she maintained her straight posture, though I could feel the strain on her as she tried not to be intimidated by the Elders. They exuded an air of power, a constant swirl of authority and influence that permeated the atmosphere.

"We have asked before that you do not tell the children stories."

As is their way, Ana's brows drew together when she noticed, once again, they didn't look directly at her. Pernax did on occasion, but it was fleeting and not quite direct eye contact.

Cascus barely looked at Ana at all.

I moved beside Ana as she said, "It's just a bit of fun."

"It is damaging to them." Pernax looked around as the last of the children left. "They are not humans and will not be treated as such. It is beneath them."

"It's important that they learn. There's power in understanding and feeling emotions rather than just using them."

"You know not of what you speak," Pernax shouted.

Ana stood her ground even as she flinched. "Sometimes

things need to change."

"Do not be a fool. Things are how they are for a reason, the Balance—"

"This has nothing to do with the Balance." Ana waved the children's book at them. "Why won't you let them learn?"

Pernax's tone returned to the steady monotone. "They learn all they need to from the community."

Ana stepped toward them, and her gaze didn't waver from Pernax as Cascus recoiled slightly. "There is more to humanity than you think. We are more than tools."

The Elders took a half-step away from her as we all sensed her anger grow.

"You are no longer one of them," Pernax said.

"But I'm not one of you either. I know, because I'm reminded every day."

Cascus turned toward her then, and when his eyes met hers, Ana froze. I stepped in behind Ana, and Cascus's gaze flickered to me for a brief moment before returning to Ana. There was something in his eyes, something communicated on an unspoken level.

This was more than a distrust of Ana.

He *despised* her with a loathing that burned through him.

I stood to my full height and firmly placed myself behind Ana, making it clear she was under my protection. Standing up to the Elders was a difficult task that should be handled delicately. I wanted Ana to feel free to speak her mind and not feel alone.

"Calm yourself," Cascus said before turning away and resting his gaze on the wall over her shoulder again.

"Why should I?" Ana shouted.

The Elders' anger rose—however much they tried to control it—we could still sense it as it lingered below the surface. Ana's fingers twitched, and I knew what she wanted. She wanted to *push* them and show them they were no better than humans. Make them *feel* the anger, admit to it, and prove that they, too, felt things.

"The Balance can be moved from within our realm, too, young one, if much force is used."

I placed my hand on Ana's shoulder as she tensed. Her distrust and rage had permeated the air, spreading across the community. "What's the problem, Pernax?" I asked.

Do you, too, fear Ana will disrupt the Balance?

It was a sense I got from Monia and some Elders, but no one spoke outwardly of it. Cascus, however, continued to push Ana and to try to control her, as if this wouldn't make things worse instead of better.

"She was telling the children stories again," Cascus said.

"I know."

I looked at the book Ana had clutched in her hand, and my jaw clenched. I was treading a fine line between understanding Ana, in most cases agreeing with her, keeping the Elders and the community happy, and the Balance safe. The Elders didn't often lose control, but they were powerful and could be dangerous if crossed. Beyond that, they possessed knowledge that the rest of the community did not, and the community trusted them to know what was best.

Who was I to assume I knew better?

Ana had strong points, but perhaps there were more layers to this than we knew.

I was on Ana's side, but I also had my duty.

Pernax pointed at me. "Control her."

"What did you say?" Ana's rage radiated off her in waves.

The Elders looked at me and nodded stiffly before leaving.

Ana spun around to face me. "*Control* me?"

"They do not understand, Ana. They are simply asking me to talk to you."

"For beings so old and wise, they are mighty stupid."

A frown creased my brow. "They have earned our respect. Please do not speak of the Elders that way." As Ana's jaw dropped, I touched a finger to her lips. "Please, I'm trying to protect you, but also do what is right. I will find a way to make sure our thoughts on the use of human emotions are better understood."

"Why *shouldn't* I speak that way about them?" she demanded, and I flinched, because she was right. "You heard how they talk about me, right? I *know* you agree with me that things need to change."

"Yes. But I also do it with *respect*. Change takes time. Too fast, and they will resist."

Ana covered the small distance between us in one step. "*They* came to *me,* Cael."

"They are protective of the children."

"I would never do *anything* to hurt the children."

I placed my hands on her shoulders, but didn't attempt to calm her through influence. She would feel the moment I tried, and I had no intention of trying to *control* her that way. I tried to ignore the thoughts that crept into my mind, reminding me I was unsure what would happen if Ana was angered further. Her fury already spilled out of her in waves that pushed the air around us both, and I'm sure others in the community would be able to feel it too. She had the emotional strength of a dozen Guardians in one volatile body. The body of the woman I loved. "I know, I know you wouldn't, and they know you wouldn't hurt the children on purpose either."

"*On purpose*? I wouldn't hurt them at *all*!"

"I know, I know." I sighed and rubbed my face. "I'm sorry." Ana's brows furrowed further as I took a deep breath. Ana and I briefly discussed the notion of her growing powers as we practiced, so she could learn to control them. But I kept to myself my fears of her instability, and that I suspected the Elders felt the same. I could tell her now, but this was already hard on her, and if my concerns about her growing power were unfounded... I sighed again. "They think teaching the children to be more human will make them less effective as Guardians. The Balance—"

"Yes, I know. The Balance, the Balance, *the Balance.* But it *won't* make them less effective, it will make them more so. Surely, if they understand the emotions they are shifting, if they understand what it's like to *feel*..." She placed a palm over her heart, and I took her other hand as she continued, "Don't they think I've learned a thing or two since coming here? That I've had so much time to do nothing but learn to channel my powers." A spark from within her ignited as she kept talking, and I felt the pulse through my fingers. The words flowed from her almost as fast as she could think. "So I can't do some of the things that come easily to others, but I feel on a much deeper level than most of you do. I think that could be put to use... if only they would let me show them."

"Baby steps, my Ana. These are not changes that will happen easily, perhaps not even within our lifetime. You cannot change a way of living that has been so for thousands of years overnight."

"Where have I heard that before?" The sarcasm dripped from her words, but her shoulders dropped when I looked at her. "It was only a story..." her voice went quiet, "... and the children like them."

"I know." I pulled her toward me and held her close. "I can only imagine how hard this is for you."

"I'm stronger, Cael."

"I know you're strong, but this must still be hard."

"No, I mean, I'm *stronger.*"

I stiffened as I held her and asked carefully, "What do you mean?"

Ana was whispering, although no one else was around. "I know we've talked about my *power* like it's something different and unexpected, but I can feel it inside me. It's like, where the human and the Guardian meet, a barrier is breaking down and forming one being. Ever since I've been here, I've felt it. A little stronger every day. I know you feel it too. But..." She held a finger to my lips as I went to speak. "...I also get why we haven't spoken much about it, and I'm guessing the Elders have something to do with it." She huffed a small breath through her nose as I pressed my lips together into a fine line. *Of course,* she'd felt it within her and had already forgiven me for not talking about it.

She's so much stronger than I give her credit for.

My chest constricted as she continued, "It's okay. I understand I'll always be a wrench in the works. You have to walk this line between your heritage and me, and I'm sorry, but I do wish they would give me more credit and speak to me themselves. *Cowards.*"

"They're afraid, Ana."

"Of me?"

"*For* you."

She scoffed quietly and sensed my hesitation before I could mask it. "I don't believe that part. But I don't feel like I'm out of control. You taught me about controlling the power when opening a Gateway. I've been putting those principles into practice internally..." She caught my arched brow and smiled at me. "I promise," Ana added, her smile dropped, and she looked at her hands as if she would be able to see her power shifting across her blue skin. "They're not the only ones who get scared. Although at least *I* admit it."

"Did you open a Gateway?"

Ana faltered. "No, not without you. But I mean, I'm in control of myself. I'm practicing to control the power before it's even a thing. You know what I mean?"

I nodded. If I focused on where I touched her, I could feel the power that surged in her blood. She was right—the mingling of human and Guardian made her formidable. Half her life on Earth, then coming here, had grown in her a power that wouldn't have come about had she had lived her whole life on Earth or been born and raised in Lucidis. Even being a half-breed would've resulted differently if she hadn't made that transition between realms after so long in one.

Ana was an anomaly, a one-off, and unique.

But I also believed being in Lucidis was a good influence on Ana, the perfect place for her to learn control. Any negative emotions she experienced were leveled out simply by being here.

I wasn't sure she'd have the same control if she ever tried to return to Earth.

But hopefully, she would never need to.

Chapter Seventeen

Culo

Kurt stood at the window, looking at the city nineteen floors below his feet. It had taken him many years, yet he had managed to work his way up from delivery driver to CEO. He had no family in the business, so there could be no accusation of nepotism. He'd relied solely on hard work and a good education and had taken advantage of every opportunity that came his way. Even if some opportunities left him broke and struggling to pay the bills at the time. If Kurt were honest with himself, he'd admit there were elements of stepping on other people to get to the top.

Lying. Cheating.

But business was business.

I knew all this from a combination of what he'd told us over beers at the local bar and what I'd read from his essence.

He was *the man,* as they say. A smile curved his lips as he looked over what I'm sure he felt was his *kingdom*.

Vikt had told us little of the grand plan, and I suspected she pretended to have more under control than she did. But *this* was part of the long-term plan—to befriend humans and become part of their society and social groups, even if it were only a fleeting part. Kurt had been CEO for six years, and the business had thrived and expanded from nine hundred employees to over three thousand.

"What are you thinking about?" Michael, a fellow Tenebrian, asked, and a tick in my jaw twitched as I watched him bounce a pen against his knee and lift his feet onto Kurt's desk.

"Just the future, and all the possibilities it holds." Kurt turned to him, and his gaze drifted past me as he acknowledged my presence with a slight nod. "How can I help you today?"

"Can't we simply come and visit a friend?" Michael said, a smile curving his lips.

"Friend is a heavy word, *friend*." Kurt sat at his desk and used a ruler to push Michael's feet off the edge. "We haven't known each other that long, and it's highly unusual to show up at my office, asking for a favor after only a few months after meeting. A few conversations at a bar don't constitute a strong friendship."

"But what if I have an offer you can't resist?"

"Or refuse?" Kurt smirked. When Michael's face remained impassive, Kurt waved his hand dismissively. "Tell me what this is all about."

"Fire half of your workforce."

Kurt laughed before the sound faded into a nervous chuckle when Michael's expression didn't shift. "I'm sorry—what? Why on earth would I do that?"

"Why on earth, indeed," Michael muttered. He stood and came around the desk, dragging his fingernails along the wood grain of the expensive piece of furniture. Kurt didn't move, though his gaze again slid to me where I stood with my hands clasped behind my back. I'd offer him no assistance—I was here for Michael to draw from my power.

Kurt didn't move as his eyes grew wide, and his gaze darted to follow Michael's progress as he approached him. Michael leaned in toward Kurt, and his eyes shifted to black in a blink. Over the years, Michael, like me, had become an expert in hiding his true nature from humans. He didn't want them to be afraid of him.

Not straightaway, anyway.

Not until he was ready to taste their pain, to experience it flooding his senses. The thought tingled my spine, and I flexed my fingers, ready to receive the delightful high of humans' pain.

"It takes a while, you know, finding the right people in the right circles," Michael said, his casual tone contrasting the stony look in his eyes as he let them slide back into blue. He leaned forward and slapped his palms on the desk, his face inches from Kurt's. "Fire half of your workforce. Do it at random. All people from all levels. No notice, just do it."

"I—"

"*Now.*" His voice radiated more power than the word alone held.

"Okay."

Michael nodded with satisfaction and sat back down as Kurt picked up the phone, relaying details for a memo to go out to his secretary. Her voice was shrill enough for me to hear as it rang through the phone, and she asked him to repeat several details in disbelief.

Kurt hesitated.

Michael nodded, leaned across the desk, and placed his hand on Kurt's.

I could sense the strain on Michael's powers to influence in this way. Humans had a strong sense of free will, and while it was difficult to make them hurt each other, things like this we could make happen. This involved no physical violence, so their willpower was slightly weaker. He had chosen his target carefully, someone high enough in the ranks to do the damage, but with a weak spot within them. Open and friendly on the outside, ruthless on the inside—a ruthlessness that could be drawn out and amplified with the right influence. I moved to Michael's side and touched his shoulder, pushing some of my power through him. The surge made Kurt blink rapidly, and Michael grinned when he felt that final shift of will.

The ripples from this would be perfect.

Personally, I preferred simple violence and pain, but Vikt had assured me that the emotional response to an act like this would have a dire effect on humans.

Kurt relayed the message with force and hung up the phone.

We waited.

The news trickled down through the levels, and Michael and I remained in place, absorbing the negative energy as it rose through the building. All those people left without their livelihoods—unplanned, unexpected, and unexplainable. Kurt sat frozen as we enjoyed the mounting negative energy in the building.

Within the hour, it had shifted from vague confusion to absolute despair, and those who still had their jobs wondered why they were spared, and if there'd be another mass firing.

No one felt safe.

But Michael was drained, and I wasn't generous enough to let him drain me. So, he sought more human pain to recharge. His lips curved as he looked across the desk at Kurt. He had now served his usefulness, and his life was no longer required.

Kurt yelled as Michael launched himself across the desk and tackled him. Their chairs clattered to the floor, Kurt's head collided with the window behind him, and they rolled together. He groaned as he rubbed his head, but was left with no time to recover before Michael's hands were around his throat.

Michael leaned in close to Kurt's ear. "You destroyed all those people's lives. Your business is ruined. Your reputation, your life, *everything.*"

Kurt's eyes widened as the realization washed over him, and he released a pained groan. Michael let him feel the results of his actions, let it fill him with dread as the future he had been picturing only an hour earlier came crashing down around him. I sucked air in through my teeth as Kurt's pain added to that from the floors below, and allowed myself a moment to bask in it. I cast my influence into the mix and fed off the pain while at the same time fueling it, growing it until it spread to the area around the building. People in the streets and buildings nearby would be pulled into the vortex of the negative energy, and I could feel each one as they were added to the fog. Michael moaned loudly with the effort expended to keep that growth moving, and I backed off, letting him take the brunt of it.

As his shoulders slumped, his fingers loosened around Kurt's throat. Kurt took the opportunity to fight back, throwing his weight into getting Michael off him. Still dizzy from the blow to his head, Kurt stumbled as he stood. Michael punched the window in frustration, a single ping the only indication of the weakened glass. He threw himself at Kurt again, feeling a burning will to live and fight back within the man.

That will make it all the better when he succumbs to death.

Kurt didn't make it to his phone on the desk, nor to the

button to call reception. Instead, he was pulled down by his feet, and his chin collided with the desk before he was dragged back toward Michael. Kurt glanced desperately at the security camera in the corner, and I chuckled.

Security had just been fired with instructions to leave the building immediately.

"Why are you doing this?" Kurt cried out as they struggled. Michael narrowly missed Kurt's head and punched the floor instead, leaving a dent as he released an enraged howl, which left Kurt with a shudder.

"You're going to die," Michael said as they both stood in their brawl, and their shoulders collided with the window again.

I saw what would happen before it did and took a step back, ready to let it unfold.

The window shifted in its frame from the force of Michael's blows, before another hit shattered it into thousands of pieces and sprayed them with glass.

Kurt teetered on the edge of the floor, which dropped straight down under his heels. The wind howled past his ears and whipped his hair around his face. In that moment, I saw *real* fear in his eyes and breathed it in.

"Help me!" Kurt reached out for Michael, but when Michael laughed, Kurt's expression went dark.

Oh, this was about to get good.

Kurt lurched forward with his remaining steadiness and grabbed Michael by his shirt before losing their balance. Michael's arms flailed for a grip on something, anything, and his rage was replaced instantly by fear when his hands grasped only the air as they both toppled out of the building.

Michael screamed in rage.

I strolled across the room and gripped the window frame before looking out. Reaching out with my senses, I found Kurt's imprint, hoping to get a hefty dose of fear as he fell to his death. Instead, I received resignation and satisfaction. His final moments were accepting of his death, and vengefully glad he took Michael with him.

Then his imprint was gone, as was Michael's, as their bodies almost simultaneously hit a parked car in the street and created an explosion of twisted metal, limbs, and blood as it was forced from the bodies during impact.

My lip twisted.

Guess I'll have to find someone else for the mission tomorrow.

Chapter Eighteen

Samael

Nine years later

It was most noticeable in my hands, I think, and often I'd turn them over in my lap and stare at the lines of them. The scales on my arms ended sooner than those on others my age, and gave way to smooth, human-looking skin, although it was still blue. I knew I was different from the other Guardians. I looked like them—mostly—but I wasn't the same. I'd known my entire life, and just in case I wasn't already aware, the community's treatment of my mother made it *very* clear. Even if they said nothing, the shift in their emotional imprints when she was near was enough of an admission. My heart ached thinking about it—how did she go day after day, knowing only a fraction of the community accepted her for who and what she was?

At twenty-two, I assisted more as the Guardians viewed and influenced humans through Portholes.

I spoke a lot to Mother about my differences. Still, my senses were consumed by guilt and shame when I was reminded of the one thing I hadn't shared with even her—that when I returned to Lucidis after a trip to Earth once, my skin had resisted changing back to my natural form. It felt as though my entire body was drawn to some innate desire to be human.

I didn't need another reason to be different from the others, so I didn't speak of it, as if saying it aloud would make it real.

The Elders had told me that living in Lucidis would suppress my human side, and I wanted to believe them. But it was a lie because I couldn't watch humanity with the same apathy as the others. I *felt* for them, followed their stories, and wished them happiness. I'd found this part of me helpful, though, and had harnessed this need to assist in spreading positive influence on humans. Using my emotional desires made me stronger than others my age, and when I saw a smile light up someone's face or a weight lifted from their shoulders, it strengthened me again. It was a cycle I could push myself into, and use repeatedly while on duty to keep the positive energies flowing where needed and the Balance.

But I saw the looks from my peers. They wondered if I was particularly adept at self-training or if I was indeed utilizing some aspect of my mixed heritage. So, some of them were still wary of me.

Mostly, I could brush off their odd looks because our duty was *more* to me than simply restoring the Balance. It was about wanting every human I came across to be happy, well, and safe in their knowledge of the future. To the other Guardians, I was a valuable asset, if a little strange to them. Only once did I try to explain to another Guardian what I was doing and how, and I even suggested that maybe if they opened themselves up to *feeling* the emotions themselves, they could be stronger too.

Some of them dismissed me, others tried and failed.

At least they tried.

Sitting in a semicircle with three friends, I shook my hands, ready to observe humanity as we did every day. There had been a spike in negative energy, and although it was only from one household, one family, every little bit helped. We couldn't solve the humans' problems, but sometimes, the air needed to be cleared of the residual fog of their emotions. The younger Guardians were often tasked with smaller spikes in the Balance as we still developed and refined our powers.

When I was younger, I misunderstood our purpose and thought I could solve the humans' problems when they were hurt. Some Guardians had explained it to me cruelly, as if I should've known automatically from birth. Maybe *they* did, but all I had in my mind was a constant inner monologue questioning every move I made and word I spoke.

I wanted to do the best for everyone, and it hurt when I couldn't.

Sulus opened a Porthole, sat next to me, and glanced at me from the corner of her eye. I returned her smile but didn't engage her in conversation. She wanted to sleep with me, and she hadn't been subtle about it—few Guardians were when it came to physical pleasure. You ask, and if they accept, you do it. But so far, I had resisted any temptation that lingered somewhere inside me. It's not that I wasn't attracted to Sulus. It was simply that I felt there should be something *more* than physical attraction, but I didn't quite know how to begin explaining this to her. So, my resistance had only fueled her to try harder. She was attractive and sought after as a mate, but she was also a good listener, which is why I was thankful to have her in my small circle of friends.

Sulus's eyes would narrow slightly each time I turned her

down, and I hoped she wasn't taking it personally. Surely not, considering I'd turned down *every* Guardian who'd come onto me. At twenty-two, typically, a young Guardian would've started bedding others by now, and may have even had several different partners.

But it just didn't feel right to me.

I tried explaining it to my parents, and Mother understood immediately. She'd told me that if I wanted to find someone I cared about first, it was completely normal to feel that way. The problem was that it was completely normal for a *human* but not a Guardian, and I constantly walked the fine line between the two worlds.

It was exhausting.

Zat shushed Viri when he opened his mouth to speak, and they both turned back toward the display in front of them. I smirked. Viri was about to try to intercept the offer from Sulus for sex, as he had been unsuccessfully trying to do for months. Viri had maintained a level of playfulness from childhood, and I was sure if he were human, he'd take it to the next level and be a prankster.

Zat was more serious about the task and thought of his duties above all else, as did most Guardians. But I had felt *something* within him—a small spark that could almost be humanity, as if somewhere in his DNA, he too was human. I'd never voice this to him, certain Zat would treat this as an insult, because it was a feeling and nothing more. But it made for a curious friendship, as I often kept company with those who displayed non-typical Guardian traits.

The Porthole loomed before us, and the image clarified as Zat shifted its location to the house in question. I turned toward the image of the humans, and tried to force my face to remain impassive as the sounds of their shouting were clear through the Porthole.

A young man with dark brown hair pulled back into a bun strode down a hallway, backpack in hand. He flinched when there was a crash and muffled yelling from the other room, but kept walking without looking back.

"David, come back!" A woman trotted after him, her cheeks flushed, betraying her stress.

"If he doesn't want me in the house, I'm not staying." David didn't break his stride but stopped short of the front door and kept his back to the woman.

"He loves you. He's your father, but he doesn't understand," she said.

David turned back toward her and gently touched her shoulder. "Mom, I'm not going to change..." he paused, and looked down at his body as if all the answers were there without him saying it. "This is who I am. I'm gay..." he dropped his hand from her shoulder when she winced at his words, "... and I can see that it bothers you too."

"I'm sorry." She reached out to him as he stepped away. Her hand fluttered through the space where he had stood, but she didn't reach further toward him.

"I just... I thought it would be lovely to have grandchildren one day, and to see your wedding..."

"I can have a family with another man." He frowned at her. "But that's not the same to you, is it?"

David slung his backpack over his shoulder. "I packed before I even told him. This wasn't a surprise to me. I was sick of living a lie, and I think you knew that."

She was crying, but didn't stop him as he opened the door. "Where will you go?" she whispered.

David paused. "Bye, Mom, take care of Dad. I love you."

He closed the door behind him.

I shrank away from the scene before me—the entire household was covered in a thick blanket of negative energy that crawled into my very bones. The house was close to the area where yet another Tenebrian-fueled incident had occurred, so the negative influence was already heavy in the area, and this family's angst was only adding to it.

I need to right the Balance.

I need to fix this.

I held out my palms toward the Porthole as my friends did the same, but unlike them, no positive energies to calm the air around the household came from me. My hands trembled as I watched the woman's shoulders drop and her breathing slow. When she stared at the closed front door, her shoulders shook as she cried, even as the fog of negativity in her home eased thanks to my peers next to me.

Go after him.

I almost put the thought into words, and the temptation to open the Porthole into a Gateway and to influence her to do the right thing was intense.

Go after him! I urged internally. But nothing happened, and she stayed staring at the door, flinching occasionally as another shout or bang would come from the other end of the house.

I kept my hands out before me, and Viri glanced sideways at me. I'm sure he could tell there was no energy coming from me, but I felt I had nothing to give.

I couldn't get David out of my mind.

I'd never been drawn to another being like I was to that human—that *one* human. But why? There was a sense of longing that had dug itself deep inside my chest, and it burst open only to fill me with a desire to make David feel better, to look after him and take away all his pain. Not the pain of all humans, only *his*. His eyes had held so much sorrow, and while repairing the negative fog around the parents' household would help bring the Balance back into line, it wouldn't make *David* feel better, and I think that's why I couldn't help.

There was no point in my being here.

Abruptly, I stood and walked away from my friends as they shifted the Porthole to search for the next surge in negative energy to be restored, having finished with that household. Move on to the next, because one human was the same as another. Each pain was only judged by its intensity, not by the human feeling it in their soul.

Sulus called after me, but I didn't stop, and used the feeling of the dew on the thick grass brushing over my ankles to ground me.

I needed to talk to Mother.

She is the only one who will understand.

Mother looked up as I pushed the door open so hard it banged against the wall before it swung lazily back into place.

"Mother, I need you to explain something to me."

"Hello, Samael." She offered me a cheery smile, with a gleam in her eye that she had when she was causing mischief. My lip twitched as she continued, "How was your day?"

"Fine, Mother, just fine."

She smirked at me. "I've almost given up on getting you to call me Mom."

"*Almost* given up? I'm twenty-two."

"I'm persistent."

"You're stubborn."

As I sat on the floor opposite her, I gently took the blanket she was sewing from her hands. Mother watched my face as I placed the blanket on the floor next to us and took her hands in mine. The playful demeanor dropped, and her thumbs brushed over the backs of my hands.

"What happened?" She reached out to touch my face, and I took her hands again and absentmindedly rubbed her palms with my fingers as her brow furrowed. When I was younger, Mother's constant displays of affection through hugging and kissing had embarrassed me, but now they were a comfort and something I had come to embrace. Although I certainly felt freer when we were alone or with Dad.

Mother was the only one who knew what it was like to be torn between two worlds.

When I didn't speak, Mother filled the silence. "You witness a lot of shitty scenes through those Portholes, I can see it in your eyes every day. You take it on board—"

"Mother, please." I closed my eyes. I didn't need her to remind me how I was different from everyone else. When I opened my eyes, she was watching me. There was no anger or judgment between us, simply a quiet understanding. "A human left his home after fighting with his parents, because he's gay."

"Oh..." Mother's gaze dropped for a moment. "This must be difficult for you to understand because it's different here." My lip twisted, but I said nothing and waited for her to explain further. Mother sighed, as if this took something out of her, and through her emotional imprint, I sensed the unease. "For

Guardians, who you love physically—and emotionally, if that were a thing here—with gender, it doesn't matter. Some people care about that on Earth. Some people don't like it... some *hate* it."

I stared at our hands intertwined together. "I don't understand what happened."

Mother pressed her lips together. "There can be religious reasons, some people simply don't understand, and some think it's unnatural or wrong. People can be very set in their views." She sighed. "Most people live side by side without issue, accepting and respecting each other for who they are and that being enough, differences or no, it doesn't matter, a human is a human. Respect is key, I think. How boring would it be if we were all the same? But sometimes..." Mother sighed again. "... like what you witnessed, it can tear people and families apart. Some humans can't accept that their way isn't the only way."

"Things are so different on Earth. What else haven't you told me?" She lifted her eyes to mine, and a brush of her pain blended into the air with my own. "I'm not accusing you of anything," I added.

"There are so many things I haven't told you, so many things that are hard to explain. Things I never thought I'd have to find a way to explain to someone." She placed a hand on my knee. "But I will never lie to you. You can ask me anything, and I will do my best to explain. I'm not *hiding* anything from you, Samael, but I never wanted to sit you down and tell you everything about humanity that is different from here. It would make Earth seem like a horrible place. But it isn't. There are so many good people and things that make it beautiful." She shook her head and let a small smile pass over her lips. "There are so many movie lines I could quote right now."

I'd witnessed Mother quoting many movie lines, and despite none of them meaning anything to any Guardian, she never stopped, and seemed content to laugh at her own jokes.

A pang of loneliness hit me with such force I almost flinched. My gaze shot up to Mother's face. Her expression hadn't changed, and she still held that slight smile, but...

Such *loneliness.*

She watched me as I thought. "Why did this get to you so much?" she asked.

"David..." I drifted off as his face returned to the forefront of my mind.

"David?"

"The man whose own family didn't accept him." Mother tilted her head, and something passed across her expression, a fleeting feeling I couldn't catch the essence of. So, I continued, "He had such sad eyes."

"And you wanted to help him?"

I *knew* she'd understand. "Yes."

But I wasn't telling her the entire story, was I? I'd had these concerns for many humans, but David... David haunted my mind and lingered in my soul. He was *different.* This was different from before. Yet, I voiced none of this and masked any guilt before Mother could pick up on it. She held my gaze and waited for me to speak.

"Yes, exactly that..." I shook my head. "What's wrong with me?"

Mother smiled sadly. "Nothing is wrong with you. It's natural to want to help other people."

"You keep telling me things are natural, but they aren't

natural, not for us. Only for humans."

"You are part human." She pouted slightly, the hurt clear through her voice.

"I know, but sometimes I don't understand these feelings." I touched my chest, where these things seemed to blossom and live. "It was like an ache, right here, like I'm being pulled toward him. But I can't help him, and that hurts even more."

Mother placed her hand over mine. "You care for him, and you can't explain it. I can't tell you why, but sometimes humans are drawn to each other."

"But I'm not—"

"Yes, you are," Mother said firmly. "You are part human. You can never take that part of you away, and I wouldn't want you to. It makes you special... one of a kind. Please don't wish to be like everyone else."

The hurt radiated from her, thickening the air between us, and I squeezed her hand, filtering my calm into her. She'd know what I was doing, and while she could've stopped me, she allowed me to do it. Mother fed off my calm and let it melt her hurt away. In return, she sent love through the connection we shared where our skin touched, and her hands warmed in mine.

"Was it difficult to learn to control your powers?" I asked, still watching our hands.

Mother abruptly ceased the energy flow between us, almost as if to prove she could.

"Some things I'm still learning." She met my eyes and smiled. "I love you."

"I love you, too, Mother."

"See?" Her eyes shone as she took me in. "Part human. All the best parts."

As the days turned into weeks, I didn't see David again during our work with the Balance. I hoped this meant he was happy, or at the very least, happier than he was in his parents' home. Every time we witnessed a violent act—and those seemed to be increasing in number—I found myself hoping David wasn't involved. Guilt would flood my stomach immediately after these thoughts. I should care about *all* humans *equally*, and I didn't want any of them to be hurt or killed or experience pain.

But I couldn't stop thinking about David.

The sad look in his eyes, and how his hand had tightened on the strap of his bag as he was talking to his mother. He had already known there was no going back.

What else might be hidden behind those eyes? What kind of person was he?

Even though I hadn't voiced it, I had already decided.

I was going to Earth to find him and find out.

Chapter Nineteen

Cael

Approaching the bench slowly, I moved cautiously, not wanting to disturb Cordus. Most of the community would've been to see him already, and he'd be tired. I'd sensed weakness in him for months, growing every day, and I knew he suspected he might be dying. He let very few Guardians physically close to him, and I suspected this was because he didn't want them to realize the small amount of life energy he had left inside. In a human reaction, Cordus may have been denying that his time had been coming to an end.

Cordus was on his deathbed.

He had a matter of hours, perhaps even minutes, left. Guardians could feel when their death approached, and sense their lifeforce drain as their energies left their body and their physical form weakened. The community was grateful for Cordus's long life of over one hundred and fifty years.

While he may not have always spoken it due to his loyalties with the Elders, I knew he approved of the changes occurring within the community. In small ways, he'd encouraged the younger Guardians to experience emotions like humanity did, at least to a certain extent—only enough to create a better understanding.

He believed that by channeling their emotions, Guardians could create more powerful influences.

I agreed. I'd seen this in Ana and Samael, and Nathaniel's actions on Earth had proved it—his pleasure in causing pain had created greater ripples than influencing alone.

I'd promised myself I'd never forget the damage Nathaniel had done, as if I had a choice. I was reminded every time I looked at Ana. The vision of her death and the feel of her body limp in my arms was imprinted on my psyche and still haunted my sleep.

Sitting on the edge of the bench, I placed a hand over Cordus's. I didn't expect him to speak, but came here to offer my respects to the Guardian who'd helped raise me, and taught me everything I knew about the Balance and humanity.

Except, of course, what I'd learned on Earth itself.

Cordus had trained me for my first mission alone to Earth, which had proved to be the most challenging undertaking of my life, and I was thankful for the training I'd had.

A slight grumble emitted from Cordus's throat, and I leaned in toward him, almost blanketing Cordus's upper body with my own.

"Cael."

It was barely a whisper, and I put my ear near Cordus's face, determined not to miss a word. "Yes, it's me," I answered.

"I am sorry, Cael. I have failed."

"Failed? How?" Cordus had been nothing but wise and good for my entire life.

"There are so many things..." He took a slow, deep breath

while I waited, and the sense of unease grew within me. "… I should have told you… told you all."

"Tell me now."

"The Tenebrians… something is changing. There's sequence… organization." His intake of breath wheezed sharply against the air, and I witnessed the shimmer in the small space between us as he absorbed what energy he could. Every word was agony, an effort, and I wanted to tell him he didn't need to speak.

But I knew he must.

"I know," I whispered.

Cordus looked like he was trying to focus on my face, but instead closed his eyes and nodded slowly. "Something big is coming…" He paused, and his eyes opened again, still unfocused. "Ana."

"She came earlier, you were resting," I whispered. Too much sound reverberated around the room, making it hard to hear, so I kept my voice quiet. The air seemed to pound against my eardrums louder than Cordus was talking.

"You must… Ana."

"I must what?"

Cordus gripped my hand with the strength of a much younger Guardian, and I startled, but didn't move away. "I'm here, it's okay." Immediately after saying it, I wasn't sure why I did. It was a human reaction to comfort those in their last moments. I almost smiled, but couldn't find the energy to make my face muscles comply when my heart was aching as I watched Cordus.

Slowly, Cordus opened his eyes, focusing on me, and he surveyed me with a hint of humor on his face, and more than a hint of pride. He pulled on my hand and brought me closer. "Listen." He breathed. His breath smelled rancid, the breath of the dead. "Do not let her back to Earth. No matter how she is provoked, no matter what..."

"But—"

"No." Another deep rattling breath followed this, and I didn't interrupt again. "She has power she knows not of... she is a danger... she is *in* danger." Cordus coughed quietly, his words a whispered strain and his eyes full of regret. "They do not want to tell you. Do not want to tell her. But you must know." Another cough. "Do not let her... do not let her go back. Half-breeds, they are unpredictable."

My brows pulled together. Ana was headstrong, to say the least, and possessed considerable physical strength. She had not yet pushed the conversation of returning to Earth, but I didn't know how I was supposed to stop her if she did.

"They will be able to feel her," Cordus whispered.

"Who? The Tenebrians?" I gripped Cordus's frail hand in desperation. "Why is Ana in danger? Are they looking for her? Isit because of Ignis?"

"If they find her, they will take her. They..."

"What? Why? I don't understand." I waited fora response that didn't come, and Cordus's grip on my hand eased as a final breath was released from his lungs.

"No!" The word came out of me in a surprised shout, and I dropped his voice to a whisper. "No, no, *no.* Tell me how to protect her. *Please.*"

But there was no reply.

Cordus was dead, and with him the secrets of Ana's power.

I released his hand, placed it gently on his chest, and folded his other hand over the top before I closed his eyes. My hands trembled with the effort it took to calm myself, and I took a few deep, calming breaths, drawing on the power of Lucidis to still my aching soul.

It was only when I had left the hut to tell the Elders of Cordus's death that the impact of his words rang in my ears, and I almost dropped to my knees.

Half-breeds, they are unpredictable.

Half-breeds, *plural?*

Were there more?

Cordus' funeral was short and simple.

While the Guardians had adopted several human customs over the generations, they didn't partake in long ceremonies. Two younger Guardians dug a hole in the burial ground, and a few Guardians gathered as the body was carefully wrapped in a biodegradable cloth.

Ana and Monia stood by my sides, stony-faced, as we watched Cordus being prepared for burial. No one spoke. There was no music or speeches as the burial process was enough to offer finality to the community. Cordus had been my mentor, my trainer, and my guide. Although Guardians shared parenthood, Cordus had, to me, been more of a father figure than most.

But now, he had died before offering his final insight of wisdom.

I turned to Ana, who looked up, offered me a sad smile, and squeezed my hand. I tried to smile back, but could only manage a lift of the corner of my mouth before I gave up.

As I caught Monia's eye, a moment of understanding passed between us. While thoughts of Cordus's warning consumed me, we both knew of the power lurking within Ana.

Beyond the dangers of Ana's growing powers were the implications that she would unleash this untapped power if she went to Earth. And beyond the threat of the Tenebrians—if what Cordus suspected was true—was the simple truth that none of us knew what to do with Ana's power, or what could happen if it got out.

Chapter Twenty

Samael

The staircase was narrow, dark, and winding as though it belonged in a lighthouse, working its way up around the inside of the old building on the city's outskirts.

I knew the purpose of this place from hearing other Guardians talking about it, and had witnessed Dad go inside once or twice. Often, Guardians would inform the man who lived here when we were coming, but I'm certain this wasn't the first time he'd have received an unexpected Guardian visitor.

The human who lived here knew about the Guardians and their duties and was here to help us if we needed to come to Earth for more than a few hours.

Surely, he was used to a few surprises.

These helpers, who had no official name, were dotted worldwide and provided clothes, a place to stay, and money when needed, so Guardians could do their work here on Earth uninterrupted and unimpeded by the inconveniences of missing small necessities.

I took a deep breath as I neared the top of the staircase. The air was thick on Earth as always, and this building held the scents of cedar and brick. I'd been to Earth more times than I could count, both as a child and a young adult, with the others my age as we took part in regular training to refine and control our influence.

But I'd never been to Earth alone.

And I'd *certainly* never been without my parents knowing where I was.

I shouldn't even *be* here.

But I wanted to meet David. I *needed* to meet him.

I needed to get him out of my head, and if he turned out not to be the person I'd imagined him to be, then I could live with that. That would be ideal, then I could put all these awkward emotions I didn't understand behind me and move on. But at least I'd *know.* The idea of David I'd built up in my mind was infiltrating my dreams, and I couldn't go another day without doing *something*.

As I climbed the stairs, I realized that for the first time, I didn't really care how others might feel about me or judge me for my actions. It was a liberating sensation, but also terrifying.

I was driven only by the ache in my chest and the longing in my heart.

I held my fist out to knock on the heavy door at the top of the stairs, but hesitated before making contact with the wood.

"Come on in, mate."

I startled, and my hand hovered in front of the door for a beat longer before I slowly turned the knob and pushed open the door. Standing in the doorway, I glanced between my feet and the man who had spoken.

"Are you going to come in or what?"

I entered the room and closed the door behind me, trying to

appear as if I belonged there and knew what I was doing. My gaze fell again to my feet, and I scuffed the toes of my shoes lightly on the floor, and shoved my hands into the pockets of my jeans. When the man didn't speak again, I looked around the well-furnished but dimly lit room. The walls were lined with bookshelves, and a thick rug was spread beneath my feet. A half-finished portrait of a woman surrounded by flowers rested against a paint-stained easel.

The Earth contact had dark, weather-worn skin, which created deep furrows around his face. His white hair was pulled into a low plait halfway down his back, but his eyebrows and beard still fought for youth with flecks of black hair peppered throughout. He had been a handsome man once, and in many ways, still was, but now his face told the stories of his life. His body was toned but hinted at indulged creature comforts. When he stood, I was snapped out of my stupor and realized I'd been staring at him, and as he straightened, his height surprised me, almost as tall as I was. Gently, he placed a cat that had been asleep on his lap at his feet and petted it with his large palm when it mewed in protest.

"How did you know I was here? Did you sense me?" I asked.

The man laughed, and a small cloud of smoke left his lips before he stubbed out a cigarette. He pointed to the monitor next to the front door. "Cameras," he grunted out. He approached me, and my brows furrowed as I'm certain his smile was at my discomfort. "You've never been here before."

"Yes, I have," I responded defiantly.

He laughed again. "Not by yourself. Not like this. You're young, too young to be here alone." His eyes narrowed even as the smile remained. "I bet they don't even know you're here."

I found myself trying to place his accent, but didn't know enough about the world outside Lucidis to do so. This small fact abruptly made me feel like a child again.

I didn't let myself shy away and stepped further into the room. "I thought you would help me."

"Oh, I'll help ya, mate, didn't say I wouldn't. But it doesn't mean I won't have questions for you first."

"Fair enough." I straightened my back. "Samael."

"John," he answered as he shook my extended hand firmly. After only brief contact, John yanked his hand from my grip and stared at me with a dark look. "Don't try to read me, mate. I've had enough of that with you lot. If you don't trust me by now, you can stop coming."

"I'm sorry. It's a habit. I meant no disrespect."

"S'okay." He was already walking away. John opened a cupboard, pulled out a cardboard box, and let it hit the floor with a muffled bang. Grabbing a few things, he handed me a cell phone and a small wad of cash and showed me the numbers on the notes. I'd handled money before but appreciated that John was trying to help, so I said nothing. I rolled the cell phone over in my palm a few times and stood patiently as John mumbled instructions on unlocking it, texting, and calling. He glanced up at me intermittently to make sure I understood. I couldn't tell if this was common practice or if John had somehow read more into the situation than I'd given him credit for. I didn't ask how he knew I might need a cell phone, and he didn't question me further as I tucked it into my pocket.

I couldn't help but watch him as he moved. John didn't want me to read his essence, but it was difficult not to catch the edges of his emotional imprint as he was so close. I tried not to pry further, but couldn't help my senses from spilling out, and brushing past the edges of his imprint.

But John was a closed book, as if years of interaction with Guardians had taught him a thing or two about calming his inner emotions and masking himself. He radiated physical and emotional strength, and I found myself wanting to know more about him.

But it wasn't my place to ask.

"I take it you know how money works? Public transportation?" he asked.

"Yes, my father taught me."

John arched a brow. "Unusual answer."

"Why?"

"Most Guardians don't mention their parents specifically... more of a community approach there." I didn't answer as John bent to further shuffle through the box's contents. "You need any clothes? Accommodation? How long are you here for?"

"Not that long."

John sat back on the couch, and the cat immediately jumped back onto his lap. He resumed petting it as it settled onto his legs, and a soft crackling purr filled my senses.

John stared at me until I began fidgeting, and twisted my fingers around my t-shirt.

Am I missing something? Is there part of this that wasn't explained to me?

"Um," I started, filling the silence. "That's an unusual accent you have."

The twist of John's lips as they shifted into a smirk before he barked out a laugh only furthered my discomfort. "Australian, mate." He waved his hand in a small dismissive circle. "Now you're making small talk with me." His brow arched even as the smile remained. "Unusual again."

I didn't know what to say, so I said nothing. Glancing at the door, I wondered if I should leave, but I was unsure how to end the conversation politely.

"Why are you here?" John asked.

I looked at him and forced my expression as blank as I could. "Why do you ask?"

John laughed again, and I bristled. "Well, you're not here to hunt a Rogue as you didn't ask for any moonstone, weapons, or a place to stay, and you look like you're not supposed to be here." My expression must have betrayed my surprise, because John added, "I don't need to be a Guardian to see that, mate. It's written all over your face."

"I'm here to meet someone." I didn't know why I was telling him anything, but I knew I could trust him. I could feel it.

"A human?"

I nodded slowly, and John grunted again. "Does she know you're coming?"

"He, and no." I steeled myself for resistance when I had corrected John about who I was meeting, remembering what Mother had said about some humans having issues with it. But John didn't show any surprise. He seemed completely disinterested one way or the other.

John nodded. "All right, but just remember you can influence humans easily here. Don't take advantage of that."

"I won't."

Despite John's standoffish attitude, I liked the man. He held a difficult position—aware of the Guardians' existence but unable to reveal it to anyone. Constantly being on call to help us out, and probably getting no real recognition for it. How had he gotten into this position, I wondered?

I could ask.

Maybe one day.

"You can't have it both ways, son."

I shook myself free of my musings. "Sorry?"

"The realms, you can't be part of both. If you're seeking a relationship, you have to choose."

I wanted to tell him about my parents, but thought better of it. "You're protective over them, aren't you? The humans?" I asked quietly.

John waved a hand dismissively at me again. "O' course, I am. Now, be on your way. You don't want to be on Earth longer than you have to. It'll mess with you."

I nodded again and opened the front door before turning back to face John. "Thank you."

John stared at me with a shadow of a frown crossing his face before his lips lifted into a thin smile. "You're welcome, mate."

Chapter Twenty-One

Ana

Slowly, I wandered back toward the center of the community. Cael was teaching a group of youths about tracking a Tenebrian—they were staying in Lucidis for this training this time—but it was something I couldn't help with. Samael would be off with his friends, possibly observing and influencing using a Porthole, maybe doing whatever Guardians in their twenties did.

I crossed my arms over my chest as I walked. These were the moments when I felt the most alone. I could assist with building the community, gardening, or sewing. I could help with the children if the Elders would allow me to, and I promised to keep my mouth shut.

But occasionally, I felt as though I were being shuffled from task to task, still lacking a solid role within the community despite my decades here.

Decades. Had it really been that long?

When I saw Cascus approaching, I looked around for someone else, *anyone* he could be here to talk to, because surely it wasn't me. He barely acknowledged me most of the time, preferring to speak to Cael as if I weren't there. My frown deepened when Cascus stopped before me, although he looked to the right of my face and didn't make direct eye contact.

"You cannot go to Earth," he stated.

My lip twisted. *Who does he think he is?*

"Is that a reminder or a threat?" I asked.

"Simply a statement."

"I don't know why you're telling me this." I scoffed, and my fingers dug into my skin as I pulled my arms closer to my chest. "Did I give you the impression I planned to go to Earth?"

Cascus looked directly into my eyes and drew my gaze toward his until I couldn't pull away. Before I could react, he held his hands on my shoulders and held me with a hypnotizing stare.

I almost stumbled. The Elders were *incredibly* powerful, and I'd not felt it directed at me before. There was such hatred in his stare. I'd done nothing to him except *exist,* and still he hated me. My anger flared, but his power squashed it as he flooded me. I tried to reverse the power back to him for a moment, but he was strong and controlled in a way that only came with age. I swayed slightly, my mind went fuzzy, and my vision went white as I lost control.

Cascus said, "You are not to go to Earth, because I said so. Do you understand? *Because I said so.*"

I started to nod slowly before a bubble of anger exploded in my belly. I felt off, strange, and the last few moments were indistinct in my recollection. But Cascus was standing close to me, and his mere presence filled me with discomfort.

Wait.

This asshole is trying to influence me.

I shrugged Cascus's hands off me. "You do *not* control me,"

I said, before I turned on shaky legs to find myself face to face with Monia.

She approached Cascus. "What is going on? What did you say to her?"

"Simply the truth." Cascus watched me before his gaze slid resolutely back to Monia, once again ignoring my presence even though I stood close to him.

Monia glanced at me, and I raised my brows, unsure where this conversation was going. I wanted to leave, but something in her stare made me stay. She turned back to Cascus. "I think she has power we know nothing of. I know you do not want to hear this, but I think the only way we will know is to teach her. We can train her, guide her, and show her how to bring herself under control." Monia's face betrayed no emotion, but I could feel the rumble of sparks of anger in the air between us. "Perhaps, some of that training should occur on Ear—"

Cascus's lip curled. "You will do no such thing."

Monia nodded but didn't look at him. "I heard Cordus wanted me to replace him as an Elder."

"I do not know who you heard that from, but they are mistaken. I will not have this conversation in front of the half-breed."

Monia nodded again. "Strange how you deny it, almost as though you do not want me in a position of power."

My skin began to crawl at what was passing in the air between the two older Guardians—complete distrust, suspicion, anger, and hatred. My brows pulled together. I thought the Elders were respected, and treated the others with respect. I'd not witnessed an interaction with an Elder and a Guardian where such negativity was being shed in their presence.

I took an experimental step back from the pair, and when neither of them looked at me, I kept moving. I didn't care if they were talking about me. I didn't want to know. I certainly wasn't going to stand by and let them plan something around me as if I were a pawn to be moved about. This *power* apparently in me wasn't news to me, though I didn't feel it was as much of a big deal as they made it out to be. Mixed heritage, growing up on Earth, then moving to Lucidis, and all of that. I was different, I got it. I didn't think there needed to be a discussion with the older Guardians about what to *do with me* as if I were a problem to be solved. I'd been here for this long and hadn't burnt the place to the ground, I think it was time they stopped treating me as though I were a bomb to be diffused.

And I certainly wasn't going to let Cascus tell me what to do.

You cannot go to Earth.

I missed Earth, but I was dead there, and I had no plans to return.

A longing, but no plans.

Why did he want me to stay away so badly that he felt the need to warn me out of nowhere?

Chapter Twenty-Two

Samael

Swirling the remaining contents of the half-empty beer bottle in front of me, I tried to resist the urge to look at the door every few moments, and carefully avoided any questions from strangers about why I was here.

Or who I might be waiting for.

I'd settled on beer when whiskey—Dad's recommendation—had resulted in an unpleasant burning in my throat. I'd finished the glass only because I felt it would be rude to order another drink before I finished my first, but I was glad when I managed to choke it down. A smirk graced my lips at the idea of asking Dad *what* he'd been thinking when he'd recommended whiskey, but the smile dropped almost as quickly as it'd come when I remembered he didn't even know I was here.

Placing the empty bottle on the bar, I waited until the bartender made eye contact before asking, "Another gentle beer, please."

The bartender smirked, but there was kindness in his eyes when he grabbed a bottle from the fridge behind him and flicked the cap off. "It's called a lager."

"Sorry." I knew my cheeks were burning, and that only made it worse. The bartender offered me a small smile before he moved away to serve another customer.

I was onto my third lager when David entered the bar, and I almost choked on my mouthful when I finally saw him. I'd picked this bar specifically because I knew David frequented this place with the friend he had been staying with since he'd left his parents' home. It was an uncomfortable feeling, coming here *knowing* he'd be here eventually, as though I were a stalker. But the only other alternative was to abuse my powers to track his emotional imprint on Earth, and that felt like more of a violation of an intimate thing than simply waiting and hoping. Despite all the time I'd spent waiting for this moment, I still wasn't prepared to see him in person. David's emotional imprint slammed into me as soon as he entered the bar—the imprint I'd gotten to know so well when I'd decided to find him again from Lucidis.

On Lucidis, I could almost fool myself into believing I was doing what I was supposed to do for my duty. But here on Earth, the truth of my actions was presented to me in undeniable clarity.

With my back turned to David as he wound his way between the round tables, I did my best to force a look of indifference onto my face. All the while, my senses were pointedly focused on him.

David sat with his friends, and in the reflection of the mirror behind the bar, I witnessed the sadness in his eyes beyond the superficial smile. That moment cemented my resolve, and I had no regrets or doubts about my actions or their reasons. I'd never use my powers here to trick David into liking me, as using them to get me into the same room as David seemed deceitful enough, but as I inhaled and allowed his essence to fill me, there was nothing on my mind but him.

Now what?

Beyond a casual exchange, I'd never tried to talk to a human before. All my trips to Earth had been brief, with my father or friends, and were only for training and learning. I'd developed my influences without having to get too involved with any individual human, and I'd learned how to misdirect humans when they asked too many questions. However, *this* was an entirely different situation, and I had no one to ask for guidance on how to do it.

Unable to stop my thoughts, I ordered a fourth beer, enjoying the slight buzzing that filled my mind. My thoughts were in contrast, telling me to move faster while simultaneously thinking I should slow down. The fourth drink hit harder than the others, and a wave of lightheadedness moved through me as David came up next to me to order.

I couldn't help it, I stared.

David caught my eye before I hastily looked away, and I sipped my beer with my gaze fixed determinedly on a spot on the wooden bar.

"Hey."

I turned toward David as he spoke, but no sound came out when I opened my mouth to reply. I was too entranced by his smile—a *real smile* with no sadness behind it.

For *me.*

It was too late to attempt to appear comfortable within my skin, but I tried anyway. "Hi."

David tilted his head and leaned against the bar. "I saw you watching me."

I stuttered my way through a response, "I'm... I'm sorry."

David smiled again, and something inside me melted. His smile was intoxicating.

"It's okay." David continued to watch me. "You look out of place here."

Hastily, I checked my hands—*had I shifted back to blue?*—and David laughed. "I'm sorry, I just..." I stuttered again, and after I cleared my throat, I blurted out, "You're very handsome."

David watched my face as if searching for insincerity. "Thank you, you're very cute."

I smiled, looked at the bar again, and pushed my messy blond hair out of my face—like my father's in his Earth form—as David picked up his drink after the bartender placed it on the bar.

I watched his hands and wondered what it would be like to have those hands touch me.

Human skin was so smooth, how had I not noticed that before?

David's fingers traced the stem of the glass.

Is he doing that on purpose?

I forced myself to refocus. "What's that?" I asked.

David held up the drink. "This?" I nodded and watched as he swirled the liquid in the glass. "It's a sapphire martini."

No drink on Lucidis was the same vibrant blue as the shades of our skin.

"Want to try some?"

"Can I? Yes, please. Thank you." It seemed David didn't stop smiling in my presence, and my chest warmed as I carefully sipped the liquid and watched him over the rim of the glass. "That's delicious."

"Can I buy you one?"

"It's okay, I can get it," I said, reaching into my pocket.

David placed his hand on mine, and I stopped in my tracks. The touch sent my senses into overdrive, and I tried desperately not to read him through it, instead focusing on the present moment. "I'm trying to buy you a drink," David said as he chuckled. "I'm flirting with you."

"Oh... *oh.*" My cheeks flushed again. "I'm... ah... Samael, by the way." Why was this so awkward? Whatever I'd imagined when I'd pictured meeting David, it wasn't the fumbling, stuttering mess I'd become. Was Dad this awkward when he'd met Mother? I'd have to ask him.

No, I'd ask *her*. If he were, Mother would *gleefully* tell me the truth.

David would lose interest in the conversation if I continued this way, and I struggled to think of something I could say or do to prolong our interaction as long as possible. I realized a beat too late that I'd given David my real name, but it hardly mattered. I wanted David to know as much of my true self as I could offer.

David kept smiling, and when I held out my hand, David took it. We held eye contact as our hands touched, a gentle brush that turned into a firm hold.

"David."

I nodded and concentrated on the feeling I got from David's shared touch. He opened up, knowingly or otherwise, and with a rush of sensation, I was inside his emotional imprint. He held so much sadness within him, a sadness I longed to make better.

But beyond that, he was nurturing and caring. He had a hint of distrust and a fear of being alone even when surrounded by friends.

Of being lonely even when not alone.

I wanted to know him more.

"Come, sit with us." David gestured at the table where a small group of his friends sat. I glanced at them uncertainly. If I were this awkward in front of David, how would I be in a group setting? How many stupid things could I stutter through because David laughed at me and never wanted to see me again?

There was the additional danger that I could get overwhelmed by their essences. A group of humans so physically close to me, it could flood the air between us with a confusing array of senses. Or even worse, what if they felt something from *me?* While they had no way of recognizing it, it didn't mean humans couldn't feel like something was *off*.

But I nodded and smiled at David even as I was concentrating inside, and made a point of further internalizing my powers to ensure I didn't accidentally release any sense that wasn't distinctly human. I followed David timidly and tried to pay attention as he went around the table, introducing me. Focusing so hard on decreasing any effect I could have on the humans, I had to snap back to the present moment to ensure I caught their names and didn't make a further fool of myself.

Was it always like this, maintaining control? After I returned from training on Earth, my body sometimes fought to keep its human form.

Was it wavering now? It felt like it was wavering.

I glanced at my hands again, still human.

Maybe I was thinking about it too much.

I relaxed my concentration slightly and found that my human form remained strong. My lip twitched as I realized I should put more faith in my human DNA. I decided I wouldn't tell Mother she was right about the strength of my human part. She'd tease me and use it against me in any following argument. I almost laughed. She's *so stubborn.*

You are, too, the voice in my head reminded me.

"This is Logan, Justin, and Nicole." David indicated each of his friends in turn, and I nodded and gave a small wave as David introduced me. When I sat, my ears popped as a whoosh of air sucked past me. Instantly, my senses were on alert. Glancing around, no one else had stirred, and the small groups of people around the bar continued to chat, and it seemed nothing had changed. My brows furrowed, and I released the hold on my essence for a moment to briefly sweep the room with my senses.

Nothing.

Turning back to the group, I realized I'd missed a question directed at me. "Sorry?"

"I said, what do you do, Sam?" Nicole asked again. She leaned forward, crossed her arms on the table, and enunciated her cleavage. I didn't feel any negativity from her as I watched her tuck a loose strand of pink hair behind her ear, only arrogance. I chanced a glance at Logan, who appeared genuinely interested in the answer I had yet to offer. He seemed a kind soul, and I decided I liked Logan.

Nicole, not so much.

"It's Samael," I corrected.

"Okay..." She smiled. "What do you do for a living, Sam?"

She played games with me, and I decided not to correct her again, taking solace enough in the slight furrow creasing David's forehead at her intentional error. As she waited for an answer, I stared at her and realized how ill-prepared I was to interact with humans. I hadn't thought this through. All I had been thinking about was getting closer to David, but now that I was here, I was out of my depth.

"I play guitar," I answered automatically.

"Like in a band?"

"No, just..."

"Freelance," David offered with a soft smile.

"Yes."

Justin smirked. "So, you don't have a job, then?"

Actively, I stopped my brows from furrowing. "I get by. Money isn't that much of a priority for me."

Justin scoffed. "The only people who say that are the ones without money."

I opened my mouth to answer, but when I looked at David, he was smiling. That genuine smile lit up his face and crinkled his eyes with amusement, and answering didn't seem so important anymore.

I didn't care what anyone else thought, only David.

And I loved to see him smile.

He held my eye contact, then Nicole cleared her throat after a moment before she turned back to Logan. "Well, back to the important stuff. Logan, you should come along."

Logan shook his head, and a dreadlock came loose from his hair tie. "I'm not really into that scene."

"I *really* think you should come along." She stared at him intently and stole a glance at me before looking back at Logan, as if I were intruding on whatever they were discussing.

I didn't care what she was talking about, couldn't she see

that?

Sneaking another sideways glance at David, my chest constricted, and I gulped down a mouthful of the martini to keep myself busy.

Logan shook his head again and turned slightly away from Nicole. "I told you no, I'm not interested."

She shrugged. "Your loss." Nicole and Justin stood to leave, and she threw a last look at Logan before they did. Logan shook his head again without looking up at her, and his brows pulled together as he took a drink. I found myself mimicking the expression, and despite myself, I wondered what she so badly wanted him to do. As they said their goodbyes, I wasn't sure I liked the glint in Justin's eye as they exited the bar.

Logan left an hour later, and although I'd found the conversation easier without the other two and liked Logan, it would be a lie to pretend I wasn't happy when he left, leaving David and me alone.

Finally.

When there was a lull in the conversation, I found myself staring at David. Unlike the people at the other tables, who talked over each other, eager to have their opinions heard, David spoke softly. He was intelligent but never seemed to say more words than were needed, and paused thoughtfully if he couldn't find the right way to explain something before he continued. He was open but suspicious, casual and easy-going, but with a level of anxiety about him.

Humans were so complicated.

"Are you okay?" I asked after a pause in our conversation.

David watched me—as usual, he didn't shy away from eye contact. My stomach leapt within me as I took the chance to study his eyes again, and watched his dark brown irises with those exquisite flecks of amber through them. David looked at me as if he could read my mind. A slight smile etched onto my lips at the prolonged stare, and David's lips shifted into a small smile. Still, neither of us spoke.

David couldn't read my mind, but I could read him.

David took another drink before finally answering, "Why do you ask me that?"

"You're sad."

"Am I?" There was a hint of amusement to his tone.

My brows flickered downward for a moment before I stared back into his eyes and briefly reached my senses out to touch David. I then replied, "Yes."

The slight smile fell from David's face. "Yeah," he answered quietly.

"Want to talk about it?"

"For some reason, with you, I do."

I tilted my head and offered a look I hoped was comforting. "Talk to me."

"This is weird, Samael. I barely know you."

"So, get to know me more."

David watched me a beat longer before his perfect lips curved into a smile. Into *that* smile. "I guess it is that simple when you put it like that." He sighed. "My parents can't accept me for who I am, and now, I don't know if *I* can accept myself. I felt so sure in who I was until I had to justify it to my family, and now I don't know who I am or if I even did the right thing. How can my self-assurance fall away like that?" The words tumbled from David as though he had held onto them so long he could no longer contain them. "If the people who are supposed to know me best in the world don't understand, then... I don't know. I know who I am, but I don't know. If that makes sense."

"I accept you, and you should too. You're perfect."

David laughed. "I'm far from perfect."

I lifted a shoulder and smirked. "You're perfect to me." This earned me another smile from David, and I decided I wanted to do whatever it took to keep him smiling. The sadness that hovered around David's chest eased slightly when he smiled, and flickered away when we shared those moments of intense eye contact without words. I eased his pain, if even slightly, and it was more gratifying than anything I'd ever done.

Because I was doing it without influence, David was happy to be with *me.*

As we talked, I asked David every question I could think of. I wanted to know *everything* about him. I learned that David used to do gymnastics but quit after being bullied, and that he enjoyed baking.

I don't think I stopped smiling for over an hour. "You'll have to bake me something sometime," I suggested as my heart did another flip. "You know, since I've never had baked desserts before."

David's jaw dropped. "Hold on."

"What?"

I watched while he looked around hastily, and leaned over to snatch a straw from Nicole's abandoned glass. "I needed something to drop in surprise. Say it again."

I chuckled. "I've never had any baked desserts."

This time, when David's jaw dropped, it was exaggerated, and he held the straw next to his lips and dropped it on the table dramatically. As we both chuckled, he placed the straw back in the empty glass. "Seriously, though? You've never had anything baked? Cakes? Muffins? Pastries?" I shook my head, and David shook his slowly. "Holy crap, where have you been?"

"I was raised in a small community off the grid."

"*Way* off the grid if you've never had *cake.*"

I shrugged again. "Probably explains why I'm so weird."

David pressed his lips together, though he was still smiling. "You're not weird." When I raised a brow, he laughed. "Okay, you're a little weird. But you're cute." There was a pause while we both took a drink to fill the silence, before David asked, "What made you come to the city?"

"To find you."

David smiled again. "Cute and charming. But mostly cute."

I slid my hand across the table, and when David intertwined his fingers with mine, a jolt of recognition bolted through me. I felt everything that made David himself, and along with that came an overwhelming urge to touch him more. My skin tingled from the contact, and it took all my strength to tear my gaze away from where our hands met and look back into his eyes. David's eyelids were lowered slightly, and his lips parted.

Fuck.

My cock twitched in my pants, and I leaned forward, an almost imperceptibly small move, but David noticed and hit me with a look that melted my heart. He leaned closer, and when his lips were a whisper from mine, he asked, "Would you like to come back to mine for a drink?"

I choked out a reply as all the air was pushed from my lungs. David's imprint surrounded me, and I tried not to think of the implications of getting physically closer when a touch of his hand on mine sent fire blazing through my senses. "Yes," I breathed out, and followed as he led me out of the bar.

Chapter Twenty-Three

Samael

David closed the door gently and turned to face where I stood quietly by his bed. Every move he made had me captivated, and I could barely breathe from the sense of arousal that flooded the room. The moment the door had clicked into place, it created a dome around us, and nothing could penetrate the sense of him that surrounded me. He was everything.

David had taken my hand once we'd crossed the threshold into his home. He'd done everything right—had offered me a drink and brushed his arm past mine as we moved down the hallway. But I shook my head and stared at the man I'd been thinking about and *dreaming* about. David was finally in front of me, and I found myself unable to utter a word.

Alone in David's bedroom, my gaze couldn't be dragged from his eyes. There was still so much pain there, pain David managed to hide whenever he smiled.

From others, at least.

I could feel his pain through the air even when he smiled. But in those rare moments when he laughed, the pain faded slightly as joy moved through his body. Beyond the sensation of simply seeing David smile, *that* was the reason I liked it so much—those moments when his essence cleared and a flicker of happiness turned into aflame.

I'd spent most of our evening together trying to make him laugh, and since David had found my misunderstandings of social etiquette and pop culture endearing, I could bring him joy even unintentionally. Initially, I'd laughed along nervously with him, not minding for a moment that the laughter was at my expense, before the ease of being with David evaporated my nerves, and I fell into a comfortable space with him. There was no malice behind David's quiet chuckle as he desperately tried not to allow his lips to curve at my blank stare when he mentioned a musician or television series he clearly expected me to know.

David approached me, and a shudder ran down my spine as he touched my shoulders before he traced his fingers down my arms and allowed his hands to rest on my wrists. I barely managed to contain the full-body tremor that threatened to take over. It was sensation overload. The physical and emotional aspects mixed on Earth were so potent... I'd heard about it but had no way to prepare for its intensity.

Still, I couldn't stop looking into his eyes.

David's fingers were calloused from his work as a carpenter, rough against my soft human skin. Involuntarily, I tensed. My training and energy on Earth were largely focused on concealing my true nature from humans, and I didn't want to make David feel nervous or suspicious around me. Occasionally, a human might experience discomfort in the presence of an unguarded Guardian. Our mere presence could reveal feelings within humans that they may have buried deep inside themselves.

I played a balancing game being this close to David.

How much should I let through?

"Are you okay? You seem nervous," David spoke softly before he lifted an arm to run his fingers through my hair and tucked it gently behind my ear when I dipped my chin and pressed my cheek into David's hand.

"I am nervous," I whispered back.

"Why?"

I lifted my head to stare into David's captivating eyes again. Every outward breath shifted the air between us and pushed his essence closer to me. I shuddered again and withheld a soft moan. "Because I've wanted to kiss you since the moment I saw you."

David didn't hesitate and pulled me to him by curling his fingers into my hair. The press of his lips against mine was gentle, and my hands shook at the sensation of his skin against mine—the vulnerability. Guardians didn't kiss, not like this, and I've wanted nothing more than to experience this.

But only with *him.*

Our kissing soon became urgent, and our hands wandered over each other's bodies with abandon—exploring, memorizing. The dam had been broken, and with our eyes closed and no longer trapped by his gaze, I gave in to every urge I had to touch David and let my guard down only enough to let my body take over. I didn't want to think, I only wanted to *feel.* I wanted to take every moment of this as a human, not a Guardian.

I responded to David's unspoken cues, hoping he wouldn't notice my inexperience.

A groan was pulled past my lips when David reached down

and rubbed my growing erection through my jeans. My jaw slackened as I opened my mouth to speak, but I could manage only another breathy moan that folded into itself and became a gasp when David's grip tightened. What was it I wanted to say, anyway? It hardly mattered. At the bar, silences with Davidwere rarely uncomfortable, and here the silences without words were filled with our combined desperate breaths, and David's encouraging hum as I rocked my hips into his touch. My arms were frozen at my sides as David explored my body over my clothes, and when David finally realized I wasn't moving, his hands stilled. I opened my eyes a crack to find him looking at me, his lips lifted into a half smile. A *knowing* smile. But he said nothing, only paused briefly before he took my hands and guided them to his chest. My fingers hovered over the buttons on David's shirt, and when he nodded, I quickly unbuttoned it.

David's eyes showed amusement as they flickered to my face, and I lifted my gaze to his.

"What's wrong?" I asked.

David chuckled. "You had your tongue half out. Does it really take that much concentration?"

I rubbed the back of my neck before flicking the final button. "To keep myself from shaking? Yeah. It's *you.*"

David's expression shifted, and something swam past his eyes as a rush of warmth passed through his essence. Without another word, he shrugged out of the fabric as I lifted my t-shirt over my head, and hastily shook it off as it tangled around my hands.

In that moment, I was torn between hating clothes and loving them. I hated them because they hindered my access to David's waiting body, but I loved them for the patience they forced me to exercise and for how they only increased the heaviness of the mood around us as we revealed ourselves bit by bit.

This time, my shudder was laced with anticipation.

David undid my jeans with one hand while he unzipped his own with the other. Shaking his hips, he stepped out of his pants as they pooled on the floor and leaned to pull my jeans down. David smiled up at me as I nervously stayed still, my hands awkwardly at my sides again.

Do something. Do something. Do something.

What do I do?

David straightened and placed his finger on my lips when I opened his mouth to speak. He shushed me quietly, and I stepped backward until my calves hit the mattress behind me.

"Let me take care of you," David whispered before he gently pushed me down onto the bed and crawled over me as I eased myself toward the headboard. When David lifted a thigh, pressed it between my legs, and rubbed against my aching erection under my boxers, I moaned and ground into his touch.

David looked down at me and stilled as he braced himself on his arms, and concern grew on his face. I raised my wide-eyed stare from David's body and slowly met his eyes.

"Don't stop," I whispered, and my voice cracked.

"Are you sure you're okay?" David brushed my hair from my face again. "You look like you're somewhere else."

I fidgeted uncomfortably under him. *I have to tell him.*

"I, um..."

"Do you want to stop?"

"No, please, *no.*" I took a deep breath. "I've never done this before."

"Anything?" I shook my head in response. "With anyone?" When I tried to shrink into the mattress, David braced himself on one elbow and leaned to the side. "Why didn't you tell me?"

"I didn't want you to... not want to be with me." I shrugged, displaying complacency I didn't feel, and looked away from David's face as my cheeks flushed.

David's expression softened. "I wouldn't want to pressure you."

"I want to do this. I want to have this with you."

"Are you sure?"

I reached up, cupped David's face in my hands, and pulled him down to kiss him hard, groaning as his tongue worked against mine. "I've never been more sure of anything."

What scared me as I spoke wasn't that I'd never been with anyone before—it was that what I'd said was the truth. I never quite fit in with the Guardians and certainly didn't fit in entirely with humans. But with David, none of it mattered. David seemed too pure to be human, and even when he was in a group, he always seemed as though he was only on the precipice of it, and not quite a complete part. As though—like a Guardian—he was simply an observer, a protector. It's not that David didn't have his flaws, as everyone did, but they all rolled in together to make him the person he was, and at his core, he was a good man.

A beautiful man.

Perfect.

It was only the two of us, and all the realms melted away.

Nothing existed beyond this room.

My breath caught in my throat as David kissed me again, and I forced down the emotions that distracted me from experiencing this. I tried to get lost in the moment, but I had to simultaneously remind myself that anything that happened tonight might not be able to happen again.

Would my parents approve of it if I wanted to see David again?

Or would it be a case of *'do as I say, not as I do'*?

There was still a stigma attached to even engaging with humans beyond the purposes of training or a mission, let alone fraternizing with them for more than physical pleasure. Sex on Earth was more powerful for Guardians than our home realms because we could absorb our partner's emotions and pleasure as well as those of anyone within the immediate area. The joy of this alone was orgasmic when concentrated upon. Add the physical act of sex to that mix, and it was no wonder Guardians from both realms sought out human partners across the globe.

But it was for pleasure only, nothing more.

Until my parents broke all the rules.

Then I saw David, and history was doomed to repeat itself.

As our tongues met, I reached and yanked my boxers down, desperate for more skin-on-skin contact. My nerves may have been aflame and tingling under my skin, but I wasn't afraid. I wanted to give myself entirely to David. David smiled against my mouth as he too removed his underwear and ground his erection against my inner thigh.

David paused again, touched my chin, and waited until I looked up from where our bodies met and into his eyes. "Are you sure?"

With a nod, I grabbed David's cock and pumped my fist over his length. David groaned and bucked into my touch, before he wrapped his hand around mine and guided me to slow my movements.

"Sorry," I whispered.

David smiled again and brushed his lips overmine. "Slowly. Let's make this last. Like this..."

I was about to apologize again when David silenced my concerns with a kiss as he guided my hand. Leaning to the side as I worked him, David opened a drawer on the small bedside table and took out a bottle and a sealed foil square. Rolling back over, David eased me onto my side and chuckled as I whimpered and reluctantly released my hold on him, before a moan was drawn from my throat as David cuddled up behind me and pushed his erection against my ass. With my senses on high alert, the flick of a lid made me jump, and David pressed a kiss to my shoulder. "Shhh... got to lube you up, babe."

David traced his fingers down my spine and over my hip before cupping the curve of my ass. I jumped when his finger made contact with my hole, cool from the lube, and David kissed my shoulder again, this time letting his mouth drag across my skin as he eased a finger inside me.

My fingers gripped David's arm, which wrapped around my torso, and I breathed in sharply through my teeth when he added a second finger.

"Relax, just breathe...." David's voice was a breathy moan, as deep and sweet as the movements of his hand. I relaxed, and in that moment, David curled his finger, and a sharp moan wrenched itself past my teeth as I was flooded with pleasure. As I let go of my nerves and relaxed into David's touch, I filtered my senses through the air and began to absorb David's arousal on top of my own. It filled me, overwhelmed me, and flooded the air between and around us until I couldn't sense anything beyond this space with him. My cock ached, and David's lips curved into a smile against my skin as I ground back into his hand, needing *more*. David responded to everything. The movement of my body, and the hitch in my breath as it left my lungs.

"That's it, relax. Tell me to stop if it hurts."

His voice intoxicated me further, and I moaned and ground my hips against David's hand. David hummed with approval, and when I was drunk with pleasure, he pulled his hand away. With another whimper I reached back and grabbed David's cock, and stilled long enough for David to pour some lube onto my palm.

"Keep touching me," David whispered as I focused my attention, but it was difficult not to be distracted by David's nimble fingers as he circled my hole.

"More..." I begged. David removed his hand from me, wrapped his fingers around the base of his cock, and braced himself behind me. His chest pressed against my back, and I gripped the sheets in front of me. I tilted my hips, willing David to keep going. The air was thick between us with our stimulation, and I looked back at David as he guided himself into me, and lowered his lips to my neck at the same time. He moved slowly, achingly slowly, pausing every inch to make sure I wasn't hurt. But with each movement, I rocked back against him, and my body opened to the penetration, moans and nonsensical sounds falling from my lips.

Until...

"*Fuuck,*" David groaned out when his hips were flush against mine. He moved his hand away, grabbed my hip, and began rocking against me, easing into a steady rhythm and building us both to our peaks.

I closed my eyes and allowed myself to drift into the moment as David bent one arm under me and hugged me around my chest while his other hand kept my hips tilted. He thrusted a bit harder, and I responded only with another moan, which David returned.

"Fuck you feel so good Samael..."

I opened my eyes, and panic flooded my chest—where my fingertips clutched the pillow in front of me, they started glowing blue. David's face was buried against my shoulder, and I bit my lip as I forced my body to change. I watched as my skin flickered before finally resting in my human form.

When I'd tensed up, David mumbled into his neck, "You okay?"

I stroked David's arm, still wrapped my chest, and forced myself to relax again. "I'm okay. Please don't stop." I didn't want to waste a moment of our time together, and while I told myself this could never happen again, deep down, I knew I wouldn't be able to stay away from him.

With a grunt, David increased his pace, and when I didn't protest but responded by shifting back against him, he kept it up and thrust harder each time.

He grabbed my arm and guided my hand down. "Touch yourself, bring yourself off."

"I've never—"

David grabbed my chin and silenced me with a kiss, and I moaned openly as I began to stroke my cock in time with David's thrusts. My jaw slackened as David moved his tongue against mine, and the pleasure made my hand tremble. David's brow glistened with sweat, and his imprint shifted as he struggled not to reach his peak.

He was waiting for me.

With another smile against my shoulder, David his angle, and hit a spot inside me that sent stars over my eyes and shoved me over the edge.

"David!" I cried out as ropes of cum painted David's sheets, and David's peak followed shortly after. The air itself could've ignited at what passed between us as our pleasure reached heights I'd never dreamed of, and David moaned as I clenched around him, not wanting it to end.

My head spun. Although I'd tried to imagine many times the pleasure that came with release, nothing my mind could conjure came even close to the physical and spiritual experience it turned out to be. Briefly, I wondered if sex would be the same in Lucidis, but it didn't matter—I didn't want anyone but David. The waves of my pleasure were interrupted as I picked up and absorbed David's desire, like a rock thrown into already rippling water, the ripples meeting and jumping over each other. The energy flow between us slowed, but didn't stop, as we relaxed. When David moved away gently and discarded the condom, I rolled over, pulled David on top of me, and wrapped my arms around him. I squeezed slightly, never wanting to let go of this man.

David laughed breathily. "Easy there, you're stronger than you look."

"Sorry." I eased the grip of my arms around David's torso, but didn't entirely let him go.

After a moment, David whispered, "Are you okay?" against my neck.

"I love that you keep asking me that." David waited until I

continued, “I’m okay. I’m much, much more than okay.”

David spoke into the nook between my shoulder and neck. “So, you’ve never...”

I pulled David tighter against me for a split second before I eased my grip again, causing David to chuckle before I replied, “No. Never.”

David lifted himself out of my grip, and reluctantly, I let him do so. He leaned on one elbow to look down at me, sprawled out across the sheets, the lines of my muscles enunciated by the fine sheen of perspiration that covered my body. “There’s something about you.”

I watched David watch me. His hair had partially come out of its tie, and bits fell in front of his face. I don’t think I’d ever seen anyone more beautiful than David was at that moment. When David raised his eyes to mine, I found he couldn’t hold his gaze for too long. I was rarely intimidated by anyone, but David’s eyes probed and enticed me to spill all my secrets.

If I looked into those eyes long enough, I just might.

“Was I okay?” I asked.

David smiled. “That’s an adorable question. You were amazing. I hope I didn’t hurt you.”

I shook my head and tucked a hand under the pillow. “You didn’t hurt me. I don’t think you ever could.”

David watched me for a moment longer. “I think we’ve gone beyond one-night stand territory.”

“Is that what this was?” While I already knew I was well past that, hearing them spoken aloud made it more real than I think I was ready to acknowledge, and discomfort crawled beneath my skin. Not because I didn’t want David, but because there were so many obstacles he couldn’t even begin to know.

"Wasn't it?" David whispered.

I lifted a shoulder in a barely-there commitment to the gesture. "I don't know. I don't think so. I didn't think that far ahead. I just wanted you... I do want you."

David planted a kiss on my forehead. "You're so innocent. I love it."

"Not anymore."

David laughed and traced his fingers in small circles around the lines of the muscles on my chest and over the bumps of my abs. "Are you tired?" he asked.

"Not really."

"Do you have somewhere to be?"

I paused. I really should go home. I'd been on Earth for hours, and I could feel David's emotions with such clarity I could almost see the air rippling around his skin in the dim light. I needed to go home and recharge. I'd been warned not to stay on Earth for too long.

But my human part begged me to stay. The part of me that finally felt as though it was at home pulled me to this realm and anchored me to the bed.

Stay. You're home now.

How could I even be sure that staying on Earth would have the same effect on me as on the other Guardians? As apart-human raised in Lucidis, I was as much of an unknown as Mother.

But realizing that I didn't care about the consequences hit me the hardest. I'd never resisted the wishes of my parents, the community, or the Elders.

But this... this was everything I shouldn't be doing.

Pushing down my powers internally, I masked my Guardian

essence as I smiled at David. "No. I've got nowhere to be."

"Then stay."

My smile widened, and the infectious nature of my grin caused David to smile too.

Chapter Twenty-Four

Samael

The next morning, I woke alone and stared at the empty spot next to me, where the sheets had been tossed aside with casual abandon. Light streamed through the gap in the curtains, creating a wedge of gold against the white sheets. Throwing my legs over the edge of the mattress, I felt the hard floor beneath my feet and took my time curling my toes against the cool wood.

The physical sensations of Earth were fading in and out of clarity.

I had been here too long.

Pulling my pants and T-shirt back on, I left the bedroom and dragged my fingers along the hallway walls, feeling the tiny air bubbles beneath the paint. I stopped to admire the paintings hanging on the walls before I found David in the kitchen making breakfast.

David looked up with a smile. "Good morning, lover."

"Good morning." My cheeks flushed, and I smiled at the floor, causing David to chuckle.

David left the stove and crossed the small room toward me. "You're adorable," he said, and kissed me on the cheek.

I touched the spot where David had kissed me as he returned to the stove and stirred the contents of the frying pan, causing the fragrance to waft through the air. "Hope you like scrambled eggs and toast. Not much else in the fridge, I'm afraid."

"That sounds fine."

Never had eggs before.

Would it be weird to say that?

"I would have baked you something, but I didn't have the time..." David glanced at the cupboards before he added, "... or the ingredients."

As he cooked, David danced on the spot, and once I was seated on a small stool by the breakfast bar, he grabbed a remote and turned up the music.

"What music is this?" I asked.

"*Nat King Cole—L-O-V-E.* I'm a sucker for the oldies radio station."

With that, he adjusted the heat on the stove and moved around the counter, singing loudly. Grabbing my hands in his, he pulled me to my feet. My instinct was to resist dancing as David swayed beside me, and he chuckled at how I seized up. While I had danced in the community, it was usually in secret, kept only to myself and a few select friends.

But as David laughed at my discomfort and danced around me, I could not resist becoming infected by David's joy. Mother's voice spoke louder in my head than the community's wishes—the joys of dance, the emotion, the abandon.

Feel it, Samael!

I let my hips and feet start moving to the music, and as I relaxed, all the dancing lessons I'd had from Mother flooded through. Years of her instilling the importance of music and encouraging me to *feel* it, not just hear it, meant that once I started, I couldn't help but move to it.

All my happiness with David took over, and I gave in.

I never had a chance to fight it.

Grabbing David's hand, I looped my arm around his waist, spun him around, and moved my feet swiftly across the tiled floor in practiced motions. David's eyes widened at the abrupt change in me, before he laughed openly, and his hand in mine grew warm as he unknowingly absorbed my energy and my bliss.

We danced, completely lost in each other and the moment, and turned in tight circles, an echo of my parents' meeting on Earth all those years ago.

As the song finished, I spun David into me, and kissed him lightly on the lips before I held him still while we caught our breath, and our chests rose and fell against each other. David laughed and clutched a hand over his heart as he guided me to sit again and returned behind the counter to the stove. He continued to chuckle as he served breakfast, and his cheeks remained flushed. Waves of happiness infiltrated the room, making me dizzy with it.

"Well, that was unexpected." David laughed as he placed a plate in front of me and handed me cutlery before he sat across from me, and we ate in silence for a short while.

"This is delicious," I said between mouthfuls.

"The secret is extra salt." David smiled. "Do you want to do something together today?"

My fork stalled between the plate and my mouth, and David's smile faltered.

"I'm... I'm really sorry. I need to get home..." After a pause, an ache filled my chest at the disappointment radiating from David, and I added, "... but I'll be back in town soon. I'd love to see you again." My words came out in a rush.

David tilted his head. "Home as in..."

"Out of the city."

"Is everything okay?"

I rubbed the back of my neck. "Yeah, everything's okay. I can't stay away for too long. My parents need me. Work to do around home, you know?"

David nodded, but the air around him gave away his confusion, and it was a stark change from the connection we'd shared only moments before.

"I'm sorry." My gaze dropped to my plate, and I pushed the remainder of my food around.

David smiled softly in the way he does, and the rush of emotion I felt toward him built in my chest again, like a wave that pulled me forward and begged me to stay with him.

"It's okay. Next time," David said, and he meant it. His essence was clear.

Confusion. That's all I'd sensed from him. Not hated or dislike, only confusion laced with a touch of disappointment. I held onto the sense of disappointment as evidence he wanted to be near me as much as I him, and tried to push away the reminder I'd been here too long already. What if I were mixing up simple emotions?

"I would stay with you if I could, I want you to know that," I said, the haste apparent in my voice as I reached across and touched David's hand, hoping to portray my sincerity without words.

Too much?

Am I too forward? Talking too much? Not enough?

David smirked. "You need to worry less—you're cute. Give me your number?"

My fingers fumbled with the unfamiliar device in my pocket, and my mind scraped around to remember what John had told me. My enthusiasm for having a means to contact David only made my motions more awkward, but David chuckled as I plugged his number into my cell phone.

"You're a bit strange, Samael," he said with a twinkle in his eye and a smile, but I still stuttered my way through a reply.

"Wh—how do you mean?"

"You always seem so concerned with how you come across to everyone. Like every action and word is chosen, but..." he narrowed his eyes, his smile still in place, "... not in a deceiving way, more like... a caring way. If that makes sense."

"I don't care what everyone thinks," I said, and David raised a brow. "Only you." The smile David gave me increased the ache in my heart. "I just want you to like me," I added.

"I do like you." After a beat, David stood and grabbed our empty plates. "Hold on. Before you go, there's somebody I want you to meet. He's a good judge of character."

I stood and shoved my hands in my pockets before removing them and clasping them in front of me while David trotted outside. I hadn't picked up on another human in the house. There was only David's essence.

Unless my powers were compromised before I realized?

I was snapped back to reality when the back door opened, followed by a scuffle and a mad scampering of claws on tiles. I stepped back as a disheveled, long-haired, gray dog barreled toward me.

"This is Jackson," David introduced as he let go of the dog's collar, and the animal abruptly stopped in front of me.

I stilled as the dog sniffed my feet. I'd never encountered a dog in person, but I was immediately overcome with an urge to scratch behind its ears. It was an odd urge, but after my father's teachings with animals, I knew not to question it.

I kneeled, and Jackson sat before me and lifted a paw onto my knee. He was huge. I was sure that if Jackson stood on his hind legs, he'd be almost as tall as me. David watched as we interacted, and I wasn't sure what he was waiting for, so I gave in to my instinct and scratched behind the dog's ear. Leaning forward, I offered my forehead, Jackson pressed his head to mine, and we stayed like that momentarily. There was an intake of breath from David, but I closed my eyes and reached out my senses to the animal in front of me.

Stunning.

Such purity and trust. Loyal and with an ever-present need to play.

I smiled and pressed my lips to the scratchy fur on his long nose.

"He's friendly, but..." David seemed rooted to the spot when I raised my head and looked at him. "I've never seen him do that before."

"He's beautiful."

"Yeah, he's a cutie." David nodded, seemingly replaying the exchange between me and the dog in his mind. I'd love to explain to him what had happened, and then maybe he'd understand what had passed between us and how rare and special it was. "He's my roommate's dog. He's often away for work, fly-in-fly-out, you know? So, it's mostly me and this guy.

But Jackson's been such a comfort to have close lately with everything going on."

"Everything?" I stood and kept a hand on Jackson's head. "As in with your parents?" I hoped there weren't other troubles in David's life.

"Yeah, I'll tell you more about it. Next time."

"Next time." Jackson leaned against my legs, and his tail wagged in long, slow sweeps, dragging on the floor. "I have to go," I said, and added, "Sorry." Jackson lay at my feet, no doubt picking up the shift in my mood.

I didn't want to leave.

David approached me. "We'll see each other soon, yeah?"

"Of course." I pulled David toward me, hugged him close, and danced my fingers over the shape of his shoulders and back, hoping I could memorize him. David's shirt bunched briefly beneath my fingers, and I ached to take it off again. David hummed against my shoulder, his hips shifted slightly, and I bit my lip against the groan I wanted to release. We stood like that for a long moment before I forced myself to pull away and slid my feet out gently from underneath Jackson.

Looking over my shoulder at David, even as I smiled, a wave of misery washed over me with each step I took away. Other than my parents, I'd never felt this closeness to another being. But of course, this was different. Far from parental love, being near David was a need that seemed to be deeply ingrained in my core.

Nothing could make me regret coming to Earth to meet him, but a pang of remorse struck my chest at having to leave.

And lie.

I took my time putting my shoes back on, although I was

only delaying the inevitable, and wasn't sure if I was making it worse or better. David walked me to the front door, and before I stepped over the threshold, I gripped the front of his shirt and pulled him forward. David's lips met mine and immediately parted to invite my tongue to play with his. The panting urgency of his breathing had my fingers curling against the fabric of his shirt as I fought the urge to stay and be with him again. Pulling away, David's eyelids were half-lidded with desire, and the grin he gave me sparked need in me all over again.

"Soon," I said, and David nodded as he gripped my hand when I still held his shirt.

"Soon."

His fingers dragged over mine as reluctantly I pulled away, and I couldn't resist turning to see him again before I walked down the side street, which was empty at this time of the morning.

Around the corner, I found a quiet spot, double-checked my surroundings, and remembered to look up for windows before I spread my fingers to summon a Gateway. When the spark happened, a Gateway flickered before it immediately disappeared, leaving only a surge of energy behind.

Frowning, I braced my feet to steady myself, then concentrated harder on the singular point in the air I would use to open a Gateway to home. This time, it happened, and I hastily closed the incidental Tenebris Gateway with a clap of my hands before stepping forward to return home.

Breathing in the smooth air of Lucidis, I stood with the sun on my face. It always felt so good to be back, and although it hurt to leave David, I reveled in the feel of my home. Stripping off my clothes, I dropped them in a pile next to me and began the shift back into my Guardian form. Opening my eyes, I watched my hands as my skin flickered to blue before it stayed stubbornly human.

Instinctively, I looked around to see if anyone had witnessed the failure of my power.

Thankfully, no one.

I focused on the sensation of my skin and forced it to undulate back into my natural Guardian form. My hair disappeared and was replaced with long, bright blue spines that quivered and spread to enjoy the cool breeze as I turned my face toward the sun. Allowing my eyes to close and my body to relax completely, I ignored the flicker of nerves in my gut at having to *force* my human form down.

There were too many emotions I wasn't used to, that's all.

I was jolted out of the moment when a hard shove landed against my shoulder. Turning angrily, I found myself face-to-face with my father.

"Where have you been?" Dad stormed.

My hands rose, and I stepped back at the rage radiating from him. While I knew he wouldn't be exactly happy with my actions, I hadn't anticipated this level of anger. It shimmered in the air between us, and my quills rose defensively. My initial instinct was to meet rage with rage, but the flame in me flickered and disappeared, and instead, I was filled with bewilderment. "What?"

"We couldn't *find you.*"

"Why didn't you just trace me?" My brows drew together. "You would have seen I was fine."

Dad threw his arms up in frustration as a growl formed in the back of his throat that edged on a screeching sound as, in his anger, he momentarily reverted to our native language. He clenched his fists and took a steadying breath. "Were you amongst humans?"

"Yes?"

"Were you..." He retook a breath and closed his eyes for a moment. The sense of his rage flickered for a moment, pushed aside by a dent of understanding. But it didn't go away, and pulsed insistently between us. "Were you hiding your identity and influence from them?"

I opened my mouth to answer, *Of course,* because it was obvious, but then the reason for Dad's anger dawned on me.

"You couldn't sense me," I whispered.

I knew cloaking my powers would make it difficult for me to be traced, but I figured my parents would at least get enough of a read on me to know I was okay.

Apparently, on Earth, I'd made myself invisible.

"*Yes,*" Dad yelled and threw his arms up again. "You hid your identity from them with too much determination, so you hid your position from *us.* How could you not have known that?"

"I didn't think—"

"You're right. You didn't think."

"*Stop shouting at me.*" After my outburst, Dad opened his mouth, then closed it again without speaking. The shock of my raising my voice halted the conversation. I didn't shout, ever.

He rubbed his face. "I'm sorry, Samael. I shouldn't have yelled at you."

"It's okay."

"It's not okay." He looked skyward and took a deep breath, forcing calm through his veins and clearing his body of anger as he tried to replace it with understanding and nurturing. I could feel the entire process from him. "I still struggle being a parent. I worry about you and your mother all the time."

"You're a great parent. Please don't worry about me."

My father smiled briefly. "It would have been simpler, before I wanted to parent more like..."

"Like a human?"

Dad shook his head and muttered, "Yes."

I smiled, but my smile dropped when my father stared me down, and his eyes flashed briefly with anger under the dark crease of his brows. I could almost see his mind working, and I could certainly feel his tenuous grasp on his rage as it began to slip again.

"Where *were* you?" Dad's quills on his back quivered with his irritation, but they didn't raise, nor did his voice.

"I was with a human."

"Why?"

I cocked an eyebrow at him. "Why were you with Mother?"

"That was different."

"*How?*" I stepped forward. "How was it different?"

"Who were you with?"

"It doesn't matter, but I'll be going back."

Dad's reply was icy. "No."

"You can't stop me."

My father raised his finger before swiftly bringing it down, evidently unsure what to do with his emotions as they piled on top of each other, creating a confusing mess of his imprint. "I am your father, and there are things you do not understand. You must not go back to Earth without my permission."

"I am an adult."

"You are still a *child*. Young by human standards, and even more so by ours."

"I thought you'd understand. I'm going to talk to Mother." I gathered my discarded clothes from the ground.

"What do I *not* understand?" Dad called at my retreating form. When I didn't stop, he shouted, "Do not walk away from me."

I ignored the waves of rage that rippled off my father and stabbed into my back, and I didn't turn around as I walked toward the community.

When I found Mother, she ran toward me, pulled me close to her in a crushing hug, and pressed her cheek to my chest before she sighed heavily. I wanted to tell her where I'd been, all about David, and what I'd felt. But in that moment, I realized I wanted to keep it to myself. David was a secret I held close within my heart, and the bond between us was one that no one else needed to know about. Besides, I didn't want Mother to worry any more than she already was—I could feel it coming off her in waves.

She didn't ask where I'd been, and I didn't tell, but I could feel the relief slowly building inside her, and I tried my best to calm her nerves. I knew she'd be able to feel me doing it, but she sighed and absorbed the energy I offered as her arms tightened around me.

"I'm sorry," I said.

"I'm just glad you're safe."

I didn't explain further.

I didn't want to explain why I'd be returning to see David and when.

Because I *would* be going back.

Chapter Twenty-Five

Culo

Sitting by myself at a table for two at a boutique coffee shop, I threw a dirty look at anyone who asked if they could take the spare chair. I didn't need it, but I enjoyed how quickly they pulled their hands away from the chair after they made eye contact. For those brief moments, I'd drop my cloaking powers and allow them to feel the negative forces behind my eyes. Fear would flash across their faces, and they'd yank their hands from the back of the chair as if scolded by the cool metal. I chuckled as I watched another human scurry away.

In years past, we were instructed to hide our natures around large groups of humans and only use our influence in a controlled manner. Sometimes, Lucidians were too keen in their *corrections* of the Balance, and we'd be quick to retaliate. But only enough, always *exactly enough* to right things again. It was a constant back and forth, and I wasn't the only one sick of it.

Sipping my latte, I chuckled again. Ignis favored black coffee, and it had become a signature among the other Tenebrians, almost like a calling card or a signal to others while on Earth that they were part of the few on this long journey to change things.

But I valued my tastes above making a statement.

A group of humans nearby were gathered around a laptop at the next table watching a video, and I listened in without looking directly at them.

"It's all about kindness and paying it forward. It's so sweet," a young woman said, her large glasses contrasting with her petite features.

"Is this going to be one of those videos that make me cry?"

"You cry at everything."

The second girl giggled. "So sue me! Just put the video on."

As the video started, a growing warmth around the group enveloped me, and my nose crinkled as I sensed it. Murmurs and general noises of appreciation echoed through the small group, and with each additional wave of positive vibes, I recoiled further, my skin crawling.

But my focus wasn't on the positivity. No, I was entranced by the laptop and the concept of being able to spread our negativity through the internet. Social media hadn't been fully harnessed before. It was used only incidentally. Hell, when we started, social media wasn't even a *thing*. The idea that we could *intentionally* rope the media into playing into our plans opened up a world of possibilities.

I must tell Vikt of this.

My appreciation of the moment didn't last long after a particularly strong wave of affection spread through the café. While people at tables nearby smiled without knowing why as the energies filled the air, I scrambled to get away, and my chair turned over as I fell to the floor. Clutching a hand over my mouth, I desperately tried not to dry retch.

A young man leaned down and offered his hand. “Are you okay? Can I help?” he asked.

I slapped the human’s hand away, and my stomach lurched at the genuine concern behind his offer. Pushing to my feet, I bolted out of the café.

As I sprinted down the street, I pushed an elderly gentleman into a group of other humans and laughed as I kept running. It was a stupidly small thing, but it amused me. I had good news about another way to spread fear to bring home, but first, there was fun to be had.

A group of humans stood around me, watching the building collapse. Each part that crumpled and fell sent up another spray of embers, and the acrid smell of burning materials filled our nostrils as the smoke permeated the air and spread toward the city center. These humans were primarily young and more easily influenced by their anger toward the world, which could be channeled into destructive acts. Weeks of work had led to this, and Vikt and I had funneled this little rebellion into something violent and dangerous. I sought out Vikt in the crowd and nodded at her where she stood in her human form. A glint in her eyes was the only indication she gave me before she smiled and turned back to watch the welcome consequences of our handiwork. This was far from the end game, but we’d shown the humans the way. It had started with simple vandalism and progressed into acts of destruction, as seen in the incident before us tonight.

After tonight, the humans would take it on themselves to further the damage.

Violence wasn't out of the question.

What were they protesting? The media would ask. It didn't matter. Their beings were so infected with our negative energy that all we had to do was keep the fog of energy around them thick, so their conscience couldn't penetrate it.

In the building, the screaming had died down an hour ago.

Maybe some homeless humans residing in the abandoned building escaped, but not all of them did. What mattered now was the approaching sirens and with them, the media, thanks to an anonymous tip that the gang responsible for recent violent acts was going to strike again.

I smiled. When news of this reached television screens, people would be devastated. *Who would do such a thing?* They would ask themselves, *Who would kill innocent people?* The negative waves would be small at first. Still, they would strengthen and multiply as they dispersed across the city, accumulating and expanding nationwide as the news spread and similar acts occurred elsewhere. It would be sufficient for us to maintain our influential foothold in the community and extend outward from there.

If there were enough minor incidents, people would become irate. They would wonder why the police and government weren't doing more, they would riot, and people could be hurt or killed.

People would definitely be killed.

A sense spiked inside my head, and I turned to find Vikt staring at me across the crowd. This time her smile was wide, as we understood this was still the beginning, and we were both eager for more.

Using the media had been a stroke of genius on my part, and despite Vikt's stubbornness, she had to give me credit where credit was due. No one talked about why we hadn't done it before, but then again, before we had been acting reckless for reckless's sake with only a vague sense of what we wanted the end game to be. Thanks to Vikt's contact, we had a solid plan.

The group dispersed as the sirens came closer.

There was so much more to come.

I flicked my hood over my head as I turned a corner down an alleyway.

First, I had some personal business to attend to.

Following Heather through the living room of her spacious apartment and into the kitchen, I leaned against the corner of the counter as she offered me a drink. Sipping at the beer, I watched Heather move around the kitchen as she made a simple cocktail for herself.

She wasn't typically my type but had caught my attention immediately.

While on Earth, I typically went for strong women who saw themselves as independent, but they would often fold the moment I charmed them. I loved watching their willpower dissipate. Humans thought themselves to be much stronger than they were. Or, I'd go for people who were physically intimidating to other humans.

Then I could show them what true strength was.

But Heather was different. She seemed oblivious to her physical beauty, but I was certain it was part of her act. More than once during the night, I'd seen her eyeing my clothes with an expression somewhere between curiosity and distaste while she straightened her brand-name dress and glanced at any reflective surface she could find. What had attracted me to this particular human was her emotional print. She felt deeply and easily, but spent most of her energy trying to conceal it as she pretended not to care what others thought. But it was a thin veil which I saw through instantly, and while she judged me on my clothes, which I'd selected randomly from the pile back home, she'd also fallen under my spell almost immediately.

Which meant—I smiled to myself—that not only was she easy to manipulate, but when I hurt her, she'd be devastated. It meant all on her own, the ripples she'd create would leave a larger negative imprint than several humans combined.

An *empath,* I think the humans called people like this—someone who felt *deeply.*

"What are you smiling at?" she asked as she leaned on the counter with her elbows and made sure to show the curves of her cleavage.

My smile widened, noting her unspoken reaction to my attention—her pupils expanded, and her skin flushed. She was taken by me. "You..." I said, shaking my head slowly. "You're breathtaking."

She blushed. "Shall we... take this to the bedroom?"

Reaching across the counter, I took her hand and lifted my arm to lead her around until she stood beside me. I ran a hand down her back, and she shivered under my touch. When I leaned in to kiss her, I used my hands to hike up her dress as

I pulled aside her underwear. She moaned against my lips and tried to move her hips away.

"Take it slow," she mumbled.

I smiled against her lips. "No, you want me." I proceeded to push two fingers inside her, and Heather tilted her head back and whined as she tried to relax her body to my rough touch.

She squirmed. "Let's go to the bedroom. Please, take it slow. We have all night."

"All right." Removing my fingers, I inhaled the scent of her discomfort and hummed before hoisting her onto my shoulder and carrying her down the hall as she giggled. Dropping her roughly on the bed, I kicked my shoes off, pulled my t-shirt over my head, and hastily undressed.

Heather looked up at me as I stood naked by the edge of the bed, and shrank back slightly against the pillows. A smile tugged at the corner of my lips. She was intimidated by me. As I dropped down next to her, she scooted away from me a fraction as she bounced on the mattress. "Can we just take it slow, please? I want this, but I want to enjoy getting there too."

Forcing my imprint to change, I smiled at her, and her expression shifted as she sighed before I cupped her cheek and kissed her again. Gently this time, softly, I worked my tongue between her trembling lips. "Let me have you," I whispered against her mouth as I slid the straps of her dress off her shoulders.

Pulling her dress down over her torso, I exposed her breasts and grunted my approval as I lowered my mouth to each nipple. Heather moaned again and leaned into my touch. Every inch of her skin tingled where I touched her, and I grinned against her skin as I felt the shifts in her emotions.

Uncertainty. Desire. Need. Arousal. Concern. Uncertainty again.

She'd said it several times in the cab on the way to her place between frantic kisses—*I don't do this. I never do this.* From our conversations at the bar, I knew she wasn't into one-night stands, but preferred relationships. She was proud of her body, and she worked hard to keep it in shape, but she didn't share it with just anyone beyond a glance from a high-slit skirt or a low-cut top. She wanted me—beyond a fuck—she wanted to be with me, *change* me, *mold* me into the perfect gentleman. She wanted conversations and dates.

I wanted to taste her pain.

After I tugged her dress and underwear off, I smiled down at her naked form. Every time I looked at her with that smile and the influence pressed through, a blush would spread across her cheeks.

First, I'd get myself off, and then break her heart.

Was it within the confines of the instructions Vikt had offered us?

Technically.

Was I taking liberties for my pleasure?

Definitely.

I pushed Heather down against the mattress and climbed on top of her. Kissing and nibbling at her neck, I worked my hand between her legs, and slapped her thighs when she didn't immediately submit.

Heather moaned when I pushed two fingers back inside her, before she whispered, "Joel, I want you, but please slow down."

"No."

Rolling her onto her stomach, I dropped my weight on top

of her and penetrated her from behind. She cried out, "Wait, you're not wearing a condom!" But further protests were lost between disjointed squeaks that escaped her lips with every thrust.

"Stop telling me to slow down..." My words were punctuated with heavy breaths as I continued to pound into her as she gripped the mattress. "... or I will make you *beg* me to stop."

Heather only whimpered in return, and when I pushed my weight on top her and trapped her beneath me, I snaked a hand under her body and found her clit with my fingers. A small, breathy *oh* was the only sound she made as I worked my hand and hips in tandem, and Heather's fingers grasped onto the sheets until they were crumpled beneath her.

Focusing on her body, I could almost see the air moving across her skin as the heat between us increased. Smiling against her neck, I felt her peak rising. She whimpered against the pillow occasionally, but had stopped making sounds of protest and had gone limp under me. Her body opened up to me as she teetered on the edge of absolute pleasure and gasped loudly.

I had two choices.

Bring her off, and use the waves from her pleasure to increase my own.

Or toy with her.

As soon as I felt the spark from her body right before she reached her peak, I took my hand away.

Her sigh of frustration and a small sob were all the edge I needed to finish, and I planted my fists on either side of her torso as I pounded hard into her. Her small body bounced on the mattress as she squeaked and grunted through the onslaught, before, with one final thrust that knocked the air out of her lungs, I pulled out and finished on her legs.

Heather groaned when I lifted myself off her, and the bed shifted as I lay down heavily.

She breathed through her disappointment, and I sighed in my contentment.

Heather rolled over, lay on her back, and gently pulled a sheet over her naked body. The air shifted around her, and I grinned at the ceiling as I probed her imprint.

Confusion. Hurt. Fear.

"Joel?" When I hummed my acknowledgment of hearing her, she continued, "Were you going to ask me out on a date tomorrow?"

Heather started twisting the sheet between her fingers at the silence that ebbed between us.

"No," I said.

"Oh, um, are you busy?" The realization that she had been used quickly took hold, and I could feel her trying desperately not to cry, as tears burned behind her eyes. She *knew* she shouldn't have trusted me. The lingering doubt had been there all night. But she was physically attracted to me enough for the influence to take hold, and for her to feel a spark of hope that maybe I liked her too.

Sitting up, I swung my legs over the side of the bed before standing and dressing. Heather sat up and pulled the sheet with her to cover her body. The negativity was already starting to swirl around her, and I didn't bother to hide my smile as she felt a sense of exposure unrelated to her nakedness.

"No, I'm not busy. There's just no need to see you again. I got what I wanted."

"I thought—"

"No. Whatever you thought. No." I grinned, but this time when I turned the expression toward her, I allowed my Tenebrian senses to leak through, and her eyes filled with tears as she rubbed her upper arm. Taking a ten-dollar note out of my pocket, I tossed it on the bed. "For being a good little whore."

"Joel..." Heather whispered.

"Call me Culo."

Heather stared at me as I grabbed the remote and flicked on the small television at the end of her bed. "Here, watch the news. Maybe you'll catch some of my handiwork." Heather sobbed as I turned to leave, my teeth bared into a sneer. I blew her a kiss and made sure I had her eye contact before I said, "When you do, you can be thankful you're still alive."

As the front door shut behind me, her sobs echoed from her room, and the fog of negative energy spread.

Chapter Twenty-Six

Vikt

Huffing heavily through the cool air, I sat on a park bench beside my co-conspirator.

"Why must we always meet in such stupid places?" I asked.

The contact ignored my question. "Why did you summon me here? I told you never to contact me. I will contact you when required, and no more."

Gazing lazily around the park, I easily spotted the other Tenebrians in their human forms as they leaned against trees or playground equipment in their attempt to look covert. But as the area surrounding the bench was full of them, dressed in a mishmash of odd clothes, they stood out. They all stood completely still and stared into the distance while listening intently to the conversation on the bench.

Consequently, humans in the park gave the area a wide berth.

"The group is growing restless, and there are many questions," I said as my contact scowled at them.

"I have told you the end game."

I resisted the urge to roll my eyes. "Then tell us how to get there faster."

"You have waited this long. You can wait a while longer. I have things in play, but they must appear to occur naturally. I will be in danger if there is suspicion that I am pushing something to happen, and the entire plan will fall."

"But—"

The contact's hand turned back into its Guardian form, and in their frustration, they scratched the bench with their claws and left four long marks along the wood. I stared at the large hand as the long fingers clenched into a fist before their skin flickered as they hastily changed back into their human form. Their skin was almost beautiful in the power it held.

I shook my head with a small laugh. "You knew I knew." I looked into the blue eyes of my contact. "You're a Lucidian."

The contact made a sound between a shush and an acknowledgment. "You can see why this is dangerous for me."

"I don't understand your motivation," I said. If they were a Tenebrian, there would be no question, as I'd assume they'd be seeking the same result we were—a new world, a darker one, where only the strongest survived.

Us.

But Lucidis was a relative paradise. What motivation could a Lucidian have for wanting to destroy that?

I dared not ask.

Whoever they were, they were decades older than me, and ten times more powerful.

"You must be patient," they said, this time their voice softer, as if they understood how badly we wanted this, and they did too. "Patience is not Tenebrian's forte, but things are coming together now. So, in the meantime, enjoy yourselves."

"Just give me something, anything I can tell them. They need structure and want to see progress. Our acts feel random to them, some can't see the bigger picture."

There was a pause because the Lucidian responded. "There's a key, a being, who I believe can be used."

"A mixed breed." I nodded. I'd felt the energy pattern, but hadn't understood the significance. I didn't trust Ignis's information years ago enough to believe mixed parentage could be of any use to us. But that didn't matter, as I had only recently encountered the mixed-breed on Earth. No doubt he'd been kept safe in Lucidis until recently, and whether they were aware of his potential use or not, I didn't know. Everything we had been doing until this point was still important and strategic, but the idea that we could move things faster if we used someone as a tool was tempting.

"Keep it to yourself." My thoughts were interrupted as my contact cocked their head toward me, failing to hide their shock I knew about the mixed breed. "I don't want your kind searching for something they don't understand."

"But what if we already know who—"

"*No.*" My jaw tensed at the power behind the word. "You must wait. I have things in motion."

Is there more than one?

Is one mixed-breed more powerful than another?

"But—"

"No more questions," my contact snapped as they stood. "Keep that part to yourself. You'll hear from me when the time is right."

They left, and the group immediately approached me, wanting answers I couldn't provide.

Chapter Twenty-Seven

Samael

My resolve to do as my father wished and stay in Lucidis only lasted a few weeks. During that time, I'd asked my friends to send David texts when they were on Earth, so David would know I was thinking of him. They didn't ask questions, and for that, I was grateful. Despite accepting me for who I was, I suspected they still harbored reservations about my human part and decided not to question my motives for contacting a human.

The alternative was that they used this small favor to me as an act of rebellion against the Elders.

Or... they were doing as friends do and helping one another out.

Unfortunately, I found the last option the hardest to accept. I wasn't blind to how some of the community still treated my mother, and I suspected I was caught in the same net. I found myself constantly questioning my friends' motives, even though they'd given me no real reason to do so, and I hated the suspicion that was never far from the surface of my mind.

The second option was a real possibility, as there was an

element of distrust between the younger Guardians and the Elders. As the activity of the Tenebris Guardians on Earth increased, the Elders assured us these random acts were not connected and that it was simply another case of Tenebrians going out of their way to cause trouble. It wasn't the first time they had done so, and certainly wouldn't be the last.

But something felt different, and while we would usually accept the Elders' word, it was difficult not to think otherwise when we could see and feel the damage ourselves.

I feared for David's safety, and as I slipped away from the community early one morning, I internally apologized to my parents for what I was about to do.

Gathering my clothes from the edge of the woodlands where I'd hidden them the night before, I hastily put them on as I shifted into my human form. Tucking my hair behind my ears, I created a Gateway, focused on David's emotional imprint, and chose a location near his home, but not so close as to intrude.

The streets were empty this early in the morning, and I slipped through the icy wall of the Gateway into the Earth's dawning orange sun. Immediately after snapping the Gateway closed, I took out my cell, texted David, and sat on a bench near a small park between two apartment buildings to wait for his reply. I didn't have to wait long before the cell vibrated in my hand.

You're up early. Just finishing at the gym and about to shower :)

Can I see you? I'm not far away. I've missed you.

Can you see me in the shower? Cheeky boy

My cheeks flushed, and David replied before I could.

Come to my place. I'll be waiting.

The cell vibrated again, and I groaned quietly as a photo of David's taut stomach flashed up on the screen. Standing on shaking legs, I remembered what Dad had said about Guardians being impossible to track if they hid themselves too well from humans.

With guilt crushing my chest for a moment, I muttered, "Sorry, Dad." before I focused my energies inward and suppressed my Guardian influences. But I went further, and found the inner part of me that was human, and focused on it to draw it to the surface. My skin tingled as I concentrated my power on this form, and when the sensation vanished, my human form stayed stubbornly and happily in place. Nodding once to myself, I glanced again at the photo from David and my cock twitched in my pants. Briskly, I started walking to David's home.

Not only did I not want to be found out by humans.

I didn't want to be found at all.

Chapter Twenty-Eight

Cael

After several rounds of questioning Samael's friends, we eventually realized Samael had returned to Earth to see a human. I barely managed to hide my amusement when Ana had reduced one of the young Guardians to cowering from her five-foot-four frame, even though he had a foot and a half on her. My barely hidden smirk dropped when I realized their eventual succumbing was because some Guardians still feared Ana as though she were some sort of ticking time bomb, unpredictable and of unknown power.

For once, however, I was thankful for this reputation.

"We're going after him." Ana's tone made it clear this wasn't up for discussion.

I reached out to her as she stormed away. "Ana, wait."

"No, Cael, this is our *son.* You've seen what the Tenebrians are up to, and I'm not having him there alone." When my eyebrows raised, Ana looked like she barely contained an eye roll. "I've heard the talk. Just because I can't see it myself doesn't mean I can't find out what's happening. If you think I'm going to stand around and hope he comes home safe—"

"I'll go find him."

Ana crossed her arms. "We go together."

"You can't."

"Why *not?*"

"Because you're dead there!" Ana's jaw dropped at my outburst, and guilt immediately flooded me from the wave of hurt radiating from her. "What if somebody recognizes you?" I softened my tone and stepped toward her, thankful she didn't move away. "What if *Penny* sees you?"

Ana stammered her way through her reasons, but her anger and panic made it difficult to articulate a concise argument. Of course, I understood her need to go after Samael. She was fiercely protective, but I couldn't simply ignore the warning given to me by Cordus, the instructions from Cascus, nor the signs I'd seen myself. Not to mention the difficulties Ana was having in maintaining her human form. Creating Portholes still alluded her, but her ability to create Gateways was almost fully formed. However, her control over her influence and sharing her powers had grown, possibly even beyond my capabilities. It seemed her human half made an unpredictable companion for her Guardian half, and *which* skills she excelled at were equally as unpredictable.

I interrupted Ana's stammering, "You can't hold your human form."

"I've held it once."

I looked at her.

"For an hour... at least..."

"Once," I said, and wrapped my fingers around her shoulders. "Once, Ana, only once."

"But you don't know how being on Earth will help that. We

both know the environment plays a big role. Otherwise, I might have appeared as a Guardian years ago on Earth." In my moment of hesitation, where I was about to tell her there were so many other factors, Ana stepped forward until we were almost chest to chest. "Cael..." she said as she clutched my hands in front of her chest. "He's our son."

"I will find him."

We looked up, still clasping hands, as Cascus and Monia approached us.

"What is happening?" Monia asked, and while her voice was calm and steady, with the same soothing tone she always used, her eyes betrayed the concern beneath the surface.

"We're going to find Samael. He's on Earth," Ana said.

I dropped my head, wishing Ana had let me do the talking.

Her response was bound to result in Cascus—

"You absolutely will not." Cascus's voice held warning. "You..." He pointed at Ana. "... are not to go to Earth."

Ana's eyes narrowed as she turned to look at Cascus, and no doubt noticed, as I had, that he was looking over her shoulder as he always did. I don't think I'd *ever* seen him look directly at her, nor get within six feet of her. Initially, his stance left Ana hurt and confused, but now anger coursed through her. "He's our *son,*" she cried.

"You will do as you're told and nothing more. We cannot have a human reveal us and cause damage. You cannot control yourself and are no better than any other human."

Ana's mouth was agape, and her shoulders shook as her cheeks reddened. Monia's face remained stony, and she watched Ana with a jumble of expressions in her attempt to keep a passive one. Her hand twitched as she glanced at Cascus.

Uncertainty tore at me. I shouldn't talk back to the Elders, but I muttered, "That was uncalled for, Cascus."

Ana whipped around to face me with rage visible in her eyes, but recognition of the step I'd taken flashed across her expression. She turned back to Cascus and opened her mouth to retaliate.

"Ana..." I wrapped my fingers around her wrist and silently pleaded before I whispered, "*Please.*"

"Cael." Ana looked imploringly into my eyes. "*Please*. I'm not stupid. I can do this."

We stared at each other for a long moment, communicating through touch alone as Ana linked her fingers with mine. I felt everything about her—her determination, love, and protectiveness. I knew her better than she knew herself, and I also knew she wouldn't give up on this. She was clinging to all she had left in this realm in a way she never did on Earth, until the end, where she gave up everything to save me and her loved ones. All she was asking was to find her son and reunite her family.

How could I deny her that?

Cordus's warning flashed through my mind.

No matter what provokes her, do not allow her on Earth.

But this was our son. Surely, Cordus would understand there were always extenuating circumstances.

Surely.

Turning to Monia, I tried not to meet Cascus's eyes. "We're going together."

Monia said nothing, and as she glanced at Ana, a shadow of a smile flickered on her lips. Her eyes met mine, and an understanding passed between us.

Ana *needed* to go to Earth.

Her powers needed to be tested. We needed to know if the power she had lurking beneath the surface was truly under her control. If not, I would be there.

If so, then all of this concern was for nothing.

Ana watched the silent exchange between us with narrowed eyes. "I can do this," she said as she met my gaze. "I can *do this.*"

"We're going to find our son," I announced again, not taking my eyes from Ana. "Then we'll come straight back."

Aside from Ana being stubborn, I wondered if a Guardian would be able to stop her physically if forced to try. I wouldn't want Ana thinking I thought so little of her that she'd be incapable, or unwilling, to keep her power under control. I needed to have more faith in her. The woman I loved was strong, and I hated that I'd had, and continued to be plagued by doubts about her abilities and the things we didn't know.

Looking at her, I realized she knew I'd been afraid. All this time, she knew.

"I'm sorry," I whispered to her. "I don't doubt you. I'm just afraid."

"I know." The corner of her lips lifted into a small smile.

Cascus stared at me. "We are losing much of what makes us the beings we are, succumbing to emotions," he started. Ana's eyes narrowed at him, but he didn't even offer her a glance, and although I could tell there was more he wanted to say on the topic, he instead pointed at Ana again and said, "Watch her like you would a child." He glanced at Ana for a split second before he looked back at me, and Ana recoiled in the corner of my eye.

He didn't quite wipe the expression from his face fast enough, nor clear the air of his lingering essence. When he looked into Ana's eyes, he was filled with pure *hatred*. My eyebrows raised. It was an extreme reaction for a Guardian, especially an Elder, and while I knew he didn't think much of her, I would never have expected him to *hate.*

What was happening to our Elders?

Ana was *nothing* to him. She was less than human, less than a tool to maintain the Balance, and he *loathed* her. A spike in the air indicated Ana's anger was spiraling as she too reacted to his gaze. Cascus started when he sensed the shift in the air from Ana's mood, and before I could call him out, he purposefully turned away and left without another word.

Monia looked between us, her face again unreadable, before she nodded stiffly and followed Cascus across the grass.

Grabbing Ana's hand, I led her to the edge of the community.

"Cael—"

"Forget it. Forget him. Let's go find Samael."

"Cascus frightens me."

I stopped. I knew she had responded to his hatred with hatred in return, but fear? "Did he say something to you?"

Her brows pulled together. "I don't think so. Nothing in particular anyway. It's more just a feeling I get from him. Everything in my intuition is telling me he's bad news."

"He's an Elder."

"He's stuck in his ways, but it's something else. He's... I don't even know how to express it."

"Come on," I said as I squeezed her hand. "We need to find Samael. He's got some explaining to do."

Chapter Twenty-Nine

Ana

My shoulder collided with Cael's as I shoved him aside as we ascended the stairs, and the railing groaned in protest under my fingers. I tensed when Cael grabbed my wrist and spun me around to face him.

"Let me go." I pushed the words out through clenched teeth.

Samael was missing—*our Samael, our son*—on Earth while the Tenebrians did God knows what. I knew Cael, Monia, and Cascus were concerned about my power and ability to control it, but this wasn't about us. This was about keeping our family safe.

And if I was as strong as they thought I was, my being here would be even better, protecting Samael if the Tenebrians tried something. I didn't think they'd target him specifically, but it was too much on my mind that he was here *again* when so many horrible events had happened so close. Something was going on, whether the community or the Elders wanted to admit it or not. Something bigger than the individual acts.

Something started by Nathaniel decades ago.

Cael increased his grip on my wrist. "Ana. Calm down."

"I'm going to find him, Cael," I hissed out.

"And we *will.*" He squeezed my hand. "But you need to stop pushing your way around, you are on Earth now, and everything you feel here is magnified." When I opened my mouth to reply, he held up a hand and brushed his fingers across my cheek as I snapped my jaw shut. "You are *influencing* Ana, without even trying. You're sending out waves of emotion. You tell us to care about humans, so *care* about them and get yourself under control."

The furrow between my brow deepened, and I slid my hand out from under his purposefully. "Don't lecture me as though I'm a child. I get enough of that from the rest of the community."

Cael snatched my hands from the space between us. Holding my wrists together, he jerked me forward until we were chest to chest and then wrapped an arm around my waist. My instinct was to lean into him, but instead, I tilted slightly back to avoid the waves of energy that radiated from him. I hadn't seen Cael angry in a long time, and beyond his words and energy, the look on his face made me drop my frustration and listen.

"Calm down," he said through gritted teeth. "Feel what's happening." His fingers lifted my top and brushed against my waist, and through the additional contact, he compelled my powers to focus on the energy we were producing. Anger swirled around us both, and pulsed outward when I noticed it. While I'd been correct about my human form on Earth—I'd moved easily from my Guardian form and it hadn't waivered—it was dangerous for me to be here if I didn't control myself.

Samael was Cael's son, too, and while perhaps I clung to him harder than I should because he was one of the few who didn't treat me differently, this wasn't only about how I felt. Cael's patience was short as he, too, had to control his anger and fear. Cael agreed something was happening here on Earth and was probably torn between the Elder's warnings about me, Monia's cryptic words, and his instincts and conclusions.

It was written all over his face. Every step he took was laced with indecision.

He was in a difficult position, one I'd forced him into.

My gaze flickered between his eyes and our hands, and I squeezed my eyes shut briefly, took a deep breath, and inwardly forced calm through my veins. Cael watched me, and didn't let go until he sensed the change in my energy and the air around us cleared.

With a sigh, Cael brushed his fingers over my cheek again, and I leaned into the contact this time. "I'm walking a fine line here, Ana," he said, and I raised my eyes to his. Pain radiated from his expression even as he kept his essence clear. "A line between trying to keep you safe from whatever is happening, and keeping you safe from..."

"From?"

"From yourself."

I pressed my lips together and resisted the urge to argue. It was the same topic again—my powers, and how deep they ran. "Haven't I proven I have control of myself?" I asked as calmly as I could.

"Samael is missing," he said, and I tensed, *as if I needed the reminder.* "You're under pressure. Sometimes, when pushed, say by Cascus? You react. Not physically or verbally, but you *react.* I can feel it coming off you in waves, but it's like they're ripples in a pond hiding a tsunami underneath."

"Do I frighten you?" I inched closer to Cael.

He leaned down and inhaled near my neck. "No. I just want my family to be safe."

"Me too." I took a few deep, steadying breaths and nodded after a moment. "Let's go."

We continued to climb the stairs, our fingers interlinked, and took each step slower than before.

"We should color your hair," Cael said.

"Huh?"

"So you're not as recognizable."

I almost rolled my eyes as I smirked. "That's the oldest trick in the book, Cael, from every fugitive movie ever made."

"Maybe that's because it works."

I grinned and flicked my hair over my shoulder. "Fine, I'll go brunette and hack it up a bit. Happy?"

Cael chuckled. "Hack it up a bit? Sounds professional."

"Oh, you know me." I stopped as we reached the door at the top of the stairs. "I never do anything without thinking it through fully."

Cael snorted quietly before he knocked, and as his fist lifted from the door to complete the third knock, it opened. "Kyle."

"John."

The two men nodded at each other and slapped their hands together for a brief handshake before we entered the small apartment. I stayed half a step behind Cael and watched John make his way around the apartment before offering us a beer from the bar refrigerator on the counter. Usually, I'd accept, because it had been way too long. But we weren't here for a social call. Cael had explained to me as we'd walked through the city that John was one of the Guardians' contacts on Earth, tasked with providing clothes, cell phones, and a bit of cash when needed when they were required to stay for more than a few hours.

"No thanks," I replied to John's offer before Cael could speak. "We—"

Cael cut me off. "We need your help."

"I guessed." John crossed his arms over his broad chest, the dark hair on his arms visible where he had rolled up the sleeves of his plaid shirt.

"Our—"

"It's the fourth time this month you lot have dropped past without prior notice." John waved a hand at us before he sighed and dragged his palm over his face. "Usually, I get a note at my door, giving me a few days to ensure I have whatever you need." He glared at Cael. "Or the Tenebrians, sometimes they think it's funny to influence me through a Porthole and make me feel like shit for a few hours, as they're way of sending a message. Assholes," he grumbled.

Cael frowned. "Have all your drop-ins been Tenebrians?"

John grunted. "Mostly. When the last lot were here I brought up with them all this shit I've been seeing on the news, which is clearly their doing."

"John..." Cael's tone edged with warning. "They could hurt you."

John scoffed. "I know the fucking rules mate, they wouldn't. But I made it very fucking clear to them they needed to cut this shit out, or never come to me again." I followed his gaze as it flickered to a hunting knife on a coffee table. "I don't think they'll be back."

"Fuck John. You shouldn't mess with them."

"Our son is here," I blurted out. I'd tried to be patient, but every moment of Cael's and John's conversation crawled across my skin as I squirmed on the spot. Samael had returned to Earth without informing us first, and we were not here to make friends.

"You're a Guardian?" John asked, his voice sounded skeptical.

My anger jumped, and I had to work to keep calm as Cael rested a hand on my arm.

"Sort of." I dismissed his arched eyebrow. "Our son, Samael, was here. You would have helped him... a cell, money, whatever. We need to know where he went, and I know you can help."

"If he wanted to be found, you would find him," John replied, once again crossing his arms over his chest.

"Don't play games with me."

John didn't even blink as I raised my voice, and arched his eyebrow further. "I assume he's hiding his location from you. Have you considered why? He'll come home when he wants or has to."

"It's more complicated than that."

"Why?"

"Because..." I hesitated and had to force my jaw to relax after I found myself grinding my teeth. I shouldn't have to explain myself to this guy, but Cael seemed to respect him, so with another deep breath, I tried to stay calm. "Samael is part human, and an extended time here could make it more difficult for him to return."

"How do you know what effect it could have?"

Cael shifted his weight from one foot to the other. "We're

mostly speculating, since there hasn't been much experience with half or partial breeds before."

John grunted, but offered no further opinion.

Cael continued, "Besides, as you've noticed the increase in Tenebrian activity, you understand why we need to ensure he's safe."

"Where's my son?" I asked again and stepped further into the apartment. I didn't want to have to ask a third time, and I resented having to ask more than once in the first place.

John and I stared at each other for a long moment.

Finally, he said, "I don't know."

"You're lying," I snapped.

John shrugged. "No."

"Track his cell."

"Can't. Old model. No internet."

Crossing the small room in a few steps, I grabbed John's neck and ignored Cael's shout as I backed John against the opposite wall. John didn't react and held my gaze as I drilled into his eyes with mine. My skin tingled where my fingers wrapped around John's throat, and as my body automatically created a path between us and read his essence, I let it. Cael might know this guy, but I didn't, and I needed to know if I could trust him given all the shit he was giving me.

John's gaze didn't waver from mine, something unreadable in his expression as I read his imprint.

Then I went deeper.

There was something inside him.

My eyes widened as we looked at each other. John didn't cave under my stare or the secret he knew I was about to dig up.

A shock of electricity passed between us, and something in

John's eyes betrayed him, the slightest flicker...

Regret.

"Ana, *stop.* You'll hurt him," Cael shouted.

John and I continued to stare at each other, and slowly, I retracted my hand from his neck and took a step back. "Who are you?" I whispered.

"Nobody." John lifted his lip in a snarl.

"Ana, let's leave," Cael pleaded.

"Who *are* you?" My voice rose with my desperation for information as I crowded into John's space and forced him to make eye contact.

I know you.

How?

"I'm nobody, Anahera," John's voice was quiet. "Let it go."

"Ana!" Cael shouted.

"*Cael.*" I rounded on him and pointed at John. "He's a *Guardian.*"

Cael's jaw dropped. "Wh—"

I turned back to John. "Tell me who you are and where my son is."

John's stare was icy, and he looked around me to find Cael staring at him. He sighed and looked back at me. "Only if you tell me how you knew," he said.

"It's true?"

John ignored Cael's question, and his eyes never left my face. "Tell me how you knew."

"I could feel it." I frowned. "Couldn't anyone else?"

"I don't like the Guardians reading me, they know this. Doesn't mean they haven't tried. But it's been so long since I've been there, I thought all traces of my power would have been gone by now."

I shook my head. "Why me?"

Cael answered, "We're still figuring out your powers, some seem to be enhanced..." I opened my mouth as Cael's voice trailed off. But he was right, we *were* still figuring me out. We'd had so many conversations, all of which revolved around the same thing.

We don't know how I'll react on Earth.

A pang of fear flickered inside me—did I even want to know the full extent of my powers?

Should I have stayed in Lucidis?

John turned to Cael. "When you stayed on Earth for too long, what happened?"

"I lost control of my powers."

"And then what?"

Cael's eyes widened. "I lost my powers altogether."

John nodded and watched as the comprehension dawned across our faces.

"Exactly... how long have you been here?"

John's eyes glazed over for a moment as he tried to figure it out, looking back through time in his mind's eye. "Give or take... I've been here fifty years."

Cael's jaw dropped, and something that could've passed for a smile moved across John's face. "What? You think you're the only one who learned the value of humanity?"

Cael shook his head slowly. "I ..." Cael looked at me, and I pressed my lips together in an imitation of a smile. "Initially, yes. But seeing how some of the others in the community have been interested... and then embraced Ana, but..." he shook his head again, faster as if to shake the thoughts out. "If Guardians were disappearing and staying on Earth, we would know about it. The Elders would know."

John's laugh was loud and harsh. "The Elders *do* know. They know everything that goes on with their absorbed knowledge from past generations."

"Why wouldn't they tell us?"

"Why wouldn't the Elders tell the communities that some Guardians choose to live amongst the humans rather than keep their powers? How would that look? It might make it seem that some Guardians know more about humanity than they do."

"That would be a shocker," I added sarcastically, and when John laughed again, something tugged at my chest. "Wait." I stepped forward and grabbed John's arm. He watched me, and in my chest was a complex mixture of hesitation and desperation. There was definitely a familiarity about him. I released his arm, rubbed roughly at my eyes with the balls of my palms, and sighed.

John's eyes softened, as if he already knew what I would ask.

"Did you know my father?"

John hesitated, then, "Yes."

Cael glanced back and forth between us as the air vibrated around me with my indecision. Everything was coming to the surface, all the pain from the moment Dad had walked out, to accepting he was never coming back, to losing Mom. My hands shook as all the unanswered questions swirled around and collided with the realization that the one who had *all* the answers was no more than a handful of miles from my front door for most of my life.

"You..." I closed my eyes as I took in a shuddering breath. "You were right here. The whole time."

"Ana—"

"Is he alive?"

John sighed. "I think so, yes. But I can't be sure."

"Did you come to Earth together?"

John smiled. "No, we met here. I'm a Tenebrian. At least, I was."

Cael immediately dropped into a defensive stance. His weight was balanced, so he was an unmovable force against attack. I stared at him. "He has no powers, Cael."

Slowly, as though measuring each movement, Cael stood. "He must still have something, since you sensed it in him."

"You've known me for many decades, mate. Have I ever given you a reason not to trust me?"

Cael's expression twisted as he grappled with the revelation, before he offered a small shake of his head and took a steadying breath.

If John had wanted to harm him, he had many chances to do so before now.

"If you knew about Ana's father, why didn't you tell me?" Cael asked.

John smirked. "I don't make a habit of spilling secrets to every Guardian who comes through that door, mate. Most of you are so caught up in the old ways, and only a few are beginning to see humanity and emotions for what they truly are—a source of strength. Change had to happen at some point, though I didn't think I'd see it in my lifetime. But I never know which side of the fence you're on..." He eyed Cael. "... I think you were on one side of thinking, then became the other."

Cael didn't answer, then asked, "Where is our son, John?"

I looked back at John and waited for an answer.

"I wasn't lying, I don't know where he is. But I do know he's with a human."

It wasn't something we hadn't already discovered from his friends, and as my conversation with Samael returned to me, I muttered, "David."

"You know him?" Cael glared at me.

"I haven't met him, and I didn't know he was going to go after him. But Samael mentioned him..." Cael waited for me to continue, but said nothing, and I dropped my arms in resignation. "Samael saw David when he was hurt emotionally, and he was correcting the Balance. He felt something for him, a nurturing, a need. He cared."

Cael's eyes traced the movement as I held a hand over my heart, and I sensed his resolve soften.

"Like mother, like son, then," he said.

I smiled, approached Cael, and placed my other hand on his chest, mirroring me. "Like father, like son, you mean."

John cleared his throat. "Can this display of affection be continued later?"

"How do we find him?" I asked.

John shrugged. "As I said, he doesn't want to be found. But you can find David, and then you'll find your son. Find humans who have been close to Guardians. They leave a distinct energy pattern."

Cael nodded and moved to leave, but turned back toward me as he reached the door. "Back when we first met, I noticed being around you sharpened my senses." He smiled. "We'll find him." I nodded and turned to follow Cael, but he hesitated as he continued to watch me. "Ana, what about your father?"

I faced John. "Give me the short version."

“Your father loved you, but he had no choice.”

“I said the short version, John, not lies.”

John chuckled. “Don’t be stubborn, it’s not a lie.”

I stared at him with my eyes narrowed. “I’ll be back for the long version another day.”

Chapter Thirty

Samael

David and I walked through the city center, close enough to hold hands, but without the overt physical contact. Merely the occasional brush of skin on skin as our arms moved past each other. Each whisper of contact sent a tingle through me, making me wish to be alone with David again.

But I was distracted. There were shifts in the Balance, which moved back and forth between the dark and light forces. But these were stronger than the usual day-to-day shifts.

Or perhaps it only seemed like it because I was on Earth and in a crowd.

The Balance was rarely ever still, but something external was forcing these changes. There had been minor chatter about the Tenebrians organizing, but I had to believe that if something drastic or dangerous were going on beyond the usual shenanigans from Tenebris, the Elders would've told us. There would have been a community meeting, and we would have worked together. But nothing at home had changed, so these shifts must be normal, and maybe I was too young to notice the difference.

A wave of guilt pushed through me.

Because none of it mattered if I wasn't at home to help if something *did* happen.

"Samael?" David's voice was edged with frustration, and when I shushed him so he could focus on an energy spike, David scoffed quietly. "Please don't *shh* me."

I turned and looked at him, focusing on the air as it shifted around his being and his mood changed.

David sighed. "You're not listening."

I ducked my head. "I'm sorry, I was distracted."

"You often seem to be."

"What do you mean?"

David gripped my hand for a moment before he dropped the contact. "Samael, you know I like you. But sometimes, it feels like you're not even here, and that's when you *are* here. You disappeared for weeks, and I got an occasional text message, and that's all. You live, God knows where, out of the city, then suddenly you're back and wanting to pick up where we left off. How can I feel like I know you and not know anything about you at the same time?"

"I'm sorry, I—" I held my hands up as a young woman collided with my shoulder.

"Shit," she cried as she dropped her bag.

I kneeled and helped the woman collect her belongings, and as I handed her a diary, her fingers brushed mine, and I flinched, looking up at her face.

She had recently been close to a Tenebrian.

Close, and *hurt.*

"I'm sorry." I caught the name on the front of the diary. "Heather."

Her eyes traced over me as she took me in, and something on her face told me she picked up on the calming influences I was pushing her way, even if she didn't understand what they were.

Heather snatched her wallet away as I went to pick it up. "It's okay." She watched me as I stood with her, and glanced at David before she looked back at me. "Thank you." Her voice was stiff.

Last time she had let her guard down, she had been hurt. My chest ached for whatever the Tenebrian had put her through, and I tilted my head. Her *thank you* was only genuine on the surface.

"Are you okay?" I asked.

It was her turn to tilt her head, and she added a frown. "Yes." The confusion in her was evident. I'd asked if she was okay the same way a family member would, not the way a stranger on the street would, to see if she had been physically hurt.

She nodded at me and left, and I watched her go.

David turned to me. "Do you know her?"

"No, she just seemed... troubled."

"I like that you care." David watched me for a moment in that way he does, as if reading my thoughts. "Do you want to get something to eat? We can talk."

Nodding, I looked back at the woman as she disappeared into the crowd, then took David's hand and held his eye contact after he looked up at me. Rubbing the back of David's hand with my thumb, I said, "You know me."

"I do?"

"Yeah." I let my walls down, only enough to allow David to feel my essence, even knowing David wouldn't understand what he was feeling. But it would be enough to soothe him. "Better than most. You know me."

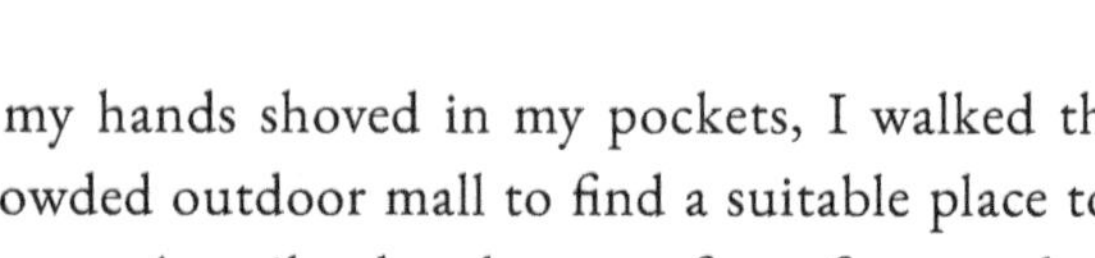

With my hands shoved in my pockets, I walked through the crowded outdoor mall to find a suitable place to open a Gateway. A smile played on my face after my date with David—over lunch we'd chatted and laughed, and when David had kissed me, it was enough to make everything else melt away. I pressed my fingers to my lips as though I could still feel him there, and my smile dropped.

David was understandably frustrated with my disappearing act, which lacked any real explanation and was accompanied by only stilted communication. I'd debated telling David the truth, but how would I begin that conversation? My parents were thrust into a difficult situation and had to deal with it the best they could. But revealing myself to David, and beyond that, the existence of other realms without any real *need,* wouldn't be approved of by the community.

Besides, commencing a relationship with another Guardian was unusual enough, and I couldn't imagine how the Elders and community would react if I wanted a relationship with a human.

"Samael."

Glancing up, I held out my hand as Nicole approached. "Nicole, hi." She ignored my outstretched hand and stopped close to me, invading my personal space.

I took a half step back, but despite her smile, I could still sense the negativity radiating from her.

What had she been doing? Or what was she planning to do?

"Can I walk with you?"

"Uh, sure." My brows furrowed. I didn't understand enough about human interactions to know why she'd asked. We hadn't seen each other since our initial introduction when I'd met David in the bar. Nicole didn't say anything as we started walking away from the crowds and into emptier streets, so I fell into step with her and waited.

After a while, I purposefully slowed down my steps, not wanting Nicole to follow me too far.

I needed to be alone to get home.

"Well, I better get going home," I said as casually as I could manage despite the uncomfortable sensation tingling up my spine.

How do you politely dismiss a human who didn't leave of their own accord?

"Back to Lucidis. Yeah, I figured." I stopped in my tracks, and Nicole continued a few steps further before she turned around, a wide grin adorning her face, and her eyes flashed dangerously. "You are so young, so inexperienced. You're what? Barely in your second decade. I can feel it."

"Who are you?" I clenched my fists by my sides and inwardly pinpointed his powers, ready to strike if needed.

"Call me Vikt. I never cared for the human names."

Her eyes swam black as I took a step backward.

Tenebrian.

"You're going to help me," she said. Her voice had changed. It was deeper and more menacing as she let her natural essence show through her human form.

"No." I backed away a few steps. "Get away from me."

"You're part human, it radiates off you. I'm supposed to wait, but I think I could use yo—"

I struck before she could finish her sentence and hurled a wave of positive energy at her. All the happiness I had inside me from the time I'd spent with David, I directed at her. Vikt recoiled, but only slightly, with barely a half turn of her body.

It wasn't enough.

She was stronger than I.

"Stop wasting time. Come with me." She held out her hand, and when I took another step backward, she approached me quickly. One moment, she was several feet away, and a blink later, she was right before me. She swung her arm out and her palm connected with my cheek in a backhanded slap that sent me crashing into the wall. My ears rang as my head collided with the bricks, leaving a visible dent in the wall from the impact. "I will explain the damage you could do to the others." Her smile was threatening and made my skin crawl. "The perfect tool." She grabbed the back of my shirt roughly and started dragging me down the street. I struggled to keep my footing as my heels slid across the pavement.

Vikt seemed to be talking to herself more than she was talking to me. "Why wait when I already have the mixed breed?" She laughed to herself, seemingly unaware of my continued struggling.

As though something burst inside me, my anger took over. Nicole—Vikt—had been so close to David, and she could've hurt or influenced him. Maybe she already had. I flung myself out of her grip and aimed a kick at her stomach. Physical fighting wasn't my preferred method, but I'd fight back in desperate times anyway I could. Vikt recovered quickly, approached me in three angry steps, and raised her hand to strike me again.

"Get the fuck away from him!" Vikt stopped at the shout with her hand still poised to strike. It wasn't the shout itself that made her stop, but the energy that radiated behind it. Vikt's gaze shifted from me as I turned my head to see the woman running toward us with an essence of rage that carried with her like a storm.

Mother.

Behind Mother, Dad was racing to keep up, and when Vikt spotted him, she sniffed the air like an animal and bared her teeth, her eyes flashing black.

"*You,*" Vikt cried, and pointed at Cael. "You killed Ignis." The air was knocked from her lungs as Mother collided with her and tackled her to the ground.

"Ana, *no!*" Dad grabbed me and threw me to the ground behind him, shielding me with his body even as I scrambled to my feet. We watched Vikt and Mother wrestle, and every time Dad tried to get close, he was repelled by the dome of energy that surrounded them like a protective shell, spreading out in pulses around them.

Mother freed herself from Vikt's grasp and stood before grabbing Vikt by her hair and hurling her along the pavement. The Tenebris Guardian cried out in rage as the small of her back collided with a pole. Mother was breathing heavily, her eyes flashing dangerously, and my eyes widened. The *power* coming off her was incredible, and when Dad spoke her name gently, she turned and looked at him, making him stop in his tracks. Her eyes were blazing, almost white, and her skin might as well be glowing from the rage that radiated from her.

Dad looked around, and I followed his gaze.

Humans were present, although not many, enough to be an issue if the situation escalated further.

How much had they already seen?

Vikt had lost interest in Dad as she watched Mother from where she lay on the pavement. Her eyes were completely black now, and although there was a slight shift as she tilted her head at Dad, the look didn't last long before her attention was focused on Mother again.

"I wanted revenge, but I want *you* more," she hissed out, and the hairs on the back of my neck stood to attention at the sparks of hatred coming from her. "Fuck, you're just perfect, aren't you? I can feel your power."

No matter how long I stared at Vikt from around Dad's stance, she didn't even look at me. My presence, which had been such a focus before, was nothing compared to whatever she wanted with Mother.

"Dad..." I whispered urgently, and he cocked his head slightly to show me he heard. "She tried to take me first. The Tenebrians are planning something—"

Vikt launched herself at Mother again. But Mother grabbed Vikt's shoulders and used her momentum against her, spinning in a tight circle before she pressed her against a brick wall. Pushing her weight down, Vikt struggled against Mother's grip before she slapped her across the face. Dad tried again to intervene and held his arm out as I shifted forward. But the power around the two of them surged again, and we were forced back a step. Mother growled low in her throat, pushed Vikt to the side, and kicked her hard in the ribs. There was a crack, and Vikt crumbled again.

Mother was strong on Earth.

Terribly strong.

As Mother approached Vikt again, she was torn from whatever trance she was in as Dad called out, "*Ana.*"

Vikt took the opportunity to scramble to her feet and run.

Mother whipped around angrily. "You let her get away," she snarled.

"What were you going to do?" Cael stepped forward, his movement hindered slightly as the barrier between them lingered with Mother's rage. There was a forcefield around her, and I resisted the urge to step back. She was my mother, but what was happening? I'd not felt anything like it before, not even from the Elders.

Dad forced his way forward as Mother's hands curled into fists at her side. "What was the plan? Kill her in front of all these people?" He gestured around us, where humans were still walking and shopping. Some had stopped and stared at the fight, but moved away quickly when Mother glanced their way.

Mother's chest heaved as she fought for control. I could feel the two pieces of her that made her whole swirling around inside and around her, battling for dominance. Whatever equilibrium she had maintained while in Lucidis had been thrown out by being on Earth, and now the parts that made her were fighting against each other, and each collision caused a surge in power.

Her focus wavered for a moment before her eyes settled on me, and she doubled down on her energies, barely containing the two sides to her that were in a dominance battle. Dad watched her cautiously as anger seeped out of her in waves, and her eyes were still slightly glazed. Dad looked where the Tenebris Guardian had been, and I followed suit and searched for the feel of her, but she had already vanished. Back to Tenebris, no doubt.

But it didn't matter. At the moment, the only thing that mattered was keeping Mother calm.

Very slowly, Dad reached back and grabbed my arm and moved me behind him as I went to move forward to Mother.

Shielding me from my own mother.

To our left, a young couple approached. As they came within a few feet of us the young woman flung her partner's arm off her shoulder and screamed at him, "What the fuck is your problem?"

"My problem?" He stood his ground, filled with equal rage. "What's *your* problem? Yelling at me for no fucking reason?"

"You are such a jerk." She shoved him, and he stepped back, his eyes dark with anger.

Dad approached them, placed a hand on each of their backs, and rushed them out of the way. They yelled at him for touching them, but the further away they walked, the calmer they became as he forced tranquil influences into their beings before he returned to us.

I turned slowly on the spot. Despite Mother's battle for stability, it was like a chain reaction had started when she had lost whatever control she had in the first place. My jaw dropped as I watched the circle of Mother's influence increase and spread out from her. Humans around us picked up on her anger, which fueled and infected them. Arguments broke out across the street, and some people started crying, suddenly weighed down by the stress of life itself.

It was spreading.

"Ana." Dad's voice trembled as he forced his energies to calm and reached out a hand toward her. "You need to calm down."

She whirled around. "I *am calm,*" she yelled with an unsettling edge to her voice.

There was a pulse through the air, and we stepped back. Dad kept me behind him, and his arm tensed whenever I tried to move around from where he stood.

"Dad..." I gripped his arm as he took another step back. "Is she okay?"

"Cordus warned me not to let her come here." He shook his head slowly as his eyes widened, and filled with sorrow that cut into my chest. "He said they might be after her, but I didn't think..." He swallowed. "We have to calm her down, Samael."

"Let me talk to her, please."

Dad pushed me back further. "Are *you* okay?"

My brows drew together. *Did he think I'd be out of control because of my human part, too?*

"I'm fine," I said.

Dad took several steps closer to Mother. Only when he was within a foot of her did she appear to see him, and he waited until her gaze settled on his face. "Ana, please," he whispered. He reached out to her again, but she slapped his hand away with a stinging swipe.

"She came for our son, Cael," she cried. "Our *son!*" She was still breathing heavily, and with every outward breath, her negativity was projected further, infecting more people and spreading around us like a dome. Her eyes, now cloudy and white with power, shone with tears. The effect was both devastating and beautiful.

Without another word, Dad launched toward her, breaking past whatever was left of the barrier between them, and wrapped her in his arms. She struggled, both physically and mentally, against the calming energies he forced into her being. Dad was physically larger than she was, but she was stronger. I could feel his fear, and knew it wasn't fear of Mother and what potential pain she could bring him, but that she might hurt herself, and he wouldn't be able to stop it.

As he crushed her to his chest, her skin flickered. She didn't change form, but there was a distinct glow to her. "I love you," he whispered into her ear. "I love you, Ana. Samael is safe. He's safe."

He repeated it over and over again, and gradually, her breathing steadied. When Mother brought her arms up and held on to Dad, I knew she would be okay. But he didn't let go or stop calming her until he saw the humans around us calm as well. Many apologized to each other, saying they didn't know what came over them, and moved on with their lives.

Dad breathed a heavy sigh and gave an almost imperceptible shake of his head when I went to move toward them.

I saw it in his eyes.

Not until I'm sure she won't hurt you.

It was a horrible thought to have, and the ache in my chest increased until it was a sharp knife cutting through my soul—to have to consider protecting me from my mother. But he was doing what he felt he had to. Mother was an unpredictable force, more than I'd ever realized or thought to consider. I'd been so wrapped up in my concerns, perhaps I'd been blind to the power within her. Or was she only unstable because she'd come to Earth?

She came here to look for me.

This was my fault.

My breath shuddered as I felt the burning of tears behind my eyes, but I refused to cry and slammed down a barrier over my emotional imprint before Mother picked up on it.

After a few more moments, Dad gestured for me to approach, and I closed the space between us with a handful of large, purposeful steps and embraced Mother, too. She relaxed into our hold, turned to face me, and wrapped an arm around my waist. There was a sob, and I felt her body shudder. Dad moved to the side so I could embrace her fully, and Mother raised herself on her toes to kiss my cheeks over and over again, just as she used to when I was a small child, her face streaked with tears that flowed freely.

"Mother, I'm okay."

"I would never have forgiven myself if you had been hurt. Never."

"It's not your fault." My voice hitched. "It's mine. I'm sorry."

Abruptly, she pushed me away, leaned back, and gripped my shoulders. "Why did you hide from us?"

"I..." I stumbled over an explanation. I had my reasons, but everything that was so clear when I was with David crumbled when I looked into my mother's eyes, so full of anger and hurt. My previous assurances that I had been doing the right thing dissolved when she was in danger, and the fear for her life and safety made everything that came before feel small and insignificant. "I wanted to see David."

Mother's shoulders dropped, and she let her hands fall from my arms. There was barely any anger left in her imprint now, and what anger remained wasn't directed at me.

"Samael..." she started.

"I know you understand." I embraced her again, and she leaned against me as though all the energy had drained from her body. “I’ll tell you all about him later.”

Dad’s brows drew together as he rubbed her back in slow circles and watched me carefully. She was dwarfed between us, and all it did was make me want to protect her more. I met Dad’s eyes over Mother’s head, and knew he was thinking the same thing.

Did the Tenebrians target me and simply come across Mother, or was she the target all along?

What was their plan?

It seemed too much to be a coincidence, and I could feel the discomfort radiating from Dad in waves as he turned it over in his mind. When I shifted my focus to Mother, I felt how drained her energy levels were, and snapped my gaze to Dad’s in a panic.

“Come on,” he said with forced calm. “Let’s go home.”

Mother allowed herself to be guided away by Dad so we could find a place to open a Gateway to get home.

“Dad?” I caught up with them and whispered, “I need to come back.”

Dad didn’t stop walking, though his shoulders stiffened. He looked hard at me, and I held his gaze as he felt it.

He already knew I’d come back.

How could he say no when he had fallen for Mother the way he did?

“Nicole... Vikt...” My stomach churned. “She was so close to David. Dad, she could have hurt him. What if she uses him to get to us?”

“We’ll talk later. Right now, we need to be home.” He glanced at Mother as her head lolled against his chest. “All of us.”

I nodded, followed them, and closed the Gateway behind us as we returned to Lucidis.

Chapter Thirty-One

Vikt

The harsh scrape of the dirt against my skin had me hissing between my teeth as I collapsed upon my return to Tenebris. Remaining on my hands and knees, I breathed in the thick caustic air and relished in the sensation of the power of my home realm as it filtered through to my core. Red dust swirled around my fingers and legs, and the heavy orange was low on the horizon, casting the tall trees in the distance into long shadows. Dark fingers that reached out, ready to strangle the life from me.

Still catching my breath, I looked around at the realm I called home.

The realm I despised.

Things were changing, and Tenebrians were tired of living under Lucidians' rule—laws laid down by history to be upheld forever.

It was time for things to shift.

We all knew the stories of what would happen when the Balance shifted, which hadn't happened since almost the dawn of time itself. When the Balance was still nearly as new as the Earth, the Shift happened, and the continents had moved. The fragile walls between the realms collapsed, and chaos erupted when Lucidis and Tenebris met on Earth—earthquakes, erosion, extinction.

The Balance wasn't centered again for thousands of years.

But maybe we needed chaos—a fresh start, survival of the fittest. My contact had been right—we *were* slaves to the Balance. A role we neither chose nor wanted, and while our acts would have been enough to bring on the Shift given the time, the half-breed would speed things up considerably.

I knew who she was. I could taste her imprint as it lingered on my skin. Did my contact seriously expect me to wait?

If she set foot on Earth again, I could find her.

Brushing the dust from my legs, I stood before I opened all my quills, shook roughly, and analyzed my body. While there were no physical scars from my injuries after my fight with Ana, I'd not forget the fool she'd made of me.

A *human.* Of part human at least, and that was demeaning enough.

I was at least thankful for the healing power of the Gateway, and had walked through slower than necessary once I'd escaped Ana to allow my body maximum time between realms. Groaning as I straightened, my body tricked me into thinking my ribs were still broken, almost as if I could feel the scrape of bone on bone within my body. But the break was healed, and the sensation was nothing more than a phantom.

I was well-versed in ignoring physical pain, but my pride had taken a beating today, and that wasn't as easily forgiven.

A small group of Guardians was gathered on the plain, their orange quills quivering in anticipation as they gazed down at their prey. One of the human Reflections lay on the ground between them, bloodied and beaten. They looked up as I approached, which allowed the Reflection time to escape. They didn't try to stop him—there was nowhere for him to go, anyway. Chatter broke out in the group as I drew level with them, and I gritted my teeth to pull back the sneer I wanted to let loose. This wasn't a game. I looked at Ceps as I stopped, and he shushed the group angrily, having no patience for chit-chat.

These several types of Ignis's followers—those who no longer cared for the old ways and had long since abandoned the unspoken call to guard the Balance and protect those within, those who looked out only for their pleasure, and those who truly understood what we planned to do.

With guidance and instruction from the Lucidian traitor, our plan had escalated.

And with the information I had now, there'd be no stopping us.

We sought to build a new world that was fit for us and any other being who survived the transition and dared to live in it.

Sul eyed my body as I subconsciously ran my hands over where my injuries had been moments before. Sul towered over Ceps, me, and most of the others in the group. She was sought after as a mate, but chose her sexual partners carefully, as the weaker males often didn't survive the experience.

"Speak," she demanded, her gaze not wavering from my eyes.

"I know how we can do it. I found the key to finish this."

"Tell us what you learned." She, too, had no patience for theatrics, and her flat nostrils flared.

"The half-breed Ignis spoke of in his final moments, and the key the traitor told me about are one in the same. She lives, and she is powerful." There was a moment of silence, then the chattering started again. I ignored them and turned to Ceps. "She is unstable. We can push her, use her. She could bring on the Shift all by herself. The fog we've created over the years was the groundwork, and she's the final step."

Ceps's lips curled into an unpleasant smile. "Power and instability are an interesting combination—"

Sul interrupted, "No doubt the Lucidis Elders will protect her. We cannot get to her there."

Ceps nodded at Sul. "Yes, but Vikt encountered her on Earth."

"She has a son, and the son has a human lover," I added.

Ceps bared his teeth. "Oh, this is too easy."

The chattering had started again, excited, hungry for action, when they had been waiting so long without even realizing what they were really waiting for. They had an idea, of course, but most were willing to ignore the final plan of causing the Shift and focus on chasing their pleasures. Ceps held a clawed hand up and cleared his throat, but this did nothing. He clapped his hands together loudly, and a low growl emitted from his throat.

Opening his mouth to speak, he grunted as Sul pushed him back. His eyes narrowed, but the bright orange quills on Sul's arm vibrated dangerously, and Ceps said nothing.

"The time has come for action," Sul shouted, and a small cheer erupted from the crowd. Several amongst the group didn't even know the plan, nor care. All the motivation they needed to be on board was the permission to torture humans and feel their pain, free from responsibility or consequences. "We need to find the half-breed and bring her here."

"How?"

Sul's black eyes glimmered as she glanced at the Tenebrian

who spoke. “She came to Earth once and will do it again.” She smiled, and it twisted her expression unpleasantly. “Humans are pathetic, predictable beings.”

The others threw in their thoughts. “We’ve waited long enough.”

“What if she does not go back?” One snorted.

Sul turned to me. “We are patient, are we not?”

“Always,” I answered.

“If we do not act immediately, perhaps they will think there is no threat.”

I bared my teeth. “Agreed.”

“Wait before going to Earth and finding the human lover...” We were almost toe to toe as she grinned, and I mirrored the expression. “Then make him bleed.”

Chapter Thirty-Two

Cael

Ana sighed heavily as I draped my arms around her body and pulled her back against my chest. We stood outside our sleeping quarters, looking at the stars and the brightness of the galaxies on display across the night sky.

"Are you okay?" I asked for perhaps the sixth time, as my chin rested on her shoulder.

Ana sighed again, which elicited a smile from me. I knew her well enough to know the first sigh was real, and the second was simply for dramatic effect.

"It's been a hell of a day," she said.

I shrugged. "Don't know what you mean."

Ana smiled. "Sarcasm. How very human of you." Her cheek moved against mine as the smile fell from her face. "I remember when I first found out who you were." I hummed in acknowledgment, and Ana continued, "I think it was then I realized that I loved you."

I hummed again and pressed my lips to Ana's neck, making her squirm as my scales tickled her soft skin. "What makes you say that?"

"Even though I didn't understand, I could feel who you were when you finally let that wall down, and all it did was strengthen the connection we already had." She chuckled. "Turns out my whole life after my parents were gone, no one knew who... *what* I was, not even me. Until you did."

Ana didn't need to lead the conversation like this, although I always enjoyed hearing how much she loved me. I pressed forward and asked, "Do you think Samael should be allowed to be with David?"

"I'm wondering if we should at least let them give it a go."

"Ana, you know it's complicated."

"I know that, but at least they have a choice. You and I were thrown into a situation and dealt with it the best we could. Finding love through that was luck."

"Maybe it was fate."

Her smile returned. "Maybe it was."

I kissed her neck again and let my lips drag along her skin. "Can we talk about this later?"

Ana sighed again as I traced the outline of her scales down her stomach and over her hip bones with my fingers. "Cael, we really should talk about—" Her sentence turned to a gasp as I pressed a hand between her legs and applied pressure in the perfect spot that I knew so well. She gripped my forearms as I focused my attention and used one hand to hold her hips still as she started to move against me. Breathing in deeply through my nose, I let her intoxicate me, and allowed her essence to seep through my fingers and skin. I couldn't ever imagine being with anyone else, especially when we were intertwined like this. She was everything that made me complete.

Ana writhed against my busy fingers, and I inhaled again as

she whispered, "Please."

"Shall we go inside?"

"Yes." Her response was a breathy whisper, but she made no attempt to move inside and continued to grind her hips against my hand. "Just... *please.*"

Smiling against her neck, a low chuckle rumbled in my throat, and with a slight twist, I maneuvered my fingers while I wrapped my other arm tighter around her waist. I pressed two fingers inside her, and the warmth of her walls pressed against my fingers as she trembled in my arms. My thumb brushed over her clit, and as Ana shook with her impending release, I jerked her body tight against mine. In contrast to the first time we were together, I didn't hold back anymore, and the impact of the motion knocked the breath from her. She laughed breathlessly before she moaned, and covered her mouth with her hand as her orgasm hit unexpectedly fast.

Completely wrapped up in the feel of her and the skin-on-skin contact, the air changed swiftly around us, and we were enclosed in our bubble of time. I let go and let our essences blend and mix together. There was no one else in this space. This space was ours. I didn't give Ana much chance to recover and dragged her backward into our shared quarters. It was still early at night, and we had the room to ourselves. Pushing her chest to the wall, I pressed my body against hers, but hesitated when she tensed up.

"Are you okay?"

"Yeah," Ana panted. "It's nothing, just don't stop."

I probed her essence and pinpointed the fleeting moment of fear that had caused her to tense. I didn't need to ask what it was. I knew her every thought.

No matter the years that passed, the trauma from her night with Nathaniel was harshly imprinted on her mind, and along with that was the fear from when Ed had attacked her. My instinct had been to move back and give her space immediately, but Ana didn't want to be coddled, she wanted to be pushed. She didn't want to let the fear win. I sensed as she shoved the fear from her mind and released a contented sigh, and I took a moment to marvel at the mastery she mostly had on her powers before she pressed her perfect ass against my groin and I groaned.

"My Cael," she whispered as the tension evaporated from her skin.

Steadying Ana with one arm still around her torso so her breasts brushed my skin, I used my other hand to lift her leg. She opened for me, welcomed me with a stretch of her legs, and lifted herself onto her toes. I lifted her slightly so her feet barely brushed the floor and thrust my hips forward, making her cry out as I penetrated her. We moaned together, and her toes curled.

This was raw us.

Watching Ana fight a Tenebrian had released the feelings I'd tried so hard to keep dormant. All those fears—*what if I lost her again?*—came to the surface and took over my body. The memories of the pain were so clear, scars on my heart that would never fully heal, and with a snarl I fucked Ana harshly. I used the feeling, and it drove me. Given time to think about it, I'd have held back. But I knew Ana was stronger than she was all those years ago, stronger than me, and she could take everything I had to give and more.

Ana slammed her forearms against the wall to steady herself

as I thrust into her, *hard*, over and over again, as she gripped me. She moaned loudly and freely as I took her, and the sense of her need swirled around with my own. She knew that the fight on Earth had shaken me. Ana would be able to feel it as clearly as though she could read my thoughts.

As much as I needed her, she needed me too.

Pressing my face into the crook of her neck and shoulder, my sweat dripped onto her skin as I took her relentlessly, and her legs dangled and her back arched as she took my cock so perfectly.

"So perfect," I mumbled against her skin, and groaned as she gripped me tightly.

"Cael..." She panted and said my name again and again. I only grunted in response as I barely held on to my control. Pulling out roughly, I spun her around, kissed her, and bit her neck before I bent to hook my arms under her knees. Standing, I lifted Ana against the wall and lowered her onto me. Instinctively, Ana wrapped her arms around my neck as her back hit the wall with an audible thud with every thrust. She was so open to me, so exposed on so many levels, and I wouldn't have it any other way. Ana allowed herself to come undone under my touch, and my senses blurred as the physical and emotional connection fogged my mind. Ana frantically rubbed at her clit, and screamed as I gripped her ass in my palms. When she came, I cried out as I reached my peak and spilled inside her.

Breathing heavily, I leaned against Ana as she stroked my back and tilted her head against mine. We stayed like that for a long while and fell into the feel of each other.

"Did I hurt you?" I asked, and brushed my lips over the tops of her breasts.

"Never." She kissed my neck, then patted my shoulder until I lowered her to the ground. When she stumbled a bit, I caught her as she laughed quietly. "Legs a bit unsteady."

"Do you need to lie down?" I crooned, and Ana laughed breathlessly again.

Chuckling, I guided her to the bed, lay down next to her, and curled around her, her back against my chest. "I love you," I murmured, then kissed her neck and shoulder. "Sometimes it still feels strange to know that."

"To know that you love me?"

"To know that I *can* love in this way. As though I would cease to exist without you."

"Love is pretty amazing."

I inhaled her essence again and sighed. "Love is amazing when you've felt other emotions your entire life. Imagine *not,* and then the first thing you feel is love."

"Is that the first thing you felt?"

"I didn't know what it was, but I think I loved you the moment I saw you."

Ana wiggled until she was cuddled against me as close as she could get, and curled her fingers into mine. "Maybe you loved me from the first moment I squeezed my boobs together for you."

"Maybe." I chuckled, then grunted as she elbowed me. "I love you, Ana."

"I love you, too, Cael."

Sighing into my embrace, she fell asleep quickly.

Sleep took longer to come to me, and while I listened to the sounds of her slumber, I was plagued with thoughts of the unknown. The interest the Tenebrian had taken in Ana unsettled me, and Samael's fears of David's safety told me I wouldn't be able to stop him from returning.

I couldn't lose Ana again, I simply couldn't.

She must stay here. I had to protect her. I had to protect them both.

But *how?*

With another sigh, sleep's embrace pulled at me as Ana's inner calm infected me, and I soon succumbed.

Chapter Thirty-Three

Ana

"Absolutely *not.*" Cael rarely raised his voice, and the shock settled over me while my arms dangled uselessly at my sides. I felt as though I should be gripping my fists in rage, or grabbing his shoulders and shaking some sense into him. But instead, I stood still as my jaw dropped. It wasn't only his tone that threw me, it was the wave of anger that followed. The anger was followed almost immediately by a tidal wave of fear that nearly had me stepping back from him.

"Cael..." I started, half expecting him to interrupt me before I could say what I wanted to say. His stern glare was enough for the words to be lost in my throat. "I... I have to know."

"You've waited this long. Until now, you've shown little interest in finding out about your father." He sighed and brushed down the raised scales on his forearms with a huff. "Until we know what's happening, I don't want you back on Earth. It can wait."

"But—"

"It can *wait.*" He snarled through the last word, and my brows furrowed.

"Cae—"

"No."

"What if they kill him?" I blurted the question out as I threw my arms up in frustration. Cael stared at me, and I took a step closer to him. "Whatever is going on—because you and I both know *something* is going on, even if the Elders deny it. Whatever it is, what if John gets caught up in it and is killed?" I sucked in a heavy breath and squeezed my eyes shut. It cut something into my chest when the realization that my most pressing concern, if John died, would be the information lost with him. *Of course,* I cared about him as a being, but now that the carrot of knowledge of my father had been dangled in front of me, I had to have it. "You're right. I never cared about my father before, and didn't think I ever would. But knowing someone who knew the truth was *so close* my entire life, just..." My hands clenched at my sides then, and I started when Cael wrapped his hand around my fist and waited until I tangled my fingers with his. "I have to know."

"Your powers," he offered weakly. "The Tenebrians..."

I nodded as I remembered the feel of power that ploughed through my veins when I'd fought the Tenebrian. Thinking Samael was in trouble was like something snapped inside me, and both sides of me fought for dominance. I could feel it, something deep inside, burning bright and moments away from being let free.

"I'll go see John, and then come home."

"I'm coming with you."

"No." I placed my fingers over his lips when he tried to reply. "I have to do this alone."

Cael grabbed my wrist. "Then I'll be watching," he snarled.

At my narrowed eyes, he sighed and added, "The building. I'll watch the building and be alert for energy changes."

"Fine."

Cael grabbed my hand, led me to a more secluded area of the community, and waited while I shifted into my human form. I paused before dressing long enough to brush my hands over my breasts, stomach, and arms, and looked up to see Cael's gaze following the movement. While I smirked at him, his lip lifted into a half smile. Cael opened a Gateway with a sweep of his hands and took a moment to position it somewhere quiet near John's home. Without a word, we stared at each other until he indicated the Gateway with the smallest jerk of his head, and I nodded, kissed him, and stepped through.

My human form stayed stubbornly intact, and even when I relinquished my concentration for a moment, it didn't waver. The Gateway shut behind me soundlessly, but I sensed its closure and closed my eyes. I could almost imagine feeling Cael's gaze on me through a Porthole. I trusted him enough to know he wouldn't intrude on the room where I would talk to John. He knew this was something I needed to do on my own.

Before I could chicken out, I moved swiftly toward John's home, climbed the stairs, and knocked.

Following John's grunt, I entered the dark apartment with a notably more timid nature than I had the last time I was here, and closed the door gently behind me.

"John?" I squinted into the dim light and turned when the orange glow from a cigarette briefly illuminated John's hands in the corner of the room. He flicked on a table lamp as I approached, sat on the couch next to him, and tucked my hands under my legs to stop myself from fidgeting.

There was no question about why I was nervous, and I knew that John also knew. But old habits of concealing my inner feelings still ran deep, and hiding was something I still used as a defense mechanism.

I'd admit it to myself, but that didn't mean I'd admit it to anyone else.

I sighed as I tried to find the words to start the conversation. John didn't ask why I was here, of course, he knew already. He grunted again and turned his head away so he wasn't blowing smoke toward me, and his following sigh was heavy as he stubbed out the cigarette into a brown glass ashtray.

"Ana..." he said while I was still trying to get the words out. "Your father..." He paused, seeming to collect himself. "... Roger. He loved you."

My spine straightened as I steeled myself against the emotion that rose in my chest. "He left me, John. He left *us.* My mother and I. He left us alone."

"He loved you and Bronte very much."

"Then why did he go?"

John sighed again, as though no amount of preparation could've made this moment any easier when it finally came. Did he know that someday we'd be having this conversation? Was it only a matter of time before I stumbled across him and he was forced to confess? Or were these words he'd assumed would never pass his lips? A secret he kept with him until the day he died.

"When you were born," he started, and I held his gaze, trying unsuccessfully to keep the judgment from my expression. "He didn't know how much human and Guardian you would be. He wanted you to be raised and to live on Earth, but he feared his presence alone would be enough to make the Guardian side dominant, so he kept his distance." John lit another cigarette but put it out before it even touched his lips. The secrets he had guarded were coming to the surface, and the struggle within him was evident as it flowed around him. For so long, he'd pushed it all to the side and lived on Earth, keeping in touch indirectly with his homeland and beings by adopting this role. But it was as though now he was letting the walls down all at once and opening his chest for the entire world to see. He was so good at hiding that he'd managed to hide from the Guardians for decades. But the fact that I could read his imprint and essence now meant he was laid bare to me, and my chest twisted as the act's implications cemented.

He *cared.*

John shuddered, though it wasn't cold. "Roger stayed around long enough for you to hit puberty, then when he was sure your human half was dominant, he decided it was best he wasn't around."

"Nice of him to decide that for both of us." I had to remind myself this wasn't John's fault, and sighed. "Why didn't he come back when Mom died?"

"I suspect he didn't know how to explain everything to you."

"That's a cop-out. He could have at least tried."

John only watched me. "I'm sorry, I don't have all the answers. I'm trying to help."

Swiping angrily at a stray tear on my cheek, I took a deep breath before I asked, "But you two were friends?"

John nodded. "This is not the first generation of Guardians to question the Elders, though there seems to be more now. Some of us have long since suspected that humanity is stronger and more valuable as beings beyond keeping the Balance. The Elders were insistent on having us keep our distance from humanity, and that wasn't enough for some. Unfortunately, the questioning of the way things have always been has given rise to two opposing sides. The side that wants to learn more about humans and be with them on a deeper level... predominantly Lucidians, and the Tenebrians who seem intent on causing more chaos than before, realizing humans' fear feels good to them..."

"There's more to it than that now."

John stared at me. "Now there is, yes, I agree. There have always been small rebellious groups acting only for their own pleasure, but that's all it was back then. I can only theorize what they're up to now. It seems bigger. But none of the ideas that come to mind are good."

"Tell me. Worst-case scenario."

"You didn't come here to discuss that."

"Tell me anyway." Whatever was going on, the Tenebrian had shown interest in me and Samael before I'd fought them off. Somehow, whatever was happening, I was tangled up in it.

What if I were the *cause* of it?

The thought struck me like a knife through my chest, and my next breath caught in my throat.

What if Ignis's death was somehow important to the Tenebrians, and they held me responsible?

What if *all of this* was some rebellion against his death?

All those people may have been hurt because of me.

"Worst case scenario? They're trying to tip the Balance."

I snapped my eyes back to John. "*What?*"

"The Shift. They're trying to bring it on."

"Why the hell would they do that? Isn't that world-ending type shit?"

John landed a hand gently on my arm and patted it awkwardly before he retreated from the contact. "It's only a theory. You asked for a worst-case scenario."

"Right, right." But I couldn't keep my thoughts straight.

"Don't hate me for this, Ana." My gaze snapped to his as his shoulders dropped. "Your father fell in love with your mother during a mission to Earth, to stop..." He hesitated. "... to stop me."

"John..." My voice was edged in warning. If he'd killed people, I don't think I could ever forgive him.

"I think he felt my hesitation in my work here when he cornered me. I was here as part of a small group, and Roger knew if I went home to Tenebris, the others would sense my hesitation, too. They'd probably tear me apart."

"So, you didn't kill anyone for the pleasure?"

His eyes widened, suddenly filled with an innocence I hadn't seen before, usually hidden behind all the secrets that clouded his eyes. "Never."

"Didn't the Tenebrians come looking for you when you stayed on Earth?"

John gave me a look that suggested it was a stupid question, then shrugged. "At first. You think the beings in the communities of Lucidis are distant from each other? In Tenebris, connections are nonexistent, and there is no sense of community. Each Guardian for themselves. They fill their days getting kicks by torturing the Reflections and sometimes each other. They didn't care enough to try too hard to find me."

"They came after Nathaniel when he was causing chaos, so

why haven't they done anything this time? There's so much going on right now."

"I told you, Ana, things are changing. They've either stopped caring, or they're..."

"Planning something bigger together," I finished. John nodded, and I asked, "When the Tenebrians come here, do you help them?"

"I have to. I'm meant to be an impartial party."

"Don't they sense who you are?"

He laughed then. "Ana, they think I'm human. They barely look at me. But I'm touched you care for my well-being." He chuckled again, patted my knee, then withdrew his hand from the contact a second later.

It had felt natural for a moment, and I'd been comfortable with John.

Like I knew him.

I paused as a memory rushed back to me, so strong and clear I couldn't believe I'd forgotten it.

I, as a small child in a playground, with my father, my mother, and—

"Uncle John," I whispered.

The color drained from John's face. "What did you say?"

"I remember you. You were there when I was young."

While John smiled sadly, his eyes betrayed the emotions he battled internally. My instincts tore into two conflicting actions—hug him, or draw away from him for lying and hiding from me for so long. In that moment, in his eyes, I was the small child who had shown him my dolls, listened when he read me stories, and laughed at the silly voices he used to make. It all came back. My entire body tensed as he dropped whatever walls he had left, and as his essence washed over me, I remembered.

"You taught me two things, Ana," he whispered, and this time I didn't bother to wipe the tears from my cheeks. "What it meant to love unconditionally, and what it felt like to have my heart torn from my chest when I had to leave."

"John..." I wanted to understand. I *did* understand. But it still hurt.

"I made a promise to Roger. My presence would strengthen and bring out your Guardian side as much as his. It was the hardest thing I'd ever done, but I had to leave, too. It hurt so much to leave a loved one again. I'm sorry, Anahera, my angel."

I choked back a heavy sob. "My parents used to call me that, too."

All the memories that had escaped my mind like grains of sand through my fingers were back, building sand castles where even the tides of time couldn't wash them away. But with it came the pain, fresh and spiking against my heavy heart as though it had happened only hours before. I looked around the room again, seeking something to distract me. Instead, my eyes landed on a painted portrait of a woman. I'd seen it on the way in, but hadn't given it a second glance. I studied it, and a furrow pinched my brow as something tugged on my heart again. The similarities were too striking, and I'm certain the painting was of my mother.

Or perhaps it was how he imagined I'd grow up to look. I glanced at John, who had followed my gaze, and I held back from asking about the painting, instead realizing that every brush stroke contained the pain he'd lived with.

No one had come away from this unscarred.

But there was still one pressing question.

"So..." I swallowed heavily and wiped my face again, "... where is he now?"

"Abroad? I honestly don't know. I would tell you if I knew, Ana," he added after the look I gave him. "I'd like to think if he died, I'd feel it." He looked at his hands. "But I'm not so sure anymore."

I took his hands in mine, and John didn't pull away this time. He also didn't resist as the warmth spread from my fingertips against his palm, reading him and pushing my essence into his.

"I'm telling you the truth," he whispered, misinterpreting my intent. I only wished to calm him, to soothe his pain.

"I know."

I stopped the energy flow but continued to hold his hands, feeling his rough skin under my fingertips and tracing the weathered lines on his palm. He looked at me with an expression I couldn't place, but from the feelings swirling around us, it felt like regret.

This is a lot. I need to think.

Abruptly, I stood. "I should get going." On a whim, I bent down to kiss his cheek quickly. "Thank you."

"What will you do with what I've told you?"

I looked at him with a sad smile. "What can I do, John?"

"Sense him, find him. You sensed me. You might be able to locate him."

"If he's been on Earth this whole time, if he's abroad..."

"Not from here, search from Lucidis."

"I don't know if I can..."

"Maybe not, but if you want to, you can try. He's your father, so it would be like sensing yourself."

I nodded at his words, but my skin itched to leave. I needed peace and emptiness. I needed to let my mind catch up on all the new memories and information. I would discuss John's suspicions with Cael soon, but first, I needed to simply *be.*

As I turned to leave, John called out, "Ana." I turned to face him, and he said, "Be careful. Something is brewing. We can't be sure what. But whatever it is... It's bigger than us."

"Do I need to be on the lookout for anything in particular?"

"Just keep your senses sharp." I nodded and made my way toward the door. "Where are you going?" John asked.

"Home."

"Be careful."

"I will." I hesitated, then smiled sadly. "Thank you, Uncle John."

John nodded and watched me leave, and before I closed the door, the rush of his emotions hit me in the back.

Grateful. Thankful. Love. Hurt. Guilt.

And *fear.*

Chapter Thirty-Four

Samael

Coming around a corner, I found my parents in a tight embrace, and Mother had her face buried in the crook of Dad's shoulder. I slowed my steps, but continued toward them when Dad looked up and nodded at me. Mother smiled at me as I approached, but her smile was hollow.

"I need some time to think," she said to Dad as she pulled away and brushed her fingers down his arm. Dad nodded and squeezed her fingers before dropping the contact, a deep furrow between his brows as she moved away.

There was no easy way to say what I needed to say, so once Mother was out of earshot, I blurted out, "I'm going back for him."

Dad rounded on me, and while his lip twitched, I could sense he was at least attempting to cover his anger. "What do you mean you're going back for him?"

My lip twisted. "I meant what I said. Why do you *think* I want to go back?"

"I don't think you understand what you're getting yourself into, Samael. What are you going to do? Hide your identity from him forever?"

"No..." Discomfort clawed at my skin. "I'll tell him one day."

"And you know him well enough to know that'll work? That he'll love you once he knows you're not human?"

"Mother loves *you*."

"That's different," Dad said.

"How, Dad?" I snapped, letting my anger filter out. "How is it different? You didn't know she was a half-breed when you fell for her, and she still loved you even after finding out who you were, *and* who she was."

Dad glared at me and offered no answer. I was part human. No matter how much time I spent trying to hide or deny it when I was younger, everyone knew it, and no one knew it better than my parents and me. Eventually, I was bound to feel things intensely, and the chances that those feelings would create complications always existed as a potential.

But Dad still doesn't want me to seek a relationship with a human.

I looked up as Dad sighed, sadness in my eyes as his gaze bore into mine. "Don't think because I'm not part human like you and your mother, I don't understand." I turned my head away and squeezed my eyes shut as he continued, "You're seeking an emotional connection that few Guardians could provide you. But your mother and I... it was different. A relationship with a full-blood human is doomed to fail. Either you would have to give up your powers and live on Earth, or you and David would have to be content with only seeing each other for brief periods, for the rest of your lives." I didn't reply and bit my tongue against the torrent of responses I could say, which would help nothing. Dad stepped forward. "I'm trying to protect you."

"I know you are." I released a heavy breath. "I didn't plan for this, Dad, and who knows? Maybe it won't last forever. But there's something between us, and I need to explore it, or I'll regret it."

"We need to talk to your mother first."

After our last trip to Earth, I hesitated. She wouldn't want me to go. "Okay."

"If you leave without telling her again, she'll lose her mind," Dad warned.

"Dad, I know. I said okay."

Dad turned back toward the community center, and I felt him sweep the area mentally as he searched for Mother's emotional pattern.

His brows furrowed, and he tried again.

"Dad?" I asked as I watched the crease between his brows deepen.

"I can't find her."

We looked at each other, and without turning, I also sent out my senses for her.

Nothing.

"You don't think she went back to Earth, do you?"

Dad dropped his shoulders and looked up at the sky as his lips pressed together. "Goddammit. John."

"She went back for John? Why?"

"He knew her father."

"What? When were you going to tell me this?"

Dad snarled. "We had more important things to deal with. She was *just* there. She must've gone back to ask more questions." Dad ran his hand over his face as my head swam with this information.

"We should go get her," I said.

Dad narrowed his eyes at me. "I should go."

"She'll be difficult to trace, we should at least go together."

Dad nodded, and gripping my elbow, we allowed our senses to mingle as he opened a Porthole and we tried to locate her on Earth. She was difficult to pinpoint, but we started near John's place. I frowned when I couldn't feel her, and Dad shook his head and changed his stance to turn the Porthole into a Gateway.

"Wait." Dad stopped, and I looked between him and the abandoned Gateway as it collapsed.

"What's wrong?" As soon as the words left my lips, I felt the ripples through the air.

In unison, we turned toward the community. Something was happening on Earth. Something strong enough to create a significant shift of negativity against the Balance.

The Tenebrians were doing something.

Dad opened his mouth to speak, but no words came. His hold on his emotions fell, and I felt guilt drop onto his shoulders and crush his chest.

Duty vs love.

His voice shook as he said, "You go."

"What?"

"I'm going to help here, then I'll come for you and your mother."

"Dad..."

"Go find your mother, and bring her home. Then you can..." His fists gripped and released by his sides. "Find David, and make sure he's safe too. Something is happening."

I stumbled as an aftershock pushed me back. Dad hadn't

moved, but continued to glare toward the community. "Maybe you should go, and I'll stay here."

Dad shook his head without making eye contact with me, and the battle of wills he fought within himself continued to rage. "No, you go get your mother. I'm needed here. Besides..." He turned to me with a pained expression. "You're better at hiding your essence than I am. Do it when you're on Earth. Hide as deep as you can." When I looked at him, Dad threw his arms up. "Don't look at me like that. I'm trying to do the right thing, but all decisions feel wrong." He trembled as his inner war raged on, and this time, when the aftershock of power came, he too stepped back. "Make sure your mother is okay, send her home, then find David. Okay?"

"Dad—"

"*Okay?*" Dad's conflict surged inside him, fighting when every decision forced him to face another one, until the air around him rippled with anger, fear, and confusion. Without thinking, I grabbed him and brought him in for a brief but intense hug that said everything I couldn't with words.

Dad's eyes shone. "Go." He turned and ran back toward the community, and I opened a Gateway.

Chapter Thirty-Five

Culo

Pulling my long blond hair into a ponytail as I walked, I didn't break stride to acknowledge the women who admired me as I passed. I had a destination, and while I'm sure I could talk one or more of them into a quick stop in a side alley, I was headed for a shopping mall in the heart of the city.

We had big plans for the humans there.

Tenebrians didn't usually resort to using weapons, preferring our hands, or perhaps blades in a pinch. The close contact you can get with someone as you squeeze the life and fear out of them can't be achieved with a gun. However, these were different times, and the goal was to inflict maximum damage in the shortest time. While humans were primitive, their weapons were certainly effective.

Catching the eye of a young woman as I walked, arm in arm with another man, I allowed my eye contact to linger and forced my influence into my essence around me. Mesmerized by me for reasons she couldn't explain, she didn't even blink when I swept her along with me as I passed, and her arm broke link from her partner. He yelled after her, but we didn't stop. After a few more steps where the sound of her partner turning to catch up made me smirk, I spun her around and dipped her down as if our stride had been a dance of seduction, and kissed her deeply. She ran her hands up my back, and when her fingers gripped the fabric and curled around the weapons hidden beneath my coat, the spell was broken.

With a gasp, she pulled away from me, and I didn't care enough to stop her and let her drop to the ground before she scrambled away. Laughing, I kept walking and listened to them argue as the negative ripples of the chaos hit my back.

As I rounded the corner into the mall, I pushed groups of people out of my way. I knew the spot—we had been here before to find the most advantageous place to make our move. According to Vikt's contact, there were specific points on Earth where the damage would be magnified, where points of human contact converged and created almost a mini-Balance on the surface. Entering the shopping center, I approached the meeting point as if I owned it. Because today, we did.

Once gathered, I stood back-to-back with the other three Tenebrians in the mall's center while the crowds on the second-story balcony looked down upon us. Humans started to gather, their curiosity piqued at the small group of men and women in black coats.

"What's going on?"

"Maybe it's one of those flash mobs?"

"Cool."

We waited as the crowd increased, and I smiled at the floor—the humans were so stupid, like moths to a flame. We made our move before the humans got bored and started drifting away.

The Bowie knives were drawn from under our coats in one synchronized move, and we each brandished one large blade in each hand. The female Guardian, Aisha, present, raised her head and watched the crowd.

They didn't move.

Did they not sense the danger they were in? Or were they just hypnotized by the speed of our movements?

It didn't matter. They were there, and they were prey.

A middle-aged man at the front of the crowd cleared his throat. "Listen, I don't think you're supposed to have those knives here."

Aisha flicked her hair over her shoulder and eyed the man. "What?"

"I'm sorry, I just meant—"

In the blink of an eye, she was in front of him, and his sentence cut off as she drew the blade across his throat. Warm blood spilled out of the wound as the blade crossed from one ear to the other, opening the skin up and covering his shirt and the floor in the sticky liquid. His hands scrambled uselessly toward the wound, trying to hold together the sliced skin, and he dropped to his knees. When he fell into the puddle of his blood, the shock of the scene broke.

Then the screaming started.

We reacted immediately, and chaos broke out in the mall as people ran for the exits, desperate to be away from the maniacal beings and their knives. The elegance of our moves went unnoticed by the pathetic humans, who were driven only by their survival instincts and desperation for escape.

A young woman slipped on a puddle of blood, twisted her ankle, and cried out in pain as she struggled to regain her footing before my knife penetrated between her shoulder blades. A security guard launched an untrained attack at me, only to be thrown into a pillar hard enough to break his spine before he crumpled to the floor in a twisted heap, one leg bent over his torso at an unnatural angle.

The screams carried the wave of terror out of the building and across the city as people fled, and those unlucky enough to be left behind were killed. Sometimes quickly, other times slowly and painfully. I glanced over to see Ceps as he watched the fear in his victim's eyes drain away before it was replaced with an empty stare as he removed his blade from their stomach and kicked the body away from him.

My fingers found the cool trigger of the gun I'd stolen from a farmer outside the city. The theft caused repercussions in the small community, furthering the negative influence we intended to spread. Everything we did, even the actions leading up to the planned ones, only helped our cause. Having never fired a gun before, I held it with my arms outstretched, and my shoulder was thrown back with the kick from the weapon. Crying out in rage as the bullet ricocheted off the ceiling, I proceeded to use the gun as a club, and brought it down across the heads of humans as they tried to flee, hard enough to break the wooden stock. I tried again, and this time planted the weapon against my shoulder. It still kicked, but the resounding shot echoed throughout the mall's center as two people fell. Those close enough to be hit with debris and bone fragments from the bodies screamed anew.

The police arrived quickly, but not quickly enough. Upon hearing the sirens, we separated, created Gateways within the mall, and stepped through them to go home.

Chuckling as my feet hit the dusty ground of home, I dropped the gun and turned to open a Porthole to watch the chaos unfold. As the screams died down and the area was cordoned off, the authorities stared at the dozens of people who had been maimed and killed, bodies spread across the floor. Several officers fled the building and slipped on the mixture of blood and innards in their desperation to be outside before they vomited. Some made it outside in time, others didn't.

Ceps came up next to me, and we offered each other a knowing glance as we watched news vans and helicopters arrive. The entire area surrounding the mall was teeming with reporters and emergency workers as the police tried unsuccessfully to secure the extended perimeter.

The fog of fear and pain across the city was thick, and with every news report witnessed, it would get worse.

Power stabbed into my back, and I turned to find a small group of Elders watching us.

"Shit," I muttered.

Ceps's eyes narrowed. "Why aren't they acting?"

The Elders watched us watch them, and neither of us moved. This was the most significant disturbance we'd caused in one area, and while we suspected they knew our other attacks weren't random, surely they could no longer ignore it.

An Elder took a step toward us and raised their hand. But before they could speak, a moonstone blade was driven into their spine by one of the Elders behind them.

Ceps and I stilled as the Elder who'd attacked nodded and moved away with the others.

Elation filled my body.

Some of the Elders were turning.

Without fear of repercussion, Ceps and I turned back to watch the chaos unfold, shifting the Porthole location to see how far the ripples had spread. Panic spread across the country as local and national news reporters teamed up and swapped information. Live streaming from private cell phones had brought the event's magnitude to light.

Because it wasn't only one attack.

With the help of her contact, Vikt had arranged twelve, and they all occurred at the exact time across the country, all in public places, and all with four people and weapons killing random members of the public.

The reporters had no answers, and the police were of no help. Who were these people? Why were they launching these attacks? Before the attacks, there had been no ransoms or chatter on the internet or social media. It was an exquisitely planned, well-coordinated, and flawlessly executed attack with no known motive and no suspects.

The news spread fast, and humans were afraid.

Chapter Thirty-Six

Ana

It took me several attempts to open the Gateway and then several more to position it correctly. Each time it sparked and fizzled out, my ability to concentrate died with it, and I had to take some moments to re-center myself before I could try again. All the confidence I'd held while I'd practiced with Cael vanished the moment there was some importance or intent to what I was doing.

Each time it fizzled out, I thought I'd attract attention.

But no one came. Maybe my Gateways weren't big enough to be on the Guardian's radar, or because Gateways were regularly opening and closing across the community.

After the discussion with John, my mind was left muddled. Beyond the talk of my father were John's theories on the Tenebrian activity, which mingled with their apparent interest in me. Despite the voice in my head that screamed insistently at me, *Earth was not the place I should be right now*. I needed to clear my mind.

And as much as Lucidis was home now, Earth would always be special.

When I tried to clear my head of all intrusive thoughts so I could focus on what John had said, only thinking of Samael and Cael made sense.

Samael had found love, and I'd decided to see David for myself.

After I'd opened a Gateway and once on Earth, I walked slowly. I was concentrating on so many factors that I occasionally forgot to watch where I was going and walked into someone. I didn't want to be recognized, and perhaps I was overthinking it, but I looked down and pulled my cap down further as I let my now brunette hair fall in front of my face.

I needed to find David, and focused on the imprint left on him after he'd been close to Samael. However, I also needed to focus on maintaining my human form. Although it held perfectly last time—and I must remember to gloat to Cael about that—my mind was plagued with paranoia of my apparently uncertain powers. I could feel them inside me, and I also focused on keeping them steady.

So far, so good.

After apologizing again for having my shoulder hit a passerby, I made more effort to look where I was going. I knew these streets, these shops, and these buildings. Although so much had changed in the decades since I'd wandered this city, it still felt the same. Being here, my heart ached for the life I could've had. I wouldn't change having Cael or Samael for the world, but if I hadn't sacrificed everything, and if Cael and I were somehow able to live our lives here, how would things have been? Would Samael have felt more at home, or would his Guardian side pose more of an issue than his human side in Lucidis?

Would Cael have had to make the same decision my father

did, and leave so Samael could be human?

My lip trembled as emotion threatened to take over me, and I hastily regained control of myself, remembering what Cael said about my effect on people if I was close and feeling things too strongly.

Getting upset about a hypothetical situation wasn't helping anyone.

Weaving in and out of the crowd, I made my way to what I assumed must be David's townhouse. Samael's imprint was in and around the house, where he had smiled and felt the hints of love, and it lingered strongly. As I got closer, I clutched my chest. Not only *hints* of love, but *real* love.

I wondered if Samael had told David how he felt.

After knocking on the door, I rubbed my hands together, started fidgeting, and rolled my necklace pendant between my fingers.

Meeting your child's partner, isn't this something all parents dealt with at some point?

I can do this. I'm just as strong and controlled as other parents are.

Think of all the things I've dealt with that most people couldn't even imagine.

But, the voice in my head reminded me, *most parents don't meet their children's romantic partners by stalking their essence through the city streets.*

"Fuck," I muttered under my breath. What the hell was I thinking?

David opened the door before I could turn and run away like a child playing ding-dong-ditch, and smiled warmly. I knew it was David immediately. Samael's essence was all over him.

"Hi, can I help you?" he asked, his voice quiet but strong.

"Hi, um..." I brushed my fingers through my short hair. "I'm looking for David."

"You found him. Have we met?" There was no malice in his voice, only curiosity.

"I'm Ana." I held out a hand. "Samael's mother."

David managed to cover his shock well, and his eyebrows lowered almost as quickly as he'd raised them. When he took my hand, an eyebrow cocked involuntarily, and I took the brief moment to read him through the skin-on-skin contact, before I let his hand go.

Confused. Closed off. Protected. Willing to love. Empathy.

"Oh, well, uh, come in." He stood back and extended an arm, closing the door behind me as he pointed before following me into the kitchen. "Would you like a drink?"

"Oh my God, yes please. Do you have any cola?"

I cringed inwardly as David's eyebrows rose again, and a half-smile adorned his face. "Yeah, sure."

When he handed me the can, I opened it with a satisfied groan, took a gulp, and muttered, "Oooh, it's been so long."

David sat across from me. "Wow, Samael said he lived out of town, but I didn't realize it was so remote that you had no soft drinks."

Chuckling, I took another swig and sighed happily as the bubbles played on my tongue. *Was it always this overly sweet?* "You have no idea." Placing the can on the counter, I added, "Sometimes someone from the community will bring back some from the city, or some chocolate, but it isn't often, and each time I forget how much I missed it."

We watched each other momentarily, scanning each other's

faces and features. "So..." David folded his arms on the counter and leaned forward while a playful smirk remained. "This is unusual. Samael and I haven't known each other very long."

"I know. I'm so sorry to drop in like this. I'm not even sure why I did..." I rubbed the back of my neck as I laughed awkwardly. "If I told you it was to see if you were a good person, you'd think I'm strange and overprotective. But then again, I'm not big on lying."

David nodded. "All right, if we're being honest, it's a little weird. But in saying that, Samael isn't like anyone I've ever met before. So I could only assume his family is a little... different."

I laughed again. "Nice safe word choice."

David smiled. "Can I ask you something?"

Shrugging, I said, "Go for it. I'm intruding on your home, after all."

"You *do not* look old enough to be his mother."

Unsuccessfully, I tried to brush my hair behind my ears, but it fell forward again. Lucidis had slowed my aging, and that combined with my mixed heritage meant that although I was almost fifty, I didn't look much beyond thirty. "Good genes, I guess."

"That's good to know. So Samael will be cute for a long time."

I smiled with a tilt of my head and focused on the air around David and how it had shifted when he'd spoken of Samael. "You really like him, don't you?"

"Yeah, I do." He watched me with narrowed eyes, but his smile didn't waver. "Aren't you going to give me the obligatory *if you hurt him* speech?"

"No." I fiddled with my pendant again. "Nothing like that. All I wanted was to meet you, nothing more. I like to think I'm good at getting a read on people."

"I get that sense from you," David said, "And now that you have met me?"

"And now I have, I can leave..." I stood and held out my hand again, "...and say thank you for your time, and ask that you not judge Samael by my actions, but do try to understand."

David took my hand and placed his other hand on top of it. "I do understand. Parents, eh?"

It was said with humor, but behind the words was sadness. I remembered the scene Samael had described to me with David's parents, and my chest constricted. My fingers twitched in his hold, and David held my gaze as if sensing I wanted to say something.

All I wanted to do was to hug him, like only a mother could.

As he smiled, I watched his face and felt the warmth flowing through him. I could see what Samael saw in him. He was hurting, there was pain under the surface, and he was a sea of contradictions—reserved and quiet but quick to open up to someone, humorous and cheeky, fast to hurt and slow to forgive. He was a complicated man, as many humans were, but beyond everything, he was kind, soft, and quiet—all the things that Samael was and made him his most human.

I grinned as I broke the contact between us. I didn't mind whether Samael chose a human or Guardian partner, but I was secretly proud he was drawn to *this* human.

In a world where I was still the odd one out and still finding my place after decades, every reminder that my son was mine was welcome.

"It was lovely to meet you, David."

"You too, Ana."

Given that my ability to relocate a Gateway was shaky at best, I decided to head back toward John's before going home. Meeting David had been more invigorating than I had hoped, and while I knew Guardians could feed off the essence of humans, I'd never done it. But simply being in David's presence had helped clear my mind, and aside from now having no doubts that David was a good person, my thoughts were also clearer as they worked their way through the jumble left after my discussion with John.

Step one was to go home and tell Cael of John's suspicions that the Tenebrians were attempting to shift the Balance. They may be nothing more than suspicions, and ultimately, Cael may not be able to do much about it when the Elders refuse to see the woods for the trees, but he needed to know.

Step two, figure out with Cael and Samael what the *fuck* we actually *could* do with whatever the Tenebrians were planning. Then, and only then, would I seek out my father. There were more important things to deal with than a long-lost family member who'd had decades to find me. Especially when it turned out he could have found me both in Lucidis and on Earth.

Sighing, the relaxing sensation of drawing the cool air into my lungs was replaced with a heavy weight on my chest that crushed the air from my lungs, as I stopped abruptly.

I'd felt him again, as clear as though he was standing right next to me.

David.

I hadn't gone too far. But David was in trouble. I didn't know how I knew, I just *knew.*

The sense of his fear crawled under my skin and into my being, and my breathing increased as I struggled to maintain control, aware that my feelings would affect those around me.

Should I get Cael and Samael and ask for help?

What if there wasn't time? David was in trouble *now.*

A spike in his fear brushed past me, before his pain drilled into my skin.

No time.

I ran.

Chapter Thirty-Seven

Vikt

Standing on the curb outside David's home, I tapped my fingers impatiently against my thigh. Incredibly, the half-breed had been here only moments before, and irritatingly, I had missed her. My attempt to follow her trail was stamped out as she was lost in the crowd of humans, and with a huff, I gave up. I doubted Ana was clever enough to mask herself on purpose, so the difficulty in tracing her must be another side effect of her mixed genes.

Grinning, I turned back to face David's home.

I didn't need to trace her because my lure was right before me.

Storming toward David's home, I shouted, "Come outside." And allowed my power of influence to travel through my voice and into the house. I hadn't bothered to direct my energies, and the occupants of the houses on either side of David's came into the street. After I snarled at them, they hastily retreated into their homes.

"Nicole?" David emerged onto the porch. "What's going on?" His brows were furrowed, and his hands twitched at his sides. I sneered—these pathetic beings never ceased to amaze me. He truly believed he'd come outside purely as a response to my words, and was completely unaware of the hidden power behind them.

"Come here." My voice was low and controlled.

David hesitated. It wasn't much, but it was enough to raise my eyebrows. Had Samael done something to him? Given him some protection? I shook my head rapidly. The young Lucidian didn't have knowledge of that sort of power, let alone the power itself. No, I was simply being faced with the will of the human himself.

"Are you okay?" David asked. He approached me willingly after his initial hesitation and stood within arm's reach of me.

Which was all I needed.

Grabbing his upper arms, I spun myself around, pulling David with me, and using my momentum, I hurled him onto the road. A small truck swerved to avoid him, horn blaring, while the driver slammed on the brakes. The wash of the metallic scent of blood was already in the air from David's hard fall, and after he removed his arms from covering his head when the truck swerved around him, he raised his wide eyes to me. David didn't speak as I approached him, but he attempted to push himself away from me, wincing when the movement further pushed the broken asphalt into the wounds on his arms. Scrambling to his feet, David held his fists before him, his hands trembling and eyes wide. I laughed.

"Nicole—"

It was as far as he got, and I put on a burst of speed and shouldered him. He fell back again, grunting as he skidded across the road. I bent to grab his hair and tilted his head back. I ignored the car that almost collided with us and didn't respond as the driver yelled out her window. David's eyes never left mine, and his hands gripped my wrist as I grabbed his neck. With a heave, I lifted him from the ground and swung him onto the bonnet of the car, baring my teeth. The sound of the metal as it buckled under his weight blended with the driver's scream as the horn abruptly cut off.

"If I wanted to, I could kill you," I whispered. David's eyes were wide with fear, but it wasn't enough. I pushed harder and let the negative forces within my being seep out. "How would it feel to your parents if you died right now? They never got to say they were sorry or hear you tell them you loved them one last time."

"You leave them out of this—" David's voice was cut off as I increased the pressure on his throat.

"Your little boyfriend Samael, I might kill him too. Maybe Logan as well, and anyone you've ever cared about. Because I can, and maybe I'll kill that mutt you live with. Maybe I'll make you watch."

"No." It was a protest, spoken quietly around the pressure on his neck. I chuckled as I let one fingernail transform back into my Tenebrian form and stretch into a claw. I punctured it through David's earlobe and pulled until he screamed as the lobe slowly separated from his head.

Inhaling deeply, I sighed with contentment. *Now* I could feel it, and the fear continued to come off him in waves. Confusion mixed in with the pain and fear, even as I stopped my assault. His eyes were manic as I ran three fingers through the blood on his neck and smeared it on his face. David didn't understand why this was happening, nor how I was so strong, and it all combined into a toxic soup of terror that radiated around him.

My chest heaved with elation as I turned on the driver of the car, and pulled her from the open window while David coughed where he lay on the bonnet. The woman screamed and started slapping and kicking uselessly at me, actions that stopped the moment I punched her—a lightning-quick shot to the nose. As I let her go, she clutched her face and dropped to the ground as blood oozed out between her fingers. The woman's nose was broken, severed almost, and she crawled away as quickly as she could before she was scooped up by a passerby who assisted her with an arm around her back. The pedestrian threw a guilty look back at David, obviously wanting to help him, too, but afraid to get close.

Fuck this felt good.

Turning back to David, I grabbed his collar before he could scramble to his feet as his hand clutched over his damaged ear. "Why are you doing this?" He asked, without raising his voice, and his maintained control enraged me.

I didn't even bother answering, and instead threw him a disinterested look. With a smirk, I shoved his hand away and tugged on his torn ear. He screamed, and I laughed.

Anger pulsed through him even as he tried to collect himself. "What did I ever do to you? I was nothing but nice to you." He leaned back as I grabbed his collar again, but his eyes didn't leave mine. "Even though you constantly tried to rope me and my friends into dangerous activities. That *you* thought were fun. It makes sense now I guess, you fucking psycho." His laugh was humorless.

"They *were* fun! Messing with humans is *always* fun." His eyes widened when I said *humans,* and I yanked him forward so our faces were an inch apart. "You are a tool, David. You are nothing but a tool, and humans will never be anything but tools. Now be a good boy and focus on the pain." I threw him to the ground again, and his palms tore on the pavement as he tried to break his fall, before I landed a kick to his gut, which had him rolling into a defensive position.

I could've sworn I felt her through the air as I looked up.

It wouldn't take long.

She would come for him.

Chapter Thirty-Eight

Cael

There was too much negativity.

All the acts from the Tenebrians had built up over the years. There was a pattern, I *knew* there was a pattern. Why didn't the Elders listen? Why were they so insistent that this was all regular activity?

Shaking my head as frustration clawed through me, I tried to focus on the job at hand, and attempted to keep the Balance rightened after the shopping center massacres. However, the intrusive thoughts continued to infiltrate my mind. The Elders had been steadfastly insistent that there was nothing bigger going on than the Tenebrians being up to their usual tricks. But the tilt in the Balance had rocked me to my core, and panic was spreading across the community. Everyone was at work because we could all feel it. The sensation of the Balance losing its hold had reverberated through our bones and itched under our skin. The acts had been placed across the entire country, creating a negative energy field that blanketed and contained the fog, causing it to fold on top of itself and become a self-feeding, ever-increasing mess.

It was no accident.

"Cael," I turned as Monia called me, interrupting my thoughts. "Where is Anahera?"

My brows pulled together as I tried to place her expression while the senses around her were clouded and confused. My fingers were still spread and aimed at the Porthole. "On Earth. Samael has gone to get her." When Monia simply watched me, I dropped my arms, and the Porthole closed with a swipe of air that lifted the scales on my shoulders. "She's in danger, isn't she?" I asked.

"She..." Monia trailed off, and there was another shift in the air.

I suspected.

I *knew.*

The truth hit me in the chest harder than the movement of the Balance, and I almost buckled.

I was being influenced.

We were being influenced.

Someone here was a traitor.

"How could I not have seen it?" Looking hopelessly back at the community center, I frowned as Cascus approached us. I watched him, and my eyes narrowed. He always seemed to be around when we were discussing Ana, so intent on controlling her, and knowing her every movement.

But then again, so did Monia.

Not my mother, she would never...

"Where is the human?" Cascus asked curtly.

"Anahera is on Earth," Monia said.

"So, she is out of the way."

"She might be in trouble," I said.

Cascus's shoulder twitched in what could've been a shrug. "I warned her. I told her she is not to go to Earth." He tilted his chin as he surveyed the chaos unfolding in the community. "She is of no concern. We have work to do here."

"Why do you hate her so much?" I forced my hands to unclench, not even realizing I had made fists.

"Because she does not belong here." Cascus looked into my eyes. "*Do not forget your place.*"

His attempt to influence me struck my senses, and I pressed my will forward as I took a step closer to Cascus. "I'm going to get her."

"Are you sure that is the best thing?" Monia's expression was still unreadable, as was her essence. "You are needed here."

"Do as you please," Cascus said, and left.

I stared after him, and tried to put the pieces together.

Ana was on Earth. Did the traitor want her on Earth or here?

Now that I had attuned myself to it, the sense of influence was palpable in the community's air. It was not strong enough to raise an alarm, but it was enough that I could find it if I searched for it.

Monia moved away to help a small group of Guardians battling negative forces through a Porthole, and I watched her as my mind raced. The chances of my being able to locate Ana or Samael on Earth with *this* fog would be nearly impossible. I tried to seek Sasha or Esco out in the crowd, but couldn't see them, and I'd need to link my powers to someone.

Groaning, I clutched at my head as if I could force the pieces into place by sheer willpower.

All this interest in Ana must be beyond her mixed heritage.

I'd allowed myself to fall victim to whatever blanket of

influence was over my home, and Ana—*oh Ana*—she was the *only* one who wasn't taken in by it. My suspicions were nothing more than bubbles under the surface of my mind, while Ana felt tidal waves of warning.

Mind made up, I spread my fingers and flicked open a Porthole.

Ana was safest here, with me.

Chapter Thirty-Nine

Ana

"*You,*" the bitch with pink hair stood over David next to an abandoned car as I struggled to recall her name. A small group of people had gathered, but no one was intervening. I couldn't blame them—even if they didn't understand the waves of negativity they felt from her, she'd feel like pure evil to them. My mind had been in a fog when I had left Earth after my fight with her, and her name returned to me after a few moments.

Vikt.

She turned at my shout, and grinned at me as I yelled, "Get the *fuck* away from him."

David pulled himself into a sitting position and scrambled to the side of the road to lean against a light post when Vikt's attention was no longer on him. He watched me approach with something akin to awe, and I threw him a look.

Stay there.

My fists clenched at my sides, and I stormed toward Vikt, not caring that the essence of my Guardian influence leaked into the air. I *wanted* her to feel my anger.

Vikt smiled. "Ah, you heard my call." She nodded toward

David.

I glanced at him again before returning my gaze to Vikt. "Are you okay?" I asked David.

"I'm okay, but she's strong. *Be careful.*"

I nodded and waved a hand at him. "Get inside that shop there." When out of the corner of my eye, I noticed he didn't move, I turned to him as my rage flared. "*Now.*"

David pulled himself to his feet using the light post, and thankfully, a bystander snapped out of their stupor and rushed forward to help him. But David stilled without following my request to seek shelter. He looked over my shoulder, and Vikt followed his gaze.

"Samael." Vikt smirked. "How nice of you to join us."

A chill ran down my spine, and I whipped around as David called out, "*Samael.*" My son turned at the sound of David's voice. "Stay away from her."

Samael's face fell when he saw David's injuries, but his shock was soon replaced with rage, and he barreled toward Vikt. Before he reached her, I swung out an arm, gripped his jacket, and yanked him around behind me.

"*Mother,*" he cried out, and rage ebbed through his voice.

When I turned on him, Samael took a step back. Even our experience during our last trip to Earth hadn't prepared him for the anger in my eyes. We only briefly held eye contact, but it felt like it stretched forever. I didn't ask why he was here, though I suspected he was either here to find me or David, and said all I needed to say in that moment.

"Go to him," I whispered.

Samael stared at me for a moment longer before he bolted to David. The stranger helping stepped away, and Samael kneeled next to David as he hooked his arm over his shoulders, and they slid to the ground again. David's face remained expressionless even as his fingers twitched where they gripped Samael's jacket, his mind giving in to shock now that Samael was close.

Vikt beckoned. "Come to me." Her voice was smooth and oozed power, calling to me in more ways than one.

I brushed her influence away as if it were nothing. "That's not going to work on me," I said.

Vikt's eyes narrowed before she recovered herself. "We can do this one of two ways. Either you come with me willingly and I leave your child and his lover boy alone, or I kill them and take you, anyway."

"Option three," I snarled out, "I kill you and keep my family safe."

"Wrong answer."

The air shifted, and my hair lifted with it.

All at once, they were everywhere.

Gateways opened in front of and behind me. The Tenebrians evidently no longer cared about hiding their means of transportation to this realm—some hadn't even bothered to change into their human forms. As far as David and the other spectators saw, people and creatures stepped out of thin air onto the street and surrounded me.

David gripped Samael's shirt. "What is going on? Who are they?" Samael shushed him, forced David to his feet, and ushered him to safety, keeping David hidden behind his body. Samael moved slowly, and I dared not turn to look at him, holding him in my peripheral vision only. I didn't want to draw the attention of any Tenebrians to his presence. But the few who glanced his way didn't care.

They were all focused on me.

I took a visual sweep of the area around me before I turned back to Vikt. "Why are you doing this?"

"We are tired of living under the ancient rules. It is time for a change. The biggest change that ever was."

"You're trying to tip the Balance," I whispered, taking a useless step back.

"Yes." Her smile was smug.

John was right. Cael and I were right. Something bigger had been going on, and even if I had managed to get to Cael and tell him John's suspicions, would it have made a difference? They'd been working at this for years, *decades.* I remembered unusual activity when I was pregnant with Samael. "Even if that change means destruction and death?" I cried out and my body twitched as I resisted the urge to step back again, knowing the Tenebrians were at my back. "The world will crumble. People will *die.*"

Vikt shrugged. "Whatever will be, will be. It cannot be any worse than living to serve the Balance. We're nothing but slaves, and always have been slaves to our duty. But with you, we will have the power to make it shift."

Me?

There was a sharp flash as a Gateway opened immediately behind Vikt, and she screamed in rage as she was tackled and swept off her feet.

"Vena!" she cried, and allowed her hands to change back to their Guardian form as she swiped at her attacker—another Tenebrian, and from the waves radiating from him, he was much older.

"You must stop this." He threw her to the ground as though

she weighed nothing, before he jogged toward me. Instinctively, I stepped back from the Tenebrian as he stopped before me. He turned and addressed the small crowd of Tenebrians, "You must *all* stop this. You cannot imagine the destruction you will bring down upon us. I understand your grievances, but this isn't the way."

There was scoffing and mumbling, but nobody moved.

Sirens could be heard in the distance.

No, I thought as I clenched my fists, *all that means is more potential victims.*

Vikt came to her feet and laughed again. "Too little, too late, Vena. We have made up our mind."

Vena stared her down, his eyes an inky black. "I heard rumors, but I did not think anyone would actually try—"

"You should have taken it more seriously, then. No one bothered to look into our activities further, neither Tenebris nor Lucidis." She sneered. "It helped having contacts on both sides, though."

My head spun.

A Lucidian helped with this? Who? Why?

Vikt continued, "You're all so consumed with how things are, *how they will always been...*" her tone was mocking, "... and you only have yourselves to blame." She pointed at me with a claw. "Take her."

Samael's cry of rage came from my right, and I turned and cried out, "No!" as he threw himself toward the nearest Tenebrian. The large male grabbed him by the back of his jacket and threw him to the ground.

I moved to run toward Samael, but Vena grabbed my arm, and I struggled against his vice grip. "You must run." His plea carried the urgency as the group closed in. "*Now.*"

"Not without my son!"

"I will help him. Now *go.*"

I stared into his black eyes.

Could I trust a Tenebrian?

But I had no choice—the Tenebrians were moving, and the few existing gaps were closing fast. Words ran through my mind as I struggled to piece everything together—Cascus's warnings about not going to Earth, and Monia's persistence that I *should.*

Who could I trust?

"*Run,*" Vena cried out again, and his voice took on the grating edge of the ancient language in his panic.

My feet remained still as I glanced back at Samael, who launched another attack to reach me, and I shouted at Vena, "Save him," before I turned on my heel and ran. They closed in around me, moving fast, and I managed to dodge past the first group of Guardians.

But not the next.

There were too many of them. They kept coming, and they were fast. As they closed around me, I watched through the gap between their torsos as Vena pulled a Guardian off Samael and helped him to his feet.

Save him.

The Tenebrians had lost interest in anyone but me and only showed notice of Samael and Vena when they attempted to break the circle to reach me. The Tenebrians passed back through the still-open Gateways one by one until the final group dragged me with them. I struggled, but every time I managed to loosen one grip, another hand would appear in its place and grip harder. Pain crawled under my skin at the direct contact, and their elation filled the air as I struggled. I could feel their imprints clashing with my own—Tenebrian meeting Lucidian meeting human—and the sensation started to burn.

Samael shouted something as I was dragged through the icy wall of the Gateway. I screamed as the sensation of thousands of dry ice needles pushed into my skin, and the pain only increased as I was pulled against the resistance from the Gateway. The Gateway tried to push me back to Earth, but the Tenebrians wouldn't let me go.

I tried my best to center my energies as we entered Tenebris, and the warm air assaulted my lungs. Channeling my power, I threw two Tenebrians off me, but there were more.

So many more.

I had to think of something else, so I went limp and allowed myself to be carried.

I needed to devise an escape plan, but all I could think about was the look on Samael's face and that Cael didn't know where I was.

Chapter Forty

Samael

The muscles in my arms strained as I reached toward the Gateway, as my mother was dragged through. The Tenebrian Guardian's grip around my torso increased, and I struggled against his strength. The more desperate I became, the harder the Tenebrian worked to contain me, until breathing was a chore through the pressure on my chest from his arm. I could've turned on him, but whoever he was, he'd helped me against the others, and I had no choice but to assume he was on our side.

"Who are you?" I pushed the words through gritted teeth as I continued to struggle.

"Vena. You can trust me."

"I trust you," I hissed out, "Now *let me go.*" I clawed at his arm. "I have to save her."

Vena spun me around roughly, grabbed my shoulders before I could flee his grasp, and shook me to gain my attention. "*Listen,*" he snarled out as he stared hard into my eyes. "I will go after her. You go home and get your father. Tell him and as many as you can what happened. We do not have much time. Tell the Elders, tell everyone."

"But—"

"No. There is no time to argue. Many years ago, Cael did not take the chance to trust me, and it caused damage that could have been avoided. Admittedly, I should've tried harder to convince him, and now I implore *you*. You *must* trust me."

"You know my Dad?"

"I can feel his imprint in yours. Now go."

A look passed between us as Vena dropped his arms before he strode away, stopping only to yell, "Clean this mess up," at me before he stepped into one of the Tenebrian Gateways and disappeared through it.

Shuddering with adrenaline, I looked at the shimmering outlines of the Gateways the Tenebrians hadn't bothered to close, and worked quickly to close them all. As I stilled to create my own, my shoulder was gripped and pulled back. I spun, ready to attack, but relaxed at seeing David's face.

"Samael! What's happening?" Panic radiated off him in waves, and I longed to soothe it.

"David, I—" I stumbled through everything I didn't have time to say. Glancing at my hands, they glowed a light blue, with wisps of milky mist flowing over my skin as my human form struggled to contain my Guardian power in the face of my panic.

When I raised my eyes to David's, he watched my hands, too.

"Who are you?" he whispered, his foot poised to take a step back from me. *"What are you?"*

Without thinking, I pulled David against me in a tight hug. David gave in, too tired and confused to fight, and the lingering sense of love I felt in his essence almost drew a sob from my throat. I took the opportunity to calm David and sent waves of my essence through his being. As David's shoulders relaxed and he leaned into me, I pushed him back gently and looked into his eyes.

"I love you, you know that, right?" I asked.

David looked at me and blinked slowly. The hurt and confusion in his eyes were almost too much to bear. But I had a mission now—I had to save Mother, and stop the Tenebrians from tipping the Balance.

Duty came first.

"I know this is a lot to take in, but I promise to explain everything. Right now, I need you to trust me."

David nodded, but his face betrayed his vulnerability, even if I couldn't already feel everything he felt as it swirled around him. All at once, I understood what my father must have gone through all those years ago and why he tried so hard to ensure I didn't face the same difficulties he had. While humans were strong, they were still human, and a sudden realization of the existence of other realms and beings was a lot to take in.

Watching someone you loved try to process the information while they remained in danger was equally as difficult.

I pulled David forward and kissed his forehead, and when I turned to leave, David grabbed my hand. "Take me with you."

I hesitated as my chest ached. "I can't."

David nodded again. He didn't understand what was happening, but he wanted to be near me, to be protected, and to protect me as best he could. That knowledge eased the ache of leaving him.

Only slightly.

"I *will* be back. I promise I will come back for you. Stay in your home."

"My parents—"

"Are okay. We will get them together later. Just stay inside, please."

David nodded again, and achingly slowly, he let go of my hand. The moment we broke contact, the hole opened in my heart again as though I had lost a piece of myself. I watched David cross the street and head back inside his home.

I had no idea if being inside would protect him if something happened to the Balance, but I needed to tell myself I'd done all I could to keep him safe right now.

Drawing a deep breath, I squared my shoulders and went home.

As I came into Lucidis, I stumbled and was immediately grabbed by my father.

"What happened? I felt it!" The panic was thick in his voice as his hands moved up and down my arms, checking for injuries. "I couldn't get a sense of your location, and if I'd come to Earth, I would've lost you entirely through the fog." Words continued to tumble from him until he finally looked me in the eyes. "What happened? The Balance is teetering."

It wasn't often that Dad panicked, and seeing him in this state shook me until I had to force myself from my shocked state. I shouted to be heard over his words. "It's Mother, they've taken her."

"I—"

"They've taken her, Dad! We need to do something."

Dad's immediate response was to get to Mother, and he spun on the spot and spread his fingers to create a Gateway. Fear gripped my chest as the sparks of a failed Gateway flickered around his fingers and died. Dad looked up at the sky, briefly closed his eyes, centered himself, and tried again.

Nothing.

"Dad, what's wrong?"

"The disturbance in the Balance... I can't get through."

Releasing a low sound of panic and grief, I tried myself. While I could feel the veil between the realms, and coming to Lucidis from Earth felt normal, it was as though the sensation was blocked, and I couldn't grasp the air to open a Gateway. When I went to try again, Dad grabbed my wrist and pulled me, and I followed as he turned and ran toward the community center.

"The Elders," Dad shouted as we rounded the edge of a hut and moved past the questioning gazes of the other Guardians as they fought to keep the Balance upheld through Portholes. The community had, of course, felt the disruption and the break in the atmosphere when so many Tenebrians had moved through to Earth all at once, and back again.

"When the Tenebrians passed back through to their home realm, there was an explosion of power," my father said as we ran. "Now I know why."

"Mother."

He nodded, and I realized what I'd felt on Earth would've been magnified here. With the energy waves generated from Mother as she tried to fight the Tenebrians off, and the resistance as she was dragged to Tenebris, it would've only pushed the Balance further.

Panic was shrouding the community, and a mass rally was

underway to reach Earth and work directly from there to put things right.

But no one could get through.

Dad stopped abruptly as we neared the Elder's hut and grabbed my shoulders. "Listen to me," he whispered hurriedly. "We were too slow to react in our passiveness, and for decades, centuries even, we haven't given humanity the regard it deserved."

"Dad, I know this—"

He shushed me angrily. "Beyond that, it seems most of the community, and likely in other communities, have been blind to the pattern of the Tenebrians' behavior. How?" When I opened my mouth to speak with answers I didn't have, Dad continued, "There's been a blanket of influence cast over the community for years. I didn't notice it until I was *looking* for it. I believe it's evidence that a Lucidian, or more than one, has been assisting the Tenebrians."

"Is the influence still over the community?"

"No, it dropped when Ana was taken to Tenebris."

My stomach dropped. "Dad..."

"So, my son, we must ask ourselves two important questions. Who would have the power to do such a thing and—"

"Who can we trust?" I whispered.

My father nodded, and I could feel the same sense of unease moving through him as it did me, and I understood his conundrum. If we were to act, who would we go to? The logical answer would be the Elders, as their power combined could help get us to Earth, but what if they had been covering it all up?

If it was the Elders, was it all of them, one, or some?

Or was it an older Guardian, not quite an Elder but powerful enough?

And if we couldn't trust anyone...

"What are we doing here?" I hissed and waved my arm at the hut next to us.

"We need the Elders' power to create a Gateway, and maybe while we're here, we'll find some truth."

Cascus appeared from the hut, showing no concern for the chaos in the community.

"Cascus." My father turned to the Elder. "They've taken Ana."

Cascus raised his head to meet Dad's eyes. "I told her not to go to Earth. I believe Cordus did too."

I snapped, "That's all you've got to say?"

Dad placed a hand on my arm, which I angrily shook off. "No, Dad... this is too much! Respect for the Elders means nothing if they don't respect us back." I rounded on Cascus. "He *knows.* He knows why she was taken, and he *knows* what the Tenebrians are doing. I can feel it."

When Cascus didn't respond, I clenched my fists as my rage radiated from my body in waves.

Dad drew himself level with Cascus, eye to eye, almost brow to brow. "Elders need to stop hiding things from the community. The only way we can resolve this is by working together. The Tenebrians know something we do not, and they have taken my partner. The Balance is on the precipice of shifting. It's never been more important for us to work together, and someone is working against us." My father's eyes narrowed. "I've never been more furious at myself than I am right now at having trusted that you knew what you were doing."

Cascus's expression didn't change. "I know exactly what I am doing. Do not question me."

"Then do *something.*"

"There is nothing to do. She is a human taken to Tenebris. They will likely kill her and be done with it. Then, we will restore the Balance."

"You're hiding something. Why did they take her?" I insisted. Was Dad expecting to be able to sense who the traitor was by mere proximity? Or was he genuinely seeking Cascus's help?

"She is a human—"

Dad snapped. "I *want* my *wife* back!"

"Wife?" Cascus smiled, though his eyes were empty. "A human term. You have finally succumbed to the humanity."

Succumbed to the humanity?

Something inside me stirred, as though my essence picked up on a shift inside my father's being. Dad's connection with Mother had always stirred something inside him. I could feel it whenever they were near each other, as though a part of him reached out to her whenever she was close. Almost the way our imprints reached out to humans to be reenergized, but it was something more. But there had been a change. I gripped Dad's shoulder and concentrated on the point. The smile dropped from Cascus's face when he realized what I was doing, and I broke the physical contact with my father before Cascus could reach out.

It was too late, I already knew.

Dad was more human than he realized.

We all were.

Cascus's slip didn't mean Dad had succumbed to the human he loved. He meant the human *inside* him. The human part of him.

"All Guardians are part human," I whispered.

Cascus laughed then. It was a small chuckle, coming from a face without a smile, but it was more emotion than I'd ever witnessed from him before. Dad dove inside himself, searching for the truth, sensing it when I reached out to touch him again and allowed him to draw from my power.

"We are, aren't we?" my father said, stepping forward and bumping his chest into Cascus's, forcing him to step back.

Cascus's tone was even. "We breed slowly, but humans procreate faster. Sometimes we use them to get our numbers up."

"But you said half-breeds were unstable?"

"They are if they are allowed to move between the realms. Kept on Earth and away from Guardians, they'd grow up feeling and being human and never knowing any difference. However, in their way, they contribute to positive shifts in the Balance. Their Guardian half, while subdued, still helps."

"You're using humans on an entirely different level..." I said.

"They are tools." His gaze levelled on me before he continued, "Eventually, we send another Guardian to them, and the subsequent child is three-quarters Guardian." He indicated to me with a flick of his wrist. "Enough to live here and function as one of us, and at times, with more effectiveness. If they are kept subdued, they need not be different from the others." He glared at me. "This one is ruined because the human mother has too much involvement."

"But the others—"

"Stop asking questions you already suspect the answers to. Humans are tools for the Balance, and they can be used as tools for offspring as well. We would not have had to take such extreme measures if they had kept their population under control, but there are so many of them that we were losing control. Guardians feared that one day we would lose our grip on the Balance for good."

There was a madness in Cascus' eyes that was unsettling, and I took a half-step away from him as his energy pattern changed, and the air around us shifted.

"You are part human," he told Dad, "several generations back now. You would be around one-eighth human by my calculation, and yes, many of the Guardians are. I told you that we were losing what makes us Guardians. I have been trying to correct that."

"Tenebrians have been using this method too?"

Cascus eyed him. "Not so much. We outnumber them, so they outwork us."

Dad shook his head. "What does any of this have to do with Ana?"

"Perhaps she represents something they hate."

"So, this *whole thing*, all these events and the damage, the attacks and kidnapping, was all because some generations of Lucidians cross-breed with humans? That doesn't make any sense."

"Revenge then, for the death of one of their own."

My eyes narrowed as the air around us changed again. Cascus had further shut himself off as much as he was shutting off the conversation. He was throwing reasons out for Mother's kidnapping as if it made little difference. But I couldn't forget Vikt's excitement as she watched Mother being taken to Tenebris. This was about more than revenge. This was years of their plans falling into place perfectly, and Mother was the ultimate goal.

Dad threw his arms up in frustration. "Revenge? Why her? Why not me? I killed the Rogue."

"You underestimate their hatred of humans."

Rage boiled inside me, and I'd had enough. I grabbed Dad's arm as I said, "This is insane, Dad. He's either guessing or trying to throw us off the truth. What else are they hiding if they can hide crossbreeding for generations?" I turned to Cascus. "I don't trust you. Why did you even tell us this? What purpose does it serve? A distraction from the truth?"

Cascus said nothing, but his eyes sparkled with something that was almost...

Happiness?

"We need to get Ana back," Dad said, his voice distant as he tried to focus.

Cascus stared at him, his eyes void of any emotion. "You cannot. She is gone. Let it go."

"We are going whether you like it or not," I snapped.

"You will die trying."

"We will save her, and everyone you've put in danger, either directly or through sheer ignorance." My father paused and stared the Elder down. "If this was all because of you, I'll be coming back for you."

Dad turned and left without another word, and I looked down upon Cascus with disgust before leaving, too. We had found nothing of worth except increased suspicion that Cascus and perhaps some other Elders were working against us, and we were no closer to rescuing Mother.

Time wasted while Mother was in Tenebris, and the Balance was being pushed.

"How are we going to get to her? We can't open a Gateway."

"Not alone..." Dad said as his eyes darted around the area, "... but if we combine our powers, we just might be able to break through."

I nodded and turned when Dad called out to Sasha. When he finally located her, she came running with Esco close behind.

"What's going on?" Esco asked.

"They've taken Ana."

There was no hesitation from Sasha. "How can we help?"

I barely had time to be thankful for Sasha's willingness to help. "We need to make a Gateway, and we can't do it alone."

Sasha nodded and turned to Esco. "Get the others." Esco raced off, and Sasha took my hand. "Let's get to it, then."

Chapter Forty-One

Ana

The Tenebrian Guardians surrounded me in increasing numbers, and those who were not part of the group that had ambushed me on Earth were no doubt attracted to the area by my pain. My skin crawled as my form shifted between Guardian and human, uncontrolled. The pins and needles sensation was the same as I'd experienced the last time I was here, but tenfold, and it never stopped. A constant sharp prick against my skin, a thousand times at once, all over and shifting all the time. There was no reprieve. A moment after the pain was gone from one point on the skin, it would return.

"P-please," I stuttered through gritted teeth. The feel of this realm seeped into my skin, as though it were infecting my blood. How long could I take this? It felt like I was going to split in two. "Wh-why are you doing this?"

Their laughter in response was cruel and grating.

"The Ba..." I couldn't even get the words out. Every nerve was on fire, a thousand tiny needles in every pore. Thoughts of Samael and Cael fueled me for a moment, and I tried to send out pulses of positive energy, but it faded into nothingness before it even left my body.

"She's worried about the Balance." A nearby Guardian snickered, his eyes empty black pits.

One clawed at my chin and forced me to lift my eyes to his. "We have maintained the Balance for millions of years. Every generation of humans is making it harder with their out-of-control emotions. You were born onto this Earth and have done nothing but ruin it. We think it is about time we allow the Balance to tip, and if it wipes you all out, then that is even better. It's our turn to be the controlling realm."

"No..." A strangled whisper was all that escaped my throat. I was losing control of my power. I could feel it with the increased frequency that my skin flickered madly between my two forms. I felt it with the pulses that left my body, driven by negative energy as my hope dwindled and I was overcome by the pain and discomfort of being in Tenebris.

Power Cael and I had known about, power we had trained me to control.

We had no idea what we were dealing with.

At every involuntary pulse of energy from me, the Tenebrians became more riled up and excited. They pushed past each other, eager to be closer to me to absorb my essence, reeling in it, exploiting it. I screamed as they began using their influences and pushed negative energy into the air around me, so there was no escape from the feelings that infected my being. The pulses built inside my body until I was sure my skin wouldn't be able to contain it any longer.

Panic gripped my chest. I didn't understand exactly what was happening to me, how the Tenebrians planned to use it, or if I would survive whatever happened.

Mixed heritage.

Decades on Earth. Decades in Lucidis.

Never happened before.

Is this what I was to them all along? A weapon to shift the Balance? The ultimate combination between Guardian and human, unstable and unpredictable?

I dropped to the ground in a heavy heap and used the hidden space under me to try to open a Gateway. I only needed to get *somewhere*, anywhere that wasn't here. But I couldn't concentrate, and managed only a few sparks before they faded out, and I was dragged back to my feet.

The Tenebrians started swiping their claws down my back and across my arms. With every scream that left me, the pulses that radiated from me increased in power, and laughter rang out from the Guardians each time a visible ripple shifted the air.

"Your humanity makes you unstable. We look forward to using you to tip the Balance, then letting you watch the destruction of your own making."

Gritting my teeth, I willed my powers under control. It worked, but only for a fraction of a second before a particularly nasty swipe across my lower back made me spasm in pain and lose the fragile grasp I had on my power. The dust shifted in a ripple that moved across the ground and out of sight.

"This is taking too long!" a cry came from the back of the crowd.

A Guardian pushed others out of their way and made their way toward me with a swagger that promised pain and horror. Their quills shimmered even in the dim light, the shades of orange standing out brilliantly against the black undertones of their skin.

He hummed as he breathed in next to my skin, and his snout of a nose pressed up against my neck. I tried to move away from him, but was surrounded and had nowhere to go. Everywhere he touched me was agony.

"I know about you," he cooed, his voice deep and threatening. Velvet and fire. "I know about your mother." I forced my gaze to shift to his eyes.

"Don't you..." Another swipe across my back, and I tried to breathe through the pain. "Don't you talk about her." My hands gripped into tight fists, and every quill on my back rose whenever my Guardian form rematerialized.

"I know how she died." He practically purred. He was so close I could feel the brush of his quills against me, and when I realized he was aroused, my stomach churned.

"Sometimesss..." he hissed, drawing the word out around his tongue as though its taste was a delight "... we like to see if we can get humans while driving to turn into oncoming cars." His laugh was a warm chuckle. "For no real reason, simply to see if they *will.* And sometimes..." He slammed a fist into his open palm, and the sound made me flinch even while I determinedly held his gaze. "We find someone in such a bad way that they do it."

I shook my head. It was lies, all lies. It had to be. I wanted to kill this Guardian, to *hurt* him, to do anything to make him stop talking. But I was frozen to the spot.

And part of me wanted to know.

There was a commotion behind the group that surrounded me, with the sound of running and shouting. In my peripheral vision, I saw another Guardian approaching. "*Stop.* You do not know what you are doing."

A young female turned toward the intruder, and using his momentum against him, slammed a palm into his chest and knocked him to the ground. "Stay out of this, Vena. You are of the old ways, and it is time for things to change." She spat at him. "Whoever dies, dies. Only the strongest will survive, and we will build a new world."

Vena twisted, pushed himself to his feet, and brought the female to the ground with the same move. He shouted above the crowd, "This is bigger than you think. All three realms will merge into one, and the transition will not be smooth. There will be death. You are dooming us all."

"We have all heard the old stories," someone in the crowd shouted at him. There was a chorus of resounding jeers as they closed in on Vena. Vena met my eyes as he was pushed from the group and enveloped in a tangle of limbs.

The resignation on his face stung more than the unspoken apology.

The Guardian, restraining me, kept talking as though there had been no interruption. "Of course, we did not know she was your mother... that was just a bonus. But that man was on the edge and had been thinking about suicide for the longest time. So, with only the slightest push, he swerved his vehicle..."

"You..." I trembled.

"... and drove head-on into your mother's car."

"*No.*" All the air was pushed from my lungs, and I barely reacted when another claw swiped across my back.

"We watched her die, slowly, *painfully.* She gasped for every last breath, trying to hold on to her life. Maybe she was thinking of you in her final moments."

"*Stop it!*"

He moved closer, seductively tilting his head like a snake hypnotizing its prey. "So really..." he watched me, enjoying my agony, "... it seems *I* killed your mother."

I screamed, and the sound that left my lungs wasn't human nor Guardian, but somewhere terrifyingly in between. The energy that left my body threw the Tenebrian Guardians off their feet, and pulsed around me in an ever-growing dome of instability. My image continued to flicker between forms as the energy waves rose around me, like flames of air, and the dust at my feet rose as it was caught up in the whirlwind. As some of the Guardians tried to stand, I continued to scream the sound I no longer had control of, and they would be thrown off their feet again and forced back.

"No," Vena shouted, struggling to get closer to me as the forces pushed him back. "You must contain yourself, human..." He paused. "*Ana, please!*"

I met Vena's eyes, and while my vision was blurred with clouded white, regret and pain pulsed through me, and reflected in Vena's eyes.

I knew what was happening, but I couldn't stop it.

The screams kept coming, physically pulled from my lungs and dragged through my throat, cutting like razors as my feet lifted from the ground and I was surrounded in a bubble of pain.

It was too late.

The entire realm seemed to vibrate until a single crack, starting small under Vena's feet, moved outward, increasing in girth and spreading.

Chapter Forty-Two

Cael

The snap was as though someone had taken a whip to my skin, and I stumbled back as it felt as though my chest was torn in two. It wasn't pain as such, more an absolute awareness that something had changed, and that the fabric that held our world together had been torn.

Samael winced as I reached out and gripped his shoulder. My fingers flexed, causing my claws to dig into his skin.

"Dad?" Fear filtered through my son's voice, even as he stood firm.

It couldn't be true.

I didn't want it to be true.

Around us, the Guardians of Lucidis looked up as a dark crack opened in the sky and spread in a rapid, haphazard motion. Beyond the crack was utter blackness, pure nothingness, as the realm itself began to fall apart. The air around us appeared to shimmer, as huts, trees, and other plant life seemed to shift in and out of existence.

I whipped around at a loud crack behind me, and couldn't move as my jaw dropped. A Gateway spontaneously opened, and the humans on the other side looked curiously at the apparition.

Looked at *me.*

"Dad, what's happening?"

The vibrations of fear sent chills down my spine, until the fear was replaced with numbness. Ana and I had suspicions about her increasing power, but it never occurred to me that she could be used as a weapon.

Why would it occur to me? She was the love of my life, my other half, and the anchor that held me and our family together.

But they'd used her just the same—dragged her through to Tenebris to make her as unstable as possible, and pushed the Balance the final amount needed to do what they wanted.

To create the Shift.

There was a laugh behind us, the maniacal laugh of a lunatic who'd finally snapped, and I turned slowly as my fingers curled into my palms.

"Why?" was all I could push out through gritted teeth.

"It is too late. We have succeeded, and there is no going back."

I muttered, "You *helped* them."

It wasn't a question, but Cascus nodded as he smiled. "Humans are so predictable. Tell them not to do something, and it is the first thing they want to do. The more I pushed the half-breed, the more she pushed back until it was inevitable." I stepped back as Cascus continued, "Monia wanted to bring her to Earth to train her to control herself, but I couldn't have that. I needed her to be volatile, to *think* she had herself under control, so that control could be broken. I needed not to have interfered too much, nor to get involved in her kidnapping. All I needed to do was tell her she was not allowed on Earth, to plant some ideas with the Tenebrians, and wait."

"Tell us why you fucking coward," Samael hissed out.

"Because humans are a curse. It was only a matter of time before they wiped themselves out and took us with them. We will take over the world and live as we were always meant to be."

"Don't you know what will happen if the Balance tips?"

"Of course, I do."

"Everything will die!" I yelled.

"Not everything..." Cascus said with a sneer, "... only the weak."

"Why Ana? If there are so many part-breeds as you claim, why Ana?"

Cascus's lips twisted cruelly, torn between mirth at his plan coming to fruition and disdain for Ana. "She was an accident. She was not one of the planned half-breeds. Then, because of you, she spent half her life on Earth and half here with our strengthening environment. She was a one-off, an anomaly, and useful because of it. We could have done it without her, but it would have taken much longer. As soon as she came here, I knew, and all I had to do was be patient."

The ground trembled again, and Samael adjusted to stop from stumbling as I stared at Cascus.

Cascus sighed, seemingly unconcerned with the growing sense of dread which crept through the realm as Lucidians were torn between desperately trying to fix something they couldn't possibly save, and saving themselves. "It is partly our fault, I imagine. Crossbreeding seemed like a good solution to the problem, but now humanity has infected our species. The younger generations are changing, growing weak." He shrugged. "Sasha is one we brought back here, a quarter-human, and look how pathetic she is, all empathy and weakness." He looked at the crack in the sky, and the satisfaction on his face made my skin crawl. "It is time for a fresh start."

When I lowered my eyes to Cascus, he took a step back. Rage flooded through my veins, and my vision went white. When it cleared, Cascus had taken another step back from me, seeing in my eyes a promise and premonition of his death.

Cascus was stronger than I, but self-preservation and cowardice ran strong through him.

He ran, and although I took a menacing step forward, I didn't follow.

"Dad?" Samael's voice trembled, and I could feel his essence shift and waver as he tried to keep his emotions under control. "Tell me it's not real." The façade of strength faded away as he gave in to his terror, and his eyes watered even as he stood tall. Fear of the Balance shifting was ingrained in his DNA, and his discomfort would be the same as what we all felt.

But there's nothing we could do.

"It's shifting." My voice was stony.

"It hasn't happened already?"

I shook my head slowly before I closed my eyes and wished for strength as another Gateway spontaneously opened and slammed shut next to us. "The Shift takes time, but it has begun."

"How long do we have?"

"Weeks? Maybe only days..." I shook my head again and studied his face. "I wish I could give you the answers."

Samael opened his mouth to reply before we both spun wildly on the spot as a high-pitched scream echoed through the realm. It was coming from everywhere and nowhere all at once, full of terror and pain, and seemed to bleed through the very air itself.

Before us appeared a distorted image, and Samael stared wide-eyed as I did. An illusion?

No.

It was Ana.

She stood terrifyingly still, seeming to hover inches above the ground, surrounded by a vortex of air, energy, and red dirt. My chest ached anew, and I reached out to her as she screamed again.

She was screaming for me.

"Ana!" I cried out and lunged forward. But I passed through her image as if it weren't there.

It was a Porthole.

In her pain and instability, Ana had done the impossible and created a Porthole directly from Tenebris, where she was trapped, to us in Lucidis.

She rotated slowly until she faced me, her eyes a milky white, and her face contorted in pain.

"Ana..." I whispered and reached out even though I knew I couldn't touch her.

I tried to change the Porthole into a Gateway, but my power stalled uselessly at my fingertips.

Then, her face changed for a moment—realization, and awareness.

She knew what was happening, and she couldn't stop it.

My arm remained extended toward her, hoping she could see me at least. I wanted to tell her it wasn't her fault, and that we loved her, *I* loved her. But no words would come, and my heart shattered when a tear ran down her cheek.

"Ana," I whispered again, and my voice broke with the tears that ran freely down my face.

The Porthole closed, and she was gone.

Epilogue

Stepping off the plane and onto the warm tarmac, I looked up toward the sky. It had been many years since I'd been back in my home country, and although this is the place where I felt I had truly found myself all those decades ago, I couldn't bring myself to return.

Until now.

Every day I'd been away made the prospect of coming back more difficult. I'd made some terrible choices, and while they were made with the best intentions, it didn't make them any easier to act on. I knew what I *should* have done, and while the lure to return home was a constant ache that lived under my skin, I was too weak to act.

The days turned into years, and the years into decades, and although I had achieved some amazing things, I had so many regrets.

But if there were ever a time to make things right, it was now, and perhaps I could make more than one thing right.

I'd watched the news for my hometown and country, and over the past few years, I had witnessed a series of violent crimes as they increased in number and intensity. Even in my distant state, I'd felt the changes. No matter my years on Earth, I was who I was.

When the final Shift had happened, it was like a punch to the heart.

And I'd felt *her*.

The plane had been seconds from landing, but those seconds dragged into hours as my fingers dug impatiently into the seat's vinyl.

I hurried toward the gate and entered the terminal before waving down a cab. I needed to find an empty space with fewer people and fewer distractions, closer to the city center, before I could even consider acting. My gaze fell to the moonstone pendant, which dangled from a simple leather strap around my wrist.

Even with the stone, I might need help.

I hoped John still lived in the same building.

It would take everything I had, but I'd get to her. I'd find her and make things right.

My daughter, Anahera.

To be continued

Acknowledgements

WHAT IS THERE TO say when I left you on such a cliffhanger?

At least you don't need to wait long for Book 3! If you've bought this on release, it's only a week away!

Thank you, as always, to my amazingly supportive friends and family. Rewriting this series has been a passion project, and a significant amount of work went into it behind the scenes. I wanted these books to be the best versions of themselves, to bring the story back to life and make it something I was proud to share with the world.

I hope you enjoyed Shattered Heart. It was a bit of a slow burn, unlike my usual writing style, as it was all leading up to this moment.

The story will be concluded in Reborn Heart.

Thank you for reading! Xx

RELA

Bonus Chapter — John

ANA

The only way to survive was to sit still.

Absolutely still.

As still as I could manage.

I was practically holding my breath, keeping each one smooth and even, attempting to slow the movement of my chest so it was almost imperceptible. Because of those eyes. Those eyes that looked down at me as they had a dozen times before. But never this close.

When there was movement, I released a slow breath and let a chuckle escape my lips.

It was silly, but I lived for moments like these. I could get lost in another world, shut off everything outside these four walls, and simply focus on the story that unfolded before me.

In this case, *Jurassic Park* on the big screen.

When the characters held their breaths, so did I. Stilling when they did, and almost screaming when they did, too—although I refrained from allowing that last bit of reaction to slip through in the theater. As much as I liked to allow myself to get absorbed in films, I wasn't sure the other audience members in the theater would appreciate my screaming along with Lex.

A revisit of an old classic was precisely what I needed. I hadn't seen it on the big screen in... well, ever. Although I was in my mid-twenties now, I still sat with my eyes wide and took in every motion, sound, and note of that perfect soundtrack as I shoveled popcorn into my mouth.

I'd regret the popcorn later—too much butter and salt. But the movies were a time to forget the outside world, including rules about healthy eating.

I'd go for a run tomorrow to work it off, anyway.

Sighing, I settled back into my seat. The fabric was almost as worn as the carpet, a faded red I was sure in its glory days would've been an impressive shade of maroon. But now, this aging theater relied almost entirely on people like me—film fans who would pay to see the same movies we loved as children over and over again. Or, for something different, B-grade movies no one had ever heard of but were always good fun, even if the special effects were terrible.

I needed this escape.

Recently, I'd started working at a new bar, and while it was a nice venue and convenient because it was closer to home, it wasn't the same as my previous job, where I'd worked since I was twenty-one. Moving on was one thing, but being forced to move on was entirely different. I'd been loyal to the owner, Mr. Banks, working many hours without pay to help him when things were tough. His name was Timothy, but I liked to call him Mr. Banks because it afforded me an opportunity to quote another movie at him. He'd wave his hand and tell me off for not calling him by his first name, then laugh heartily when my response would be *"Confound it, Banks!"*

But he was gone now.

The first thing his son had done after his father passed was fire half the workforce and hire his friends in their place. I knew there was no point in following up with an unfair dismissal claim, and I wasn't sure I'd even want to work for Timothy's son, anyway—the dumbass.

My new boss, Pete, hired me straight away and noted that he was impressed by my references.

I hadn't provided any references.

Timothy had passed, and his son sure as hell wasn't going to put in a good word for me. Not with the single-finger salute I'd offered him as I'd left. Pete had shrugged and said that word tended to travel in this industry in the city, and he had heard good things.

That was a first.

Cursing under my breath, I hated that the thoughts of Mr. Banks, which flooded my mind, made me feel this way. I could almost feel the sadness seeping through my body as I sank further into the seat. I didn't usually get close to people, as they always left in one way or another.

Of course, leaving by taking death's hand wasn't his fault, but I could add his name to the short list of people whom I had allowed to see the real me underneath my defenses and were now gone. Then, I'd be left with a gaping hole where my emotions had once been before I shut myself off to the world.

Closing myself off was a process that had begun when my father left and was finalized when Mom died.

Patting myself rapidly on the cheek, I lightly slapped away the thoughts. Swiping angrily at a stray tear, I refocused on the film and allowed myself to go slightly doe-eyed when Sam Neil came on the screen—a pre-teen crush of mine.

Who was I kidding? A *current* crush of mine.

When the movie was over, I stood and stretched, and my black t-shirt lifted to expose my hip bones and flat stomach. When the movement caught the attention of a young man walking down the stairs near my seat, he winked. I arched an eyebrow at him, not declining his advance as such, but the look said precisely what I intended.

Try it... If you dare.

He didn't dare. I chuckled.

Shrugging, I sat to wait for the end of the credits. There was nothing after them, I knew that, this wasn't a modern-day movie, after all. But it was a habit I couldn't break. Plus, it seemed wrong to sit through a film I loved without acknowledging the people who had worked so hard to bring it to life.

The rain began as I left the theater, and I hesitated momentarily before I shrugged and stepped out into the rain. It increased in intensity as I walked, and I was drenched by the time I rounded the corner to my street. The blanket of rain was so thick that the street was lost in a gray haze, casting it in a depressing light, although it was barely evening. Running now would be pointless. Besides, I was in boots, not running shoes, and I didn't want to twist my ankle for the sake of a few seconds.

Penny looked up as I entered the apartment, her expression halfway between amusement and concern. "Raining?" she asked with a smirk.

I scrunched my nose and made a face at her as Penny laughed.

A wave of exhaustion came over me as I stepped under the warm rush of the shower a few minutes later. The temperature was uneven as always, moving between comfortably warm and almost too cold, with dashes of scorching hot water thrown in. The building was old, and I was used to it. I liked my comfort zones, and this apartment was one of them. Once again, I had been here several years, and after I established myself in a home or job, I'd generally only move when forced to. However, the *no-pets* policy of this landlord was wearing thin on my patience.

I wouldn't mind a small dog or cat.

Or two, or three.

Slumping my head against the shower wall, I realized my error wasn't new, in fact, it was the one I kept making.

Not enough sleep.

Being warm like this only made me drowsy, a pattern I was doomed to repeat unless I got my shit together. Often working late nights and having my dreams haunted by another loss of someone I cared about, I figured it would be months before I got a decent night's sleep again. Tonight, I had my second shift at the new bar, and I'd struggle through until three in the morning and then collapse. Maybe if I let myself get completely exhausted, I would sleep most of tomorrow.

"I've got to get to work, Penny," I said as I stepped out from the bathroom, pulling a clean top over my head and grabbing a jacket from the back of a chair.

Penny looked up from her laptop. "You look like hell."

"Thanks."

Penny's voice softened with her expression. "No, I mean it. Are you okay?"

I held Penny's gaze for a moment and studied her face. She looked tired as well. Studying to be a nurse while working her way through was beginning to take its toll, but she soldiered on.

Really, I had nothing to complain about.

"Yeah, just still sad about Mr. Banks, you know?"

Penny pressed her lips together and nodded, understanding that when I said I was *sad,* I really meant *devastated*. It meant I was torn up inside, and for months, I'd be even more of a recluse than I usually was. It meant that, as always, I felt pain deeply and without apology. Penny couldn't take the pain away, but she could help me through it.

"If you need to talk..." Penny paused when I raised my brows. "...Or just want some company, I'm here."

My lips twitched into an almost smile. "Thanks, Penny. You know I appreciate it." And with that and a small wave, I was out the door again.

JOHN

Sundays were likely to be quiet in the bar, and thankfully, when I arrived, the crowd reflected my expectations. A few people who perhaps didn't have enough fun on Saturday night, or wanted to drown away the oncoming Monday blues. But it was mostly a quiet lot, and they kept to the tables and couches dotted around the room, listening to whatever music was being played and chatting amongst themselves.

Sitting on a bar stool, I folded my hands, one on the other, as a bartender approached with a smile. She had long ash-blonde hair, and the moment her eyes fell on me, her gait shifted into something that showed the sway of her hips.

Fuck.

I was old enough to be her father, but it didn't stop my gaze from trailing over her body.

"The usual?" she asked.

My eyebrows shot up, and in a nervous reaction, when I rubbed my beard, her eyes darted to the salt and pepper color, which did nothing to dim her smile. In fact, it seemed to widen, and she visually traced my body as I had hers. Muscular enough—or so I thought, I liked to keep fit—with a long ponytail that trailed down my back.

"How do you know my *usual?*"

She studied my face and smiled at me, allowing every flirtatious muscle in her body to work its magic as she tucked her hair behind her ears. "What do you mean?"

"I haven't been here in a few months."

She slid a beer across the bar, and my eyebrow remained arched. She had remembered correctly.

"Guess I've got a good memory for handsome faces."

The corner of my lips quirked in amusement, but I couldn't help the slight tensing of my jaw. "Am I that recognizable?"

"To me, you are." She winked. "I'm Erin."

She held her hand out across the bar, and I hesitated. Slowly, I took her hand. "John."

When our hands met, I felt something on the edge of my senses, and glanced at the blonde bartender at the other end of the bar. My fingers flexed in Erin's when I recognized Ana, and I glanced away quickly to find Erin staring with a Cheshire-cat grin. Ana chuckled and resumed serving the other patrons, and I released a slow breath.

After Ana had looked away, I stole another glance at her. She was beautiful, much like her mother. While I figured eventually, I was bound to run into her, given we both lived in the same city, I hadn't planned on it being more than a lingering passing in the street. Ana had a life, and I hoped she was happy, but it wasn't my place to contact her against her father's wishes, as much as it pained me.

I didn't realize she'd already started her job here.

"Don't bother." Erin smiled.

"Sorry?"

Leaning across the bar, Erin took advantage of the angle to give me a view down her top. She bit her lip as my glance slid automatically from her face, down her neck, and paused on her breasts. My lip quirked again as I stole a look at the skin she exposed to me. Erin tilted her head, and she watched me as I raised my eyes back to hers.

"I saw you looking at our new girl, Ana, but don't bother."

"I wasn't going to—"

"It's okay. She might be a closed book, but I'm open for business."

As Erin grinned, I barked out a laugh. "You don't mess around, do you?"

"All the time." She winked again. "But life's too short to play games." Erin leaned over the bar, catching my eye contact and biting her lip as I steadily held her gaze. "I see a dominant streak in you, John, and I'm tempted to push you to see what would happen."

This wasn't what I was here for, and I could see Ana in my peripheral vision, smirking our way, no doubt used to Erin's antics. Her offer was tempting, and I could certainly see myself lifting her onto this very bar and covering her mouth to muffle her moans while I—

"So..." She drew the word around her tongue, ending with a pout of her lips, colored with sparkling pink lip gloss. She was so close, I could smell the faint scent of watermelon that I assumed came from the gloss. My cock stirred. There was no denying she was beautiful. Enchantingly so.

But she wasn't the reason I was in the bar tonight.

Maybe another time, another night, another lifetime where I didn't have responsibilities that outweighed my desires.

But not tonight.

She ignored the other patrons, and some stood uncomfortably close to me, attempting to gain her attention. Glancing at Ana again, she was run off her feet. It seemed a group had decided it was time for the next round. But her face showed only amusement, no irritation at Erin's behavior. They must be friends, or at least Erin had endeared herself enough to Ana that she put up with letting her pick up the extra work while Erin worked only at flirting.

Or maybe the look was fake, and underneath it, she was gritting her teeth.

Maybe I was thinking too much about what Ana might be thinking.

It was difficult not to feel protective.

Erin stretched an arm to me and trailed her fingertip along my wrist in small circles. When I reached up and gently clasped her wrist, her eyes flickered up to mine, wide with anticipation and lips parted with a silent gasp.

Fuck.

Grinding my teeth, I gently moved her hand away from mine. "I'm sorry. I can't tonight."

Her face fell, but she recovered quickly with another grin. "So, there's hope for another night, then?"

I chuckled. "Maybe."

"That's not a no." Sliding her elbows back across the bar, she winked and moved away to serve someone else in the group of increasingly irritated people waiting.

As I moved away from the bar to stand in a corner, I watched as Erin and Ana exchanged a glance. Ana raised her eyes to me again, and I looked away, pretending to scan the bar for someone. I could feel her eyes on me and wished she'd stop.

Breathing a sigh of relief when she started working again, I watched the other bar-goers.

Looking for someone hadn't entirely been a cover, I *was* here for someone. While I didn't know his name, I'd know him when I saw him. His face was imprinted in my mind. We'd met a handful of times, but were never formally introduced.

Tenebrians didn't have a habit of politely introducing themselves.

They didn't belong here. Not like this, and that was the problem.

It wasn't my duty to stand here and wait for him. I should have little to do with these beings from another realm. But after hearing him talk about this bar and the things he had planned for it, I couldn't stand idly by and let it happen.

So many humans wouldn't be able to wrap their minds around the idea of visitors from another realm, but I knew all too well. Usually, I'd see them only once or twice a month, at most. But this was something different, I could feel it in my bones. Not the duty they were here for, but something for personal pleasure.

A Rogue in the making.

Nursing my beer as it grew warm in my hand, I waited.

As the night wore on, I began to question myself. Had I heard the Tenebrian correctly about the location? Even if I had, I wasn't naïve enough to believe that these weren't the sort of beings to change their minds on a whim and go and wreak havoc elsewhere if it struck their fancy.

I'd shifted further toward the back of the bar and slumped on a stool by a small table in the corner where shadows partially hid me. Erin and Ana kept glancing at me, and I wished they wouldn't.

When he entered the bar, my back straightened.

Finally.

The man was tall, all Guardians were, and his bright blue eyes stood out underneath his dark hair. The sharp lines of his face drew the attention of several women, and men, in the bar, including Erin, whose eyes lit up as though all her Christmases had come at once. I could understand her reaction. He radiated a danger that seemed to draw women to him. Even the sort of women who would proclaim they never went for the *bad boy* type had difficulty not looking at him.

Scowling as the Tenebrian smiled at Erin, I thought, *He bloody knows it too, the smug bastard.*

Waiting in the corner, I finished the dregs of my beer, scrunching my face in distaste at the flavor of the warmed liquid. Without taking my eyes off the man, I placed the bottle on the table. Apparently, a bit too loudly, as it drew a look from Erin, who tore her eyes away from the dark-haired man long enough to smile at me. That confident smile almost became a simper as she looked back at their new customer.

I was pleased to note Ana didn't react the same way to him as Erin did. She had drawn herself away to the other side of the bar, throwing glances at the stranger that bordered on concern. She wasn't falling for the strong, dark, and handsome thing he had going. Maybe she could see past it and knew that he wasn't a good man inside.

He wasn't a man at all.

I waited while he ordered a drink and sauntered over to where I sat as though we were old friends reuniting.

"Better stand up and greet me, John, or people will think something is wrong."

Grinding my teeth, I stood and held my hand out, and had to resist the urge to punch him in his handsome face when he drew me into a tight hug. His fake laughter rang across the bar while he patted me on the back, harder than necessary.

As we sat, he smiled. Nothing was friendly about that smile, which radiated the darkness inside him. "I don't think we've ever been introduced. Can't say I've ever bothered. But, since you're here, you can call me Cain."

"You're shittin' me, right?" I asked, not bothering to keep the disdain from my voice. Although perhaps I should consider my words more carefully, as power radiated from the Tenebrian even in his human form. "*Cain?*"

Cain laughed loudly and used the opportunity to glance around at the women who had turned at the sound, throwing them a smile coupled with the dark influence behind it, that had their knees buckling. "Might as well add some flair to my persona here, don't you agree?"

"I don't think we'll agree on much," I grunted out.

"So, to what do I owe the pleasure of finding you here?"

"I heard your plans, and I'm here to stop you."

Another laugh, this one grating against my ears like nails on a chalkboard. Although it did give me some pleasure to know that even my questioning of Cain was enough to make his control slip, only enough that his laugh sounded as sinister as he was inside.

But perhaps making him lose control of himself wasn't a good idea, either.

An out-of-control Tenebrian was a dangerous being.

It was nearly impossible to talk to Cain with respect. "You're not going to burn this place down."

"Well, I mean, I am." Cain smirked.

"No."

"I don't see what you're going to do to stop me."

"Why here?"

Cain's lip lifted into a snarl. "Some Lucidian took me down years ago here, I don't like the vibe."

I stared him down. "I'll send you back."

"Excuse me?"

I straightened my spine. "I'll send you back to Tenebris. You think I don't know how?"

Cain's eyes raked over me as though trying to tell if I was telling the truth. When I slid a hand inside my jacket pocket and thumbed the knife, Cain was still watching my movements. He didn't need to see the knife to know it was there, and when his eyes darted back to mine, I saw absolute rage there. I should probably be more afraid than I was, but I also knew the owner of this bar, and I wasn't about to let it be reduced to ashes. I wouldn't let Cain do it even if the bar was empty, and I sure as hell wouldn't let him do it when it was filled with innocent people.

My eyes flickered to the two women behind the bar, and I realized my mistake too late.

Cain followed my line of sight, and his smirk morphed into a devilish grin as his eyes fell upon the women. "Ooh, like that, is it?"

"No, I..."

Cain's face darkened, and I saw that tell-tale flash of black cross his eyes for a moment. Clenching my fist around the knife in his pocket, I stilled. I hated that Cain had gotten under my skin so easily. I was stronger than this, but Cain had found my weakness, and I knew he'd have no issue exploiting the weak spot.

Innocence.

As Cain stood, his chair slid out behind him and toppled over, the sound attracting the attention of those surrounding them. Few people were left in the bar, but as I stood with equal vigor, almost all eyes were on us. I risked another glance at the bar to find Erin and Ana watching me, and cursed under my breath when Cain chuckled.

"I was going to torch this place, but I think I've found something more fun."

While I was prepared for the move, I wasn't ready for the physical strength the Tenebrian displayed. In his human form, Cain was almost as strong as he was in his natural form, and when I moved to grab him, Cain snatched the front of my jacket and threw me over a nearby table without any effort displayed on his features. The patrons at the table screamed as I was slammed onto its surface, their glasses scattering to the floor and breaking, adding to the commotion.

Cain wasn't bothered by the attention he was gaining with his show of strength. His nostrils flared as he breathed in deeply, filling his lungs not only with the thick and sticky air of the bar but with the fear now permeating the room. The humans were afraid of him, made stronger because most of them found him attractive in one way or another, until a moment ago. Now they were questioning themselves, wondering if a handsome face could so easily sway them that they didn't see the darkness in his eyes or didn't pick up on the flash of lust for violence that flared in his pupils.

The people were afraid, and Cain reveled in it.

His eyes flashed. He wanted to make it stronger.

I grunted as he gripped my jacket and lifted me toward him. He grinned before he snapped his head forward and collided his forehead against my nose. The crunch of the cartilage breaking sounded in my eardrums as blood exploded from my nose, and my head cracked against the table as he shoved me back against it.

His breath was hot against my face. "I could take them both. Maybe I'll fuck them on the bar while these pathetic humans watch on helplessly. I wonder how they sound when they scream." My head throbbed as he glanced at the bar again, and Ana wrapped her arms around herself as she shivered. "Oh, I think I've found my victim. I always did like blondes."

As Cain moved away, I toppled over the table's edge and grunted as I hit the floor. Cain strode across the room toward the bar, his eyes flickering hungrily between the two women behind it. He placed a palm on the bar and vaulted himself over the top, his feet knocking into the shelf behind the bar and breaking several bottles along the way. He approached the women, and grinned when Ana planted herself firmly in front of Erin despite being shorter than her. She held her arms out as though she could stop him, and I stumbled as I tried to get to my feet and force my head to stop spinning.

Cain laughed and approached until Erin and Ana were backed up against the corner of the bar. He leaned in, breathing in the scent of Ana's hair while she trembled. "What's your name, sweetheart?"

"Fuck off," she spat.

He threw his head back and laughed again, glancing at the handful of men approaching him, shouting at him to back off. He wasn't concerned and took another whiff of her scent, raising his hand to take a lock of her hair in his fingers and smirking as she jerked away from his touch.

"That wasn't very nice," he said, and she trembled again. I felt it through the air as he let the darkness exude from his voice, allowing Ana to feel only a hint of the power and influence within him. It was enough to spike her fear, even if she didn't understand the source of her terror.

To Cain, it was ecstasy.

He hummed. "You should be nice to me... it will be much easier on you if you are."

She stretched her neck away from him as he slowly moved to cup her cheek. Erin gripped her shoulders, whispering, "Ana..."

His eyes darted from Erin to Ana, and Ana squeezed her eyes closed momentarily.

"Ana," he purred. "Now I'll know what to shout when I—"

Cain stumbled forward a step as a bottle was broken over his head, and simultaneously, I was relieved someone was finally stepping in as I struggled to pull myself together, but feared what would happen to them if Cain was aggravated. Whoever had the nerve to attack him hadn't taken any chances with a small beer bottle. No, that was a full bottle of bourbon, the thick glass breaking and covering him and the women in the amber fluid. Turning slowly, Cain licked his lips as the bourbon dripped from his hair and down his face. His attacker shrank under his gaze as Cain drew himself to his full height before aiming a kick at the man's stomach, sending him hurtling across the floor. Hurried whispers of people phoning the police sounded as the other men hesitated and someone rushed to the fallen man's aid.

Gritting my teeth against the spinning in my head, I ignored the blood that dripped from my nose and coated my lips and forced myself to my feet. As I lunged toward the bar, my fingers fumbled with the knife in my pocket.

"It may be against the rules for me to kill you, Ana," Cain whispered as he turned back to her. "But when I'm done with you, you'll wish I had."

"Don't move," I said through gritted teeth.

Cain froze as I held the knife to his back. It wasn't a large knife, but it didn't need to be. The edge of the blade pressed against Cain through his shirt. All it would take would be a twist of my hand, a slash, a stab, and I would remove him from this realm.

But not here.

Not in front of her.

"How's your face?" Cain smirked.

"Still pretty despite your efforts."

Cain hissed through his teeth, and his eyes fell on Ana. "Don't feel fucking hope yet you bitch."

Ana's eyes widened as her jaw dropped, and Erin wrapped her arms around Ana and pulled her against her chest.

Cain shifted, but paused when I pressed the blade pressed firmer against his back. Cain was fast, but could he move fast enough to grab the knife before he was injured? I doubted it.

He wasn't allowed to kill me, either.

"Things would be so much easier if I could dispose of humans as I saw fit," Cain muttered.

"How about you go for a walk, mate?" I growled and leaned against Cain, pressing the blade to him, leaving him under no illusions that I would use it. "I think it's time you went home."

Cain licked his lips again, weighing his options. He glanced at Ana again, his eyes resting on how her chest rose and fell with her rapid breaths. She was still on edge, poised to attack or run.

Cain scoffed. "If I allow myself to be taken down by a *human*, I'll never be able to show my face in my community again."

"Leave." I snarled.

Cain's eyes travelled over the people around the bar as they stood and watched the scene unfold. They couldn't hear what was being said, but Cain remaining still with his hands raised was enough to ease the fear in the bar.

"You know..." Cain started casually, "... I think maybe I ought to be going home now."

But he didn't move.

"Don't fuck with me, Cain," I said as I pressed the blade into Cain's back, forcing him to arch away from the tip to prevent himself from being cut. "I'll do it in front of all these people if I have to. You'll have to explain to your Elders what the *humans* saw and why I won't allow you anywhere *near* this city again."

Cain chuckled. "I won't be coming back, John. You're too much trouble." Cain straightened and adjusted his shirt collar. He turned slowly, his hands kept up to confirm his surrender. As he turned, I allowed the blade to trail around his body and pressed it into his stomach when we were face to face. "Can I just say goodbye to my new girlfriend first?"

Cain laughed when Ana stiffened behind him. He no doubt felt the spike of her fear puncture the air. He looked down. I twisted the blade and cut the front of his shirt, the sound of the fabric ripping loud enough to gain his attention.

"Don't test me, Cain."

Cain's smirk was full of amusement as he watched me, his gaze taking in the dried blood on my face. He tilted his head. "You need to let me by, so I can leave."

After a pause, I stepped to the side, flicking the blade toward the exit. My gaze followed Cain as he ducked under the hatch and out from behind the bar. The remaining people gave him a wide berth as he stalked toward the door.

"You won't be seeing me again, John, but it's been an absolute pleasure," he said with a flourish of his hand.

"Fuck off, mate."

Cain laughed once more, and the sound of the door closing behind him rang in the silence that stilled the bar. Hastily, I pocketed the knife and turned to leave. When I felt a hand on my arm, I shrugged it off before turning to see Erin behind me.

"Thank you," she whispered, rubbing her arms. "I mean... thank you."

She didn't know what else to say, and really, there wasn't anything else she could say.

"Yeah," Ana added. "Thank you."

Although she looked uncomfortable, I knew it was a genuine *thank you*, and sighed in relief, knowing I had cleared the danger for now. I couldn't always protect everyone, but at least tonight I had made the right decision to be here. Not meeting Ana's gaze, I nodded at the floor. I'd made too much of a spectacle of myself already. It was in my best interests and my preference to fly under the radar.

I wouldn't be able to come here again.

Walking the length of the bar, I snatched a bottle of whiskey from the shelf, growling as I poured a generous amount on my nose before taking a few decent mouthfuls and swallowing loudly. Replacing the bottle and making my way to leave, I could feel the eyes of everyone on my back.

Strongest of all was Ana and Erin's gaze.

I needed nothing from them, no thank yous, no payment. I had reasons for being here, and had done what I came to do.

It was nice to see Ana. I hoped she was happy in her life.

ANA

My shoulders trembled again as I watched the man who had saved us leave the bar. I couldn't shake the feeling I should've done something more, hugged him, maybe? Offered him a drink? Although he had taken what he wanted, and I had *no* problem with that whatsoever. Hell, if our manager had an issue, I'd pay for the damn whiskey myself.

He should've taken the whole damn bottle, he deserved it. The strength that guy had shown had been terrifying, and beyond that was the sickly feeling that oozed from him. Like he was darkness personified. I bet that's what it was like to meet a serial killer.

But he had stood up to him—John, Erin said his name was—and somehow made him leave.

Slowly, after several people had asked if we were okay, and someone had tended to the man who had been kicked, the noise level in the bar returned to a subdued norm. Hopefully, the police would be here soon, and we'd all have to give statements. As Erin moved to clean up the broken glass and blood from where John had been thrown to the table, I grabbed her arm.

"Erin, you need to do me a favor."

She looked at me, and her voice was normal despite her blotchy face and trembling lips. "What is it, babe?" she asked.

"When the cops get here, don't tell them John's name."

She looked taken aback. "What? Why?"

I couldn't find the words to explain properly. "I just... get the feeling he doesn't want to be known. I think he wants to be left alone."

"But... he saved us."

"Just do it for me, please?"

Erin stared at me for a moment and bit her bottom lip before nodding, and I released her arm as she moved to clean. I began sweeping up the glass behind the bar, and the broom became congealed in the sticky liquor on the floor.

Erin had also volunteered to call Pete and explain what had happened, and I didn't argue. She had been here much longer, and he was less likely to have an issue with someone he knew. The man had given me a job, but he still valued money, and repairs were expensive. I didn't want to be the new girl who trashed the place on my second shift.

As the night moved on, the stool where John had sat remained empty as some silent homage for the man who had been brave enough to stand up to the attacker.

There was something about him, some small light flickering in the back of my mind—a beacon to something I couldn't find.

And I couldn't shake the feeling that he'd taken some secret with him when he'd walked out the door.

Connect with Me Online

ANGELS AND FIRE BOOKS

Find our exciting stories at:

www.angelsandfirebooks.com.au

READER GROUP

https://www.facebook.com/groups/588038442170571

NEWSLETTER

https://www.subscribepage.com/angelsandfirebooks

GOODREADS
https://www.goodreads.com/author/show/21761217.Stefanie_Dawn

BOOKBUB
https://www.bookbub.com/authors/stefanie-dawn

AMAZON
https://www.amazon.com/author/stefaniedawn

WEBSITE
http://www.angelsandfirebooks.com.au/

FACEBOOK
https://www.facebook.com/stefaniedawnwriter

INSTAGRAM
https://www.instagram.com/stefaniedawnauthor

About the Author

Stefanie Dawn writes steamy paranormal and sci-fi romances, as well as dark and urban fantasy. She strives to give her readers stories they can escape into as they become absorbed in the worlds created, and fall in love with the characters.

Stefanie adores creating romances that will keep you hooked, with HEAs and paranormal fantasy, elements of instant attraction, and of course lots of steam!

When she isn't writing, Stefanie might be painting, reading, or watching movies. She loves the process of producing films as another form of storytelling. There's also a good chance she'll be baking some delicious treats—pretending she won't later regret consuming them—or simply enjoying a cocktail with friends.

Stefanie Dawn lives in South Australia with her ever-supportive partner and a lovable gang of rescue cats.

You can stay up to date with Stefanie and her books at

www.ingramcontent.com/pod-product-compliance
Lightning Source LLC
Chambersburg PA
CBHW020327030826
48979CB00021B/469

* 9 7 8 1 7 6 3 8 7 0 5 4 3 *